Tricia Sullivan was born in New Jersey in 1968 and studied in the pioneering Music Program Zero program at Bard College. She later received a Master's in Education from Columbia University and taught in Manhattan and New Jersey before moving to the UK in 1995. Her novel *Dreaming in Smoke* won the Arthur C. Clarke award.

Find out more about Tricia Sullivan and other Orbit authors by registering for the free monthly newsletter at www.orbitbooks.co.uk

By Tricia Sullivan

MAUL

DOUBLE VISION

doublevision

TRICIA SULLIVAN

www.orbitbooks.co.uk

ORBIT

First published in Great Britain in July 2005 by Orbit
This paperback edition published in April 2006 by Orbit

A CIP catalogue record for this book is available from
the British Library.

ISBN-13: 978-1-84149-173-8
ISBN-10: 1-84149-173-X

Typeset in Palatino & Myriad by M Rules
Printed and bound in Great Britain by
Clays Ltd, St Ives plc

Orbit
An imprint of
Time Warner Book Group UK
Brettenham House
Lancaster Place
London WC2E 7EN

www.orbitbooks.co.uk

For the Heim sisters
Gertrude
Catherine
Marion

And for my daughter
Rhiannon

With love

something like lunch

Maybe it's the bonelessness messing you up. Like, if you aren't feeling too confident about things, maybe it's because you're all folded over on yourself, limp as a piece of wet Charmin that clings to anything it touches.

You can hear guys discussing your situation. You can even feel them handling you, but you can't see them from here. All you can see is a bunch of sheds and a ship surrounded by scaffolding – and, looming beyond this, a distant chunk of the Grid. It's flashing in and out of reality in its own special, hostile-fungus-with-horrible-geometric-properties way. This doesn't contribute to your overall grip.

Plus, Serge isn't exactly cheerleader material.

'I hope that hankie's gonna fly, Lewis.'

Captain Bonny Serge's voice percolates in her throat, phlegm effecting the same break-up of tone by white noise as the interference on a walkie-talkie so that she can be standing two feet away from you and sound like she's in Paraguay. Now she hovers on Gossamer's dorsal side while Lewis fine-tunes Goss's receiving systems to take into account the electrical disturbances that have been plaguing the flyways since the stand-off at N-Ridge began.

The scaffolded ship kaleidoscopes and then vanishes as the tech untangles Gossamer from herself. Now you can see clearly. The Grid fills your field of view, pulsing, until it's obscured by Serge's body as she moves around to ventral. Her stocky trunk always appears mismatched with her stork legs, just like her Texas accent doesn't jive with her geisha-girl features. Maybe the physical comedy of her appearance is what makes her aspire to such hardassedness: fear of being laughed at just for existing.

Lewis, kneeling, leans over you to snap her kit box shut. She says, 'Gossy's good to go. If she makes it to N-ridge, the nex will take her recordings straight to Machine Front. I think we're on top of the interference problem, too.'

A grunt from Serge: the most courteous response she ever gives at this hour of the morning. It's enough to satisfy the tech, who smiles and stands up, relaxing.

'I still can't believe the golems could of sabotaged the friggin' MaxFact,' Serge adds, blotting her forehead with her sleeve. 'It's Machine Front passing the buck again. *They* f%#ked up and now we're gonna pay for it. You lose control of your rocket-guidance system, you might as well give the Rompers a 695 because you're going to Wisconsin in a bucket.'

You don't know what a 695 is but Serge doesn't expect you to answer – the nature of the nex means you can't. She just wants to hear herself saying it. She's like a guy talking to his dog.

Lewis doesn't realize that Serge's commentary isn't directed at her, so she tries to contribute to the conversation by saying, in a manner lamely imitative of Serge's backwoods drawl, 'Captain, we got to hope that rocket don't come back to visit us in quad-ruplicate. We got to hope it ain't landed in the well.'

The conversation has taken on a rehearsed quality. You don't know whether it's being repeated for your benefit, since every-thing you hear is transmittable to Machine Front, or if it's just shop talk and in fact Serge and Lewis have been trading remarks like this for two weeks, ever since a golem raid on N-Ridge culminated in a misfired rocket, downed communications to the mines, and the disappearance of N-Ridge's command officer, Dr. Arla Gonzalez.

Serge should really hawk and spit, but she just lets the phlegm go on clogging up her pipes as she says, 'Yeah, well, I need this like I need a leopardskin pillbox hat.' She glances at her watch and gives a little jerk. 'Come on already, when are Machine Front giving their report?'

Serge sticks her finger in her ear and wiggles it spasmodically, as though scratching a furious itch. An instant later, Dante Perelli, the Machine Front bimbo of choice in Serge's army, appears as a projection above Serge's yellow-and-green Swatch.

'Hi, Serge,' he purrs. 'Ready for the numbers?'

The numbers come swarming out of the Swatch like little green Space Invaders. Dante's brow furrows sympathetically: no self-respecting ArtIQ could fail to anticipate the human reaction to news like this. But Serge isn't just any human. You can tell more about the nature of the data from looking at little digital Dante than from the reaction of Serge herself.

All she says is, 'There has to be a better way of stopping them.'

'You know the algorithms,' says Dante. 'The more we kill, the faster they come. The faster they come, the more we have to kill or they'll take apart the equipment.'

Grunt. Pause.

'I won't be forced into a torch operation. Not while we still got a guy out there might be alive.'

Whatever you may say about Serge, you can't say she doesn't look out for her guys. Everybody else has given up on Gonzalez.

Dante answers her angry stare with, 'I'm only here to offer information and assistance.'

'What's on the card for N-Ridge, then?'

'If they keep multiplying by current rates? Eleven thousand for your neck of the woods. Maybe nine-five, maybe twelve.'

Serge is quiet for a second. 'Dante, Dante,' she says at last. 'This is not what I like to hear. What do S&T say?'

'Strategy says they predicted this in March. Tactics say that Logistics didn't allocate enough hardware to deal with the swollen figures on N-Ridge. Research say the well's hottest in N-Valley and Logistics say, quote, you try schlepping fourteen hundred tons of plastic up the side of N-Ridge when there's Iowa boys and girls throwing themselves under the treads and screaming to Jesus as they die, unquote.'

'A golem is a golem,' says Serge flatly, 'and they don't come from Iowa. I thought we was past all that emotional hoodwinking.'

'We won't be past it until you girls have gone home. Machine Front is here to do what you wetheads can't.'

'So what now? What's the actual position at the mines?'

'Standoff. Us on the road, heavily armored. Them blockading the mine perimeter, waiting for us to kill them so they can reproduce.'

It's an inadequate description; you know because you've seen it for yourself, from the air. Nevertheless, Serge seems to have the imagination to visualize it for herself, because she says:

'Yuck.'

'We have to penetrate, Captain. I know you babes don't like killing—'

'That's why we're here, dopehead. To *not kill*. Because the boys got carried away and now look at all the friggin' golems.'

'As I was saying, I know you don't like killing golems but in this case it's essential that we get through to N-Ridge. The third wave of unmanned relief vessels is already launched and en route to us. Once they get here, you can all go home and leave the battle to us machines. But the new ships won't be able to make their targets without Grid-specific logic bullets, and N-Ridge is the only place to get those. Ergo—'

'Yeah, yeah, yeah. I intend to retrieve Gonzalez. I ain't gonna deviate from that plan without a direct order to the contrary from X.'

'The clock is ticking, Captain. If Gonzalez is alive and knows what went down up there, great. If not, Machine Front has to move in.'

Before Serge can respond, you feel Goss shudder and stiffen. She's reacting to a chemical signal in the Grid that the humans can't sense. Gossamer's action catches Serge's attention and gives her an excuse to snap the image of Dante into her Swatch.

'It's about time we was movin' on up.'

Gossamer is already standing on end. She – and you – have been lying loose like a shimmering cloak on the repair rack, but now that she is aroused for flight she stiffens like a sail in the wind. You're picking up input in her olfactories. The Grid communicates with her by scent as often as not and, at the moment, it's calling. She squirts a reply from her ventral slits, and then, without further warning, launches into the sky. There's a momentary jockeying for power between you and the Grid with its beckoning scent: both seek to use Gossamer. Then you assert control. It feels good. Once you're in the air, all your uncertainties vanish.

'Don't get shot down,' Serge shouts, like you're in a WW2 movie with Zeros over the Pacific and shark's-teeth snouts, with those symbol thingies numbering your kills.

But you're not a pilot. In the air you *are* Gossamer. You're a living rainbow: people have to be in the right place at the right time to even see you. Along the length of Gossamer's belly you feel every slight variation in texture and temperature and pace. Your ventral side is so sensitive you feel like the pea-wakeful princess in the old story; sometimes you swear you could sense the undulations in the Grid below through the very air, if you shut your visuals down. Gossamer's wings have been mapped onto your human fingertips and her tail, more oddly, has been mapped onto your lips. You think this is something to do with the density of nerves required to process the sensory information. Gossamer's tail is particularly subtle and since the Gossamer-equivalents of olfactory nerves are located there you guess that crossing it with your human lips and tongue makes some kind of sense. But it means that sometimes, after flying, you can't speak properly for awhile. It also makes food taste funny for a couple of hours.

None of that matters, though. Because when you fly, you're real. What a feeling. You're so thin and light that you're just a membrane relaying information. You almost lose your self, your sense of subject: you almost become a verb.

You scan incessantly for relevant data. This isn't as easy as it sounds. While you're flying over the dun baldness of X, the Landing Zone, everything's straightforward enough. In the very center of X are the intensive gardens – seven levels of them. Encircling these are the command buildings and residence units, then the factories and signal towers. Each arm of the X has a landing pad. You cross over the last of the signal towers and pass above the security net, which consists of an energy barrier to keep out golems. It's patrolled by indigenous Fliers; but unlike Gossamer, these are wired directly to Machine Front so as to sound the alert if golems try to enter X. You choose a roadway from among the many that radiate from X like beams of light from the heads of saints in medieval paintings. To aid with orientation, you'll follow the N road as far as it takes you into the Grid.

You take a last look back at the lights and the straight lines, the blandness of human architecture basking in a dull, diffuse light that doesn't necessarily seem to come from the sky. You can see Serge's team as they load into the Machine Front convoy that will crawl after you while you fly overhead. You can see a couple of jeeps puttering over the tarmac toward the scaffold-covered ship. You can see dark rain clouds scumbled over the flat surface of featureless white cloud and, below them, the emerald green of the gardens like a little piece of Oz.

Then you stop looking back and start looking forward, and there it is. The Grid.

Sometimes you'd swear you could see it breathing; but the limits of the Grid are hard to perceive, and if it does respire then it exhales confusion. Even its name is misleading. The first explorers inaccurately called it the Speed Jungle because its structures reminded them of trees that could move, snaking and changing positions like beans sprouting on time-lapse film. Later, the First Wave soldiers who escaped immersion in its well called it The Headf@*k, and when the generals saw what end the Grid's captives came to, that name was reified by the fact that no more soldiers were sent in. But those who control the names of things now call it the Grid – a euphemistic, deceptively neutral label that suits the purposes of the war-makers. Ostensibly they chose 'Grid' because the phenomenon in question functions as an armature for the soft stuff of the planet's life codes. Also you figure it's because from the air the Grid looks more like a spider web than the forest it resembles at ground level. Especially at night, in the absence of the blond light that can etch the details of each terminus, each leaf, each flower spiralling into cloud, the faintly luminous Grid seems two-dimensional, reducible. It seems a statement, not a question. It seems localized and therefore finite. Yet, by daylight when you have flown in close like Gossamer has, then the hairs and tendrils of the Grid become apparent. Its essential seediness asserts itself as you realize you are flying through a delicate life-pod like those blown from dandelions on Earth, only far more complex. You perceive that the identity codes of the Grid are sticking to you and Gossamer like motes of pollen, looking for a fertile place to replicate themselves and ultimately, by their persuasive powers, to make you into something for the well.

Something like lunch.

Gossamer is a human-modified indigene. Thanks to the efforts of the Machine Front engineers, she is carrying a spy kit consisting of electronics so low in mass that they don't even register on a standard Dataplex scale. Without these silicon prosthetics, Gossamer would be just another native entity – unusual, yes, because so few of the planet's organisms are independently motile, but not extraordinary.

The extraordinary part comes about because Gossamer carries you, Cookie Orbach, all one hundred ninety-seven pounds of you, within those slender, body-electric-powered filaments. You: Cookie: World's Chubbiest Spy: You fly above it all.

What the Grid's well would make of Gossamer's Earth-made parts if it ever got hold of them is a matter you have refused to consider on the basis that you might flip out. The well makes golems of human bodies; it swallows armored vehicles whole, and strange tree-cities spring up in their place. Missiles, too, are transformed, and red lights like malevolent swamp-eyes hover in the froth of the Grid's upper layers when the well has been cooking the weapons of the terrestrial colonists. But what would become of Gossamer's Earth-made eyes if Gossamer fell in the well is an unknown belonging to that broad category of things you would rather eat cake than think about.

Of course, you are aware that Gossamer is a prisoner of war. It has no cortex as such, and therefore possesses neither intelligence nor consciousness nor selfhood, so there is really nothing to feel guilty about because Gossamer doesn't know that it's being exploited. It was picked up by Machine Front in an opportunistic nest-strike. It was taken away from the Grid and loaded with spy tech; then it was returned, with you on board thanks to the beauty of the nex.

Your job, apart from hanging on to the nex and translating what Gossamer sees, is to make sure that Gossamer stays clear of the Grid and its integrity-remixing properties. This act of will exerted upon the relatively simple nervous system of Gossamer does require a degree of communion with the indigene, however vague. It is the nature of the nex to fold you into Gossamer a little, as egg whites into angel food cake. Finding the end of your-self and the beginning of Gossamer is sometimes like finding a contact lens in a white shag rug. But that's a subtle point, not one you often consider.

So:

You don't understand your job, but you do it anyway. The more you learn about people, the more you believe that's not so unusual.

Besides, no one understands this war.

LOOK FOR BURN SIGNS, Serge reminds you unnecessarily. She's nervous today. That makes two of you.

Burn signs are important because if Dr. Gonzalez has been forced to commit suicide, she will have self-immolated to prevent the Grid making golems of her.

Serge is relaying a message from Machine Front.

SAT SAYS YOU GOT A STORM BREWING AT 60 DEGREES, AND THERE'S A GAP IN THE GRID AT 22 APPROX THREE KILOMETERS FROM PRESENT POSITION. CAN YOU CHECK THE GAP BEFORE WEATHER HITS?

The storm is no surprise: nobody's been able to fly over the mines since the incident thirteen days ago. The Grid brews impossible weather and magnetic conditions. But this alleged gap doesn't sound right to you. You know this area well. You've never seen any break in the continuity of the Grid around here.

You can't answer Serge, you can only direct Goss as best you can. You move towards the location she transmits, but there's nothing immediately visible. Sat's got it wrong – but they're not wrong about the storm. The wind's already kicking up and the sky's gone black over your starboard side. Goss shivers, detecting small electrical disturbances.

Then you see it: a break in the Grid as clean and precise as if somebody has cut a hole in the planet's topography with scissors. In the same moment, sensory cross-mapping with Gossamer gives you a sickly-sweet taste in your mouth as

Gossamer's olfactories go into overdrive, trying to read all the scent messages the Grid's giving off. They hit you on an unconscious level, making you feel twitchy and out of control.

A flood of primary emotions floods your chest and guts. You don't have time to analyze or even name them *fear, anger, elation, loneliness, hunger* because they follow one another in such rapid succession. You let them run over and through you, like you learned in that book about Paul Atreides: *Fear is the mind-killer*, you tell yourself this. And your discipline kicks in. You are a conduit. You are not to get involved.

RECORD – URGENT TRANSMISSION – RECORD ALL

You start sending pictures, angling Gossamer carefully to catch as much of the new phenomenon as you can in one bloom of data. It looks like a good hundred vertical feet of the Grid have been shorn off, exposing its foundation and the gnarled, knotty bases of what had been an intricate and mathematically sophisticated structure. There is an implied violence about the sight, not least because on the perimeter of the event the Grid is dead.

Dead, like gray flesh around a wound. Without light, or color, or movement: dead. It's just a brittle skeleton. Deep in the gray pit, well-fluid still gleams. There is something else down there, too, but you can't make it out before Gossamer's pass is finished and you lose sight of the gap.

How did this happen? No machine could chop up the Grid on such a large scale – and you're nowhere near any of the roads that machines use, anyway. It can't be golems because they don't build things or even use tools. It's one of the ways everybody can be sure they're not like humans. They don't have to use tools: they don't need shelter any more than they need food or sleep. They're like mushrooms. They spring up full-grown, clad in the battle gear their progenitors died in, and they do it literally overnight. They disappear into the well again just as easily.

You bend all your effort to recording a clear and focused image despite the best efforts of the Grid to repel your sight.

The storm's visible now, its wind bending the stalks of the upper Grid and sending petals and clouds of pollen your way. Gossamer doesn't like the smell. She's like a horse scenting cougar. She wants to get the heck out of here.

But there's something funny about the living Grid in the region *around* the hole, as well. You don't know if you're imagining it, but you'd swear there are the beginnings of a visible order within the seething mess. You think you can detect angular structures within the freeform. They probably wouldn't pass an ArtIQ test; but to your subjective eye, they are there. You lean hard on the nex and transmit:

URGENT. NOTE APPARENT STRUCTURES. AMPLIFY BANDWIDTH.

Here comes the storm. Gossamer has no bones to feel the weather in, but her primitive nervous system is screaming warnings; in a minute, she'll flee or risk being crumpled up like a used Kleenex and tossed away. Magnetic dirt blocks your transmission. You see everything, but Machine Front will get only fuzz.

All the same, you force Gossamer to come around for another pass, scanning for clues. Your prosthetic eyes record a few more anomalies in the Grid: rectangles where there should be parabolas, spaces where there should be form. Nothing you know how to interpret. You take Gossamer on a wider circle now and pass through a series of scent-phrases that hit Gossamer's olfactories like Pop Rocks hitting a kid's tongue, temporarily overriding your sense of taste and obscuring whatever hidden messages may lie beneath.

Gossamer makes a bid to surge upward – whether seeking to avoid the storm or the crackling and singing upper extremities of the Grid, you can't tell. You manage to keep control of her, but you figure: enough already. You get the hint: time to go home.

You turn Gossamer around and start going back. And just then, her eyes give you the prize.

Serge's lost soldier is sitting in the Grid, high up at the very edge of the mysterious gap, overlooking the well. Just like a little statue, except for the automated blinking flare on the back of her helmet that is meant to alert fliers to her position.

Can't leave now.

URGENT. TRANSMIT. HAVE SIGHTED MAJ GONZALEZ. REPEAT HAVE SIGHTED MAJ GONZALEZ. URGENT.

You can't do anything. Goss has no supplies and she couldn't carry a field mouse, much less a hundred-and-twenty-pound soldier plus full equipment. You note the coordinates and hope they're right – the Grid can mess with orientation and does, especially with the storm front doing its thing in your left eye – then you decide to try and signal Gonzalez. Your data strip offers a 'stay/wait' sequence that Gossamer can pulse on scent towards the soldier's position so that she won't be tempted to wander off and get herself more lost than she already is. You start to implement the command.

Gossamer is not interested in carrying out your instructions. She has never rebelled against you before, so either you've lost your touch, or the storm is worse than you are able to perceive and she's shutting down non-essential nervous activity.

You judge by the rush of body-electricity and concomitant bladder-dump that it's the latter. Goss's survival reflexes are kicking in bigtime. She executes a neat maneuver, literally turning on her tail, and flees the coming storm, dropping the nex.

You're nowhere. You're blind, deaf, gagging – *choking*, actually, and—

—'Cookie! Pizza!'

the department of extraplanetary hauntings

Ah, *sugar*. I'm back.

I sat listening to my heartbeat for a few counts, getting accustomed to myself again. My feet were asleep. My hands, palms-down on the reception pad, were cold and sweating. The TV screen was blue. I smelled Old Spice.

'Cookie? You out yet?'

'Yes, Gunther,' I whispered.

'Good. We'll debrief in five.'

He sounded crisp and impatient. I wondered if it was his fault I lost Goss. Why had he been calling me, anyway? I licked dry lips, about to turn in my cheap plastic chair and ask him what was going on, but I heard the door of my assignment room snick shut and knew he was gone.

Five minutes. I had just enough time to go to the bathroom and get a Coke from the machine. Popping open the can, I shuffled along to Gunther's office, feeling awkward and dislocated, like a sea mammal on dry land. The post-flying bad taste in my mouth was even worse than usual. It was a funeral taste, like orchids, or something that had died – or both. I sipped Coke but it only seemed to complicate the nastiness.

Gunther is singing along to Billy Joel's *The Nylon Curtain* and shooting baskets with a nerf ball. I'm a little out of breath and my upper lip is sweating so I sit down on his leather couch and pretend to be interested in his little performance.

'You missed Gloria's birthday party,' Gunther said. 'I think they saved you pizza and cake.'

I blinked. 'What time is it?'

Outside Gunther's window I could see maple trees tossing in a warm breeze, and traffic passing on the Garden State Parkway, which runs right behind the Dataplex building. The traffic was heavy.

Gunther shrugged and fished in his desk for his watch. 'Six . . . eleven.'

I put my hand to my mouth. I had entered the nex at ten o'clock. 'I had no idea . . .'

'Yeah, I know. I was hoping the pizza shout would get your attention.'

He grinned. Gunther's going bald but otherwise he's not bad-looking, he's not married, and he's not stupid. However, he has some work to do in the sensitivity department. He seems to think my weight problem is funny.

'It was really rough out there today,' I said. Gunther didn't pay any attention. He and Billy were singing something about Sesame Street.

'Gunther, there's some kind of structured effect going on in the Grid on N-Ridge. Near the mines. I couldn't get Gossamer in for a close enough look, but from what I could see it was pretty weird stuff. The Grid was actually chopped off. I've never seen anything like it.'

Gunther went for a bank shot and screamed, 'PRESSURE!'

'Gunther! Don't you care? What kind of debriefing is this?'

He startled and dropped the nerf ball.

'Sorry,' he said in a different tone. He switched off the boom box, cleared his throat and sat down, loosening his tie. He picked up a pencil and tapped the eraser on a legal pad. 'OK, tell me everything.'

I opened my mouth to speak, but didn't. He was staring expectantly at me. I stared back.

'The tape recorder, Gunther?'

'Oh! Right. Yeah.' He reached into his desk drawer and dragged out the tape recorder. He cued the tape and turned it on.

'This is Gunther Stengel debriefing Karen Orbach on July 2, 1984 at . . . six-thirteen p.m. Go ahead, Karen. What happened out there today?'

He assumed an attentive pose and maintained it throughout. The thing about Gunther is, he's so fake he's real. I used to hate him, then I liked him, and then I started to wonder if there was something, like, *wrong* with him. By now I've given up trying to understand what he's all about.

It took me a long time to tell my tale, but if he checked his watch I didn't see him do it. When I was finished, my face felt hot and I must have looked excited.

'Well!' he said. 'Well!'

He sat back.

I added, 'Serge thinks she can get Arla out of there. It's remarkable that she's still alive, but there are so many golems in that area that Serge could be walking into a trap. If I were advising her—'

'You're not.'

'What?'

'You're not advising Serge.'

'I was only saying.'

'Don't. I'm telling you this for your own good, Cookie. Don't make it personal. *That's what the Grid wants.*'

I hate it when Gunther decides to play big brother with me. I said, 'How do you know what the Grid wants?'

'It's obvious, isn't it? It plays our own fears against us. It uses our own hardwiring to short-circuit us. We can't let ourselves be fooled by that.'

I knew he was right, in a technical sense. But: 'My hard-wiring, as you so unromantically put it, is all I have. If I can't trust my instincts, what am I doing in there?'

'You are a set of eyes for Machine Front, no more, no less. Leave it there.'

I shrugged, trying not to act offended.

'You want me to go back to N-Ridge, then?'

He picked up the nerf ball and stood up. 'That's not up to me.'

In other words: *I know my place, and so should you.*

I stood up. Gunther took a jump shot with the nerf ball and while his back was turned I glanced at what he'd written on the legal pad. But there was no writing at all, just a drawing of Fred Flintstone.

'The Grid has no respect for human life,' Gunther said, retrieving the ball from behind his wastepaper basket. 'Remember that.'

I left.

How could I argue? I never went to college. This job pays over forty grand a year and I don't have any other skills. I can't even type. I'm fat. I've never had a boyfriend. This is the one thing I can really do.

I couldn't find Gloria so I went into the break room and picked up a piece of cold pepperoni pizza. There was some RC cola left over, too, so I poured that in a paper cup, but I didn't sit down. Thinking:

Do I really want to keep doing this?
Then again, what choice do I have?

I started out as a police psychic but I was too good at that. I started getting death threats from some guy who got out of prison on parole and wanted revenge because my information had led to the discovery of one of his victims' bodies. I tried to get police protection but even after all my help the police didn't want to do anything for me. I was a nervous wreck and in danger of losing my job as a file clerk. Around that same time I developed my TV allergy. I thought it was just stress. Then I answered the ad for DEH and found out that what I thought was an illness was actually a talent. So I came here.

The Department of Extraplanetary Hauntings is hidden within Dataplex Corp under the moniker Foreign Markets Research Division. Which is accurate enough in its way; I mean, how much more foreign can you get than another planet? We're at the back of the building next to Programming. All the geeks and weirdos in one pen. The programmers don't bother us and I don't think we even attract their notice.

I always said I would accept no money for my work because I am a real psychic and to profit from it would be greasy and uncool. But there are a few other factors in the equation. For one thing, all the other Fliers collect a paycheck. As far as I know they aren't psychics like me, they don't get premonitions or messages other than from The Grid, they're just spies. None of us trust each other, I guess, and anyway we're not allowed to exchange notes. But I've seen their faces after they come out of their assignment rooms and I know we're all in the same boat. And all of us have to live. As the war drags on we spend more and more time Flying. There comes a point when you realize that you deserve some compensation for the stress – and, in my case, the weight gain.

Gunther drives a BMW. I just have a Rabbit, but there are

reasons for that aside from money, chief among them being my stupid pact with Gloria. I could get a better car if I wanted to.

Speaking of Gloria.

'Hi, Cookie, what's up?' She came into the break room in a cloud of Vanderbilt perfume.

I turned, swallowing a lump of congealed mozzarella.

'Happy Birthday!' I said thickly.

'Thanks. And thanks for the present, you crazy woman.'

I smiled. 'I expect you to learn how to use those.'

I had given her two pairs of nunchuks: expensive, heavy wooden ones covered with Japanese writing, and a light, foam-covered pair to actually practice with. Gloria and bruises do not mix.

'What are you still doing here? Come on, we can walk out together.'

I'd only had time for two bites of pizza – it tasted like gardenias – but I put the food down and followed her. Gloria is very tiny and delicate, with gorgeously fluffy dark hair. She's always well dressed and neat-looking, and she wears lots of cute gold jewelry, charm bracelets and stuff like that. I lumbered after her down the corridor past a series of conference rooms. She had to stop at Maryann's desk to tell her about some message from a VP in the Milwaukee office.

'*Lexus,*' came the voice of a man with a Southern accent from the nearest conference room. Another focus group. '*Out of that name I get luxury, sex, and nexus.*'

'*What's a nexus? Is that like solar plexus?*'

'*No, I think it's like a locus.*'

'*Plague of Lexusus.*'

'*Focus, people, focus! Ha-ha.*'

It's hot today. Even in the air-conditioning my thighs are sticking together under the silk skirt I got for forty percent off retail at Annie Sez on Route 46.

'What about a swarm of women, you know, like locusts? Around some guy? A plague of sexy Lexuses?'

Gloria caught the expression on my face. 'Shut up – Cookie, don't say it. Come on, let's go, I have to get ready for my big birthday dinner.'

We went outside, smacked by a hot pillow of air coming off the road and into our faces.

'I'll think of you tonight when I'm eating my lobster thermidor and drinking Margueritas,' she joked. 'You are gonna sweat, that's for sure.'

'I don't know, maybe . . . I'm kind of tired and it's *sooo* hot . . .'

'Hey!' Gloria gave me a little shake. 'You better train, Cookie. Whatever happened with Gunther, just take it out on the makiwara or something.'

We had reached her Lincoln Town Car, and she opened it and started rolling down electric windows to let out the heat.

I said, 'What did Gunther tell you?'

She made a face and lowered her voice to a whisper. 'Nothing. But he's been acting all bitchy all day. I think the head office is giving him a hard time about his results.'

'He didn't seem stressed to me. He seemed . . . out to lunch.'

'You aren't thinking about leaving again, are you, Cookie?'

I shrugged. About a year ago I found out that the Dataplex branch in Milwaukee employs psychics to dream up new military technologies and to try to find out what the Soviets are up to. I sent over my resume and they called me for an interview, but before I could go Gunther got wind of it and dragged me into his office, where he shocked me by bursting into tears.

'You CAN'T leave us,' he wailed. 'You're our BEST FLIER.'

I was flattered but I told him about the stress thing and the weight thing. He pulled out his checkbook and told Gloria to call the Jenny Craig Weight Loss Hotline. All the while he was saying things like, 'They're useless bastards over at Military Telekinesis. All they've invented so far is a device that lets you reload your gun by mind control. Does that sound like something you want to be involved with, Cookie?'

Gunther knows that I don't like the idea of violence, but I couldn't really see how working for Military Telekinesis could be any worse than what I was already doing. But I pretended to agree. I felt I owed Gunther and anyway, I've never been too good at standing up to people. Every time I do, I end up losing my temper, and I don't like to lose my temper. So I stayed, and when I got bored of Jenny Craig microwave meals that weren't big enough to feed my cat, Gloria started dragging me to her karate class and made me sign the pact. For whatever good it's done.

'Well, whatever Gunther's problem is, it's Gunther's problem. Right? Not yours.' She pointed her finger at my nose. 'You! No "maybe" about training. We have a pact, remember?'

'OK, OK. I'll be there tonight. See you.'

I dragged myself over to the Rabbit and unlocked it. As soon as I was faced with the distressingly small space that I was supposed to sit in I remembered the pact all too well. I had to train four nights a week and I had to cut down on my eating, no matter how weird things got over the nex. I'd asked Gloria to enforce my decision. She leaped at the chance. She made me sign *in blood*.

The wheel of the Rabbit dug into my stomach and I barely had room for my elbows when the door was closed. I wasn't allowed to get a new car, either, until I'd shown that I could fit comfortably behind the wheel of this one.

Stupid.

Having squished myself into the hot car I turned on the radio as I swung out onto High Mountain Road. Hall and Oates were on PLJ. I made a face but couldn't get anything funkier because all the other stations were commercials. I wondered what those golems were up to. Had they built those structures or had the Grid grown them? And why? In my experience golems had two functions: 1) to die messily, and thereby multiply even more, and 2) to sabotage/steal/destroy Machine Front equipment.

Since when did they do landscaping?

And why, given the numbers of them on N-Ridge, hadn't they gotten hold of Arla Gonzalez yet?

I swung onto the Parkway and dug for quarters so that I could take the exact-change lane at the tollbooths. At the same time I found some Lionel Richie on the radio, even though I had to steer with my knees. I've always liked doing two things at once. Or more. It keeps my mind occupied.

Among the quarters I found a couple of fuzzy Tic-Tacs. But they couldn't quite kill the icky-sweet taste of Flying in my mouth.

Nebula greeted me at the door of my condo. I was late because I'd had to stop at A&P for cat food, among other things. She stood on my feet and tried to climb up my leg, talking the whole while. I put the grocery bags down on the counter and immediately saw that she'd been digging in the spider plant again.

'Bad Nebbie,' I said. 'Insouciant Nebbie. What did you do to my book?'

My latest paperback, *Crystal Singer* by Anne McCaffrey, was buried under the soil that was supposed to be in the spider-plant pot.

'I'm tempted to put an embargo on your Tender Vittles,' I told Nebula. 'You are a wicked, wicked, puss.'

She took this as praise, rubbing her jaw on the dirty book-cover.

There was a message from my mother on my answering machine. Was I OK? I hadn't called in a month. Guiltily, I called her back.

'Are you eating good?' she asked.

I told her I'd lost a little weight.

'As long as you keep your strength up,' she said. 'I hope you wouldn't be subscribing to none of these fad diets just so you could look like some model. A man likes a little something to hold on to, Cookie.'

I ignore the part about men and tell her that I'm very strong thanks to karate. She says, 'OK, as long as you remember to hit the other guy before he hits you. Don't get hit, Cookie.'

I give her a little lecture on Bushido and how it's uncool to attack, how you are only supposed to defend yourself in an honorable way.

'Don't let your Grandma Angela hear you say that,' she said darkly. 'She used to carry a rolling pin in her purse, and she didn't wait to find out what was gonna happen. She saw a situation developing and *wop*, she let 'em have it. Got the butcher that time when he tried to overcharge her on lamb chops.'

I guess everybody's mother drives them crazy.

'She had to go all the way to Hasbrook Heights for her meat after that, but the upshot was the butcher there heard about what happened and gave her a ten percent discount on everything, just out of fear! How's work?'

'OK. Busy.'

'You socking your money away?'

'Yeah. I don't spend much. Plus I have a lot of stock in the company. You get the check I sent you?'

'I got it, and it went right where all your other checks go, honey. Straight into savings bonds for my future grandchild. I'm counting on you, baby. I think your brother's gay. He ain't told me about no girlfriend in five years, and now he's talking about taking this job in San Francisco.'

'Not everyone in San Francisco is gay, mom. Maybe he's just not ready to settle down yet.'

'Yeah, that's how it is with my kids. Nobody wants to settle down these days. I just keep hoping you'll meet some-body nice. How's your friend Miles?'

'He's OK. You know he's just a friend, Mama.'

'Why is he just a friend, girl? He's got a good job, doesn't he? He respects you, doesn't he? You think he's shy?'

'We're just friends.'

'You should cook for him. Those Jewish families, they eat everything so bland. Hey, I just thought of something. Do you think he's not interested in you because he wants to marry one of his own?' She lowered her voice to a whisper. 'Do you think he's a racist? Doesn't he like black girls? Or . . . would he expect you to . . . *convert*?'

I made a face and tugged at my hair. A part of me wanted to laugh and I guess if it had been anybody else's mother I would have laughed. Instead, I snapped, 'I don't know and it's none of my business and anyway maybe I'm not inter-ested in him like that, didn't that ever occur to you, Mama?'

'OK, OK, you don't got to get all huffity about it.'

'Can we just change the subject, please.'

'As long as you're *happy*, Cookie.'

The warmth in her voice brought tears to my eyes. I wanted to break down and tell her everything that was going on at work, but that was impossible. Not only wouldn't she begin to understand, but she couldn't help and she'd only get upset.

'Tell me about your tarot class,' I said.

'Ooh, I'm designing my own deck. I'm gonna call it the

Mavis Deck. It's all in pastels and I'm gonna put gold filigree on the back, and I got my calligraphy set to write out the interpretations. I'll send you a copy of the card I just finished. It's Strength. You'll like it.'

By the time I hung up with her I was late. There was no time to make dinner, so I just brushed my teeth about six times to kill that flower-taste (it didn't work), got my gi and stuff and packed my gym bag, grabbed a water bottle and the car keys, and went out again. I wasn't actually hungry, which was surprising, but I don't like missing meals. I start to feel I don't know who I am if I don't eat.

Supposedly this is all part of my overall problem/talent. I'm so suggestible that it's probably a good thing I can't watch TV anymore, because I'd be at the refrigerator every time a food commercial came on. Hyper-suggestibility, they call it. In a way it's a talent, because it makes me able to take the crusty nex and experience it as real. Gunther says one day he'll prove it's not just an illusion, that Fliers like me *really* experience the alien environment. He says that places like the Grid are indistinguishable from Earth to us. 'I can prove that you see what happens there just like a dog hears a dog whistle. I'm just not publishing what I know because the world isn't ready for it.'

Well, he seems to know a lot about it. Only he doesn't seem to know how I can become thin. I'm sure that my fat is just me paying the price for being a Flier. It's like this: I'll be sitting around reading an Anne McCaffrey novel and she'll refer to Master Robinton spreading cheese on a piece of bread and I'm off to the Fridgidaire with the book still in my hand. The first chapter of *The Hobbit* is responsible for at least 3,000 calories every time I read it. And the more sensitive my Flying becomes, the bigger my problem. Gunther's right: I'm like a dog, I just can't stop myself.

The food/book thing has been going on as long as I can

remember. I vividly recall reading a Trixie Belden book when I was about seven or eight, and there is a scene where the girl shamus and her friend Honey are drinking lemonade and eating slices of homemade cake. I can remember that cake so clearly, even though it was only cake in a book. I could eat a hundred cakes in real life – and probably have – but none of them can capture the essence of *that cake*, a cake that isn't even real.

Well, if that's true, I should be able to subsist on imaginary food. My problem is that I keep trying to make those imaginary foods real. I'm a *food channeler*, that's what I am. And let's face it, with the nex doing a number on my head the way it does, I have to have some kind of escape. I've only been truly fat since I started working at Dataplex. Before that I was just moderately plump. I think that I've become so sensitive and suggestible that any resistance to food I might have once had is totally gone.

So off I go to karate, to discipline and reform myself.

Minnehaha is a small town sitting well away from any major highways. There are no supermarkets, but the main street has a tiny movie theater, an ancient department store that seems to trade mostly in corsets and hats judging by the drab window displays, and a handful of little shops that sell things like cameras and children's shoes. A small sign with KARATE stenciled on it in Chinese-restaurant Oriental lettering points to the dojo, which is tucked down a narrow alley in between an insurance agency and Tony's Pizza. Beyond the alley is an empty lot and then the banks of the Minnehaha River with its cheap, often-flooded houses.

I walked into the dojo, saw that there were no higher ranks than me nearby, and so bowed in the direction of the masters' photographs on the wall. We have to bow to the highest rank when we enter and leave as a sign of respect.

There were some kids and their parents in the waiting room, and I saw Miss Cooper sitting behind the desk, taking checks. She smiled at me and we bowed to each other. I inhaled the familiar smell of old, foot-sweaty carpet. I hadn't wanted to come tonight, but now that I was here I immediately felt better. This place had become my second home. When I'd first started training here with Gloria, I'd been terrified and had felt intimidated, but after I passed my first test and got my orange belt I started to feel really proud. I had seen a lot of white belts come and go, and all of them were in better shape than I was, but I was learning katas and drills and techniques that your average person just doesn't know. And the black belts might look impressive and scary, but they're just regular people underneath it. At first this seemed to spoil my fantasy of living in a little slice of medieval Japan, but then it became nice. Especially because Miss Cooper, who is anybody's definition of a woman warrior, started encouraging me a lot. It's thanks to her that I ever got my purple belt. I never thought I'd make it this far.

Miss Cooper is here every night. She teaches the kids and sometimes she teaches the adult beginners' class. Sensei is busy in his office most of the time and only comes out once or twice during a lesson to give instructions or say a few words to the class. All of the real work falls to Miss Cooper. On top of all this, she has to do her own training. She runs, she lifts weights, she hits the makiwara, practices her katas, and trains for the demonstration team. Sensei likes to put her forward as an example of how a smaller person can defeat a bigger opponent. He also teaches her naginata, a woman's weapon which is like a curved knife on the end of a stick. She gets to wear a special costume for this in demonstrations.

I got changed. I haven't gained any weight since I started training, which does give me some hope. But my gi looks like a jib sail, especially because of the way you have to wrap it around your body. I looked down at my stomach. I ought to be very hungry, but that nasty bite of pizza had kicked up a fuss in my stomach and made me felt nauseous. Probably the heat, but I had decided not to stop at McDonald's just to be on the safe side. I now felt tense and scared.

I was wishing I'd at least grabbed some fries or a Coke as I left the dressing room, and because I was preoccupied I nearly bumped into Sensei himself. John Norman was in his mid-forties, fairly tall, with dark hair that he parted on the side, a big nose, no chin, and heavy, black-rimmed glasses. He was a big guy but kind of clumsy and not in shape, as such. Not to meet the eye. Of course, that doesn't matter if you're a master because of all the secret techniques you know. The most dangerous masters of all look like doddering old men.

'Good evening, Miss Orbach,' he said, smiling without showing his teeth. 'You're here early.'

'I have to do my cleaning,' I said. Sensei has assigned each of the women with a cleaning job around the dojo. He says he asks us to do it because the men wouldn't do a very good job. Gloria's job is vacuuming the carpets. My job is to keep the bathroom clean. It's all part of showing good karate attitude.

'Well, keep up the good work,' he answered, and went upstairs. I passed his office to get my cleaning supplies out of the closet and saw that he had been watching a video showing his own teacher, Sensei Ingenito, doing a kata. The katas get changed a lot depending on who's in charge of the organization and I guess Sensei has to keep up with that. I averted my eyes. I didn't want anybody to think I was snooping.

I only had a few minutes to clean the toilet; then we lined up according to rank and bowed in. I struggled through the warm-up. Miss Cooper was leading. She can do a full split.

She told me and Gloria to call her Tanya, which we do when we're outside of class. In class, everybody uses last names and titles out of politeness. Politeness is very important in Japan, and also using titles reminds us that we are doing something serious here. We have a different identity in the dojo than we do out there in the ordinary world. What we're doing in here is deep, historic. Spiritual.

I felt a little dizzy, and during push-ups I lay on the floor more than usual, but nobody seemed to notice. It was a full class, and the counting rang out in Japanese. Soon the walls were sweating and people were slipping on the wooden floor. Sensei came out after warm-ups and broke the class up into groups

I always train with Gloria. Always. We joined together, and we always partner up. But Gloria's not here tonight, and Sensei has decided we're going to practice sparring because he wants to enter a tournament next month. I've never been in a tournament, and I've only sparred a couple of times.

I'm excited.

Miss Cooper paired me up with Cori Knight. I'm a purple belt and Cori is a green belt with two stripes – almost a brown belt, which is a pretty big deal. She was out for over a year recovering from a knee injury, so even though she outranks me she hasn't been around for most of the time that I've been training. Cori is skinny, poor because she's a graduate student, and always whining about something. She has extremely long brown hair that she wears in a braid; she never wears makeup and she seems to have permanent PMS. Tonight she's in a good mood because her boyfriend gave her a couple big hickies over the weekend, and instead of trying to cover them up she's wearing a tank top under her gi. I'm jealous that she's skinny and has a boyfriend, but I'd rather be fat and single than be stuck with her personality.

I heard that once Cori got her nose broken in a tournament. She also wears a knee brace on her left knee. She's incredibly lazy in class and totally sucks, but she still outranks me and Gloria. No matter what we do, we can't catch up.

We square up to fight, smiling fakely at one another.

'Watch my nose,' she says. 'And my knee.'

'Yeah,' I said, 'And your stomach.'

She had surgery to remove a cyst or something so she's funny about being hit in the stomach. So, that leaves as possible targets her chest – no, can't hit her in the boobs, she's a girl – OK, so what am I allowed to hit?

She's got lots of targets on me, though. I mean, come on, it's like hitting the broad side of a barn.

Cori started dancing around. She would come shooting in to hit me in the body, leading with her face – but I couldn't hit her in the face, remember? I mean, I couldn't even fake a hit to her face or focus a hit near her face, in case I made a mistake and damaged her precious once-broken-already nose. So she'd hit me, smirk, and dance back out of range again. If I went after her she'd remind me, 'Keep your form! Square your shoulders! Chamber your opposite hand!' which of course she's allowed to say because she outranks me. Meanwhile she's totally relaxed her own posture so as to extend her reach and hit me more easily. And I'm supposed to just stand there and take it.

She got me a couple times pretty hard in the gut.

'You better tighten up when you get hit,' Cori said, panting. She was bouncing up and down in her front stance like she was on a trampoline. Sensei told everybody to loosen up when they spar, and this kangaroo stuff seemed to be her interpretation.

'I am tightened up,' I said. 'That's just fat.'

'Well, it's sticking out so I get to hit it.' And she smiled at her own humor.

I was getting annoyed. I can remember coming in with a couple of faked punches to the face, disobeying the rules she'd set. This freaked Cori out and she put up her arms to block, which was when I gave her a roundhouse kick in the left kidney. To give me some credit, I didn't actually hit her in the face, although the idea was tempting. As she was crashing sideways from the force of the roundhouse I guess I did sweep her right leg out from under her for good measure, and she crumpled to the floor. I wasn't sure what I was supposed to do at this point but I gather you are not supposed to then jump on the person, straddle their chest and start slapping them around the sides of the head.

It was sort of like instinct. Playground stuff.

I mean, Cori p'd me off, you know? I was trying to play by the rules and she was taking advantage of it. I don't like that. I am a nice person and I don't like it when people think that means they can do whatever they want to me.

There was only one other black person in the class, a green belt called Troy. He was kind of cute and he knew it. He actually pulled me off Cori and dragged me away. He kept saying, 'Whoa, whoa, easy, girl,' like he was talking to a horse. I started crying.

'Come on, baby, you're all right,' he said in my ear. 'Don't let them see you flinch.'

I snuffled mightily, wiped my face on my already-sweaty gi sleeve, and nodded. Don't let them see you flinch. Story of my life.

without a babysitter

When you first get the nex back, you don't know where you are. You have to call Machine Front to get your own coordinates.

GOSSAMER UNDAMAGED BY STORM, you add. DETECTING NEW OLFACTORY AGENTS. RECOMMEND FULL FILTRATION FOR GROUND STAFF.

When they send your coordinates, Machine Front add a warning: OLFACTORY SAMPLES BEING TAKEN BY ROBOT PROBE FOR ANALYSIS HERE. GROUND CREW ALREADY ON FULL FILTRATION. INFORMING WOULD ONLY COMPROMISE MORALE. KEEP CLASSIFIED.

But it isn't the ground crew you're worried about: it's Gossamer. You've never lost contact with her involuntarily, until now. The Grid has somehow overridden Machine Front's neural controls of the indigene, and you're afraid it has something to do with this new smell.

Serge's team will be well on their way to Gonzalez's coordinates by now. You scan the lattice of fibers that rises, tree-like, from the well system. The Research guys don't know precisely what lies under the surface – the 'roots,' as it were. You do know that the Grid's structure follows a familiar fractal pattern as it rises: branching, becoming thinner with height, carving space into intricate, lacy shapes more subtly than Earthly trees do. The solid 'boles' that rise from the Grid's base eventually become filaments, then wisps, then nothing more substantial than odors on the wind.

But the odors say it all. Machine Front has never figured out a way to understand the significance of the changing scent patterns that penetrate the Grid. The way you understand it is that all the insect guys got together and cobbled out a rough vocabulary and syntax for the scent language, only to find out there is a whole 'nother level to the thing: the Grid also exudes psychotropes. Machine Front routinely samples the air, as its quality can be a predictor of what the golems will do next. Some of the odors stimulate the nervous system in specific ways, affecting golem and human alike while leaving indigenes like Gossamer – and Machine Front – unmoved.

Meaning that delusions, hallucinations and assorted phobias/compulsions are a matter of course for ground staff in the Grid. Is it any wonder that the First Wave guys wanted to call it The Headf@*k?

Yeah, you figure you've got a pretty good deal with Gossamer. Not that you don't have problems of your own to contend with. For example:

You are so busy looking down at the Grid that you don't notice the grave balloon until Gossamer swerves to avoid it. Your gaze, focused on deciphering the weird mathematics of the Grid, suddenly goes arcing away and you see the smoky curve of the horizon punctuated by red lights like the EQ readings on a good stereo. You see the lines and a section of the chute that holds up the grave balloon you are about to collide with. Then Gossamer corrects course and you're able to steady your vision.

It's an old grave balloon: you know this immediately because the corpse is male. The bauble floats in the sky with its sealed cargo, usually mauled or at least bloody but this time seemingly just locked in a pallid sleep. He reminds you a little of David Lee Roth but with short hair. You feel sad for him and a little smug, that this perfect body could be dead while yours remains, alive and flabby and barely used, mouth tasting of orchids, on Earth. You avoid looking at the identifier. Once you did and saw the guy's name and social security number: Leroy Jones 131-79-4247. You went through hell trying to imagine what his family would go through when they heard the news. The fast uplinks are reserved for your unit, espionage having highest priority. News of the dead comes much later – if ever. You felt awful, knowing and not being able to tell. So now you make sure you don't look at identities, but you're going to remember this guy's handsome face forever. You remember them all. You can't help it.

You can hear Serge's team below. They may look like little ants, but they're loud. Serge's voice twangs along the subtle auditory pickups of Gossamer's body, and you dive towards her.

'How many times I gotta tell you, Klaski? Huh? You wanna learn this the hard way?'

Serge is prowling around the camp dragging a Hefty bag with handle ties, collecting people's Coke cans and Kit-Kat wrappers. Looks like she caught Klaski and Hendricks making friendship bracelets out of spearmint Wrigley's wrappers.

'We wouldn't of dropped them, Captain, ma'am, honest,' says Klaski. She's eighteen but looks about twelve: small, blonde, unfinished, with a protruding lower lip that pouts all too readily.

'This shit's against regulations and you know it,' Serge says. 'You can sit watch tonight, and *you* –' she turned to Hendricks,' – the next time we rendezvous with the machines, you can defog the trailbreak headlights.'

Now that is a disgusting task. The trailbreaks kill the most golems, and messily so. The soldiers stay in the caravanserai where there are no windows. They belt out songs so they won't hear the golems screaming. There is no actual need to clean the blades of the trailbreaks and the treads of the caravanserai, because the gore is illusory and has no effect on the machines.

Even so, the hulls of the machines are painted and textured so that specks of blood and gristle can pass unnoticed. The girls will cringe and look away if they see more obvious evidence of death, like an eyeball stuck to a hatch cover or a bone splinter protruding from a gun turret, and that stuff's terrible for morale. So Serge's proposed disciplinary measure goes against everything MF are trying to achieve. It's sheer pigheadedness.

Hendricks's jaw drops. She's sitting Indian-style on the ground, her long back curling like an apostrophe. Her dark skin is so sweaty that it seems to shimmer in the flickering light.

'But ma'am, isn't there a cleaning function on the trailbreak lights?'

'Yes, there is, honey, but it's gonna be busted. You got something to say about it?'

Hendricks shakes her head, not looking at Serge. Nevertheless Serge sniffs something she doesn't like.

'You think you got it hard, Corporal Hendricks?'

'No, ma'am, I don't.'

'You think I'm some kind of racist?'

'I never said nothing, ma'am.'

'Because your girlfriend here has a worse job than you, Corporal.'

'Yes, ma'am.'

Serge turns to the little blonde. 'This is your first time outside X, right, Klaski? You understand what it means to sit watch?'

'Look out for the enemy, ma'am?'

Serge snorts. 'Hendricks, you want to enlighten Corporal Klaski?'

Hendricks clears her throat. 'You got to . . . you got to sit out in the Grid while everybody's sleeping, and watch for golems.'

'Oh-h,' said Klaski uncertainly.

It doesn't sound that bad, does it?

'But you're not in the enclosure, so you have to breathe whatever the Grid throws at you, and the suit filters can't clean up everything.

At night it usually gives you stuff to make you hallucinate. You don't know what you're looking for anymore. And if a golem gets through to the enclosure, or steals equipment, it's your fault.'

Klaski's frowning at her half-constructed friendship bracelet.

'If the Grid is so powerful, why doesn't it just gas us to death?' she said.

Everyone's ears perked up. Good question.

'Because,' said Serge, 'the Grid's like a cat. It likes to play with its prey.'

She makes as if to go, and then flings over her shoulder, 'And Klaski, when you're done crying you better pick up your Kleenex. The Grid loves them name-brand tissues.'

If Klaski hadn't already been about to cry, she's crying now. Serge doesn't care. 'These kids aren't hard enough,' she tells Lewis as Lewis brings Gossamer to the Grid for fuel. 'They haven't seen any real shit yet. Being nice don't do them no favors, that's for sure.'

Lewis glances up and sees you. She smiles. 'Whey-hey. Look who's here.'

'It's about time,' snaps Serge. 'Juice it, Lewis.'

Lewis attaches electrodes to Gossamer to recharge her batteries while the indigene feeds. Gossamer fixes her mouthparts to a nub on a branch of the Grid and begins drawing nectar, oblivious to Lewis's work. You can feel her body prickle as the Grid loads her with chemical energy.

Lewis glances after Serge and murmurs, 'Next shift's gonna be a motherf@*ker.' She pulls out a copy of *Redbook* from her thigh pouch as she activates the charge. When the juice hits Gossamer, you feel it as a blast of many-layered sound, not unlike a Foreigner record. Distantly, on Earth, you are conscious that your nose begins to run.

You remember the last time you had to spy for Serge on a recovery mission. It was only her and Lewis then, and she abused the pants off Lewis, taking out her every anxiety on the tech. In the end they found the guy's body suspended in the well, dragged it out, and torched it with some special incendiaries Serge always carried. Then, with Gossamer's help, Serge hunted down five golems that had sprung from the corpse and killed them, too. By the time it was all done Lewis looked five years older and you were eight pounds heavier back on Earth.

This time Lewis is playing it cool. She hasn't bitten her nails down yet or broken out in hives; she just checks over Gossamer while Serge looks at your recordings and then addresses the group.

'Now, Gossamer has sighted Gonzalez in this area,' she tells her guys, pacing from one end of a Grid-branch to the other as she speaks. She steadies herself by occasionally grabbing a vinelike side shoot like a subway straphanger. She's at ease in the webbing; the others are not. They huddle on the lumpy foundation beside a patch of thin well, looking intimidated. Serge says, 'Her physical condition would appear to be good, but we don't know about her state of mind. My guess is, she's snapped by now. This is why I'm so strict with you puppies. I don't want to waste precious time hunting after your ass to bring you back to X so you can get drugged up and shipped home. And I don't want to see you get killed and then I get to deal with your golems. I need you guys alive. *Comprende?*'

'Yes, ma'am.' They all say it, but Klaski says it with rote church-lips.

'Klaski, you are a big risk to me right now. You want to go back and sit in the truck? Because we can arrange that.'

'No, ma'am!' Klaski looks offended, as if she can't imagine why Serge is picking on her.

'You gonna insure you aren't a liability to this unit?'

'Yes, ma'am. I will insure it.' But her tone doesn't satisfy Serge.

Serge waits until Klaski looks at her. She superglues her gaze to Klaski's for a good few seconds. Then, apparently mollified by the submission in Klaski's milk-pale eyes, she resumes pacing and giving orders.

'The fact that Dr. G's kept her helmet on this long is a good sign. Use your Swatch to maintain your fix on it. Don't be surprised if the signal jumps around, though. The Grid plays games with stuff like this. If in doubt about which way to go, check with Machine Front. Or me. If you spot Gonzalez, what do you do, Hendricks?'

'Tell Machine Front immediately.'

'That's right. Do not take action on your own. If necessary, run away from Gonzalez until you have instructions. Understood?'

'Yes, ma'am.'

'I don't want any heroes. And don't let me hear you whining that Dante makes all the decisions. That's what he's there for. To have the information, and to use it to save your butt. I'm not interested in independent thought at this juncture.'

Independent thought. You find yourself wondering about that while Gossamer finishes recharging and the guys yawn and down their rations and Klaski says a bunch of hailmarys under her breath. Is independent thought really possible in the Grid, where every breath you take, every move you make is machine-monitored, machine-directed?

'Ma'am?' whispers Lewis to Serge. 'What about the Max? Are we looking for that, too?'

Serge shrugs. 'We are the only unit capable of moving off-road, so I guess we got some kind of shot at finding it if we get close enough to the mines. But that's not our primary objective. Our objective is to get Gonzalez out of here and find out what went down at the mines. She gave the *dis*-tress call but didn't self-immolate' – and she really pronounces it that way, with the emphasis on the first syllable – 'and if we can get her alive, then I'm a happy groundhog day because the Front has to get to the bottom of the event up there. If in the process of getting Dr. G we can find out what's going on up in N-Ridge, or locate the missing artillery, then that's a added bonus. However, I am fully intending to leave the big stuff up to the Big Guys, and that means our convoy. They're gonna be a few days behind us most of the time and they can deal with whatever we might find in the way of hardware. We stay mobile and stay alive. That's our job.'

The others are eavesdropping. Serge raises her voice to address them all.

'Any ideas you guys had about going home and leaving this one to Machine Front, you can forget about them. This is our last mission before the Third Wave arrives, and we are gonna make it a good one. And I don't mean that like just for show. We blow this task and the whole easterbunny will have been for nothing. If we give up control now and let the golems get to X, then the Third Wave will be landing in the middle of the enemy camp and on that basis they might as well not even come.'

After she says that, it's not really a party atmosphere in the camp.

There are no days or nights here; not as such. You've never actually seen the sun. There are only periods of light and darkness that come with no regularity, so MF has scheduled sleep cycles, and Serge's guys are getting ready to start one. It's tempting to drop the nex, go get an RC and some Doritos in the real world, and come back; but you have no way of knowing how much time will pass if you do. Time in the Grid. Yarks, it's enough to drive you crazy. Once you pulled an all-nighter, glued to the action, only to finally come off the nex to grab a few hours' sleep in the Dataplex reception couch when nothing seemed to be happening. When you went back, a month had passed and nobody even remembered the outcome of the mission. Other times, a sleep cycle in the Grid has lasted you weeks back home. You kept puttering through your routine, checking in with Gossamer every day to find that no time at all had passed, so you'd go home again. There's just never been any way of predicting it.

They finish their rations and shove the packaging into belt-mounted recycling units the size and shape of flashlights. Serge has erected a temporary enclosure, which houses the equipment they've been carrying. She sits in there, oblivious beneath headphones, brooding over the latest from MF, while her guys wind down for the night.

'She takes herself way too seriously,' says Klaski to Hendricks as Hendricks starts brushing her teeth with a battery-powered Snoopy. Klaski's face twisted, trying to imitate Serge's accent. '"It'll be Milwaukee in a beer keg for y'all if you don't pick up them god-damn wrappers."'

'Shh!' bubbles Hendricks through a mouthful of Aquafresh.

'She can't hear.' Klaski rolls her eyes.

'No, the Gossamer,' hisses Hendricks, jerking her head in your direction. 'It might be recording.'

You're not recording.

'It's not recording,' says Lewis mildly, flipping to *Top 10 Tips for Better Nails*.

Klaski goes on, 'I bet she's a lesbo. I bet she's just frustrated because she wants you, Hendricks.'

'She's not,' says Hendricks seriously. 'You can say a lot of things about the Captain but she ain't no dyke.'

'How do you know?' Lewis asks, no longer pretending not to be interested.

'Because I know, that's all,' answers Hendricks in a low voice, not looking at the others.

Klaski's like, '*How* do you know? Come on. Give!'

'Look, it's really private. I can't tell you.'

'Serge has a *private* life? Oh come on, just give us a hint.'

'I can't. I told you, it's confidential. Professional code of ethics. I can't talk about it.'

'Aha!' Klaski crows, slapping her knee. 'She's actually a *cyborg*. I saw it on *The Bionic Woman*. Except Serge doesn't look like a stewardess.'

'Maybe she's really a man,' says Lewis with a chortle, rolling her eyes, and Klaski says, 'Ewww! Then again . . . hey, you used to work at the clinic at X, didn't you, Hendricks? That's why you can't tell us.'

'She's a woman, OK? Now drop it.'

'Then it must've been VD. Or birth control?'

'Who needs birth control here?' says Lewis, a faint note of derision in her voice. 'There's like two and a half men on the entire planet.'

'I know, doesn't it suck?' says Klaski.

Serge appears from around the far side of the enclosure and looks at them significantly.

Lewis stands up. 'Let's just get some sleep, how about.'

They don't have tents or vehicles. They have colored lamps like headlights that attach to the Grid with what looks and sounds like velcro. Each guy stands under her light like they're taking a shower, and it beams down on her, then solidifies like shrink-wrap. By the time it's all finished, the guys look like helpless little packages, action figures in factory molds. The 'light' builds up until each guy is a waxy lump, not particuarly human to look at.

Except Klaski, who sits watch, alone.

'It sounds like Rice Krispies,' she says of the Grid. And her hair does stand on end.

She stays awake for two hours, answering the alert-noises that her Swatch gives off to prevent her from falling asleep. You wish there was a way you could read a book or something. There's nothing to do but look at the Grid doing its snake-dance, charming you with its endless shifts and slithers. Following its motion is like following a weird train of thought, one that never quite lets you remember where you've come from, so that you always have a subtle sense of having just missed some kind of possible meaning.

Whatever drugs the Grid uses to play spin-the-bottle with the heads of the human colonists, they can't affect Gossamer. Therefore, it's not a chemical state, this place you find yourself. It's a mental Grid-state, a result of hanging out inside this ontological Juicemaster. You're slipping into a place beyond words. You're losing awareness of even your own breath. You melt into a nasty hypnosis that's like a bass line: it carries you on its alien heart beat.

Still, in spite of all this, you're more with it than Klaski, who stopped trembling forty minutes ago and has been in REM for eleven minutes plus even though her eyes are still half-open.

Therefore you see them before she does.

They creep out of the well so big-eyed that they remind you of insects. They also move quickly, as if they live according to a different timescale. But their motor acts are sketchy, cartoonish: they lack precision. They're dressed in maladapted scraps of larger people's clothes: trophies, presumably. They're all female.

They seem happy.

That's the first impression you get, and it will never quite go away, no matter what's to come.

Of the rest: you crawl underneath a blanket of dread. This is too much like everything you never wanted. No seven-course meal is going to take this away.

Because they're all young. Very young. Too young to be soldiers; too young to be out at night; too young to be left without a babysitter. They come out of the well and disperse into the Grid like a hatching of spiders. You count eight as they swarm around the campsite. They make no sound. You can't even hear them breathing.

They have long toes, and there's something odd and primeval in the flicker of their hands – something familiar – but you can't quite place it.

They're scary.

Yes, you did mean that: you're scared of them. Isn't everyone afraid of children? Of their lawlessness? Their inability or refusal to recognize the forms and masks of adult status? But this is something else.

You're scared *of* them because you're scared *for* them.

And who ever heard of a child golem?

You alert Machine Front, and Machine Front sets an alarm

shrieking inside Klaski's ear. Her drooping head snaps up and she grabs for her gun. A golem is standing a few yards from her. Klaski and the golem stare at each other.

'Oh my God,' breathes Klaski.

The golem breaks the tableau by laughing, then scurries side-ways and slides between Klaski and the purple lump that was Lewis. The sound of the golem's laughter is watery and joyous, a glissando of high spirits that makes no sense in its context. Klaski seems to take it like a personal insult. She comes up onto her feet, fast.

'Ma'am Captain Serge ma'am, there's golems in the woods!'

In a shutter-fast flicker of movement, the golems ascend and vanish among the shadows. The equipment enclosure opens a slit and Serge's head shoots out, obscenely. She doesn't look sleepy.

'I don't see anything, Klaski. You had a nightmare.'

'They're only babies, ma'am! Only little girls. I couldn't shoot. But they're watching us. I bet any money they're sitting just out of range of our lights, watching.'

'If they are they don't show up on my scope,' Serge answers coolly, poking at her Swatch. 'You check your air filters lately? Gossamer's showing some sh#*t's almost the same as quaaludes, there's a funny old edge in the air. Or maybe you been too busy knitting booties for Hendricks's babies to check your air-quality meter.'

'I know what I saw, ma'am.' Klaski is shivering and her upper lip is wet with snot.

'You like flow charts, don't you, Klaski?'

'What?'

'I can tell. You're that type. I bet your accessories always match your outfit, too. I bet you know what gifts to give people depend-ing on what anniversary it is. True?'

'What?' Klaski repeats. She draws the back of her hand across her nose, disarmed into perking up. 'You mean paper, clocks, stuff like that?'

'Yeah. You want everything clear. You read the instruction manual before operating.'

'No-oh-oh. Not necessarily, ma'am. Just because I don't like being in a place where your shit could attack you if you don't bag it right, or if you drop a Lifesaver it could turn into a bullet – I mean, I don't think that makes me a dweeb.'

'I never said you was a dweeb, I said you like flow charts. You want to know what you're dealing with. It ain't like that here, Klaski. Take it from me. You got to open your mind.'

'I have an open mind! I believe in UFOs and astrology and stuff—'

'Ah, that's just the same shit as flow charts but dumbed down for the masses. People sitting in a room trying to see each other's auras? Seeing what they *want* to see? F%@king self-delusion, Klaski. The Grid knows what you want to see. It knows what you're afraid to see. It'll feed you it on a spoon.'

'Ma'am, if you don't believe me, you can check with the Gossamer.'

'And I will. Go to sleep, Klaski.'

Then Serge turns to you, checking your records, just in case.

You weren't recording, so there are no images. Serge routes through Dante to ask you what you witnessed. You tell Dante you saw them. Dante relays the information to Serge.

'We can recall Gossamer and have the visuals checked,' he offers.

'Yeah, and go the Grid blind? Pffff!'

Serge snaps the Swatch shut.

She keeps watching, but they don't come out. Towards the end of the sleep cycle she drags out a Marlboro and smokes it, distractedly.

trailbreaks

Gloria was waiting for me when I came out of my assignment room.

'I heard you clocked Cori!' she said, squeezing my forearm. 'What happened?'

I shrugged, preoccupied with the Grid and everything. 'Nothing much. She was acting like I was her punchbag, and I hit her.'

'Well . . . good for you.'

'Yeah, well, you're the only one who says so. Sensei told me off in front of the whole class. Big speech about bushido.'

Gloria giggled. 'Bushido,' she repeated, mocking a Japanese accent. 'Bull-sheet-oh. I'll bet she was asking for it.'

I was fuming, though. It was all coming back to me. I said, 'He made me go sit in the corner for half the class.'

She took a long look at me, and I realized I sounded incredibly bitchy. 'Are you OK?'

'Not really,' I said, and felt tears welling up in my eyes. 'I'm not having a very good day.'

In fact, I felt dizzy and I had a headache. The taste of orchids was even stronger. I wasn't sure if it was all because of what had happened in the nex, or if I was just faint because I hadn't eaten since lunch yesterday. I felt pretty sorry for myself, though.

'Who told you?' I asked.

'Bob Baroni called me and asked if I wanted to be on the demonstration team, and I said only if you were, too. That's when he told me.'

'I doubt I'll be allowed on the demonstration team after last night,' I said. 'You should do it, though. I bet it'll be fun.'

'Not without you. Besides, I don't have time. All that extra training.'

I took a deep breath and let it out. 'Thanks, Glow.'

'Thanks, schmanks,' she said. 'Whatcha doing tonight?'

'Lifting weights,' I said. 'Remember, the pact?'

'I thought you might want to go for a drink after work. Gunther's in a meeting in Paramus all day, so we could sneak out early.'

'Uh . . . maybe I better not.'

I could tell that Gloria was halfway between worried about me and hurt by my refusal, but she didn't ask me why I didn't want to go. I didn't want to tell her. I thought if I kept quiet about the fact that I couldn't eat, I could keep control. She said something about going to the Xerox room, but I wasn't really listening. I was worried about my debriefing with Gunther. After Gloria walked out, I decided to get it over with and dragged myself to Gunther's office, only to find him gone.

Stupid. Gloria only just *said* Gunther wasn't here. What was the matter with me?

I sat down at Gloria's desk for a minute. It was 2:30 in the afternoon. I needed to eat. I felt weak and tired.

Gloria kept a candy tray on her desk. It was full of snack-size Baby Ruths and Mounds bars. Normally I'd find these irresistible. But not with the orchids on my tongue. My stomach pitched. I was sure I'd feel a whole lot worse if I tried to eat any of them.

Then I remembered that I owed Gunther sponsorship money for his MS walkathon. I had said I would give him a dollar a mile and he had walked nine miles so I owed him nine bucks. Gunther is always doing stuff for charity or for kids or both.

He keeps the paperwork on his desk, next to his in-box underneath a photo-cube filled with pictures of his nieces and nephew and his bloodhound Andy Rooney. I picked up the envelope with the cash in it and slid a ten-dollar bill in, then put a check mark next to my name and returned the papers to their place.

Then I spotted my own name on a memo. It was the second page; I couldn't find the first page so I didn't know who it was to or what the date or topic was.

without doing a pyramid search, which doesn't fit within the client's budget. I enclose a brief list of test targets filtered from the most recent Karen Orbach transcript, with accompanying numeric accuracy ranks from 1–10 with 10 being a perfect hit.

I've never seen five tens before, and I think I'm safe in guessing that you haven't, either.

Trailbreak Granola Bars	10
Max Factor Mascara[1]	9
Radical Crunchies Snacks[2]	1
Swatch	10
Dune: the movie[3]	4
Charmin	10
Max Headroom[4]	3(?)
Pop Rocks	10
The Gap	10

[1] Shape of product resembles torpedo, reflected in transcript.

[2] We all know that this product bombed before it even hit the shelves. This was our control, and it worked: Orbach didn't even register it.

[3] Our software analysis interprets the transcript as showing awareness of the product coupled with rejection of it. Orbach refers to the book *Dune* but not the film.

[4] Our software analysis indicates the introduction of a character called Dante, whom we believe may be Max. We don't take the low number as a predictor of failure. This is the only truly unknown quantity on our list, and although the number is initially low we believe hit potential exists.

Naturally, Bob, I'm in full agreement with you that our goal is to be 100% system-driven and that we can't rely on agents like Orbach indefinitely. But I'm a practical man and these numbers speak for themselves.

On the basis of Orbach's recent performance, I propose that she be escalated to Tier One. Simultaneously, we will analyze her performance and initiate software development to mimic it. Coupled with the low-risk, low-gain methods we have been using up until now, the deployment of Orbach could boost our numbers by as much as 71%. In light of the fact that Western Syndicates are talking to Hope Industries, our direct competitors, I suggest we take advantage of this opportunity to retain their contract and to move ahead of the pack.

I hope we can discuss this further at the meeting
tomorrow. I will bring additional studies and graphs
to back-up what I'm saying. Looking forward to
seeing you then.

G.T. S.

GS/gl

A voice said, 'I don't think it's a good idea to go in somebody's office when they're not there.'

I turned and stared at Priscilla, executive secretary to Vice
President Bob Hagler, hardly believing my ears. She was
standing there in a purple knit suit, black stockings and
patent leather shoes, a goddess of corporate uptightness.

'Oh, it's OK,' I said, laughing and wanting to believe that
she was joking, too. But I could feel my face burning with
some kind of guilt – I wasn't really sure what kind. The memo
was about me, so in a sense I had a right to read it. 'I was just
putting in my money for the MS walkathon. It's cool.'

She inclined her head and gave it a little toss, body
English for *Come out of there at once, underling*.

My response was automatic and I didn't really think
about it until later. I hurried out of the room. I could feel my
boobs bouncing up and down and my thighs swinging from
side to side, I moved so fast.

'I hang out in Gunther's office all the time when he's not
here,' I said, trying to sound confident. 'We're buddies.'

Priscilla looked at me like I was a roach. She closed the
door behind me and locked it.

I tried to pretend that nothing had happened. I went back
to my assignment room, but I wasn't ready to go on the nex.
Instead, I went home.

*

While I was driving I had that feeling again. I call it the I Want a Cookie feeling, and I guess it grew out of my childhood nickname. I Want a Cookie is that babyish feeling you get. When things go wrong, you want a cookie to make you feel better. When things go right, you want a cookie to celebrate. When you're bored or flat, you want a cookie. When you're nervous. Tired. Sentimental. Watching TV. In a hurry. Killing time. In the car. You want a cookie and you have one, but instead of feeling better, instead of everything changing into happy cookieland, you just get fat and then you hate yourself, which of course calls for more cookies.

In this case I guess it was down to my conversation with Priscilla. I am one of those people who never knows what to say during a confrontation – or what should be a confrontation but in this case had been a non-confrontation thanks to me not knowing what to say. Usually, rather than get upset, I just pretend nothing's happening and wait for it to be over. Afterward, I think of several plausible responses on my part that would have ended with me feeling satisfied with myself, if only I'd had the presence of mind to speak up.

But it's always too late.

So I left work early, thinking about food. I stopped off at A&P to pick up a few things for dinner. Well, it started out as a few things but pretty soon I had a whole shopping cart full of goodies for Nebbie and me. This very cute guy got in line behind me with only a bag of Fritos and a six-pack of Coors, so I let him go ahead.

'Thanks,' he said, and smiled briefly as he squeezed past me and my stuff. He was about six-two, lean, with fluffy brown hair and a strong jaw. He had blue eyes and a tan, which always looks good but looked especially good on him, and he was dressed like a construction worker right down to his boots. It's too bad they were the lace-up kind, because I love old-fashioned boots like from *The Three Musketeers* or medieval times, where the leather kind of comes up over the calf and then folds over. I wish they'd come back in style. He'd look so good in clothes like that. I started fantasizing that he was F'lar from *Dragonflight* and he was just about to go out and risk his life flying Thread on Monarth. I'd be Lessa: tiny, fierce, indomitable and beautiful – also risking my life on a daily basis despite F'lar's efforts to tame me.

I stared at him, but I tried not to be obvious. I hasten to add that I would have let him go first even if he was the ugliest person I'd ever seen. I was just being courteous, and I wouldn't want anybody to be standing behind me with two items, seething that they were stuck behind some big fat moose buying half the store. But as I looked at him I could feel him pulling my eyes like a magnet. I followed him out of the store and watched him get in his pickup. There was a German Shepherd in the front seat, too. It licked his face when he got in.

I got in my own car and told myself to forget the guy in the store. If I really think about it, I guess one reason I was so frustrated with Priscilla's bitchiness had to do with the people I'm working with *in* the nex. Flying with Gossamer is one thing: I mean, OK, she's not emotionally bonded with me. In fact, she doesn't even have emotions that I know of, she isn't sentient, and I don't get to ride her like a dragon. Fair enough. But flying with Gossamer is still the most exciting thing I've ever done, and I love it. On the other hand, being down there with people like Serge and her team, fighting a war over this planet that everybody wants a piece of, wants to tear up, build roads on, steal its raw materials, and generally render tame and boring – that's not my idea of a good time. They're so . . . base. There's nothing heroic about what they're doing that I can see. They aren't even nice, except maybe Lewis, and she has her nose buried in *Ladies Home Journal* half the time. I admit the golems are nasty and scary, but they're also somehow sad and nobody seems to see that. I don't even know whose side to be on. With Commander Galante I felt like I was working under a real leader. With Serge I just feel off-balance all the time. And frustrated.

When I'm frustrated, I eat. And eat. I put food in my stomach like a bricklayer trowels cement, brick by brick building my wall.

I put the car in gear. I decided to go home and have a really good meal. I'd feel better. I wasn't going to let them get to me. I know there's such a thing as good. I know there are real heroes out there. I just don't know how to find them.

The guy in the A&P might be hero material. I doubted it, though. Now that I did karate, I knew that you had to be a black belt before you were anything special. When I first saw the black belts, I knew I'd finally found my own people. I'd finally come home. They were a cut above. They were people of honor. They were special. And I'd do anything to be like them. Maybe then my real life could start to be as interesting as my life on the nex – and with me acting in it, not just watching.

I got home in plenty of time to iron my gi and get ready. I had my dinner all planned out. A sirloin steak, baked potato with sour cream and two or three ears of local Jersey corn on the cob, smothered in butter. I didn't worry about the pact with Gloria because I had, after all, been fasting since yesterday and I owed myself some calories. So I had also picked up a seven-layer cake for dessert, with a little tub of Haägen Dazs on the side. I normally don't cook on a Wednesday night, I just pick up a TV dinner or something, and it felt a little strange to go to all this trouble just for myself, but I needed something big and delicious after the day I'd had.

I figured what I'd do would be eat the main meal, digest for an hour, go to karate and then afterward I could come home and have my chocolate cake and curl up with Nebbie and a good book.

My stomach was growling away while the steak cooked, so I decided to eat the corn first. I spread butter on a piece of bread and then rubbed it over the corn. I threw plenty of salt on there, too. Then I picked up the corn-holders and brought the pale, gorgeous ear to my mouth.

For some reason, I paused. My mouth remained closed. I could smell the corn, and the steak cooking, and the butter. But I couldn't seem to take that final step. I couldn't bite into the food.

Strange. Annoying. I was really hungry. With all my will, I closed my eyes, opened my mouth, and put the ear of corn between my lips. The salt stung my lower lip where it was a little chapped. I tasted the butter. And I tasted the orchid flavor of the Grid. I started to take a bite and instead found that I'd put the ear back down.

Maybe I needed some music. I got out a record by Asia which I'd bought because it had a picture of this awesome green dragon on the cover. The music is a little too white-bread and stiff for my liking, but it had a few good songs on it, like 'Sole Survivor.' I put it on and synthesizer music filled my apartment, masking the hissing and popping of the steak, which I now removed from the grill pan and dumped on my plate. The corn was starting to look cool and puckered, sitting there in a pool of salty butter.

I sat there for forty-five minutes, wishing I could eat. But I couldn't.

I thought: *I wonder if this is how an impotent man feels.*

Well, I was supposed to train and I couldn't very well train on an empty stomach. Desperate measures were called for.

I went to the goodie cabinet and forced myself to eat a half-pound-size Cadbury bar. It overpowered the orchids and tasted pretty good, and I read some *Crystal Singer* at the same time, determined to feel better. When I was done with the candy I had a vague headache, but I kept reading.

Killashandra had a vague headache, too, but it turned out to be only her Milekey Transition, and totally worth it. So I ignored mine.

Then I threw up.

I couldn't believe it.

I'd read about dancers and actresses who made themselves sick so they wouldn't get fat. But that's not me. I didn't mind being fat. I didn't want to throw up. I wanted to eat food and keep it down. I liked being big. I wasn't sticking my fingers down my throat.

What was going on here?

And what was I going to do with all my emotions, if I couldn't put them in my mouth and eat them?

That was what I wanted to know.

I went to the dojo. No one else was there yet, so I decided to practice on the water bag. I pretended I was Muhammad Ali training to fight George Foreman in Africa. I danced and whacked and dodged. The bag was heavy, but it was swinging and squealing on its chains. I was having a pretty good time.

Miss Cooper came out of the bathroom behind me. I saw her in the mirror and checked myself, sweating and puffing.

'What are you doing?' she laughed. 'It sounds like a construction site in here.'

I laughed, then jabbed and hooked a few more times for good measure, imagining Gunther's smug face on the bag at my eye level. The bag jolted on its chains when I hit it.

'Keep your shoulder down when you punch. And make sure you chamber the opposite hand. You're not standing square on. You should be punching center-line. And stay in a good stance. Keep your feet planted and your knees bent – you keep coming up on your toes. The objective is to have good form, not to just hit as hard as you can.'

I nodded, swallowing. Accepting. So much for my Ali

impersonation. Dutifully I got in my front stance and I was still taking instruction from Miss Cooper – and not moving the bag an inch – when people started showing up and doing their stretching.

Cori Knight showed up. When I went to get my towel, she was sitting on the sidelines in her knee brace, watching the class.

'Hi, how ya doin,' I said, and she launched into her usual litany of I'm-overdue-on-my-credit-card-my-car's-on-the-blink-I-have-to-study-for-a-biochem-exam-I-twisted-my-knee-again-getting-out-of-the-shower moaning and groaning. That's how I knew she wasn't holding a grudge. Probably she thought me hitting her was just another layer in her cake of pain. Or else she liked being injured. She sure seemed to be having a better time sitting on the sidelines watching than she ever had in class. And she probably enjoyed getting to sit near the black belts' section, flirting with Mr. Juarez while I sweated and fell on my butt.

Besides, because I am black I didn't think that she would want to be seen to be hating my guts. She's like that. Probably felt sorry for me. Probably thought I wished I had her skinny white butt, even though it looked like a piece of dead fish.

Gloria was there, too. We stretched and then started practicing our katas. Gloria's form is so pretty. You should see her do the sumo stances in Sei-enchin kata. They're deep and symmetrical, and she doesn't have to waddle to get from one to the other, she just flows. Her hands are graceful, too. I wish I could be like that.

Mr. Juarez took the warm-up and then told us that tonight the color belts would start learning breaking in preparation for the tournament and demonstration. Sensei came out of the office and started explaining all about focus and how, by focusing your *ki*, or spirit energy, you could direct your power into your hand and break a brick without hurting yourself. Then he asked Mr. Juarez to demonstrate punching through a brick that had been set up on special blocks. Whenever he wants to show us something hard, he asks either Miss Cooper or Mr. Juarez. He didn't ask Miss Cooper to break the brick because, he said, the ladies probably wouldn't want to practice breaking because of our nails. Miss Cooper gave a weak smile as if she'd heard it all before.

It took Mr. Juarez a couple of tries, but in the end he did it. Everyone clapped. We were to start practicing on boards. There were some half-inch thick sheets of white pine, and we were to strike them with the grain. There was a lot of talk about what part of the hand to use, how to gather your *ki* ahead of time, how to drop your weight, where to focus, and so on. I listened avidly.

When Gloria and I came to take our turns, Mr. Juarez said, 'Now, ladies, you don't have to do this if you don't want to.'

'Good,' said Gloria. 'I don't want to.'

Mr. Juarez nodded to her, she bowed to him and went to the back of the line.

'How about you, Miss Orbach?'

'I'll give it a try,' I said. Instantly Miss Cooper was by my side.

'Come on, you can do it,' she said. 'Just line up your hand in the chamber. Make sure you drop your right knee as you come down. Look at a spot about two inches below the board, focus your energy, and . . . *punch!*'

Whack!

My hand bounced off the board, knuckles skinned.

'That's OK, that's OK, it's a good first try,' said Mr. Juarez. Miss Cooper led me away and told me not to worry.

'A lot of it is psychological,' she said. 'You're afraid of hurting your hand, so you pull back instinctively. You have to learn to punch *through* that point.'

Gloria, listening, offered, 'Yeah, that's what they told me

when I was having Scottie, they said to push through the pain and you know what? It hurt worse and I had about a million stitches and bled like a pig.'

Miss Cooper smiled thinly. 'Stick around for a little extra training tonight, Cookie,' she told me. 'I'll help you.'

So I stuck around after Gloria and the others went to Tony's for pizza. Troy was hanging around the heavy bag with some of the brown and black belts; they were challenging each other how many different ways they could break a brick. ('Do it with your head, man, I saw that on ESPN once and it was awesome'.) Troy saw me standing there and came over.

'Hey, I saw you hit that piece of wood. You could punch harder than that. How come you wimped out?'

I like Troy. He's a cute guy but he doesn't intimidate me like most cute guys, he has the kind of energy of a guy you can actually talk to and he doesn't make you feel like a fat slob. He has a girlfriend and a couple of little kids; they're in the kids' class and that's how he got interested in training.

'I didn't wimp out,' I said out of the side of my mouth. 'Miss Cooper was correcting my form. I was afraid of doing it wrong.'

'Nah, you can't do it wrong,' Troy said. 'You afraid you're gonna hurt your hand? C'mere, let's try an experiment.'

He set up a couple of cinder blocks to make a platform and stuck a brick across them. Then he went out into the alley, tiptoeing around barefoot by the garbage cans and whooping, 'Ooh! Ee! Ah! A rat just ran across my foot!' so that I had to crack up. He came back with an old phone book and laid it across the brick.

'Here. Now you got some nice padding. You just got to get used to hitting something hard.'

I looked at my skinned knuckles. 'I don't know . . .'

'Come on, Cookie, don't be a chickenshit.'

'I am not.'

'Let's see you hit it, then.'

So I hit it. It still hurt, but not as much.

'You call that hitting? My girlfriend hits her face harder than that when she putting on makeup.'

So I hit it again. Harder.

'Come on, is that the best you can do?'

I hit it again. And again. Finally, Troy said, 'Here, lemme in there.'

He tore off some of the pages of the phone book.

'Enough already, Troy.'

'Come *on*, you big moose.'

'*What* did you call me?'

'Hit it.'

'I'll hit you in a minute.' I hit it. He tore off more pages.

'Again. *Mooo!*'

I hit it again. Really hard. My hand was killing me.

'Come on, bitch.'

We were drawing a crowd, and the other men were laughing uneasily at what Troy was saying to me. I could feel my face getting hot and my heart pounding.

'I've had a really bad day, Troy, let's call it quits before you make me mad.'

'Ooh, don't want to make the fat mama mad, do I?' scoffed Troy. 'She might break a nail or—'

Bam!

The brick fell on the floor in two pieces. A couple of thin sheets of telephone directory pages drifted to the floor.

I gaped.

'Ah-ha!' shouted Troy. 'I told you you could do it. You got to unleash the inner beast, girl!'

'Just what is going on here?' It was Miss Cooper. She walked in with her naginata and saw the scene.

'Oh, uh, Miss Cooper, we was just playin' around and – look, Cookie broke that all by herself!'

I looked sheepishly at the floor. My hand was bleeding.

'I think you can all go now,' Miss Cooper said, and the guys all split, even Mr. Juarez who is also a black belt. Troy winked at me as he went around the corner.

'You'd better put some ice on that hand,' she said to me. 'What's going on here? Are you trying to prove something? You're only a purple belt. You shouldn't even be thinking about breaking a brick yet. If Shihan knew about this he'd have my head on a stick.'

I apologized.

'All right,' she said, kindly. 'I wanted to talk to you about the other night. What happened in sparring. I'm concerned that you don't seem to have the right idea about what we're doing. I know you would never want to hurt anybody, but—'

'I wouldn't!' I said. 'I hate violence, I can't stand to see it. I don't know what's wrong with me. I can do the form OK in the kata, but when it gets to sparring I just lose it.'

'That's why you have to have Bushido. You have to follow the code. You can't just go around hitting people. You have to have control over everything you do.'

'Control,' I repeated. 'OK, I'll keep trying. Control.'

Then we did a little light sparring. Miss Cooper would feed me techniques so that I could learn to deal with them without freaking out. She let me come in and hit her, too. 'Good!' she'd say, or 'Too hard. Watch your left foot, I could sweep you there.' At the end, she said, 'Better. Much better. You have to have that kind of control. Otherwise you're too dangerous.'

Me, dangerous? What a thought.

Control. I'm going to have control.

But it wasn't control that broke the brick, was it?

referred pain

Next shift, Serge orders you to fly a wide patrol right over N-Ridge while her team goes after Gonzalez on foot.

'We're getting real close to the mines and according to the Front, there's enough golems up here to fill Shea Stadium. I don't want no Halloween present from the Grid when I get up there, you know?'

Gossamer rises on a warm wave and banks sharply to avoid a high point in the Grid. You smell the flowers through Goss and try to identify the psychotropic signatures that come slithering through the atmosphere, falling harmlessly on Gossamer but probably not so harmlessly on any humans in this zone. You package up everything you can get on the chemicals and send this to Machine Front for analysis as a matter of routine.

Then you start looking for golems.

If they were smart – and it's difficult sometimes to know whether or not they are smart, because they operate according to Grid rationale, which is really no rationale at all – they would send some of their members away from the set that is supposed to be massing near the mine entrance to swarm around behind Serge's convoy and make sure it could never return to X. You're going to have to spot them, anticipate their plans, and keep

Serge ahead of the game so she can find a way back without having to engage thousands more golems.

You head for the road to N-Ridge to see if your fears are founded on anything real. Well, real in a Grid sense. Because golems are like those flower sculptures you see in Asia made in the shape of people. From a distance it looks like a real person but when you come in close you see it's all gardenias or whatever. That's what the golems are. When they die, there's a lot of initial gore and they leave behind a mess, but then they pretty much evaporate into a cloud of Grid-pollen. They are only made real in a fleshly sense by human perception.

Humans feel they need to perceive things in terms of agents and they make a big separation between actor and acted-upon, subject and object. Humans organize, perceptually dividing the Grid into golems and apparently inert webbing, but MF cameras can't record golems. This invisibility-to-MF is a problem, because their non-corporeality doesn't stop golems from taking stuff apart and chucking it into the well. That's why robot planes wouldn't do any good in your job, although, through you, Gossamer's prosthetic eyes are able to record the existence of golems.

It's not long before you see a band of them moving like monkeys in the webbing. Gossamer's eyes can pick up motion through several layers of Grid, though detail eludes her. The golems are making for the ragged trail that Serge's Machine Front backup convoy has left, a wound in the Grid. You lock on to the golems and track them. Eventually you glimpse one clearly through a break in the Grid. It has been fully reconstructed, geared up in a custom battleskin complete with thermal regulator and water-purifier. Yet it is also unarmed, and a closer check reveals that it's bereft both of breathing filters and of communications equipment.

There's nothing surprising about this. Current Grid theory posits that the golems need to breathe the raw air so that they can read its scent-messages. You follow the golems until you are satisfied that they don't present an immediate threat to Serge; then you move on, making a wide sweep and scanning a fan-shaped area behind Serge's convoy. When you are satisfied nothing wicked is following them, you urge Gossamer faster and head for the logic mines on N-Ridge.

The grave balloon has gone its own way, the storm has cleared, and everything looks benign and pretty. You steel yourself, wondering what to expect. And again and again you glimpse something that looks like structure – but only when seen from the corner of your eye. When you try to look at it straight on, the apparent order disappears in the jumble and jump, only to return when you look away: on the periphery of your visual field, you are teased by impressions of castles and towers and bridges.

You turn Gossamer and head back, planning to survey a neat triangle around and between Serge and the mines. It's an area you know pretty well, so you have to double-check your coordinates when you see what it's looking like these days. Where before the Grid's open lattice had gradually evaporated into cloud, now there is a grayness. At first you think it's a burn scar; but no. Just as it was in the clearing you saw before the storm drove you away, this part of the Grid has been sucked dry of all activity. It's still there, it simply isn't alive anymore. It doesn't move, or glow. Instead of endlessly shifting branches, there are skeletal forms frozen in mid-writhe, like trees long battered by sea winds and contorted into shapes that suggest motion though they are still as death. This devastation stretches long and narrow like a road, beginning only a mile or so from the mine perimeter and reaching into the wilds of N-Ridge.

By contrast to the rest of the Grid, the stillness is shocking. Nothing moves. Nothing.

You fly over this 'road' for some time, scanning from side to side for clues as to its origin. And in the living Grid nearby, you pick up golems. A lot of them. They are heading in the same direction as you, parallel to the wasted Grid; but they are much slower and you soon pass them. You give Gossamer her head and she increases speed: she's following a scent-trail, and you can guess where it's going to lead even before Gossamer's eyes show you the very same shorn-off clearing that you were driven from before. This seems to be the end – or the beginning – of the dead zone.

What the heck has been happening here?

You start to pull pictures for Machine Front. Much of the well has been reduced to dust; but not all of it. There is something submerged in that dull gleam, though you can't see it very well from this height. Gossamer's eyes don't seem to work as well in the dead Grid. It's almost as though her eyes are adapted to see the order within randomly moving aspects of the live Grid, and she doesn't know how to decipher the fixed forms of the Grid in death. You have to strain to see through her eyes. And even the live Grid adjacent to the ruined area looks different. It looks more ordered – just as you noticed the first time you were here. And certainly, the dead, skeletal areas seem to have an almost mechanical—

SOS!!

Serge is calling you.

AMBUSHED. SURROUNDED. MAYBE 100 GOLEMS. WHICH WAY SHOULD WE BREAK?

She sends a position, but it's not within your sights at the moment. You send a question through MF.

ARE YOU NEAR DEAD AREA? GRAY THING?

NO. WHAT GRAY THING? SHOULD WE GO THERE?

NO! HOLD YOUR POSITION. ON MY WAY.

Then you hare off back over the live Grid, in the direction of her signal.

Gossamer is scanning with all her powers, but the only movement you pick up is that made by golems. A lot of them. Their movements are impressions of flickering shadow and light, suggested but not clearly articulated within the chaos of the Grid. Yet you can perceive a general pattern, like ants moving on a scent trail. They are coming from all directions, converging on a point.

I WAS AFRAID OF THIS, you tell Machine Front. HOW ARE THEY MASSING SO QUICKLY?

Machine Front doesn't bother to answer. It isn't accountable for your emotional condition; no one is. MF takes your images and sends back a little army of calculations led by a general conclusion. It has pinpointed the center of the golems' attention, the point on which all their movement converges.

Gossamer goes there like lightning and, sure enough, it's Serge. She's only a quarter-mile from Arla's last position, but there are hundreds of golems in the space between, and more are emerging from the well all the time.

You know that Serge's backup convoy is plowing its way up from the main road, but it moves with agonizing slowness.

CAN I GET TO GONZALEZ FROM HERE? Serge wants to know.

I GET THE FEELING GONZALEZ IS BAIT. FORGET IT.

TELL ME WHERE THE GOLEMS ARE WEAKEST AND LEAVE IT AT THAT, GOSS.

Right. Well, it *is* your job. You have picked up Gonzalez's signal. But you don't like the look of this. From the air it seems to you that Serge is being led into the dead area of the Grid.

GOSS, I DON'T GOT ANOTHER 20 YEARS TO HANG OUT HERE.

Ok, then. Have it your way at Burger King.

GONZALEZ IN SIGHT. FOLLOW MY BEACON.

And you throw her a light, down through layers of Grid pollen and bright and shadowy branches, a light to guide her towards Arla Gonzalez.

The team gets panicky when Serge orders them onward. They keep jumping and looking over their shoulders at the golems who hem them in, watching them from above and below and between arms of the Grid, who rise from the well to stare at them. The golems have not attacked yet, but Klaski is already hyperventilating and you read Lewis's lips as she says, 'f%&k rescuing Gonzalez, let's worry about ourselves!'

But when Serge goes bounding off through the Grid with the energy of a rabid squirrel, they follow her. Golems close in behind, cutting off any chance of retreat.

Klaski switches goggle settings repetitively, toggling her options so fast that her helmet chirps like a tree-frog chorus, until with a definitive *snap* the manual fitting breaks. She makes a violent move as if to throw it in the well, checks herself, and instead sinks to the foundation in a faint.

Hendricks is all over it. She drags Klaski up and makes her follow. Serge looks up, locates you, and signals you to proceed.

There are so many golems surrounding Serge that it seems pointless to carry on. Lucky for the team, most of the golems are hidden in the Grid; but they're all too apparent to you from the air.

It's all you can do to hang on to the nex. You don't want to be here; there's nothing you can do, why do you have to see it, this is all a form of torture . . . but you keep lighting the way to Gonzalez.

It all happens too quickly. One minute, Serge's rescue party looks like Bruce Springsteen and the E Street Band being swarmed by fans, with golems converging from all sides, rising out of the well, dropping out of branches overhead in obscene numbers. There is a swollen moment of held breath while you hang, weightless, an unwilling witness to imminent atrocity; and then you notice a little red light flashing from amongst the golems.

Gonzalez is coming this way.

Serge doesn't see her – there are too many golems in between them. The team doesn't see her. But you do. Only you. You consider recording what's happening, but a sense that this would be a perverse, voyeuristic act holds you back.

The golems seem to part around Gonzalez. Then they begin to

draw back from Serge and the team, slowly at first, and then with more and more momentum, tumbling over one another like pebbles and shells being sucked into the base of a gathering wave of immense proportions. But this is a wave that never strikes. The golems simply dissolve into the riotous bloom of data that is the Grid, leaving Serge and company turning in amazed circles, their faces pale with disbelief at their luck.

You fly over Gonzalez and try to pick up more information about her, but she's changed directon again. Now she's moving rapidly through the Grid in the rough direction of the mines. You start to follow.

Serge suddenly looks up and sees you. Her hand goes into one of her thigh pouches and out comes a scent beckon. She brandishes it like a doggy treat. You try to resist, but Gossamer is susceptible to the aroma.

GONZALEZ. HAVE SIGHTED GONZALEZ, LET ME FOLLOW.

'Come on, Gossamer,' Serge says her best dog-wheedling tone. You have no choice but to let Gossamer go to her. And you lose Gonzalez.

Serge catches you out of the air.

'Just work with me, butterfly,' she croons to Goss. Her breath smells of canned mackerel. Her eyes are alight with adrenaline and triumph. 'This is a friggin' miracle. We'll get Gonzalez, but we need backup.'

She hands you to Lewis for a quick once-over, then checks in with Dante.

'Where's the metal at? The sooner we get Gonzo and get the frig outta here, the better.'

You already know that there's a big chunk of dead Grid between here and the convoy's position, but Serge needs to get filled in.

'What do you mean, *dead*?' she asks Dante, and then frowns at the images you took earlier as they are played across the air above her Swatch'd arm. Eventually she shrugs.

'OK, but what's stopping you from driving through the so-called dead zone?'

'We don't think that's advisable, until we know more about it,' Dante tells her. 'We can't afford to risk the machines.'

'So what, then? Mountain's gotta go to Muhammad?'

'You'll have to make your way back and cut your own path.'

Serge rolls her eyes. 'How long's that gonna take? And in the meanwhile Gonzalez disappears?'

It's Dante's turn to shrug.

'You could rough it for a few more days.'

Serge snorts. 'Yeah, except Klaski will be speaking in tongues if she don't get to a jacuzzi and a Shop-Rite in the next ten minutes.'

'Lieutenant Klaski was a very bright pupil at MIT.'

'She should of stayed there, then, 'cuz she's a ditz and a half.'

Serge gets rid of Dante and yells at the others to get a move on.

She marches them straight toward the dead zone, but doesn't actually enter it. The altered structure of the Grid adjacent to the dead area seems to give Serge pause.

'I ain't never seen none of this before,' she mutters, waving at you to come in closer.

It's easy enough to fly at low altitudes, because there is less visual noise in this part of the Grid. The interconnecting arms and lattices don't strobe as much, and the pathways are much clearer. There are implicit walls and floors, windows.

'It's a structure for sure,' says Lewis, scanning it with her sensor gun.

'Who built it? Golems?'

'Don't be stupid, Klaski, golems don't build things,' Serge snaps.

'It certainly hasn't been built by anyone,' Lewis says thoughtfully. 'But it could be an example of paradigm adaptation. The Grid might be absorbing the principles of human architecture through studying our machines, and applying those principles to its own structure.'

'But why?' Serge was climbing upside down like a kid on the monkey bars. 'Human architecture is for humans. The Grid doesn't need shelter and all that.'

'Experiment?'

'Maybe. I don't trust it, though. Gives me a creepy feeling. Like it's mocking us.' She dropped to the ground and clapped her hands, dispersing a cloud of pollen.

'They told us in basic that it's a first-grade error to attribute human foibles to the Grid.'

'You are asking for a slap upside the head, Klaski.'

'Sorry, ma'am.'

'Strange back there, the way the golems just scattered,' Lewis says. 'Why didn't they stay and fight?'

'Who cares?' Hendricks puts in. 'Long as they're gone, I'm happy.'

But you're thinking about Arla Gonzalez, and how the golems gave way before her.

YOU ARE CLOSE TO DEAD ZONE, you send to Serge. ADVISE STAY BACK.

'The problem with the Grid,' replies Serge, acknowledging you with a wave, 'well, one of the problems, is that proximity don't mean doodle. Just because this part is next to that part don't mean they got nothing to do with one another. You could tweak this branch here and get a reaction like fifteen miles away, and you'd never even know.'

'Ooh, that sounds like referred pain,' Hendricks says. 'My chiropractor told me about that.'

Serge ignores her. 'OK. We got a big structure that looks human-like, and then not too far away we got a dead section, and then we're practically on top of N-Ridge where the mines are— Klaski! Quit looking panicky. This is what it's all about, right here, right now.'

'Ma'am, I have to go to the bathroom.'

'Klaski, I ain't gonna tell you again to get your act together. I am not your fourth-grade teacher.'

Serge makes a jerking motion of her head and Klaski leaps up and stumbles off behind a chunk of the Grid, snatching a proffered wad of toilet paper from Hendricks's hand as she goes.

'I'm sorry, I just can't go in front of people, OK?' she hisses at Hendricks, who is laughing.

'As I was saying?' Serge glares at the others.

'Proximity,' Lewis volunteers.

'Proximity. And beyond that, what I call generalized weirdness. It's not our cells that the Grid wants. You can pee in it, brush your hair, even bleed in it. That won't come back to haunt you. It would rather have the label off a jar of spaghetti sauce, or your New Balance sneakers. It would rather have the stuff that's in your head, when you die, to make golems from. That's what's dangerous about it. That's what's f@*ked. It eats *thought*.'

Hendricks is hanging on to a loose cable of Grid and swinging slightly, looking at her feet. She looks like a bored preschooler.

Serge takes Lewis aside and tells her to get to work gathering survey information on the structure. 'We're not in a good rendezvous position for the convoy. I don't want to stay exposed too long, but I can't see going back and walking away from this thing without knowing what it is.'

She doesn't mention Gonzalez but it's pretty obvious that she's thinking about her. You know Serge. If she really wants something bad, she never says anything about it. She never tells you what she intends to do. Seems to be some kind of superstition with her. Like she has to sneak up on her quarry and grab it from behind; she never gives herself away. You can see something in Lewis's face, too, that says she knows this about Serge.

'Right,' Lewis says briskly. 'Let's get down to work, then. I'll just take a look at our perimeter and then we can figure out where to start.'

Serge says nothing – she's distracted by the readings on her Swatch again – and Lewis takes silence for assent, hustling the others into action. You know that Serge is brewing something, but Klaski and Lewis seem to think they're on a coffee break. They wander around the structure, stretching, peering, acting relaxed and happy for once which is a real change from the grim faces you're used to seeing when they're on the move in the Grid.

'I like it here,' Hendricks announces. 'It's almost like a house. We could hang some curtains over there, the TV could go in the corner . . .'

Above them, Klaski is clowning around on the same monkey-bar-like configuration that Serge climbed.

'Dibs on the top bunk,' she calls.

'OK, cut it out,' Lewis growls, trying to sound like Serge. 'This ain't the Swiss Family Robinson. Let's start recording.'

You're busy then, helping the group take readings and make measurements; but you can't help but notice the way Serge stays out of it. She keeps wandering off to the north, or glancing that way. You know that she's looking in the direction of Arla's last position, which she can presumably locate with her Swatch. The others are too busy with their work to observe the change in her disposition. Everybody seems relieved not to be slipping and climbing and looking out for golems in all directions. There's a Friday-afternoon feeling among them.

After a while Serge says, 'I'm going walkabout. You guys stay put. Goss, get a quick charge while you can. You're with me.'

orchids

I was tired and depressed when I came off the nex. I didn't actually feel hungry, but stepping out of my assignment room my first impulse was to get a candy bar, and I found my feet had taken me to the machine automatically. I stood there staring at the bile-provoking chocolate bars before I finally picked some sugar-free Dentine, hoping to kill the nasty taste in my mouth.

Wendy came along as I was unwrapping my gum. We were only the barest of acquaintances, and I hadn't seen her recently, probably because we'd both been putting in such long hours in our respective assignment rooms. She was a middle-aged bleach-blonde Flier who was always in a hurry; always manic. Today was no exception. She hustled down the corridor in her pumps and started slamming quarters into the vending machine. She was wearing a peach silk ensemble and her hair was perfect. I could never see the point of dressing this way when you work in a little booth in an obscure corridor behind Accounting and no one ever sees you all day except Gunther and, maybe, Gloria. But Wendy is always the consummate professional – whatever that means.

In this case, it seemed to mean being so rude as to ignore the fact that I was standing two feet away.

'How are things in your world?' I heard myself drawl, more for my own amusement in seeing her jump out of her skin than because I cared.

She glanced at me, gave an off-balance smile, and banged on the machine to dislodge some M&Ms.

'The stress is killing me,' she said. 'Dog Walks Fence never mentioned the vision quest could give you heartburn. I wish I had some peyote, I mean I'm only human and that Gunther is impossible to please. Now he's going to replace me with a computer if I don't do better.'

We weren't supposed to talk shop, so I was surprised by her answer. We Fliers know better than to allude to events of the war outside the sanctity of a debriefing.

'I mean, I just bought a condo in Seaside Heights. I have responsibilities, you know?'

I nodded, bemused.

'It's hard to imagine being replaced by a machine. But, you know, maybe we'll all be better off when the Third Wave comes,' I said. 'I'd rather be reassigned somewhere more peaceful.'

'Third Wave? He's not that warrior with the rifle, is he, because—'

She clapped her mouth shut. Priscilla was coming down the corridor.

'I got them on sale at Marty's,' I said, doing a little jog in place in my sneakers. 'You should really try them, those heels are no good for your back.'

'Ladies . . .' said Priscilla. 'Everything all right?'

'No,' snarled Wendy, winking at me. 'The machine ate my quarters.'

She hit it again. I wondered if all Fliers were full of violence; maybe it was part of the job qualifications to have hidden reservoirs of rage. I left Wendy and Priscilla bitching at each other and started towards Gunther's office.

'He's not there,' Priscilla called after me sharply. 'He's out at a meeting.'

'I have to do my debriefing,' I said.

'I'll show you what to do,' Wendy said, breaking away from Priscilla. She ripped open the M&Ms and offered some to me; I shook my head. At Gloria's desk Wendy pointed out a tape recorder and a stack of cassettes.

'Just put it on the tape for him and label it. Gloria will file it after lunch. Is she a bitch or what?'

'Gloria?'

'No, catwoman over there.'

'Oh. Yeah. Hey, what was that about a rifle?'

Wendy's eyes widened. She put her finger over her lips and rolled her eyes. Then she leaned over and whispered very faintly in my ear.

'Bugged. Never, never talk here.'

Then she raised her voice and said clearly, 'Yeah, that Priscilla is a total c*%tface. I wonder if she was a Nazi in her past life.'

Wendy grinned at me and walked out of Gloria's work area, pointing significantly at the overhead sprinkler system as she did so.

And they call me crazy.

After I'd recorded my debriefing, I dragged myself home. I still hadn't eaten. It was freakish.

I called Miles and told him about the taste in my mouth and he said a lot of stuff about ketones and Gandhi and then told me not to worry about it but to try to drink water.

There was no training that night, and I decided I was going to eat, no matter what it took. It took me several hours to work myself up to it. I had some cold shrimp in the refrigerator. I made dip with ketchup and mayonnaise and shared the shrimp with Nebula. It took all my concentration to make myself eat the shrimp. Getting it in my mouth was like threading a needle in a hurricane. It was like my hand just didn't want to obey me.

I ate six jumbo shrimp and two pieces of Arnold's Country White bread. Normally this would have been just a light snack, but I couldn't squeeze in another bite. I managed to drink some caffeine-free Pepsi. Afterwards I listened to the Dr. Ruth show on the radio – this was the closest I have ever gotten to sex other than being groped by Jim Szabo in the movies when I was 22.

Then I crawled into bed. The orchid/corpse taste was still there.

I woke up at 1:47 a.m. with shooting pains in my stomach. I had curled into a fetal position on my left side while in my sleep, but it wasn't enough to relieve the pain. My insides felt like they had hot lava in them. My stomach was bloated, distended with gas, and I felt so nauseous that I barely had time to take in the readout on my clock radio before I was on my feet and racing for the bathroom.

I almost didn't make it. I lifted the toilet seat with so much force that it banged straight down again, hitting me on the back of the head as I brought up the remains of the shrimp and bread. I heaved a few more times, but nothing else came up. Then my bowels kicked into gear, and I had to quickly turn around and sit down while the lava shot out of my rear end. The smell was so horrible that I flushed, turned around, and retched again. Nothing came up but bile.

I ran the cold water and rinsed out my mouth. I was shivering so hard my teeth chattered, and my legs would barely support me. I sank to the bathroom floor and curled up on my side. I didn't dare go back to bed because I could sense that it was all going to happen again, and it did. I went through the same cycle three times, until I was so weak that

I could hardly move and my whole body ached from the effort of vomiting my stomach empty. My butt felt like I'd had an enema with battery acid. Nebbie watched me curiously, jumping up on the bathtub and meowing until I turned on the tap at a drip for her.

I crawled onto the bath mat and listened to her purring echoing in the bathtub as she washed her paws and face in the dripping water.

Imus in the morning woke me up. It took me a while to figure out where I was: I could hear faint strains of the Thompson Twins coming from the radio as the traffic report finished. I sat up.

I felt terrible.

I thought about everything that had happened last time at karate, and then being sick, and the fact that I hadn't eaten, and I wondered if I should stay home and see a doctor.

Then I remembered Gossamer. I dragged myself up.

a good untarnished fact

Serge is climbing through the structured Grid with relative ease. Inside her helmet she is listening to an archives report by Dr. Arla Gonzalez, recorded at the time of Gonzalez's appointment as commander of the N-Ridge mine. Dante is beaming the statement to Serge via Gossamer. That means you get to hear it, too. Gonzalez has a low, softly modulated voice whose beauty can't be ruined even by its distinct Bronx twang.

It might be tempting to assume that because I'm coming to this post as the former director of the X medical center, I'm not a likely choice to supervise a mining operation. But nothing could be farther from the truth. I enlisted because I felt compelled to contribute to the understanding of the Grid, and I still feel that way. On the medical side of my career, I saw the realities of survival in the Grid on a daily basis. And on the research side, I have consistently sought to increase our chances of gaining and maintaining a profitable foothold here. The way to do this, as I see it, is to understand the Grid. And the logic mines are the key to that.

Put simply, we don't know what the Grid is. We don't know if it's a substance, an organism, a species, or some kind of created structure. It doesn't behave like anything we've ever seen before. We might be tempted to say that it's an organism with different organs and systems: the foundation, the well, the branches, the pollen, the fliers . . . but it would then be an organism which comprises the entire environment, which is a contradiction in terms. So we could accord to it the properties of an ecosystem, but the members of this system exchange places according to processes we can't detect.

For example, knowing what happens when a body goes into the well and returns ninefold as golems is a little like trying to trace the decay of a corpse and the transfer of its molecules into other organisms, without having so much as a microscope to explain what is happening. There is a large element of guesswork and a reliance on concepts that are extrinsic to the Grid itself – on analogy.

We do know that the logic bullets seem to be the key to this organization. With the right interfaces, we can get our machines to mimic the behavior of the Grid, through the use of the Grid-logic templates embedded in the logic bullets. Naturally the initial applications are going to be military, and even the word we use to identify these objects is derived from war: but the products of the logic mines aren't really bullets. And they aren't really mined, they're harvested. Logic bullets are discrete, densely organized structures that are found within the Grid's substrate, usually below the level of the foundation: hence the use of the word 'mine' to describe the access points.

We retrieve them using conventional excavation equipment, beginning with large-scale machines and progressing down to finer and finer tools including computer imaging of various types. The logic bullets are non-identical and therefore the more of them that we can collect, the broader our scope of understanding will be.

It is through the logic bullets that the prosthetics used in Fliers have been developed, as well as the golem-detection sensors used in X and other defensive systems. The initial design of the Third Wave machines is based on logic-bullet analysis and, once primed with new and subtly different logic bullets, we anticipate that these devices will be fully equipped to take over all control of the Grid, leaving personnel safely at removes from golem warfare and other environmental hazards.

And that, finally, is where my interests lie. I'm here to save lives.

It's almost too easy, as if Dr. Gonzalez is looking for Serge just as Serge is looking for her. The signal from her helmet beacon comes through with no interference, and then later you see the woman herself, hanging from a strand of Grid like a subway passenger. She's looking up at you, smiling like you're the mailman bringing her tax refund.

Arla Gonzalez is petite, wide-hipped and a little plump, with small feet and hands. Her hair is plastered to her head in shiny dark ringlets so that she looks like she just stepped out of the shower. Her smile is wide and white, and she's obviously unconcerned with the fact that she's holding her helmet under her left arm and her goggles are flipped up on her forehead.

Serge is panting from her exertions in climbing and fiddling with her helmet to clear the sweat and fog from its faceplate. At first she doesn't have the breath to speak.

'You don't recognize me,' Gonzalez says to Serge as if they've just met at the bus stop. 'I know who you are, though, Bonny. We'll talk about that later. For now I'm just glad to see another person out here. Where is the convoy? We're off the main route, aren't we?'

If you were Serge, you'd be put right off your stride by Gonzalez's welcome-to-my-parlor manner. Serge doesn't bat an eyelash. She adopts her rules-and-regs tone.

'I'm Captain Serge, Major Gonzalez, and by authority of Machine Front I have to issue you a direct order to put your helmet on immediately and activate your goggles to setting zero point nine one. Please.'

The last word is thrown out there so uncharacteristically that you decide to come in a little closer to get a better sniff of Gonzalez. Serge never uses polite extras, even with people she respects.

But there's nothing in the air to explain the quirk in behavior. Besides, Serge is using her suit to full capacity. She isn't taking any chances with the Grid, and you can see why. It's unnerving to see Gonzalez standing there bare-headed without a care in the world. You zoom in on Gonzalez's eyes and see that they are yellowed. Her nail tips are turning a little blue, too. She's being poisoned by the Grid, no doubt about it.

Gonzalez shrugs and puts on the helmet.

'Does it really matter?' she says. 'I guess it does. I took it off the other day after your flier went over and didn't even pause. I guess because I was giving up hope of being found. I wouldn't want to die like a coward.'

'There's nothing cowardly about wearing your helmet,' Serge says in that same fire-safety-lecture tone. 'And we wouldn't let you perish out here. It was only a matter of time before we tracked you down. Now, I need to ask you some security questions. Have you seen any golems?'

Arla's brow furrows with concentration. She looks earnest,

like an old lady who has just witnessed a crime and wants to help the police, but neither thinks nor speaks very rapidly anymore.

'Yes.'

'When?'

'Several times.'

'Start with the most recent.'

'About ten minutes ago.'

Serge's eyes flash and for a second you think she's going to jump straight in the air like people sometimes do with Gridshock. She hails you.

'What's this all about, Goss? You didn't report no golems in this area just now.'

'They went in the well before your flier appeared,' Gonzalez says helpfully, squinting up at Gossamer.

'Were you threatened? Have any of these encounters come to blows?'

'No to both questions.' Gonzalez grins, like she's warming to the game.

'Did you witness any deaths? Were you out here alone the whole time?'

'I just told you I haven't been alone. The only deaths I witnessed were within the mine perimeter, during the raid. Before the attempted missile strike.'

Serge only looks angry for a second. Then she masters herself.

'I'm going to escort you back to the position of my team, and then we can examine you for damage and discuss this further. Are you injured?'

'Not that I know of.'

'Come on, then. This way.'

But Gonzalez doesn't move. She stands there like a horse, totally impassive.

'I'm so happy to be alive,' she says.

Serge closes her eyes. 'Dante, I got me a problem,' she says to her wrist.

Arla reaches out and snaps the Swatch shut before Serge can jerk her arm away. She leans in close to Serge, who is much taller than she is, and says:

'I'll tell you why I'm here, Captain. And then if you know what's good for you, you'll follow your own scent path back where you came from, and you'll say you can't find me.'

Serge looks at her for a long moment, and you wonder how she's taking the facts that a) Arla's not respecting her authority and b) Arla just touched her and Serge couldn't do anything about it. Arla starts to smile, thinking she has the upper hand. But after a little while Serge whispers, 'You got a lot of explaining to do, kitten, but you don't got to do it to me. Come on back with me, quiet-like, and I'll be real appreciative.'

Arla isn't listening to Serge. This, you feel, has got to be a mistake. Serge had a rattlesnake look in her eye.

But Arla says, 'It started before the problems at the mines began. I was out taking some air samples and I saw the children.'

'Ah, not this again. They're not children. They're golems.'

'I saw them, Captain Serge.'

'Then you're stupid, Dr. G. You know the rules are there for your own protection. You had no authorization to leave the mine perimeter.'

Arla smiles tolerantly.

'How do you think the Grid is making children, Serge? How could it do that? It needs dead bodies to make golems, doesn't it? One dead body and it can produce hundreds of golems, but there are no children here. So how is this possible?'

'If they exist – and I doubt they do – it's really not my problem,' Serge says. 'I'm going to come over there and take your arm, and I'm looking for some cooperation or I'll have to use force.'

Arla shows no sign that she has heard this. She frowns and continues, 'I thought maybe they could regress the bodies of the dead somehow. It seemed logical. But then I saw them up close and personal, Serge, and something strange struck me. After a while, I managed to piece together what had happened.'

'That's real interesting, Doc.'

Serge tries to take her arm and Arla neatly avoids her, slipping to another loop of Grid with more agility than she ought to possess. Serge stumbles and has to stop herself falling.

Something is stirring in the well below.

'Major Gonzalez, you been out here on your own too long,' says Serge. She moves as she speaks, creeping from branch to branch, delivering her words slowly and deliberately like a trainer approaching a rank stallion. 'You been hallucinating and you been going around with no helmet. That means that, inside-your-head-wise, pretty much anything goes.'

You are trying to get Serge's attention through MF, but she ignores the flashing on her Swatch. Below Serge, heads are rising in the well: white-helmeted, with the cusps of fists spread out to either side of each one, as if each golem is Superman flying up through the murk of the well.

Arla continues to retreat, but Serge has recovered her concentration and she keeps moving to stall Gonzalez's escape.

Serge says: 'Now you got to focus on the pertinent facts. My orders are to rescue you, Major. I'd like to do that. I'm risking guys' lives up here to try to do that. But if you resist me, I'll torch you. That's my job. I don't know how you survived the raid on the mines, but you won't survive me if you make me hunt you down. That there's a good . . . untarnished . . . fact.'

She says the last three words individually, and in between each one she makes a swift move towards Gonzalez, so that on the word 'fact' she has shot a stickyweb from her Swatch and trapped Gonzalez in the crux of two Grid branches. The stickyweb starts turning colors as it reacts to the surface of the Grid. Simultaneously, Serge notices her Swatch flashing: it's the warning signal from you routed through MF.

She springs back just as heads and fists break the surface of the well and the children come shooting out like frogs.

It occurs to you, watching, that you've never seen Serge really scared before.

Making this a first.

'This is impossible,' she splutters, flailing the spiderwhip around her head defensively. 'It's a headf#*k. It's an illusion.'

But she's stumbling over her own feet going backwards. For their part, the children slide out of the water in their *Mad Max* ensembles and swing into the branches of the trees without coming properly into focus. There's something odd about the visual effect that they have on Gossamer. They aren't easy to see when they're moving.

Arla smiles. 'It's not a head#*k. It's just a good untarnished fact. I'm not ready to come back to X yet.'

Serge toggles helmet visual settings rapidly. Evidently she's having the same focal problems that you are. Soon the children are all but invisible in the branches of the Grid. But there are strange sounds coming now from the webbing and the spaces between it: sounds of water and electricity; racing heartbeats; protolingual cries.

'You better come with me, Doc, because I don't think you want to get your butt incinerated.'

But Serge's threat is empty: that's obvious to everyone. Apart from that, you spot golems moving towards her through the Grid. You send a warning again to the Swatch. Arla says:

'I'll come with you after you've seen the things that the Grid needs you to see, Captain Serge.'

Serge shakes her head, releases a spurt of angry laughter. 'What the Grid needs me to see? This is worse than talking to Jehovah's Witnesses.'

She turns to her right and raises her spiderwhip just as a golem comes within her range. The whip goes away from her with a wailing cry and catches the golem around the neck; a jerk of Serge's wrist and the golem is dragged to its knees, clutching its throat. Serge gives a movement as practiced and near-invisible as a fencer's parry and a shining violet thread wraps around the golem and ties it to the Grid in several places. It struggles but cannot escape; meanwhile Serge is doing some fancy footwork on the branch to set herself up to meet the next opponent.

Arla takes the opportunity to exit. It's as if she knows the Grid intimately, because she makes for the deepest, densest area she can, where you can't track her. Soon she has vanished.

Serge dispatches a few more golems and then retreats, laughing coldly.

'You're playing hopscotch on the wrong sidewalk, Doc!' she calls. 'You got Dinty Moore beef stew for brains if you think you can get the better of me.'

Serge is still flushed when she reaches the camp.

Klaski leaps to her feet. 'There they are! They were following you, ma'am. Look! Right over there! I just saw a whole bunch of those little girls – look, ma'am, I'm not joking. Oh, crap, they've disappeared again.'

Serge fixes her with a hateful eye. You can see the bruising of sleeplessness in the hollows above her cheekbones, the crusts on the tear ducts, and the ubiquitous pucker between her eyebrows solidifying itself into a wrinkle.

'Let's have some grub,' she says, as if Klaski hasn't even spoken. 'Hendricks, you're cooking.'

Lewis charges Gossamer in the usual way. She's humming a tune that you eventually recognize as 'If Ever I Should Leave You' from *Camelot*. The usual meal preparations get under way, but everyone is on edge after the events of the shift. Serge is actually physically twitchy. You know her well enough to figure she's questioning her own sanity right about now.

You know how she feels. You're thinking about getting out for a break, even if it means risking continuity.

'Hey,' says Serge suddenly. 'You ever hear the one about the Japanese chef who surprised a burglar? He *wokked* him on the head, hahaha, get it, he *wokked* him? What's the matter Klaski, you look like you ate a bad snail.'

Klaski seems to cringe. 'It's just . . . my boyfriend back home, he's from Japan. I was wondering if he's cheating on me yet.'

Serge snorts. 'I should of guessed.'

Klaski twists some hair around her finger.

'Ma'am, didn't you ever get your heart broken?'

Lewis's eyes show white as she restrains herself from gasping at Klaski's audacity. Serge is equable, though.

'Not as such, no.'

'Never? Really? Not even *ever?*'

'Ah,' says Serge. 'Well, I guess there was this one guy. Six Fingers Mike. I was assigned to his team during Second Wave changeover, you know, when the guys got sent home. He showed me the ropes. That guy broke a lotta hearts – not mine, of course. We was just buddies who . . . you know!' She looks into the depths of her Lipton mug and grins, and you could swear she was blushing even though her complexion doesn't lend itself to it. No one says anything, but amazed glances are exchanged. '*And* he was a gifted mechanic,' gushes Serge. 'You should have seen him reconfigure a commando rig.'

She sighs, remembering. Hendricks elbows Klaski and you can hear the hiss of her breath in Klaski's ear. 'You don't have a Japanese boyfriend!'

Klaski elbows her right back and in a high voice says, 'Did the extra finger, like – was it—?'

Serge scowls. 'Klaski, don't be crude. And don't be such a wimp. Don't you know that people get assigned to worlds where you got to recycle your own piss, 'cos there's no water? Or them places where you got to study for years just to learn the aliens' language and then you get there and find out your contacts just lost a war and you're speaking the language of the oppressed underclass, good luck getting out of there without a slave collar permanently welded on your neck. No, I'll take the Grid any day. Get your procedures worked out, pay attention, don't let it freak you and you're basically OK.'

Klaski chortles into her Spaghetti-O's.

'What's so friggin' funny, Klaski?'

'Oh, nothing, ma'am.'

'No, I wanna know. Why are you laughing?'

'Well, ma'am. You just make it sound so easy. Some of the greatest minds of our time have devoted thousands upon thousands of pages of analysis to the question of how to deal with the Grid without getting 'freaked' as you put it, ma'am. Pharmaceutical companies have devoted millions to the problem of olfactory cortical attack. The defense industry—'

'Aw, can it, Klaski. I never said it was *easy*. Your problem is' – and she stabs her spoon in Klaski's direction – 'you expect to lose. You're all brain-fried before you even get here just based on some junk you *read*. If you ask me, that's too much friggin' imagination for your own good. You smart kids – Lewis, this don't include you, you're an exception – you smart kids can't even survive in a world without Charmin, how you gonna cope with real shit? Haha, get it? Charmin? Real shit?'

Dutiful laughter. Lewis appears gratified by the backhanded compliment.

Machine Front is calling you.

GOSSAMER REPORT TO N-RIDGE AIRSPACE FOR SURVEILLANCE DUTY IMMEDIATELY.

Gossamer is tired. You send back a weak protest, but MF is insistent.

GET UP HERE NOW.

Meanwhile, Serge's Swatch is chirping at her to tell her you're being recalled. She checks it with a flick of her eyes, then looks at you.

The rest are still chortling and passing each other the Ritz crackers. Serge walks over to where Gossamer is plugged into the Grid and disengages her.

'Machine Front have decided to attack the mines,' she says in a low voice. 'You better go.'

the cosmic information

Gloria was at the door of my assignment room. I could smell her perfume, but I kept my eyes on the blue screen, trying to orient myself to the real world. I realized she had been knocking.

'I'm sorry to interrupt you, Cookie,' she whispered. 'But there's an urgent personal call for you. A woman called Brenda? She says she's your mother's friend and it's an emergency.'

'Where's the phone?' I got to my feet, swaying.

'At my desk,' called Gloria after me. 'Line one.'

I ran down the hall and picked up line one. Brenda works with my mother at Macy's. I looked at my watch. It was the middle of the afternoon. She'd still be at work.

I blurted, 'Brenda, what happened?'

'Oh God, Cookie, I'm so sorry to have to tell you this.'

I only half-listened. Brenda's voice was quaking and strange, and her story was garbled. It seemed to go on forever. About halfway through I realized where it had to be leading.

'Is my mother dead?'

'Well, because the granddaughter had chicken pox, see, and she couldn't drive us, so . . .'

My mother was dead. That much was obvious. It took a while for me to make sense of the rest. Brenda and my mother had gone out to lunch with a former colleague who had retired last year. Brenda's car was in the shop and my mother had given up driving years ago because of her nerves, so the colleague had picked them up at work and driven them to the restaurant, but then had to leave early to pick up her grand-daughter from school because the granddaughter had chicken pox. Mom and Brenda had to be back on time to take inventory in the stockroom, so they had taken the bus back to Willowbrook from Clifton. Sitting in traffic on Route 46 my mother had collapsed. Brenda had witnessed the whole thing.

'We did CPR the whole time waiting for the ambulance,' she assured me. Her voice was hoarse and thick at the same time. 'The paramedics were very good. They worked on her all the way to St. Joe's. It wasn't no good, baby. She was gone to the Lord.'

Bile rose in my throat at the platitude, but I tried to quell my anger. Brenda was in shock.

'And she wasn't feeling good but we thought it was the Pizza Palace all-you-can-eat buffet, you never know with the mayonnaise in this weather. There was just no sign, nothing.'

'Are you OK?' I asked.

There was a pause. 'It's you I'm worried about, Cookie. I'm so sorry, baby. I'm so sorry. Just tell me what to do, how I can help .'

I didn't know what to say. A thick, half-caring feeling had come over me.

'I guess we'd better go to the hospital,' I said finally. 'Is she still there?'

Brenda burst into tears.

'I'm sorry,' she wailed. 'I'm sorry to break down like this but you sound so calm, I feel even worse. Cookie, you want me to come up there and get you?'

'No. I'll meet you at St. Joseph's. Give me like an hour.'

When I came out of Gloria's work area, everybody was standing around the Coke machine. It must have been three p.m.

'Hey,' Gunther said to his audience, 'Did you hear the one about the anorexic nun and the polar bear?'

He saw me out of the corner of his eye and his face fell.

'Cookie, are you OK?'

'I have to go, Gunther. I'll call you later.'

I didn't want to talk to him, but he followed me to my car.

'Are you sure you're OK to drive, Cookie? Is there somewhere I can take you?'

I shook my head. A stiff, hot breeze was blowing the smell of diesel and hot asphalt from the Parkway. Loud insects crouched in the furze beside the parking lot. My car felt as hot as a glede, whatever that is. I read it in Tolkien.

Gunther was still following me.

'I'm OK.' I thought of Troy and the brick. *Don't let them see you flinch.* It was just like something my father would say. Now I'd have to call him, and tell him.

'Cookie, I'm not trying to be a buttinsky, honestly. Will you let me know if there's anything I can do?'

'There's nothing,' I said, starting the Rabbit. 'Nothing you can do.'

Isn't it strange, the things people don't wonder about? Like, I have no idea how a Xerox machine works. Or a carburetor, actually. I don't understand the stock exchange either. And if evolution is this trial-and-error process, then why aren't there a lot more fossils of really weird-ass-looking things that nature tried out but they didn't work? But I don't ask because it's pointless. Like once I asked Gunther how the soldiers got to the Grid and he said they were launched via a gravity-torsion generator in New Hampshire. My friend

Miles from high school says Einstein's theory of relativity means you can't have faster-than-light travel. But they have Warp Nine in *Star Trek*, don't they? And nobody minds. So maybe Einstein was wrong. Or maybe *Star Trek* was right. A gravity-torsion generator. That sounds pretty funky.

There are just too many things I've never wondered about, and I'm feeling like the joker of the century as I accelerate onto the Parkway.

I never wondered about this. Not since I was a little kid and really needed her.

An image of my mother in the doctor's office. She is standing in front of a Winnie the Pooh height chart. I am five. I am getting a booster shot. She tells me I have to be brave. I can think of nothing in the world worse than somebody sticking a needle in my arm. My mother kneels and puts her hands on my shoulders and says,

'Now, Kiki, you got to face it like a big, brave girl. You gonna let a little needle make you scared? I don't think so. You give that needle hell. My Kiki, I'm your mama and I know how much you want to cry and run away but you are a big girl and I know you can do this.'

Then she turned to Dr. Collins.

'Make her cry and I'll belt you one,' she said.

I didn't cry. I can still taste the cherry lollipop.

Brenda met me at the hospital. She was stuffed into a tight pair of jeans and her mustard polyester blouse was puffy and crooked at the waist where she'd hastily tucked it in. She had on Nike court shoes and a huge pocketbook was slung over her right shoulder. I couldn't help thinking that she'd probably kill her training partner in a pocketbook-and-broom demonstration.

Then I saw her face.

'It's for real,' I said.

Brenda nodded slowly, lips quivering, and held out her arms to me as her eyes wobbled with tears. I let her enfold me but I tried not to inhale her perfume or relax into her softness. I didn't want to indulge in that kind of comfort.

Brenda was sobbing.

'She didn't suffer,' she said. 'I want you to know that.'

'OK,' I said. 'OK, I hear you.'

We drew apart. I looked at Brenda's shoes. She's on her feet all day at the gift department cash register, but no one ever sees her feet so I guess she gets to wear whatever she wants below the level of the counter. Still, the idea of Brenda on a basketball court made me want to laugh again. Inappropriate remarks flooded my mind.

'You knew, didn't you, Cookie? I mean, you called her just the other night – she was telling me. You must have sensed it. You two were so close.'

I nodded. It was easier to go along with her than to fall on my knees and cry and say that, no, I hadn't known; Cookie, the psychic daughter of a psychic, I never suspected a thing. To admit that I still didn't believe it and was hoping it was all a mistake. To add that I had only called because Mom had called me first and I'd felt guilty.

'We were going to go to the Bahamas in the fall. She booked a cruise. We got an off-peak deal. We were going to have piña coladas, you know, just like in that song.'

'I'm sorry,' I heard myself say, and Brenda emitted another flood of tears.

'What is the matter with me? Cookie, I'm talking stupid, I'm sorry, just tell me what you want to do, honey. Brenda's here for you, baby. You want to talk to the nurses who worked on her? The doctor went off shift but you should probably talk to somebody.'

'Do I have to?'

*

They took me to see her. I was struck by the sheer mass of her. And at the same time, how much more visible her bones seemed to be: she looked like an animal, especially around her jaw.

She had freshly painted nails. Lynette at *Lynette's D-signs* would have given her a manicure over the weekend, while they discussed the price of tomatoes and the fact that I didn't have a boyfriend yet.

It's almost impossible to say anything else about her quiet body without losing it. I felt like a big, trembling tear, I was brimming over with so many memories. At first they were just images. Flashes. Smells. Her hands on pastry dough. How she'd slap the TV to get Channel 11 to stop flipping on vertical hold.

Then the little story-memories.

'Party in the dark' when I was seven. She invited my little friends over and we switched off all the lights and played 'find this' games. Then we lit candles. It cured my terror of the dark better than any reassurances she might have given.

Or shopping, how she laughed at the skinny girls with their cigarettes and cans of Tab and their posing.

'Life's too short,' she'd say, shaking her head. 'A man can get a little piece of that any day of the week, flash some money, no problem. If he likes you for that reason, he's gonna dump you as soon as you get yourself a little older. You might as well enjoy yourself.'

Then she'd buy me ice cream.

'In our family, women are big. We're big women. In every sense of the word. Big woman, big heart.'

Big woman, big heart attack. Dead woman.

Not fair.

There would be no more unconditional love, no more platitudes, no more predictable mom-responses. Poor me.

*

We called a funeral home that Brenda knew. 'They're nice, they got a good makeup girl and they won't rip you off.'

Then we looked for my mother's class lists for her tarot group to cancel tomorrow's lesson. Brenda offered to call everybody. She'd called my mother's pastor and he wanted to come over and see me and pray with me but I begged off. Brenda looked disappointed.

'How 'bout some chicken soup? I can hear your tummy growling.'

I managed to convince Brenda that I was better off on my own. Brenda meant well, but her sympathy rolled off me. I just wanted to be miserable. My mother was gone and all I could think about was myself. I went home and cried to Nebbie. I railed at my loss.

'Who will I keep secrets from?'

Then I remembered Rocky, my mom's Maine Coon cat. I went and got him right away. It was good to have something to do. Emergency, emergency, stop everything.

But I didn't run into anyone at her building. No Rosalinda, no Joe and Vanessa. Everything was quiet and normal. I might have just been dropping by for some pork chops and cherry pie. I looked around her place. The clock was still ticking, which you don't expect, somehow. There were dishes in the sink. Her Snoopy slippers, that I'd given her.

I wandered around with Rocky at my heels, looking for some clue. A trigger? An explanation? A bottle of heart medication, a letter to me, a traumatizing message on her machine . . .

Nothing. Coupons for 9 Lives cat food. A dry-cleaning ticket. Unopened water bill.

I called Darren but he was still at school. He teaches math to underprivileged kids in San Diego. His work number was in my mother's address book and I started to dial it. Talking to my brother would be a needed form of collapse. But I hung up on the first ring. There was nothing he could do, and dragging him out of class in the middle of the day was only going to make things worse for him.

'Just slow down, Cookie,' I said.

I flopped into her couch and picked up the earrings she'd left on the coffee table the night before. Some psychics can pick up information from personal effects like this. Not me. Rocky jumped into my lap.

My mother called him Rocky not because of the boxer but because she said in his past life he'd been a ship's captain who, drunk, ran his crew aground, off the coast of Portugal. Of course she believed in reincarnation. She remembered several of her own past lives, she said.

'We keep meeting the same people again and again. It's like a theater company with the same actors, always doing different plays.' She held seances, crystal-ball readings, and tarot workshops. She threw the I Ching every day.

She used to drag me to the Baptist church on 118th Street, too. And when as a teenager I challenged the contradictions between the Bible and the other stuff she was into, she got all upset.

'All religions are the same. People just interpret the cosmic information in different ways. Like different styles of art. I like going to church, and I like wearing a nice hat and seeing my friends, and I like to give praise in singing. Whatever else I might do with my time, that's between me and God.' She fixed me with round white eyes. I guess I must have been looking unconvinced.

'Do I tell you what to believe? You can become a Jew or a Hindu for all I care. I don't even mind if you want to become one of them Trekkies, which for you I gotta say is probably closer to what's really gonna happen. Just be happy, Cookie. God likes happy people.'

I didn't see the logic of this but since Mom didn't believe in logic there was no point in saying so.

'We're all just . . . out there,' she was fond of saying, waving her hands like she was shaking water droplets off them. 'Doing our thing, and it's all happening, praise the Lord.'

As soon as I got my first job, I moved out.

When the hauntings first started, I didn't tell her. I knew she would jump on them as proof of her belief system. And she'd talk about me to her friends, want to parade me in front of her tarot class to tell about my 'chilling psychic experiences,' just like the boa-constrictor stories.

Ironically (and annoyingly, considering what she had said to me about becoming a Trekkie) the first visions happened during *Star Trek*. I was working as a file clerk for the Rockland County utility company and I had a tiny apartment in Suffern. I used to watch *Star Trek* reruns every Saturday night at six o'clock on Channel 11. I'd bring home a pizza and a bucket of Breyer's Neopolitan, and I'd sit Indian-style on the floor in front of the TV as the opening credits rolled. I'd sing along 'ooh OOOH, ooh, ooh-ohh,oooh . . .'

Nebbie was just a kitten then, and I was keeping her secretly because my lease said no pets. She'd drag her own pizza into a corner like she'd brought down a buffalo, and gnaw it.

It was the episode where Spock smells these red flowers on this planet and starts having emotions. He laughs, he cries, he starts to kiss a woman—

—and I see the assault. From below, like I'm an ant on the floor as opposed to a fly on the ceiling. It starts in a pool hall, four men on one. The underdog is a lean Hispanic guy in his twenties in jeans, a T-shirt, and out-of-style Adidas. The other four are also Hispanic, same age group and same overall look. You'd think they'd all be friends. I don't know what starts it. But I vividly see the way their weight moves across their legs and feet as they punch,

pummel, knee, elbow, and head-butt. The one being attacked doubles over almost immediately and staggers across the room. I see a forest of legs follow him. He hits a table and then slides under it, only to be dragged out for more beating.

I covered my eyes, then peeked again.

They are talking Spanish, mostly curses from what I can gather. They deliver blows, making ugly grunts, and their victim wheezes and gasps and chokes. His head lolls.

Eventually they leave him on the floor. His T-shirt is pulled up almost over his head. I can see his flanks heaving as he gasps for breath. He rolls on his side and curls up. The attackers run. The floor buckles beneath their weight; I can feel that somehow. I have lost all sense of my apartment and Nebbie and the pizza. I watch for several minutes as the man just lies there, his back to me. Then one of the men comes back into the room. He goes into the men's room and comes out half a minute later. He takes a gun out of the back of his jeans. He points it at the guy on the floor.

I see his face. It is wide, with strong cheekbones and a flat nose that speaks of some Indian in his heritage. He isn't very tall, but his body is strong, especially his legs. The muscles of his legs are clearly visible beneath his black stonewashed jeans. I see the gold crucifix around his neck, too; it's one of those that have an actual figure of Christ hanging on the cross.

I hear shouting. I hear the shot, too, but I don't look at the gun or the bullet or the man being killed. I look at the Coors poster over the killer's shoulder. I keep looking at it. I don't dare look anywhere else, and I don't have any way back to my own room where the TV is just an object that my cat likes to sit on for the warmth.

Eventually a Gillette commercial came on.

When I had recovered enough to reach for more pizza, I found that it tasted of roses. I spit it out.

In the weeks that followed, there were more hauntings, seemingly at random, when I watched TV. All of them involved the man with the gun. Sometimes I'd see him in his car – a beige Chevy Nova with a cranked-up rear end and gray body-shop paint on one side panel. Sometimes I'd see him eating lunch at a deli in Jersey City. Sometimes I'd see him sleeping in his house in Hasbrook Heights. I saw the address.

Then I saw him outside my apartment. I don't mean I saw him there in reality. I saw it in a haunting. I'd been watching *Bowling For Dollars* and then I saw the street outside my own building, and there was the guy looking at my mailbox and writing something down on the back of an envelope.

I had no way of knowing if this was happening in real time or not, but there was absolutely nothing I could do. During a haunting, I am paralyzed. I have no motor control over my own body that I'm aware of, and all my senses are engaged in the haunting. He could open my door, walk up the steps, and reach my apartment and there was nothing I could do. He could break into my apartment and attack me, and I'd still be sitting in front of the TV, watching it happen.

That was what scared me most.

It still scared me, even though all this happened years ago and the guy had never had any cause to take revenge because he'd never gone to prison because the police didn't believe me.

For all that I could see, my visions were useless. It turned out that there was nothing I could do to make the outcome any better.

I guess that's why Dataplex had come to mean so much to me. My work there gave me a chance to make things better. To be more than just a helpless observer; to be an agent of change.

But here I was again: my mother gone without warning. Nothing I could do or say to change it. I'd been reduced once again to helpless observer.

I guess that's why, though I was still in shock probably, I experienced such a strong urge to fly while my mother was not yet even buried.

max fact

It feels like you've been gone a thousand years, but you only lost about thirty seconds of flight time. You are right back where you were, leaving Serge and the others behind at their new camp and striking off towards N-Ridge and the climax of the conflict at the mines.

It's not long before you come across the infamous gap. You are supposed to head straight for N-Ridge with best speed, but the temptation to look more closely into the ruined Grid is too great. You fly in over the original break, changing eye settings so as to look down into what remains of the well fluid as deeply as you can.

Something is in there, all right. In the green and violet murk Gossamer's eyes descry at first a vague bulk; then you start to concentrate. You add layers of interpretation and probability arrays, and the shape refines itself to become an oblong. The first thing that comes to mind is a shipwreck; then you think *torpedo*. After that the form resolves itself nicely into a shape that is shadowy but unmistakable. It's a MaxFact missile, still live: undetonated.

There are filaments extending from the downed missile into the well fluid. Soft lights glow from within the thing's main body; which doesn't make sense because you know MaxFact missiles to be densely constructed of metal. Yet this one looks translucent – almost gelatinous. It has begun to swell in the middle, pregnant with some unknown quality. The shell of its guidance fins has the soft look of warm glass, and you can see circuit boards and other components silhouetted within.

How did it get diverted so far from N-Ridge? And why didn't it explode on contact with the Grid? And if it hasn't exploded, what's the reason for the dead Grid . . .?

Gossamer is picking up airbornes. The fragrances match your catalog of malevolent agents. Once again, Goss is being chased away from this scene. The Grid doesn't like you spying on it – and come to think of it, Commander Galante won't appreciate your being late, either. You take a last look at the basking missile and bring Gossamer back to her original course before she can break away from you.

Gossamer tears towards N-Ridge on a stiff breeze. At a distance, the Grid soon becomes less threatening. Seen from a height the Grid reminds you of oil making art on water. It's like soap bubbles and candlelight; it's like the swerve of wind-sculpted stone that's taken ages to assume this form but looks as if it could deliquesce at any moment. The Grid is feminine like that; like the sea, like anything subject to change, like any body that yields and sacrifices its nature and transforms itself. Like any thing that pretends to lose and, in so doing, sometimes does lose. And sometimes, against all odds, that wins.

But these are armchair evocations; you can lie on the wind and dream all you like. You are not down there inside it. You are up high, reading the pollen, untangling the grammar of the winds, and in the end, you are speculating.

Nothing's at stake for you, in truth.

Probably you like it that way.

You follow the dead Grid to the mines. It has extended itself since the last time you were here. It ends at a point closer to the mines, and the Grid nearby is taking on the same signs of human-like structure as it was in the place where Serge made camp.

Such darkness as the Grid knows has settled over N-Ridge, and as Gossamer comes wheeling over the mine encampment and looks down, you think of cotton candy and Las Vegas; but only for a moment. The blossoming luminescence over and in the mines is a result of a major MF assault. The perimeter has been entirely surrounded by heavy machinery, and although golems swarm from branches of the Grid to counterattack from the rear, Major Galante's machines are smooth-surfaced and virtually impenetrable. These must be the vanguard of the Third Wave you have been hearing about: fully automated strike forces, unencumbered by humans with their emotional weaknesses.

Major Galante's forces have blown the perimeter fence in three places and as you watch they occupy the compound. The air above the Grid shakes and sings, and you spot two other fliers being blown X-ward across their flight planes, rippling like wayward kites.

You wonder briefly whose eyes lie behind the eyes of the other Gossamers recording the operation. Wendy of the candy machine? It's hard to imagine that. And you wonder if you are the only flier who is ambivalent about whether this assault is a good idea.

After that, there's no time to think anything. You are wholly occupied in watching, registering every detail. You see golems scatter and suicide; some hide within the mine compound. These you locate for MF, which targets some with micromissiles; others are hunted down on foot by Major Galante and her elite elimination force. Golems go up like torches as Galante takes back the mines.

The burn scars of the mines' former personnel are still visible. You can see where golems have hacked off sections of heavy equipment, as well as the places where they have dragged lighter pieces of machinery out of the buildings and left them, partially dismantled. The mines themselves remain sealed, but they won't be for long. Galante and her strike force leap back into their carrier and get set to blow the mine entrance.

'I'm waiting for the all-clear from my fliers,' she tells MF, who are anxious to get inside. 'We don't want any stray golems on the ground when we go in there.'

You and the other two anonymous fliers make your final passes, checking for golems. Another flier spots a band of a heavily armed golems hiding behind a water tower. While they are being targeted and disposed of, you see two of the Grid's children sitting on the perimeter fence, swinging their legs. Watching. You look away quickly and instinctively. There are limits to what you will see, and by seeing it, what you will be a party to.

Gunther's words come back to you. Something he said to you a long time ago, when you first complained about the ugliness.

It's what the Grid wants. The Grid will use your disgust against you. It will use your fear against you. Your morality. You play right into it when you let it manipulate you.

The child golems are dangerous. You have to report them. It's your duty.

GOLEMS ON WALL AT B-17, you compose. You try to send the message but the nex jams. Gossamer is resisting you. She actually turns around in the air and flies over a different part of the mine. You tug at her, wrench her mentally, but she will not obey.

What is happening here?

The third flier spots the girls, anyway. You turn in the air just in time to see a series of micromissiles strafe the perimeter wall where they were sitting. They jump down and land *inside* the mines.

Stupid fools. Gossamer lurches, goes flying in. You get the weird feeling that the flier is trying to protect these creatures – as if she could.

The girls are running for the breach in the wall. Their hair flies behind them in wet banners; their bare feet dance over rubble and through dust. Missiles stud the ground around them. The first one dives through the hole in the perimeter and seizes hold of a Grid branch like Tarzan grabbing a vine. An explosion throws the second one through the same breach. She lands in a ball, rolls, comes up disoriented. Foot soldiers are pelting after her. She crabwalks backward, one foot black and bleeding.

Major Galante herself is at the head of the team. She halts, steadies her arm to fire her weapon. You try to set yourself for what you know will happen.

Only it doesn't. In an eye-blink, the well opens beneath the child and swallows her. Major Galante's ray gun fires into the fluid, which bubbles with radiance and then subsides.

Suddenly Gossamer is pliant again. You bring her around and continue to sweep the area, alarmed that this could have happened. No one seems to have noticed that you spotted the girls first and failed to alert MF. There are no accusations or questions coming your way.

Gossamer is an indigene. Does she have some loyalty that she's never expressed before?

But how could she, without a cortex?

Eventually, the all-clear comes through and MF sends you back to Serge. You don't get a chance to see Major Galante personally, which is disappointing. It would have been nice to reconnect with someone you respected, to remind yourself that you're one of the good guys. But it doesn't happen.

And when you fly back over the Grid, you'd swear you could hear music. It's elusive, like the blurred bass of a car stereo as the car speeds by, or the inchoate warble between radio stations. But it's enough to drive you off the nex, seeking refuge.

the pimpernel gets nobly drunk

In those first days after my mother's death, I felt a terrible need to be doing something. I had to clear out her apartment. At first I toyed with the idea of moving in there, keeping it – well, keeping it ready for her. Which just made me cry more and get all hysterical. So I decided to bring her stuff to my place. I worked at it obsessively. It was my mission.

I routinely tortured myself by recalling the last time I'd seen her/spoken to her/touched her there in the hospital. I dragged out photographs. I made funeral arrangements. All of that was a strange pleasure, or at least a form of relief from pain. It was as if I could retroactively help her. Which was dumb, but I couldn't help it.

Darren's plane wasn't coming in until the day of the funeral, and he was going to stay with friends in the city – which was just as well because my apartment was chock full of my mother's stuff as well as my own, and the cats were always fighting. It was Friday night, D&D night at Miles's house, and I decided to go because our party was in the middle of a sticky situation in some ice caves where we'd been ambushed by these troglodytes after our weapons were attacked by some kind of animate ice and frozen solid within it. Last time, my paladin had been using his 18+54/100 strength to try to wrench his sword out, King Arthur-style, but with no success, and our magic-user was bleeding to death because the cleric was lost in an ice-maze and we'd run out of Cure Serious Wounds potions. I thought I oughtn't to let the group down.

That's me, 'the ever-reliable Cookie,' as Mom would say. Sniff.

Who would know the Cookie-stories to tell at holidays? Who would be able to say: '. . . and just as I'm about to roll up my sleeves and show the plumber what I mean by a fair bill, all of a sudden my little one pipes up and says, "Did you know your cat has a lung tumor?"' This one always brought a lot of laughter, both for its portrayal of my mother as a would-be bare-knuckle boxer, and of me. 'You dark horse, Cookie,' people would say to me, and pat me on the head. Or my mother would talk about the time we almost got evicted for having a cat against the lease and how I had suddenly come up with the piece of information that our downstairs neighbor had a boa constrictor in his bathtub. 'She was never in that apartment!' my mother would insist. 'How could she know about that?'

I have only a vague memory of the events: I was about five when the boa thing happened, but my mother was still retelling the legend years later. I remembered innocently saying something that seemed perfectly obvious to me, the equivalent of 'Your shoes are in the hallway,' and everybody over-reacting. My mother was really proud of what she called my 'spontaneous visitations' which she claimed were 'stress-induced.' She tried to get me to use Vedic meditation practices to control them. She said we could win the lottery or at least make money on the horses. But I never could make the flashes happen. Instead, I learned to keep my mouth shut whenever there was a confrontation.

'Make nice, Cookie,' she'd tell me, the hypocrite! But I did make nice. I didn't want to be like her, always in trouble.

Now I'm not so sure. Maybe if I opened my mouth during a disagreement I wouldn't find myself stuffing so many Ring Dings in it afterward.

'So they aren't coming? Just like that?'

So much for my psychic powers. I wouldn't have driven all the way to Miles's house if I'd suspected the rest of the players weren't going to be there.

'Bastards,' said Miles. 'Recalcitrant tree frogs. Hopeless thugs.'

'Maybe it's just as well. I don't feel like I'm on form.'

'Car trouble on the Pennsylvania Turnpike, or so they tell me. They probably just decided to stay at Villanova for a keg party. Never mind. I bought extra Cheez Doodles. And those new things, Cheez Combos? They're like little pretzels filled with soft cheese – they're fantastic.'

He actually had lined a bunch of said Cheez Combos up in front of the lead figures we use to represent our characters and monsters. A troglodyte wielding a double-bladed axe was just about to take a swing at the Cheez Combo, which looked like a miniature Lincoln Log. I sidled closer, trying to sneak a peek at Miles's DM notes or his graph-paper map, which he kept hidden behind a cardboard shield with all the charts that told you what happened in combat. I picked up a four-sided die and spun it like a top. It knocked over a destrier bearing a wizardess.

'Try one!' urged Miles, picking up a handful of the snacks and shoving them in his mouth. For all that *he* lives on junk food and sits on his butt all day, he never gains weight. It isn't fair.

'No, that's OK, I'm not really hungry,' I said.

Miles shrugged. It would never occur to him to ask if I

was OK, if I needed to talk. That kind of thing just isn't in his repertoire.

'You want to go down to the basement and play air hockey?'

I shook my head. 'I'm feeling kind of weird tonight,' I said.

'Weird how? You mean about your mom?'

I sighed. 'I wish I could explain it, but I can't. See, it's easy for you. You're the Pimpernel. The Pimpernel can deal with any situation.'

Miles rubbed his hand through his wild hair. 'Well, I wouldn't go that far,' he said, smiling in embarrassment.

'Really? Well, what does the Pimpernel do when he feels like he's losing his grip?'

Miles grinned and patted me on the head.

'The Pimpernel gets nobly drunk, of course.'

Miles went down to the garage and got a couple six-packs of Amstel Lite. We put them in the freezer and started drinking the four he had already in his fridge door. To my amazement, the beer didn't nauseate me. He offered me some leftover Kentucky Fried but that *did* nauseate me, even if only in principle. Once the beers in the freezer were chilled, we took a couple outside and hung out in the driveway. It was dark by now except for the streetlights, and the kids next door had gone in. You could hear them watching *Hill Street Blues* on TV. Miles tried to shoot baskets and I leaned on his car, drinking as fast as I dared and swatting at mosquitoes.

'I don't really believe in it,' I told Miles, tracing circles in the condensation on the roof of his Oldsmobile with my beer bottle. I waved the Amstel at the world at large. 'None of this actually signifies.'

Why did I use that word? The Significator is the most important card in the tarot. Am I starting to sound like my mother?

I heard myself say: 'It's an elaborate illusion and I think

deep down everybody knows it. Look at all this concrete and asphalt. When me and my mom . . .' I heard my voice crack. 'When my mom and I came back from the Bahamas last year we were circling over the metropolitan area for like a half-hour. All you could see was rows and rows of houses, and buildings, and roads.'

'Yeah?' said Miles, 'It's all very well to have bucolic fantasies about trees and mountains, but you can't have that and still have photocopiers and take-out pizza and multiplex movie theaters.'

'Maybe we only need those things because we got rid of the stuff that was really important. Or hid it where it can't be perceived.'

'Maybe we got rid of scarlet fever and polio, too. Or hid them with Aunt Edna's vacation slides of Tampa Beach.'

'Oh, Miles, you're so hard-headed sometimes. If you could see the things that I see you might not be so sure.' I was slurring, which made me snort with a private laughter. Then I slapped a mosquito against my forearm and thought mournfully of Gossamer.

Miles shrugged. He sat down on the hood next to me, blotting his forehead with the bottom of his T-shirt and revealing a hairy, pot-bellied tummy that sat beneath his scrawny ribs like a kangaroo's pouch.

He said: 'I'm not a man of action. I'm a man of ideas. I need to be indoors. I need to be fed regularly. I need a dishwasher. I don't want to have to worry about going out and shooting my dinner out of a tree. It's all a bucolic fantasy.'

'A what? An alcoholic what?'

'*Bu*colic, not alcoholic!'

'Bubonic alcohol?'

I was really plastered. We both started giggling.

'You know what?' I said. 'I'm thinking about retiring my paladin.'

Miles leaped to his feet, twisted his ankle in a pothole, and staggered sideways.

'What? You can't retire Monty. I just designed a whole burial complex for him, presided over by a lich.'

'If you ripped it off from *Tomb of Horrors*, you shouldn't have bothered. I already know about the room that automatically drops you down a hundred-foot shaft and kills you instantly, OK?'

Miles swelled with indignation. 'I can do better than ripping off a *module*. Gary Gygax, he annoys me so much, why is the guy so egotistical? He really thinks that just because he wrote the rules he's, like, God. The real God would be more modest.'

I smirked into my Amstel Lite bottle. Miles obviously hasn't listened to himself when he's just finished a cunning piece of programming. Hasn't heard himself talk up his work on the phone to gaming distributors. I didn't say anything, though. *Spazmonia* had hit a snag and its creator was behaving like Sherlock Holmes in between cases. Except, instead of cocaine, Miles was into Dr. Pepper and Cheez Doodles. Lately I'd noticed that a fine dust of orange crumbs coated the surfaces of his computer and his living room – where he actually worked – had the dull odor of deeply ingrained stale cheese farts.

'I'm going to create a new character and she's going to be Neutral.'

'Lawful neutral? Chaotic neutral?'

'Just neutral.'

'How boring,' moaned Miles. 'Please, think it over. If you knew how much fun my lich was going to be . . .'

'Miles,' I said. 'Something scary is happening to me. I'm dividing into parts, but they're all still me – no, it's like, I feel like I'm stretching in all directions. Like I'm on a rack. My head is going this way, and my arms are each going that way, and my legs are getting stretched out . . .' I balanced on the hood of the Olds, trying to illustrate. 'I feel all distorted, dragged out of my own shape. I'm living in too many worlds at once. In my mind I look like a starfish. I'm being pulled into these different dimensions and pretty soon there will be nothing left in the middle.'

Miles made a big obvious effort to act sober. 'Could this be a medical phenomenon?' he said. 'I mean, there *isn't* as much in the middle. Of you. As before.'

I stared at him. 'Do you have to be so literal-minded?'

Miles said, 'OK, so this is for real. I can just see the newspaper headline: *Cookie Starfishes*. A Fair Lawn, NJ woman has mysteriously disappeared, to be replaced by an abnormally large starfish in her bathtub. The starfish was discovered reading *Ringworld Engineers* and eating a Hershey bar. No, don't go! Come on, Cookie, we're having such a good time, the Pimpernel commands you to stay!' He was running after me. 'Please? I have Yodels.'

'Yodels can't tempt me anymore, Miles,' I said in a superior tone as I crossed his tiny patch of lawn. I got in my car and tried vainly to insert the key into the ignition. The key kept stabbing the steering column and sliding off. The car seemed to be breathing, expanding and contracting around me. I felt sick.

'Well, you can't drive. Come out of there. You'll kill someone.'

'I don't care.'

'Yes, you do. Come on, come on, I've got *Raiders of the Lost Ark* on Betamax. Oh, I forgot, you can't watch it. OK, I'll tell you what, I'll read to you. All right? I'll read you *The Voyage of the Dawn Treader* – would that make you feel better?'

I sniffed. Miles had never read to me before. It was a sweet offer.

'Make it *Watership Down*,' I said. 'But first I have to be sick.'

grateful dead to the humpbacks

'—Total waste of me being here if all I get to do is follow her around and be her punchbag.'

It's Klaski, and it doesn't seem like much has changed with Serge's team since your last visit.

Lewis is laughing. 'I used to work in a hair salon,' she said. 'They made me sweep the floors and make coffee for six months before I got to even mix up the hair color. Apparently I was regarded as a risk to the clientele. You're a risk to yourself, Joanne. And us. You just don't know the ropes yet, and that takes time.'

She's running through your channels and checking your files from the day before to make sure nothing's been corrupted by the recharge in the Grid.

'I'm not trying to insult you,' she adds. 'But you're really green.'

'I know already, OK?' Klaski snaps. 'But I don't want to learn to be a soldier. Learning to follow orders isn't any good to someone like me.'

Lewis's lip curls but Klaski doesn't see it. She's deep in her mug of Cup O' Soup (Chicken Noodle).

'If you don't want to be a soldier, what are you doing here?'

'I want to study the Grid. I told my adviser that when they

recruited me. I was told there were a lot of research opportunities open at X.'

Lewis smiles. She tosses you into the air; by now the group has begun to move off, Klaski sucking up the last of her noodles as she walks.'I'd forget what they told me in the recruiting office if I were you. Just concentrate on surviving in the Grid. If you don't, you're dead.'

Klaski wipes her mouth and sticks the plastic cup in a thigh pocket of her utility suit.'Thanks a lot.'

Lewis nods at Serge to indicate that your retrieved files have been moved to her Swatch. Serge motions to the others to precede her and then scans the material quickly, nodding. When she sees the footage of the girl-golems running for their lives and making it, she whistles softly.

'I guess it's all going to end up academic,' she mutters. 'Galante's made a good job of it. She makes it look easy. Soon we'll all be home.'

She sounds like she's anticipating a prison sentence.

You rise over them. Their conversation as they move through the Grid sounds like fuzzy radio to you. You test your eyes, changing focal lengths and banking from side to side. The relative structure of this region of the Grid makes it considerably easier to track the humans moving within it.

'The grid is like a whale,' Lewis is telling Klaski.'You see it as big and scary until a whaling boat sticks harpoons in it and chops it up into big chunks, and then it's pathetic. But if you get too close it's scary again, even when it's dead. It might be a whole world you could lose yourself in. It might make everything irrelevant, from 7-11 to taxes and death. Or it might just land you on your back in a military hospital reading *Ladies Home Journal* and eating Jell-O. Either way, you're an idiot if you don't pay attention to what it's doing, every single minute you're here.'

Klaski says, 'See, but that's my whole point! At MIT I took a course on the Grid and the professor said if the Grid is intelligent we should be able to communicate with it, but the government never tried to do that. When they found out about the logic bullets they just went in like it was the California Gold Rush.'

Lewis flaps her hands at Klaski. 'Shh! Don't talk to Serge about—'

'Too late,' drawls Serge. 'Serge heard y'all. 'S OK. Y'all can talk to me about anything. Don't think you'd like to hear what I got to say on that topic, though, Klaski.'

Klaski clears her throat and keeps her eyes focused on where she's placing her hands and feet.

'I'd be very interested in your point of view, ma'am.'

Serge grunts. 'Yeah? Well, speaking of whales, did you ever hear about those guys who hang out piping improvisational music down to the ocean to talk to the whales? Playing the Grateful Dead to the humpbacks, asking 'em to jam. So far the whales couldn't give a shit. Now, these guys are talented and they believe in what they're doing, but they can't even communicate with a whale, which – am I right, you tell me, you're the college kid, Klaski – a whale's pretty close to a human, ain't it? At least we come from the same planet, and they do have big motherf%#king brains! If you can't get a whale to say good morning Miss Jones, how the ju-ju are you gonna talk to the Grid? How, Cousin Nellie? Tell me how.'

'Uh, there could be some flawed logic in—' Klaski slips and falls, the wide branch she was walking on catching her in the crotch. She gasps a bit. 'Um, whales might have big brains but maybe the Grid *is* a brain.'

'Then where's its body, chitlin?' Serge laughs. 'I sure wouldn't want to know.'

She stops and looks back at Klaski struggling to her feet. 'I'm just an old soldier, kid. And by the way, I ain't Japanese. Just in case you was thinking I knew your boyfriend.' She winked, then turned and scrambled up a net of sparking filaments to get to the next wide branch.

Hendricks had dropped back to give Klaski a hand. 'I told you she was smart. She sees right through you, Jojo.'

Serge gets the call then from Dante, asking if Major Galante can borrow you a second time. Paranoia grips you. Has Galante figured out that you nearly sold out your own side yesterday? Does she know you overlooked the children? Do they all know you are losing your nerve?

You wonder if you have to go. Maybe Serge will refuse to release you. She needs you to find Gonzalez, after all.

But Serge nods soberly and gestures to you to take off, then continues to climb.

Maybe she knows, too. Maybe everybody is in on it.

As you take Gossamer up and away, you follow Klaski's stare fixing on Serge's strange body from behind. Serge looks like a chunky spider missing four legs as she swarms up the side of the Grid.

'She has a dominance complex,' pronounces Klaski, sniffing.

When you reach the logic mines, a short, slim woman with a Major's rank-insignia on her shoulder comes to greet you. She has dark hair, blunt features and sapphire-blue eyes. Her hands as they reach to catch Gossamer from the air are stitched with silver scar tissue like a patchwork quilt. Your first thought is that Major Galante doesn't seem angry with you. So she doesn't know about Gossamer's behavior yesterday.

'Hello, my friend. I'm just in the middle of an argument with Machine Front – what else is new? Hang on. I may need you to back me up.'

Persia Galante knows perfectly well that you can't reply, but she always behaves as if you and Goss are a person. She flashes you a smile and turns back to the holographic cigar-smoking zebra projected above her Swatch – her personalized exit portal for the collective wisdom of Machine Front. You've often wondered what it says about her that she has a zebra where Serge has Dante. It's almost as if Serge wants to date Machine Front, and Major Galante wants to make sure she never takes it too seriously.

It's pretty obvious from her first words what the argument's about.

'There are no logic bullets in the mine perimeter. It's that simple. You want to come up here with a metal detector and check it out? Oh, I forgot, you're just a bunch of statistics – you can't actually walk. Well, I can tell you because I was there. The logic bullets are gone. They're not in the mines, they're not in the processing units, they're not in the storage facilities and they're not in the transports. They're not in the cafeteria or the barracks, either. We checked everywhere. We checked the damn latrines. There isn't one single logic bullet in the entire area.'

'You haven't looked hard enough,' barked the zebra. 'Nothing passed the perimeter between the time that the MaxFact missile was launched and the arrival of your convoy that sealed off the mines. The Gossamer has ample records to indicate that no golems escaped during that interval.'

On cue you call up Gossamer's visual memories associated with the golem raid from two weeks ago and confirm that this is true. There was a brief period of chaos at the beginning of the golems' assault, but once the MaxFact failed to strike its target all personnel in the mines were obliged to automatically self-immolate to prevent themselves becoming golems. The marauding golems then set about dismantling superficial equipment and dragging it into the Grid, but within a very short time Galante's convoy had surrounded the camp perimeter and prevented most of them escaping. The golems subsequently besieged in the camp might very well have entered the mines after that, but there was no way out of the camp without crossing the perimeter fence, and Galante's blockade ensured that didn't happen.

'Then they must have been removed beforehand,' Galante says.

'There is no evidence to indicate that they were. You need to make a more complete search. Take the Gossamer and cross-check all the reference files with what you can see now. We need to find out what's changed since the raid began.'

Galante blows out through her lips like a horse.

'My people have just successfully raided a golem camp that was said to be impenetrable. We have not lost a single soldier. We haven't even lost a major piece of equipment. And now you want me to go on a research hunt?'

'We need the logic bullets. You know very well that the effectiveness of the Third Wave depends on close pursuit. Close pursuit is impossible without the logic that predicts how the Grid will behave. Until the logic has been recovered, your mission remains open.'

Galante slams her Swatch shut and punches the air. She opens the Swatch again and shouts into it.

'Gossamer saw the raid. We have footage. No golems escaped my equipment. How could they have removed the logic, then? I'll tell you what happened. We've been stuck up here waiting for the right moment to go in and get the logic bullets, and all the time they were never here. They were removed weeks ago. And I bet I know who removed them.'

Machine Front is implacable. 'You will double-check every inch of the perimeter. You will check all flier records and you will do a detailed forensic analysis on the mine shafts themselves. The possibility that the logic was removed earlier will be explored by us. But don't rely on it being true.'

And so you end up spending six hours combing the air, and your own records, for some indication of where and when the logic bullets went missing. A distinct mood of disappointment, followed by anger, settles over Galante's guys.

'There's no end to what they want,' one of the elite soldiers grumbles as she fits a miner's lamp on to her helmet. 'Next thing they're going to say there's a fuel shortage and ask us to fly home powered by our own farts.'

'We'll get home, Hotchkiss,' Galante reassures her. 'It won't be long now. Did you see the videos of the Third Wave tanks? Poetry in motion. We'll get the logic and we'll all be having a barbecue in no time.'

You wish you could always work with Galante. You can't imagine Serge at a barbecue, that's for sure.

Arla Gonzalez is hanging out with golems these days. It's not clear to you what their relationship is. You don't witness them talking. But they seem to follow her, and her wishes and their actions seem somehow causally connected; but it's hard to be sure exactly what's going on.

You have seen golems disembowel soldiers with their own weapons, or with Grid-generated versions thereof. You have seen them butcher a man and toss his body parts in the Grid, like Horus into the Nile. An you have seen the hands and arms rise from the well in multiples of nine, groping blindly: the Grid always makes nine copies of everything. You have seen heads rise, eighteen eyes look around, only to sink again. But mostly the golems leave bodies intact – that's the only way to get more fully functioning golems. The best soldiers make the most dangerous golems.

Why have they not simply killed Arla Gonzalez?

Serge has got to be wondering the same thing. Again she has located Gonzalez, but the presence of so many golems lurking around her like spidery bodyguards prohibits Serge from making a capture. Gonzalez is pleasant and soft-spoken as always. She looks emaciated.

'There's something you should see before you bring me in,' Gonzalez says. And she leads Serge to the gap where you first spotted Gonzalez, the gap that holds the MaxFact missile (and suddenly you remember that you never reported that to anyone, and you wonder if you forgot by accident or if, as Mom would have said, you forgot by accident-on-purpose).

Serge beckons you down, into the dead Grid.

It's not at all nice.

Now that you see the blackened, rigid forms of what once had been branches and boles and roots, the live Grid compares as a kind of Disneyland, a moving panoply of pastel happiness and life-affirming energy. The dead Grid makes a sound like thunder, and the patterns of shadow in its wasted skeleton write on your animal cortex in a terrible, primeval script. It has no smell. And you can't help but suspect that it has no weight, either – no integrity. Judging by Serge's behavior, she has the same intuition. She creeps near to the edge of the living, throbbing Grid, but stops a few paces clear of the gray region. She can't seem to bring herself to go any closer to the gap, and her voice trembles when she sends instructions to MF.

'No one else is to come over here,' she tells Dante. 'Under any circumstances. Gossamer: you come down here with me. I don't want you going directly over it, just in case something happens to you.'

No problem there. Gossamer has no intention of going near the wound in the Grid; in fact, she seems to be physically repelled by it, like a magnet of the same charge. You come in among the upper branches, sinking faster as Goss picks up more mass in the form of Grid pollen, until you hit a branch near Serge and stick there.

'Record this,' Serge says, 'But don't try to send it yet. We'll have to test the air waves first.'

She takes a few steps across the gray foundation like a nervous ice-skater. She lightens her goggles by one setting, and you take the corresponding restraints away from Goss's machine eyes. The Grid starts to boogie and shake, but you edit that out and focus on the dead zone. The branches are flashing alternately black and white; then they change to ultraviolet; then everything goes dark. The strobe pattern makes Serge grab her head, and she takes the opacity on her goggles back up a notch.

'I hope you're getting this, Goss, because I can't even look at it.'

You can see everything in the clipped instants between flashes. There are shining parcels wedged in the cruxes of branches and dangling from cords. There are tools and snake skeletons. There are casette-tape casings with what your zoom function tells you are rodent guts in the place of audio tape. There are oil paintings of human faces and human body parts, rendered with a technique referred to by art historians as photographic; but no photograph could make a human elbow look so gorgeous and disgusting at the same time – the body parts are almost *appetizing*.

Most of what you see is metal. Stereo components and gun fittings.

Surrounding what's left of the well is a dust bath. Its surface stirs like vapor from dry ice. Rising from this is a weird tower of heterogeneous components: stereo woofers, antennae, Barbie dolls like little totem figures strung on the cat's cradle of the Grid. The tower looks like a satellite receiver as might be envisaged by a Pink Floyd album-cover designer.

Serge looks at this scene for a while without touching anything or venturing too near the dust bath. Then she goes into the live Grid again and stands there, looking silently at the dead zone.

'I think it's just a freak-out,' Serge says after a while. 'Psychological warfare. It's just another game.'

Arla answers her; Serge must have forgotten that she was there, because she startles at the sound and then looks resentful.

'You saw the structure in the Grid. Lewis doesn't know what to make of it, does she?'

'Yeah, so? It looks like some friggin lost temple of the Jungle Ungawungabungas,' says Serge. 'Place is ripe for a wanna-be alien archaeologist. That ain't what I'm here to be.'

She turns away from the dead zone and starts moving back into the gleaming Grid lattice with a purposeful air. She's missed the real point of coming here; you swiftly send a message.

Machine Front will probably tell you off for not informing them first.

MAJOR LOOK IN THE WELL. THE MAX FACT LANDED HERE.

Serge doesn't break stride. Gonzalez is following her, talking.

'The altered Grid isn't an ancient artifact. We both know that. It's been built more recently.'

'Yeah? By who?'

'Ah. The question you should ask isn't *by whom,* it's *for whom*?'

'I got a war on here,' says Serge, swinging herself up off the foundation and into the Grid proper. You sense that she just wants to get away from the dead zone, and Gossamer's only too glad to lead her. After a while Serge stops and scratches the back of her neck. She's lost. You send her the camp coordinates, and she immediately sets off again, following your directions without acknowledging your presence. 'I'm gonna be needing a real good reason not to torch this whole sector.'

'I can show you a reason.'

Before Serge can retort, you both hear a voice. It comes from your dorsal side, behind Serge's back. It's a light voice; a young voice. But it doesn't speak with words. It makes an utterance derived from playgrounds and mental wards: long, guttural, with tongue waggling around ineffectually in mouth, and ending in spittle.

By the time you locate the position of the speaker, the utterance has changed into something perfectly recognizable – familiar, even.

It's a child, and she's laughing.

'Don't run this time, Bonny,' Arla says softly.

'I ain't got no intention of running. I already decided what I'm gonna do if you call up your baby goons again.' And out comes Serge's trusty spiderwhip.

She peers down into the shadows that drape the well.

'I know you're down there,' she says loudly. 'Come on and try to kill me. Come on! I'm not afraid of you turkeys.'

Down below, the surface of the well stirs. Serge stiffens and you can see the muscles in her body coiling. You can smell her excitement.

A head breaks the surface, then a body. Serge's hand tightens on the spiderwhip. She is going to release it any second now. The creature surges out of the well, moving from shadow into light, shaking its head and opening its eyes.

But Serge doesn't do anything. With the swelling music has come augmented Grid-light. A clear ray now streams down on the golem, though Serge herself is in deep shadow. It reveals a small body belonging to a child no older than five or six. The child is a girl, with straight black hair and eyes elongated by epicanthical folds, and ears that stick out like a leprechaun's. She holds up a hand.

It has six fingers.

Serge staggers back as though struck.

'Arla, you sonuvabitch,' Serge says. She's just clinging to her branch, trembling like a plucked piano wire. 'No!'

'You didn't get a good look at them before this, did you? Are you frightened?'

Serge's trembling resolves into smooth, aggressive action. She whirls and lunges for Gonzalez, taking the other woman by surprise. She gets Gonzalez by the throat and presses her up against the bright webbing. The Grid is still playing its horrible symphony.

'I see them all right, but what I'm seeing can't be right. It's just some nightmare shit.'

Arla smiles.

'Nightmares by definition aren't real.'

'How did that thing get in the well?' Serge snarls. Her nails snap against the alloy of Arla's collar.

'You know that I used to run the medical facility at X. Your very own Corporal Hendricks worked on my team in those days. We handled all kinds of problems. Including sexual-health matters.'

'Go on.'

'Paper waste and anything that might contain data useful to the Grid was incinerated within the compound at X, to prevent verbal and conceptual contamination. But sewage and the like was routed directly into the well. So were the contents of the biological waste-disposal system at the clinic.'

'That's a nice thought.' Serge makes a face.

Gonzalez shrugs. 'It's a matter of practicality. As you know, the well has never shown any reaction to human bodily fluids or tissues in isolation, only to actual corpses, and these need to be fairly intact from a structural point of view in order for the well to make golems out of them. Considering that we had no other way of disposing of waste, the well was the logical dumping ground for inert materials.'

'Inert materials.' Serge says it with an edge sharpened by irony. She is shaking her head back and forth.

'Yeah. Now, in certain cases involving reproductive health, we used special sealed containers to hold waste. Just to be safe. But there was a seal malfunction in the lab, and some of the materials leaked into the well.'

'Materials.' Again: the dead voice. You've never heard Serge like this before. She looks on the verge of tears.

'During the crossover period, when the majority of the male forces were being replaced by female soldiers, my staff recorded terminations of seventeen pregnancies, most of them in the very early stages.'

Serge's face is on fast-twitch. You can hear her panting.

'I don't believe this. I don't believe what I'm hearing. Are there others, then? Other children?'

Arla shrugs. 'Maybe. But I don't think so. Even the Grid has limits. Thirteen of the terminations were performed very early. Only four happened after twelve weeks – and I think it's one of those that we're looking at.'

'But that can't be right.' Serge has a fervent air, and she shakes

Gonzalez as she says it, as if the force of her conviction can make her words true. 'That was only four years ago. These kids are older than that.'

'I never actually said it was four years.'

'These kids are older than that,' repeats Serge.

'How did you know it was four?'

'You know how I know,' says Serge. 'Quit playing me like I'm a dumb bunny.'

Suddenly she lets go of Arla, who stumbles and goes down on her butt on the foundation. The children scatter into the Grid like spiders.

Serge's teeth are chattering.

'What the hell *are* they, Gonzalez? They can't be human. If you know what's going on, you better tell me right now.'

'I don't know what they are. But I know what they aren't. They can't be picked up by scanners while they're alive, so you're right: they're not human. They aren't golems, either. Because they also don't disintegrate on death. They can die, for real.'

'How do you know this? What evidence have you got?'

'I know they can die because I killed one of them,' Gonzalez says softly. The way she says it somehow manages to make her sound graceful, even saintly.

You want to go home.

'When the raid started, I shot one of them off the perimeter fence, and then I went to check for damages and I found it lying there. It was still alive. I took it inside. I'm a doctor. I know a living thing when I see it. I know a human being when I see her – even if the cameras don't. I put her in quarantine and tried to medicate her, but she died. I couldn't allocate surgical resources because we were under golem attack. I told MF what I'd found, and I sent the body back to X. Hours later, MF launched a Maximum missile. It was supposed to wipe out the surface of the camp but leave the mines intact so that the logic bullets could be recovered afterward. MF would then come in and take care of any remaining golems. It was our worst-case-scenario plan. We would all die: we knew that. But at least we wouldn't be killed and dragged into the well by golems.'

'But the missile never hit, doc. It was a misfire.'

'It wasn't a misfire. They pulled it down outside the perimeter. The well grabbed it and it didn't explode, but little by little it killed the Grid all the same. You can see the destruction gradually working its way towards the mine.'

'Who pulled it down? MF?'

'*They* did. These children. *Your* children.' She pauses. Serge has not flinched. Gonzalez adds, 'They pulled it into the well. With that apparatus you were looking at.'

Serge turns back toward the dead zone and the impossible quasi-machine tower made of body parts and stereo components. 'They built *that*?'

'They appear to have a great deal of mechanical aptitude. I've watched them.'

As the two of them are talking, the children flit among the Grid's branches with monkey grace. Again you notice a curious disjointed aspect to their movement. They look like badly spliced film. Serge must be able to see them in the periphery of her vision, but she doesn't let herself be distracted.

'Why don't Machine Front know about this?'

'Because I didn't tell them,' answers Arla.

'You f%*king traitor. You're crazy, all right – crazy like a coyote. No wonder you're still alive. You're on *their* side. You're helping the golems.'

'Hey, what do you want from me, Captain? I took a physician's oath long before I came here. When I told Machine Front I had a specimen of a human born in the Grid, they didn't change their tactics to take that fact into account. Instead, they went even more hard-ass and tried to blow up everybody in the mines.'

'Yet you said yourself it was a worst-case scenario . . .'

'You just don't get it, do you? Everything is alive here.

Everything. The Grid is nothing less than miraculous. Our orders are bulls*%t.'

'That's not for you to say.' Serge is swinging her head from side to side like a bull getting ready to charge. 'You don't know enough to make that judgment.'

'I don't have to be able to lay an egg to know when one's rotten.'

'What do you mean by that, Major?'

'I mean what kind of crazy s*%t it is!' Gonzalez's neighborhood accent comes shining through. Her voice rises to a squeak. 'Mining for logic bullets. Fighting with the indigenes. Taking samples of organic molecules for study. What about understanding the Grid? Nobody's trying to do that.'

'It's too soon. There are stages, steps to be taken.'

'Baloney. You don't just march in and invade. That's where all our civilization went wrong. Just watch *Star Trek*.'

'*Star Trek*, Jesus Christ, Arla . . .'

'This thing is smart,' Arla says, slapping the Grid with her palm like she's complimenting a horse. 'Machine Front is playing games with you. The Grid isn't your enemy, Machine Front is.'

'You're sick. You need help. Don't you realize that without machines we'd be dead?'

'Would we?'

'I don't follow you and I'm not sure I want to.'

'Let's take the concept of the ArtIQ test,' Arla says. 'It's easy to get an ArtIQ to duplicate an image – to make a photograph, say. But ask an ArtIQ to create a painting and it can't do anything but copy. It can't put its own interpretation in. It doesn't have that creativity. Now, people have compared the Grid to a highly sophisticated computer. It takes dead bodies and reproduces them, synthesizes them, and animates them. It even manipulates their neural structures so that they can function with a modicum of intelligence. So far, so good. But what about an embryo? Something in an early state of gestation has been torn from its human host and dropped in the well, and somehow the Grid has grown this thing, developed it, and taken it past the point of what would have been birth and into its childhood. How is that possible? How could it know what to do? It's an extraordinary leap, and I would argue that the only way it's possible is if the Grid is able to actually identify with the developing embryo and sense its wants and needs, and then provide them. If the Grid is identifying with us to that degree, why are we fighting with it and not talking to it? If it is coming to us in the form of our own people, shouldn't we see that as a bridge to communication, and shouldn't we cross that bridge?'

'But they're not talking to you, Doctor, are they?'

'Not yet, not as such. But the situation raises the question: if a dead embryo could be brought to life by the Grid, what about a live person? Could a live person become a conduit, a—'

'—Channel? A psychic medium? Gypsy Rose Lee, Fortunes one dollar . . .'

'You can laugh about it, but the only way forward that I can see, Captain, is for a living human to go in the well and see what it does to her. Meet it halfway.'

'And is that going to be you?'

'I'm working on it,' says Arla.

'Ho,' says Serge. 'I see a pattern here. Weren't you supposed to suicide up at N-Ridge with all your subordinates? And if you were gonna jump in the well for thrills, haven't you had enough time to work up the nerve? You know the way I see it? I think you like the romance of committing suicide but you don't got the necessary pumping action. You can't do it.'

'We'll see what happens,' says Arla in her sweet voice.

Serge grunts, 'I doubt it. I know your type.'

'And I know *your* type, Captain Serge. I know your type all too well.'

'So then you know what I'm gonna have to do about this.' Serge gestures to the well without looking at it, as if afraid that she might meet the gazes of one of the children.

'And I don't think *you* have the requisite pumping action, Captain.'

Serge swallows.

'Why don't you tell me about my . . . offspring. Go on, then. I'm listening.'

Arla's voice drops to a whisper.

'You're shaking, Captain. It's a good front, but I can see you shaking from here.'

Serge's eyes flare. She gropes in her pocket.

'Want a Snickers?'

You are getting too close. You can see the poison in Gonzalez's eyes. You have to bring Gossamer around in the air and take her higher, or risk getting entangled in the Grid. And in doing so you lose sight of them, just for a few moments. Just as Gossamer goes into a banking turn, the golems come.

It's very fast.

You use the Swatch to shriek a warning at Serge. She springs back from the nearest golem with a curse.

'You don't need friggin' rescuing,' she hisses at Gonzalez. 'What are you doing? Are you controlling them?'

Gonzalez shakes her head sadly.

'No, I'm not controlling them. That's your job.'

'What the skunk you talking about?'

'Machine Front are just using us. Always have been. They need us to die, Captain Serge. Without us, no golems. Without the golems, no one to take apart the machines.'

Serge snorts. 'That's bass-fishing-ackwards, Gonzalez.'

'You go up to N-Ridge and look around, Captain. Then you can tell me about bass fishing or fly fishing or any other kind of redneck killtime you can think of.'

'I can't buy into this paranoid fantasy crap,' she said. 'A fl*kup's a fl*kup's a fl*kup. And this is one, I can feel it right down in my toes. Because if I believe that some disposal-seal malfunction resulted in the dead embryo going into the well, and the kid that resulted from it was hell-bent on putting machines into the well to make them alive . . . well, it could be true but if I was to follow this popcorn trail of logic to its natural end, I gotta be believing that the machines done it all on purpose. That they want to be alive. And that's just too Frankenstein for this Kansas girl, Toto.'

Gonzalez doesn't say anything for a moment. Actually, she looks like she's going to cry.

'Maybe when Machine Front have manipulated you the way they've done me, then maybe you'll understand. If you can still think, which I'm starting to realize I can't.'

And she retreats into the webbing, leaving Serge with her spiderwhip and her Swatch, surrounded by golems.

'Is she a downer or what?' mutters Serge.

You start to call Lewis for help, but Serge stops you.

'They're going,' she says.

And the golems do leave once Gonzalez is out of sight. But you can still make out the children, half-secreted in the Grid's netting, watching Serge.

like my hiney

I dropped by Miles's house to pick him up for the funeral. He didn't want to drive his car into Clifton; he's funny like that. I've known Miles since high school and we both went to Rutgers. He didn't even have a car then; I liked it that he stayed friends with me even after I dropped out and started having mental problems and he started making all kinds of money doing his hobby, computer games, even before he graduated. Now he had an expensive, if staid, Buick, and he kept it washed and waxed and never subjected it to stress. It's not like Clifton is exactly the South Bronx, but that's Miles for you.

I got there early and he was still working. I sat down and reveled in the air-conditioning of his living room. Outside, it was scorching.

'I'm just tweaking a few things with the graphics,' he said. He showed me the screen of his Apple. It was covered with letters and numbers and symbols in short rows going down the screen in a long column.

'I don't see any graphics.'

'This is the code.'

'But how do you get the pictures out of those symbols?

Spazmonia! moves, it looks like a cartoon. Where are the actual pictures?'

He showed me again and tried to explain, but I still didn't get how a code could be a picture. Much less a whole actual action game.

'Looks like magic to me,' I said.

'It isn't,' sighed Miles with his usual air of faint condescension. 'It's just a collection of rules. Nothing supernatural about it.'

Then he showed me his test game. It was about a spider spinning a web. I looked at it for a few seconds and felt a migraine coming on.

'I can't look at it, Miles. Sorry.'

'It's a shame,' Miles said. 'I was going to give you a trial copy. I thought you might like some kind of . . . diversion. You know.'

I looked away. 'I would. And I wish I could escape into a game. But I don't know how to use a computer, anyway.'

He rubbed his nose and pushed his glasses back.

'I could lend you my old Apple IIe. I'll bring it over and set it up. I'll give you some text games. Those shouldn't trigger your problem and they shouldn't bother your eyes, either. You ever hear of *Quark*?'

I shook my head.

'*Hitchhiker's Guide to the Galaxy?*'

'Heard of the book.'

'They're both pretty cool games. *Quark* is kinda like D&D on another planet, but with a humor element. *Hitchhiker's Guide* is *really* funny. They don't have any pictures. Playing is like interacting with a story.'

'I don't know. I'll think about it.'

D&D on another planet sounded a little too close to what I was already doing at Dataplex. Not exactly recreation.

*

The funeral service didn't take very long. Mom had wanted to be cremated and her ashes laid to earth in Bear Mountain State Park, where my dad had proposed to her. I felt sorry for my dad. He had taken off work to come up from N.C. He was even more biceps and shoulders than I remembered. He was wearing a gold chain.

'Hi, Mr. T,' I said when I saw him.

My father is not the world's most emotionally articulate person, and I think it was hard on him to watch me put my mom's ashes under some ferns near the summit of the mountain where he'd given her a ring with a speck of diamond in it some twenty-seven years ago. I don't know if he had any romantic memories about this place, or if he thought my mother had specified it just to get his goat. The latter I doubted. She wasn't spiteful like that, and besides she had always maintained that he would predecease her, gunned down in the line of duty – even after he left the force to start his own security business. He'd laughed at her predictions.

Another wedge in the relationship, I guess. How he and Mom ever got it together long enough to have me and Darren is the biggest mystery. Talk about hard-headed. My dad has about as much imagination as a railroad car full of cinder blocks. He's good with people, though, in his own way. He's got a kind of instinct about people where he can guess what they're up to not by what they say, but just by looking at them from a distance. It must be that he's got an eye for detail. When Miles got me reading Arthur Conan Doyle, I kept being reminded of my dad because he is socially bizarre in the same way as Holmes is. Once he spotted a pickpocket at a hot-dog stand in Central Park and made a citizen's arrest. At the time he was chaperoning us on our junior high field trip to the Natural History Museum and for the rest of the day I was cool and everybody wanted to hang out with me, because of my dad. Afterwards, he tried to rationalize it like Holmes. ('Oh, I was watching him. It was obvious he was up to something because his breath smelled of falafel.' Like, huh?) But you know it's really all about my dad having a nose, even if he doesn't want to admit it.

We don't talk very often. He doesn't like it that I don't listen to him. He told me to go to college and I dropped out. He told me to go on a diet and get a boyfriend and I went to work at Dataplex and got fatter. He told me not to buy a Rabbit because they're death traps. He thinks he knows everything and I guess he's worldly-wise about some things. He's very successful in his security business.

My parents had an ongoing dispute about how much reality I should be exposed to, as if life were radiation. My dad wanted to toughen me up, put me on my guard. My mom wanted to protect me from nightmares and cosmic negativity. She kicked him out of the house when I was twelve because he left crime-scene photos from a homicide on the kitchen table. 'You ain't doing that kid no favors,' he yelled at her through the double-bolted door. 'I didn't think, I'm sorry, I was careless, but I could talk to her about it, explain . . .'

'Nothing is an accident, Thalo,' she sobbed at the inside of the door. 'On some level in your mind you did it on purpose and you'll do it again and she's too fragile, I'm telling you because I know.'

'Let me in and we'll talk about it.'

She didn't let him in. They divorced. I started reading Stephen King, just to spite my mother. I covered up *Carrie* with the dust jacket of a fairy-tale anthology (which was actually scarier). Was I *fragile*? I didn't know if I wanted to be fragile or not.

My mother swore blind they didn't split up because of me, and I guess I believed her. They were totally incompatible and hardly a day went by where they didn't argue about pretty much everything from politics to laundry duty to what to call the cat.

'If anything, we stayed together as long as we did because of you and your brother,' she told me once when we were making Toll House Cookies and eating all the batter before we baked it. After the break-up, we'd both gotten into food at a semi-professional level.

Well, whatever he might have been feeling deep inside on Bear Mountain, my father looked like he wanted to get a beer and go to a ball game. It was a gorgeous summer day, and the park was full of picnickers and cyclists and kids on summer vacation. All my mother's weird friends were there, burning incense and chanting over their crystals. I liked them. Their presence made me feel like she was still around somehow, and I began to wish this wasn't going to be the last time I ever saw most of them.

I didn't want it to end. As long as we were all here, talking about her, remembering her, it didn't seem so bad.

Everybody went back to her apartment afterward. The furniture was still there, but I'd taken out most of her effects and so the appearance of the party was more like a house-warming. There were cardboard boxes lying around, and I'd taken the contents of the liquor cabinet and piled them in and around the kitchen sink, which was full of ice. I stuck to sparkling water. It had been fun drinking with Miles the other night, but I couldn't take any more throwing up. I was afraid my teeth would rot from all the acid.

The Psychic Friends were in full cry. They smoked weed. After a while, they got the munchies, and then they got gossipy. Several of them left to bring back pizza. Agnes and Lorna, an astrologer and a Kirlian Energy Therapist, respectively, hung out in the kitchen talking about my mother. I was waiting to use the bathroom and I could overhear them, whether I wanted to or not.

'—Scheduled to give a workshop on the African Celestial Tarot after the annual Psychic Pancake Breakfast in White Plains. She drew a huge crowd last year. Maybe we should have a special service this year.'

'It depends on what Ayeisha's spirit wants. We should meditate on it. Does the daughter . . .?'

I didn't look over. I sipped my sparkling water and pretended to be interested in the bathroom door. The voices grew hushed, as if they were afraid I'd overhear.

'. . . Darker forces . . .' I heard. Then: '. . . She told . . . after the police . . . Woodcliff Lake.'

Yep. They were talking about me. I walked over there, feeling threatened for some reason I couldn't pinpoint.

'Cookie!' cried Agnes. 'We were just talking about you. Honey, is there anything I can do for you?'

I shook my head.

'You know, I'm just so glad that at least your mother signed that deal last week. Her African Celestial Deck will be her legacy to the tarot community, and a nice little nest egg for you.'

I blinked. 'She sold her deck?'

Agnes nodded triumphantly. 'To Renaissance Flower for exclusive distribution. She was going to surprise you. She made a real nice chunk of change.'

My lip quivered. Mom could have quit her job at Macy's. She might never have been on that bus. Why didn't she tell me?

'The money was for you, anyway,' Agnes said. 'She wouldn't have spent it on herself.'

'Maybe one new dress,' said Lorna.

'Oh, yeah, well, you gotta live.'

Lorna added, 'It's a funny old universe. Just when you think you're getting somewhere, the Powers That Be come along and change your direction.'

'Maybe they needed her elsewhere.'

'Excuse me,' I said. I wanted to get away, but people seemed to be making it their mission to talk to me. Brenda kept giving me puppy-eyes and offering to wash dishes, which I let her do because the smell of food made me feel sick. Someone I'd never met wanted to know if there was more guacamole, and two kids were throwing pot holders out the window. I started to wish I could vanish, cut the nex, wake up somewhere else . . .

I spotted my father popping Maalox in the corner and looking at my mother's friends like he was thinking about busting them for possession. The air had gotten a little rich after the pastor left. I waded over to him.

'How's the Rabbit?' he grunted.

'Thinking about getting a Honda next year.'

He nodded. 'Good car. Nice suspension. You need any money?'

I shook my head. Didn't I just say I was getting a Honda?

'Job pays good,' I added.

'That's OK, then. You . . . uh . . .' He cleared his throat a couple of times. 'You ever want to come down, you know, stay with me. We could go out to the Barriers for a few days, rent a beach house.'

I nodded. 'Maybe in the fall.'

He shifted his weight from foot to foot. Something was coming. Dread crept through me. I hoped he wasn't going to get all emotional and start talking about making up for lost time or how beautiful my mother was when they first met, or how much he regretted—

'So what's with the forearms, Cook?'

'Huh?'

He pointed with his beer can. 'You got muscles.'

Trust him to notice.

'Oh,' I said shyly. 'I lift weights now.'

'Yeah?'

'Uh-huh. I do karate, too.'

'Karate's for wusses. But I guess it's OK for a girl. You any good?'

'I will be.'

He smiled and rocked back on his heels.

'This reefer smoke's making me sick,' he said. 'Think the Yankees got a shot at the pennant this year?'

I snorted. 'Like my hiney they do,' I said.

My dad left at midnight, just after Gunther and Brenda. Agnes and Lorna seemed determined to stay to the bitter end, but I shook them off by attaching myself to the Ever-Elusive One, who had cornered a pained-looking Gloria.

'My mission is simple,' said Miles. 'To deliver computer gaming from the mindless button-pressing of the arcade to the inner realm of the arcane.' He gestured theatrically. 'To bring the inner world to your home computer.'

'I don't have a home computer,' said Gloria in her depths-of-Bayone twang

'To your Atari, then.'

She seemed to weigh this up. 'The kids have Atari. That *Haunted House* gives Tony nightmares. Cookie, do you have it?'

I shook my head. 'Atari makes me hallucinate seagulls.'

Miles gave me an annoyed look.

'Well, most people do. And you probably will have a home computer by the year 2000.'

'Miles knows about these things,' I told Gloria.

Gloria shuddered. 'The year 2000? I'll be 48! Please! Don't wish my life away!'

'I *do* know about these things,' said Miles, ignoring her. 'You see, I may appear to be just a regular guy in a *Mad* magazine T-shirt and Wrangler jeans, but I have another identity. In my own world, I'm a hero.'

'Aren't we all,' deadpanned Gloria.

'Miles,' I said out of the side of my mouth. 'Isn't the Pimpernel supposed to keep his identity secret?'

'Sink me,' said Miles. He bowed to me. 'My lady, you are correct. Guacamole, anyone?'

eat jerky

Serge is subdued in camp. Her jaw is set like somebody trying not to cry. Nobody makes eye contact with her. Klaski keeps dropping things in an effort to avoid Serge.

When Lewis wants to charge Gossamer and send the data to MF, Serge nixes it. Doesn't tell anyone why. She looks at you significantly, though, as though daring you to say something. You want to laugh: you can't say anything out loud, and even if you could, what would you say?

'I guess Machine Front are interested in all kinds of data,' Serge says, kneeling beside Gossamer on the pretext of peeling scum off her boots. 'I guess we rely on them as a matter of faith.'

Lewis is clued-in to Serge's moods enough to take a stab at the problem.

'You want me to make some kind of special report, ma'am? About what we found today?'

Serge looks at her sharp, and you realize that for a second Serge thought Lewis was talking about finding Arla and the child golems. Then Serge realizes she's talking about the altered structure in the Grid. She says, 'Not yet. We'll work up some more angles on these structural features tomorrow.'

She says it calmly, but in such a way that Lewis closes her mouth.

You wonder what she means to tell you, though. Does Serge *want* you to share what you saw with MF? You realize that you don't want to do that. You know what will happen. More weapons, more attacks, in an effort to exterminate the developing golems – if they are golems. In light of what Dr. Gonzalez has said, you just don't think MF need to know right now.

Serge is watching Gossamer, who lies completely inert, giving away nothing of your thoughts.

'I'm a company woman,' Serge whispers to you. 'You do what you got to do. In the morning I'm gonna let you go, and I expect you to make a report. In full. I know that's your duty. I won't hold it against you.'

Her eyes are black with conviction.

She turns to the others and says, 'Y'all need to understand something. Machine Front is all we got out here. The Grid will mess you up. It ain't just air filters you got to worry about. There's something about the Grid, something in what it does to your eyes, something in its shape and the way it sounds – you guys ever take a good listen to this thing? It does stuff to you makes you not trustworthy in your own head. That's what your Swatch is for. That's why we have Dante, and I don't need to remind y'all that Dante is made out of pure, hard facts. He's not a person. He doesn't have an agenda. He's a representation of the facts that we know to be true, and you got to listen to him.'

'OK, Serge,' says Lewis softly. She looks a little freaked, and exchanges glances with Hendricks. But Klaski, with her usual appalling sense of timing, chimes in with the kind of over-sincerity that disguises contempt.

'Follow procedures at all times, right, we got it.'

Serge draws a long breath.

'Goddamit, Klaski we play by the procedures because the procedures is all we got. You want to be High-Risk Betty, do it right.

Take your risks intelligent. Any sh%&head can jump out a plane and pull the cord. Here you got real problems. You walk into a patch of cyanide – your fault. You ignore Dante's advice – your fault. You climb out over the well without checking storm differentials on the branch you're on, don't blame anybody but yourself if you take a couple thousand volts. If Hendricks here dies and you don't take care of business immediate-like, don't be surprised if you don't wake up in the middle of the night with Hendricks golems stealing your air kit and com link.'

'Yes, ma'am,' Klaski whispers.

'I don't care what anybody says,' Serge goes on. 'As long as we're out here, Machine Front is what we got and we better use it. I'll sit watch, Klaski.'

Klaski looks stunned and frightened by the reprieve, as though it must be a set-up for something even worse. 'Get in your cocoon and get some sleep.'

You don't make the report. Not that it seems to matter. Because the next day Serge gets new orders, delivered via Dante.

'We're sending you reinforcements. Personnel carriers, survey equipment, and weapons experts. Your orders are to recover Gonzalez at any cost, as soon as possible. We need her alive or dead, and we need her now.'

Serge's brow furrows. Her lower lip pouts childishly. She glances at you.

'So I take it you got a report from my Gossamer.'

'No, why? What new information do you have for us?'

'Never mind. You want to play games, you're gonna find I'm up for it.'

'No games here, Captain Serge. Just an urgent mission to recover Arla Gonzalez. Isn't that what you've been campaigning for?'

'Well, then, let me do it the way I do it. I don't need no reinforcements.'

'We'll be the judge of that, Captain Serge.'

'I've got a bead on Gonzalez. She'll be in quicker than you can say *Late Night With David Letterman*. Don't worry about it. Nothing will compromise my sense of duty.'

She sounds a little desperate. You know she thinks you told MF about her aborted fetus and its . . . consequences. You know she thinks they're giving these orders because of her conflict of interest.

Only you didn't tell them. So what's going on here?

Klaski and Hendricks are whispering together. You can only imagine their joy at the idea of personnel carriers coming, and their horror that Serge isn't accepting the help.

Dante bulldozes on. 'Major Galante will be in charge of the unit. You'll brief her on everything you know, and then take your instructions from her.'

Serge cursed loudly. 'You got to be kidding my pants.'

'Machine Front expects your cooperation in this matter,' said Dante in a tone that was meant to be stern but only sounded nasal in the Swatch's audio processors. 'Major Galante will be with you within three shifts. Please hold your position until then, and use the Gossamer to track Dr. Gonzalez.'

Serge says something so bad-mannered it makes you cringe.

You want to tell her that the reason MF are so hell-bent on getting Gonzalez is because they believe that she has the logic bullets. Nothing to do with the child-golems, whatever they are. But you can't talk to Serge without also talking to MF, and you can't figure out how to compose a message that won't somehow compromise Serge.

She sulks for a few minutes, then sends Lewis and the others to catalog the dimensions and boundaries of the structured elements in the Grid.

'I'm going into a danger zone,' Serge says. 'If I don't come back, wait for Galante and follow her orders. On no account does any- body come after me.'

With a martyred look at you, she sets off alone into the tangled Grid. You hang with the group for a while.

'Where's she going?' Klaski wants to know.

'None of our business,' Lewis informs her. Klaski sticks out her tongue at Lewis when Lewis isn't looking.

'She was acting weird last night, though.'

'Time you learned not to look a gift horse in the mouth,' says Hendricks.

'Oh, you too, then? Why is everybody so serious? I thought we discovered something important. And the convoy will be here soon! God, I can't wait to take a shower and play some Cyndi Lauper. Shouldn't Serge be happy?'

'She won't be happy until she gets her guy back.'

'Well, I'll be happy when the convoy gets here. We can't stay exposed anymore, five work cycles is the legal limit. It says so in the manual.'

Lewis says, 'I wouldn't put too much faith in the manual if I was you. We'll meet the convoy when the Captain is good and ready.'

'But Lewis, that's illegal. We have to go *now*.' Klaski's on the verge of tears.

'Can it, Klaski. Now get up there into position – I want to you to triangulate this reading for me.'

You leave them taking measurements and gossiping.

It takes a while to find Serge. Gossamer's eyes aren't used to picking up movement in this altered region of the Grid, and you have to pay close attention to detect her presence. She's cradled in the arms of the Grid like a guy in his hammock who's supposed to be mowing the lawn. She looks decadent, almost sensual, with her armor-clad limbs draped around the thrumming contours of the Grid. If you didn't know better you'd say she was drunk.

She's talking to herself.

At first you can't hear her over the Grid interference. The Grid is humming, a slow alternation of the same two pitches, *ee-oo, ee-ooh*. It's like the sound of an English fire engine heard through maple syrup.

Gossamer drops lower, and you increase your receiving power on audio.

'I know y'all think I didn't care about you or I wouldn't of done like I done. See, that's just not true. I didn't want you to have some s%&t life like I did when I was little. I didn't want you growing up with no daddy in some sh%&hole apartment or trailer park and me getting a job as a auto mechanic or repairing refrigerators and us hating each other by the time you was thirteen – I didn't want that. See, I just couldn't bring myself to do that. I'd of been a failure. I should of stayed away from Six, I know that. I doubt he even remembers who I am. He's too busy getting off with some other girl wants him to love her, well, that's not me, no siree Hankie, and I'll tell you what, why should I be the one left holding the sack of potatoes? Huh?'

There is no verbal reply. But now the humming seems to divide into two strands of sound: a deep, rhythmic thrumming overlaid with a soft, uneven whine.

'Nothing personal, of course. See, what y'all don't realize yet is that I am NOT TO BE F%@KED WITH. Got that, everybody?'

Serge sits up suddenly, sticking her head way out on her neck. For a second she looks like somebody's hunchbacked grandmother. Then you see what she's looking at.

A whole collection of the child-golems is arrayed on the edge of the nearby well. They are half-in, half-out of the fluid, in various attitudes, still as garden statues. The Grid is still humming, and now another track of click-clacking kicks in, like deep swamp noises. Serge waves her hands at the girls.

'And OK, at the moment I might look like the biggest jerk on God's green— I was gonna say on God's green Earth but I can't even say that, can I? The biggest joke there is, maybe I look like a jerk but I done what I done for reasons. Maybe they weren't as good as I thought but they looked good at the time and I ain't never said I was perfect.

'I wish Jezzy was here.'

The noise is growing more complex all the time. It seems to creep into your mind through a back door. You hear elements of sound that remind you of the squeaking of fingers across steel guitar strings and frets – the incidental noises of a guitar without the music, as such.

'No, cancel that request, she'd just complain they don't got no MTV.'

Serge is starting to worry you. You have never seen her get emotional in this way. You're taking a chance routing through MF to send her a message, but you have to reassure her that you're still on her side.

LOGIC BULLETS MISSING. NOT AT MINES. MF THINK GONZA-LEZ HAS LOGIC. THAT'S WHY BACKUP. NO OTHER REASON.

Serge snorts, receiving this. Gives you a little salute.

'Don't f@*king matter now, does it, Goss? Don't matter why. The end product is the same old poop.' She sighs, squeezes her battleskin-clad knees with her gloved hands.

'Yup. The whole trailer-park thing is looking pretty good to me now. I could get a job fixing VCRs and we could live out near the Indian reservation, park ourselves someplace cheap. Eat jerky – God, I miss jerky. And spam. Drink Pepsi. Maybe go down to a ball game on your birthday. If you were born, which you won't be. We could shoot squirrels like them Indians. Being poor's not so bad if you don't watch TV or go to the mall. Don't know what you're missing and it's OK.

'Like not being alive, right? Don't mind losing what you never had.

'Not that I could speak for y'all.'

Serge looks at their goofy faces and their spatulate fingers, six on each hand. They say nothing back to her. But the Grid is adding weird harmonies and disrhythmias to its chorus. Serge shouts at it now.

'How dare you do this to me? To US? Jesus God, what are you that you think turning dead embryos into golems is funny? Dead people is bad enough, disgusting enough, but this, this, this is beyond shame, you S?*T.'

She pauses.

'What is this supposed to be, some pro-life Mothers of America apple-pie bullshit because I'm a soldier goddamit and what was I supposed to do? I already told you about the friggin trailer park and like how was I supposed to know? Plus, already, where was the guy in question, where was six-fingers Six, I ask you?

'Are you listening? Are you here? What is the point of being God if you turn your back on people at a time like this YOU FRIG—

'Sorry. I'm sorry. I didn't mean that, JC. It's just that, well, if you really want to know it's just that here's me telling people not to contaminate the well or drop any Coke cans in it and look what I dropped in it and sacrificed, a whole person, a helpless person y'all hadn't even finished making yet and I—'

She gulped and sucked, her diaphragm spasming in tearless sobs.

'I feel like a total A-hole.'

The singing came on. Funny how Serge was talking about humpback whale song this morning. The Grid makes whales sound tonal – symphonic, even. Its repertoire of noises has a curious effect. It reaches you with pitches just on the edge of hearing. It plays rhythms that make you feel crazed. Serge doesn't pay any attention. She's talking to herself, or God, or whatever, but however you read it, she's gone somewhere else in her head.

'OK, there's only one thing I can do.'

She takes something out of her pocket that looks like a hand grenade. You haven't seen one of these in a long time; it's an old-generation robot report unit.

'This is Captain Serge. I'm calling for an emergency destruct sequence to be initiated across the Grid from the points to follow. I have identified pernicious danger to the Effort and I doubt I will be able to get out to make a report personally. I'm downloading a briefing into this probe which will back up the destruct order. Do not wait to analyze it all. I cannot overemphasize the urgency of my request. This whole sector has got to be torched by any means necessary.'

Serge sticks the probe onto her Swatch and the unit chirps a few times as data are exchanged. Then she chucks the probe in the air. It goes sailing past you at a decorous pace. At that rate, the thing will take days to reach X. Maybe weeks. What is she playing at? She could have given you a direct order.

She looks up at you.

'Sorry, bud. Don't mean to hurt your feelings, Goss, but you're indigenous and I just can't trust you to give the order to kill your own planet.'

This is spooky. How does Serge know that Gossamer would protect the children? And how can she just . . . order them to be torched?

'My uncle JJ used to say trying to know your self is like trying to read the sky backwards. There's better ways to spend your time. But I can't help thinking about it. I don't think these kids is mine anymore than the rocks on Ardent beach is mine. The Grid took the embryo I got rid of and figured out what makes it grow. It made a lotta copies and filled their heads with whatever ideas it gets out of the candy-bar wrappers that idiots like Klaski manage to drop in it. Somebody musta dropped in some weird *Greatest Hits* albums to make it sing like it's doing.

'Now, Goss,' she adds in a conversational tone. 'Now that I sent that order, how much you wanna bet we get a visit from a bunch of golems right about now?'

You don't understand her. Does she have a death wish?

But Serge isn't wrong. Gossamer detects movement. Something's coming.

The children react first. They sink into the well without a sound or a ripple. An instant later, Serge startles.

'Whathef%#k you doin' here, Klaski? Who told you to follow me?'

'Nobody, ma'am, only I thought—'

'You didn't thought nothing. Go back now.'

Klaski breaks down in tears.

'Ma'am, I came to tell you I got to get out of here, I can't take it anymore, I have to go home, I'm sorry, I know I'm a disappointment to you and I don't want to let anybody down but—'

'F%#king Maybelline and Sugarfree, kill the speech and get your butt back to the convoy before you get hurt. Of all the friggin' ways to behave, Klaski – Jesus, just get up and go, that's an order.'

'I can't, I can't, I'm sorry, please don't yell at me.'

'We are in a ambush position, Klaski. You sit there any longer we're both gonna be hold the pickle hold the lettuce flame-grilled meat. Now get *up*.'

She grabs Klaski forcibly by the arm and drags her to her feet.

'Ma'am, I can't, I can't, don't make me, don't be mean, I—'

Serge speaks in a whisper.

'Some of us *don't snap*, Klaski. You can't let yourself snap, not out here. Some of us are strong enough that we hold it together no matter what.'

'I don't want to be that strong, ma'am. I was brought up nice and I want to go home. I'm only here because my adviser at MIT said it would look good on my application to grad school. I don't want to be like you and if you don't like it you can go ahead and kill me.'

Serge looks up at Gossamer.

'You get that?' she calls. 'She's asking me to kill her.'

She gives Klaski a shake. 'What in tar-fu%*ing-nation good's that gonna do, princess and the pea?'

Klaski said nothing.

'Come on. Back to camp.'

'I thought the convoy was coming but Lewis said no, and rules and regs says we got to go back, it's all I could do to hang on in there this long, it's not fair, ma'am—'

'Shut up. Put your feet one in front of the other. There's a good girl, Joanne, come on, walkie-walkie, you can do it. Now we're gonna climb over this here branch and *Dante are you reading me get Lewis up here yesterday with a rehab kit and a radio cloak, I got me a freaker* there you go – see, that wasn't so hard, was it? I need you to climb for me, just like on the monkey bars at the playground, you go on up, I'm right behind you I got you don't worry you ain't gonna fall and if you did I'd catch you—'

'It's no use, Captain ma'am, I just can't.'

At which point Serge hefts up Klaski's body like a sick dog's, fireman-carries her at a run-stagger across the Grid's foundation—

'—come on Lewis come on where are you—'

—until, chest heaving and wheezing, Serge coughs up something purple-green that lands on the side of a Grid-arm with a splat and a sizzle. Klaski pulls out a travel-sized package of Kleenex and tries to offer it to Serge, but fumbles and drops it in the well.

Serge emits a primal roar and drops Klaski.

'—Brand-name contamination, I don't believe this, where's my flamer—'

Klaski doesn't protest. Lewis arrives, snorting and grunting, and Serge says, 'Get her back to camp, she's out to lunch, I gotta clean this sonuvabitch up before the Grid processes it—'

'What is it, ma'am, what contaminant?'

'It's a brand-name plastic wrapper, goddamit, now get the kid out of here, I'll see you in a minute.'

Lewis retreats, dragging Klaski in an improvised cocoon.

You see the children rising out of the well, in synchrony, coming up in all directions – must be seven, eight of them. And then men, battle-clad, armed, shedding Grid-fluid like boxers shed their silk robes on arrival in the ring, and you try to alert

Serge but she's cut you off, she's angry, she's scraping plastic off the Grid and frying it with total intensity, total purpose, as if by eliminating them she can purify this whole situation, fix everything, feel better, and forget about it.

'Getthef%*kouttaheregossamer, and I mean NOW or sohelpmeGod I'll shoot you thefrigdown.'

You're flying straight for Major Galante, to beg for help.

But the nex cuts off, leaving you breathless.

cookie starfishes

'Cookie, I need to see you right now.'

I felt dizzy as I followed Gunther to his office. He never just jerked me out of the nex that way. It must have been an emergency. When we got inside, he thrust a sheaf of papers at me.

'I need you to do this worksheet for me right away.'

'Worksheet? But—'

'Cookie, just do it now, okay? The computer is down and I've got Headquarters on my back. I don't have time to do a debriefing and consult the system.'

I was looking at a Xerox with a long list of brand-name products – all kinds of things. I didn't recognize all of the names.

'I want you to circle the ones that come to mind when you remember your session just now.'

I felt my face screwing up with indignation.

'What? Gunther, you pulled me out of the nex for this? I'm right in the middle of a—'

He pointed to the document. 'I'm very serious,' he said.

It was a long list. I scowled at it. Now that I thought about it, some of the names did ring a bell. I immediately recognized Maybelline, Sugar-Free Dentine, Burger King, and Kleenex. I was about to circle them when I also noticed Bird's Eye Peas, Pepsi, *Late Night with David Letterman*, *Girls Just Wanna Have Fun*, MTV, and Swanson's Apple Pie. There were a lot of other names on the list, too, but these all happened to be ones that came up in my last flight.

I recalled the memo page I'd seen on his desk. 'What's this for, Gunther?'

'Marketing survey.'

'But what's it got to do with the war?'

'Ours not to ask why, Cookie. Are you finished yet?'

I was circling names, but not the ones I suspected were 'right'.

'Are you sure about these?' Gunther said.

I nodded. I'm a terrible liar.

'I'm sure.'

'Great. That's great. I'm sorry to rush you. I know this is a hard time for you. Was there something else you wanted to talk about?'

'Not really,' I mumbled.

'Thanks again, Cookie. This is just what I need to keep Headquarters happy.'

'OK,' I said, and he gave me such a big smile that I wondered if I was imagining things. 'Um, I left the walkathon money in your envelope. Just so you know.'

'Yeah, yeah, thanks,' he said, ushering me out. He handed my paperwork to Gloria and told her to fax it. Then he winked at me.

'Take the rest of the day off.'

I didn't want to take the rest of the day off. I wondered what might be happening in the nex without me. I tried and failed to eat. I read all my old favorite books but they just didn't do it for me anymore. I had finished *Crystal Singer*, disappointed because there was no high heroism in it, and for all that stuff about there being music in the crystal, nothing ever happened with that, either. I started reading it again anyway.

At 5:30 I got a call from Gunther. He sounded tense and clipped.

'Cookie, I think you'd better take some time off.'

'I did,' I said. 'I took the whole afternoon, but I wish—'

'No, I mean like a month. Take a chance to get yourself back together. You've had a bad time lately.'

'I think working would be more therapeutic,' I said.

'We'll pay you,' said Gunther. 'No problem. Just . . . take a step back, OK? I'm saying this to you as a friend.'

I was stunned, but what could I do? I couldn't confront him with my doubts about the 'worksheet' and the memo I'd seen. I just couldn't. I mean, he's such a boy scout, how could I suspect him of anything underhanded? At the moment he's selling compilation tapes to benefit the homeless, and every summer he throws a huge party, paid for out of his own pocket, with steak and endless quantities of German beer and Wyckoff bakery sheet cake, and invites everybody from work and their families. He always knows Letterman's Top 10 list, and he's gone to bat for his people with management on more than one occasion over vacation time and a microwave for the break room and the casual-clothes Friday.

It couldn't be his fault. It had to be my fault.

'OK,' I relented. 'But they're getting Major Galante to help Serge, right? Will you let me know what happens?'

'I'll do everything I can do, within security protocols,' he said stiffly. 'Now, don't worry about anything. Just take care of yourself.'

I went around feeling foggy and indistinct for two weeks. I stopped being hungry. I stopped trying to eat. I barely even read any books. I took a lot of baths, which Nebbie liked. I thought about going to the beach but I couldn't face buying a bathing suit. I did karate a lot. I listened to Prince.

Then I remembered my dad's birthday was coming up, so I dragged myself out to look for a present to send him. Stopped at ShopRite for some cat food. I had double coupons for Fancy Feast Beef and Liver. Not that I needed double coupons considering that my food bill these days was nil.

I wandered up and down the aisles in a sentimental fashion, remembering all the foods I used to love. Fudgetown Cookies. Bachman Pretzel Logs. Nestle Quik. Cocoa Crispies.

I stopped. There, between Apple Jacks and Lucky Charms, I saw something that made me forget Cocoa Krispies.

Cookie Starfishes.

Little brown starfishes dotted with chocolate chips.

Miles's nasal voice sounded in the imagined space between my ears.

'I can just see the newspaper headline: Cookie Starfishes. *A Fair Lawn, NJ woman has mysteriously disappeared, to be replaced by an abnormally large starfish in her bathtub. The starfish was discovered reading* Ringworld Engineers *and eating a Hershey bar.'*

I glanced around furtively. Nobody seemed to be looking at me, but I felt like the eye of the world was boring into the back of my head. I had a sense of malevolent, overarching awareness lurking somewhere above and behind me, invisible. I reached out and picked up the box.

They must be new. I'd walked down this aisle every week for years, and I'd never seen this cereal. There was a free rubber starfish toy advertised on every box.

I steadied myself. 'Whoa, now, girl,' I muttered. I pushed my cart to the customer service counter and waited behind a woman with four kids who had to return a jumbo box of Yankee Doodles because it was stale. I wondered how old the Yankee Doodles had to be before they got stale. Maybe about 400 years, considering that the half-life of a Yankee Doodle was about an aeon thanks to all the preservatives. Gotta love 'em, though, right?

'Are these new?' I said when it was my turn.

'Don't tell me those are stale, too!' said the clerk, sighing. Then, when I explained, she said, 'Yeah, they just came out. There's a coupon in our circular – do you want it?'

She handed me a newsprint advertising flier. *Save fifteen cents on Cookie Starfishes*.

'You can collect the box tops and get a free action figure from the show,' she added.

'The show?'

'Yeah, it's a cartoon, you know?'

I tried to laugh but coughed instead.

'You got kids?' she added. 'If you had kids, you'd know the show. I guess you don't watch much daytime TV.'

'No,' I said faintly. 'I'm usually at work. Um . . . what's it about?'

She laughed. 'Oh, I don't know, you'd have to ask a kid if you want to really understand it. These famous wizards, they got turned into cookies by this evil sorcerer, and they're in the shape of starfish, and they, like, go spinning through the galaxy trying to get back to being wizards again but they never can, but they, like, save a lot of planets from destruction and stuff. It's silly. My kids love it, though. Go figure.'

I bought the cereal and went to my car in a daze. Like a thought-daze, but without the thought.

You keep finding yourself at a loss. You're trying to wrap your head around something and you don't know what it is, and neither does anybody else. You can't nail down even one corner of it and every time you try the friggin' thing comes whipping back and slaps you in the face like a wet bedsheet you're trying to hang out on a windy day. But you don't even realize this much, not when it's happening, because everything's going off on a level below any phrasing or imagery that you ever ran across.

All you know is: you can't sit still.

You want to eat the entire menu of the Palace Diner but you can't even choke down a rice cake.

You shake all over.

Have I been saying 'you'?

Well, there you go. See?

I don't even know which world I'm in anymore.

The fact that Cookie Starfishes existed at all gave me a pins-and-needles feeling all down my face. I drove to Paramus Park feeling like an automaton.

I parked near A&S. Then, just as I was getting out of my car, some guy took a handicapped space even though he could walk just fine. There was a big sale, and everybody else was lining up for spaces and cruising around looking – I'd been circling for twenty minutes – but this jerk figured he was special and just took a space right by the door. He didn't even have the courtesy to limp.

I guess it was the not-eating part that made me speak up. They say if you feed a dog raw meat it'll become vicious. I hadn't been eating raw meat or hardly anything else at all, and I was going through most of the day feeling trembly and weak. When I saw the guy take that parking space, though, my blood seemed to return from wherever blood hides when you don't feel good, and heat rushed though my body. I started gasping for breath, and I felt my heart pounding as if I was running. It beat so hard that it hurt the inside of my chest. I was also shaking violently.

I marched up to the guy and tapped him on the shoulder. He looked surprised as he turned around.

'These parking spaces,' I said, 'are reserved for the handi-capped. You have no right to park there.'

He turned away even before I'd finished speaking. 'Mind your own business,' he threw over his shoulder. 'Fat bitch.'

'I might be fat but you're an inconsiderate jerk,' I shouted after him.

He gave me the finger.

I threw my hands up in the air.

'You so have it coming to you,' I said. 'We'll see about you.'

But nobody was paying attention to either of us, and within seconds he vanished between racks of Lacoste shirts on sale for twenty-five percent off.

I was supposed to be buying a present for my dad's birth-day but I clean forgot about it. I turned and went back to the parking lot, still oozing anger from every pore. I saw the guy's car: it was a blue Chevy Impala.

I stood off the car in a horse stance and gave it a side kick. I didn't focus. I didn't do a test kick to see if I had the right 'ma'. (Fight distance in Japanese. See? I know my termin-ology.) I just kicked it as hard as I darn could.

To my shock, a dent appeared in the door.

I put my hand over my mouth and looked around. I half-expected police to materialize from out of helicopters and drag me off to jail, but no one even seemed to notice.

I checked out the dent. It was pretty good.

I wanted to do it again and find out if it was a fluke, but I was too scared. I scurried off to my own car and pulled out of my space. A rusty station wagon containing an enormous family of Middle Eastern-looking people swiftly replaced my car. An old guy in a Mercedes hit his horn, disputing their right to the space, and they gestured colorfully at him, laughing. He scowled at me as if it was my fault, so I flicked my chin at him, Italian-style.

I've never done anything like that before. My mother always taught me better.

But it's kind of fun.

That night, I didn't even bother to try eating. I ironed my gi and raced off to class. I dented a car!

When I got to the dojo I went straight up to the water bag and whaled it with a side kick. It rocked and spun and the chains holding it up squealed.

'Whoa-ho!' called Troy from the weight room. 'Yo, Adrienne! Eye of the Tiger!'

Troy was really into *Rocky*.

'That's all right,' I said. 'You could make fun of me. I don't mind.'

'No, seriously, I wasn't kidding, that was some kick.'

I looked away, embarrassed. Miss Cooper came over and said, 'Well, you've got some power going on there, Cookie. Now, can I make a suggestion?'

I bowed to her. Could she make a suggestion? She's a black belt and I'm barely a purple belt. Could she make a suggestion!

'Try the kick slowly.'

'I can never do it slow,' I said apologetically.

'Just try. Stand on one foot. That's it. Now when you pick up your other foot, make sure you keep it level.'

Make sure you keep it level. I'm gonna fall over in a minute . . . I'm shaking and swaying.

'That's it, now extend it out sloooowly . . . keep your foot level, oops, try again . . .'

Miss Cooper worked with me for about ten minutes but I couldn't get it.

'That's OK,' she said. 'You'll get it, you just need to work on your form.'

I thanked her profusely and bowed several times.

The thing is, after that I couldn't kick at all. Whatever grace my outrage had lent me, it was gone. For the whole class I kept kicking like a spaz, and once I actually slipped in somebody's sweat and fell over. In spite of this, after class Miss Cooper came up to me and asked if I wanted to join the demonstration team.

'I need another woman for the pocketbook-and-broom segment,' she said. 'We meet after class on Monday nights and go over the routine. I'm sure you could learn it.'

I doubted that, but I had nothing else to do. I said yes.

The next day, I marched back into work and told Gunther that I was fine. I wanted to fly.

'I admit things haven't been going that well without you . . .' he began. He looked at some papers on his desk. He was flushed and his tie was askew. He chucked his pencil across the desk and sighed. 'I just don't know if it's a good idea. We're in a very tricky position right now, and I find it hard to believe you're going to be up to it.'

'This is what I do. This is what I can really, really do. Let me do it. Please.'

Gunther sighed again. 'OK, we'll give it a try. Just remember, it's my head on the block.'

it bakes cakes

The sunless light is failing by the time you find your way back to Serge. You know Galante can't come in time, but you have to do something. At first you think you've got the wrong coordinates. You see the lake-sized well; you see the submerged missile; you see the shorn-off sides of the Grid. But you don't see Serge.

Then you realize that the well has changed its configuration. Serge is there, surrounded by golems. Her ray gun and incinerator have fallen in the well, but she's still got a crossbow and she's using it. Machine Front crossbow bolts have been engineered with what you assume is some kind of nerve agent, but derived from the Grid itself. They have the power to temporarily shut down a golem if they hit a vital point. Their beauty lies in the fact that they don't give the golem the satisfaction of martyrdom and multiple replication, yet by temporarily putting it out of commission they can save a soldier's life. Problem is, a guy has to be a hell of a good shot to disable a golem in battle armor.

Serge must be a pretty good shot. You can see several fallen golems draped over sections of the Grid or lying in shallow pools on the edges of the well. Most of them are big: males, remnants of the First Wave soldiers whose bodies were taken by the well. You wish you could get in closer, but that's impossible for

Gossamer, who already has to execute some pretty slick maneuvers just to get a clear view past the drifting tendrils of the Grid's upper layers. Up here, cloying odors drift across you and Gossamer like rainbowed smoke; you try to ignore them and focus on the details of Serge's situation.

It looks like she's on an island, surrounded by the well like a moat. She has solid Grid in a radius of maybe twenty feet around her; there are three golem bodies here. The rest are scattered in the shallows of the well or on the foundation of the Grid on the other side of the moat-like channel. You can see where the Grid has rearranged itself to isolate her, and slowly, chillingly, you realize that the well is closing in on Serge.

You are so upset to discover this that you have to take Gossamer up and out for a little while. You can't hold the nex when your mind is all emotional and distracted. Your own body makes too many demands when you're upset. So you go for a sunshot glide in the beautiful topsmoke, soaking in the colors that the sourceless Gridlight makes when it hits all those motes of pollen and refracts. The light is softening. Darkness will come soon.

Sometimes when you fly at night you think you could maybe get a handle on the Grid. But how do you get a handle on a verb? The thing isn't a 'thing' at all, it's a function, it's a process, it's the very shiftingness of information states in the world. That's why it changes depending on how you look at it, what you are, how your very own tissues are interacting with its billion-packed substrates of variable sets and supersets. It's a flash in the mind's eye, a tease, the fleeting breath of life in a moment of possibility. Miraculous, really, that it hangs together for you at all, and a testament to the solid-state behavior of your species's hardware. And nothing more.

And yet.

And yet.

And yet, darn it.

It makes things. It bakes cakes. If it had known you were coming it would have.

When you watch these people play out their behaviors against the backdrop of the Grid, you edit the scenery heavily. You make branches and foundation and well, you make up and down, you make color, you make continuity. You must, because they must, and their visual filters force the Grid to conform to shapes that their minds can process.

But what about Gossamer's mind? Gossamer is an indigene. You are an Earthling. The two of you are sewn together with a crummy piece of experimental hardware that may or may not offer you a true rendering of each other. Surely it should enable you to see into things more deeply than the guys on the ground can. Gossamer is part of the Grid. She answers its calls, smells its moments, suspects its desires and anticipates its whims, which are written on her in flight-shape and windtaste.

The guys never take off their goggles, because if they saw the Grid too clearly their little brains would shrivel up and croak – or, in the case of Klaski, croquet.

What about you, Cookie the Spy?

Could you find out more if you tried?

Do you plan to buy the party line until everything's too messed up to save?

There are no transmissions from Machine Front, who must have received your distress call by now. Galante is on her way, but the convoy is too slow. Too slow.

You can only watch. The well of the animate isn't made of water. It's a complex of cells and its consistency is variable. It seems to be able to configure itself into solid Grid or liquid – this according to rules that nobody has figured out yet. That's how the Grid keeps you guessing: wells form and disappear and re-form in different places. Boles liquefy and pollen hardens and the whole package seethes and wavers in Gossamer's eyes, which are also somehow made of the same stuff as the Grid.

There is Serge in her battle armor. Battle is our defining metaphor for progress. When really it's about hanging on. Sheer persistence. The romance of battle never dies, even though it usually messes up a lot more than it saves. Gossamer lets you watch Serge being surrounded, by feet and then by inches. The golems stand around in the branches and on the foundation, some of them partially submerged in the well like corpses half-risen from a mass grave. They watch as Serge's footing begins to give. She tries to attach herself to branches with cabling from her battle suit, but the branches melt away and puffs of drugged smoke replace them. She staggers, keels, sits like a cat recovering from anaesthetic: all grace gone.

Beneath Serge, the Grid begins to melt.

It takes her like quicksand. It takes her like a snake eating a mouse. It takes her head last.

You watch the whole thing.

Gossamer hangs like a handkerchief in the windless sky, accumulating pollen and sinking slowly so that you find yourself zooming in to see Serge in ever-increasing detail as she is swallowed by the Grid. You are forced to watch her taut, concentrating face as she turns her mouth to the sky. You see her breathing quicken to an impossible pant. You see her pupils dilate. Her smoky skin takes on a cool hue. She doesn't attempt to move. You admire her discipline: she knows that if she moves she'll sink instantly. To the last she hangs on, refusing to panic, because rescue is still possible.

She knows this because Gossamer is there, bearing witness. Gossamer must be bringing her hope.

Better hope than despair, right?

You wonder what she's thinking. You want to look away, but you don't let yourself. You see the fluid of the animate flow into her mouth and fill it. She coughs it out several times before it finally covers her. Her eyes are still open as her face blurs. She sinks by inches.

Major Galante arrives four hours later. It's all over by then. The golems have gone back into the well. Gossamer is near exhaustion and wants nothing but to go to roost in the canopy. A mass of metal and plastic and flashing lights breaks the stillness. Queen songs blare out into the Grid announcing the arrival of the rescuers; but it's too late. Serge has vanished in the depths.

The message comes in, as cold as Machine Front knows how to be.

YOUR PERFORMANCE UNSATISFACTORY. RETURN TO X FOR REASSIGNMENT AND REPROGRAMMING. NOW.

That's bullshit but you are in shock. You don't argue. You start to rise and take bearings for your journey back to the convoy, but you can't get height. Gossamer struggles and at first you think she's just too tired to rise. Then you feel the rending of your wing. You feel the air rush turn wild and bumpy against your ventral side. You see the Grid whirling toward you and then away as if you were a spinning yo-yo, and in the last instant before you lose the nex, you glimpse a small figure in batle armor squatting on a looping arm of the Grid. You are falling directly toward her. Just as she brings her crossbow down to her side and smiles up at you with satisfaction, you recognize Major Arla Gonzalez.

all members commit feedback

I sat in my plastic chair, looking at a blue TV screen for nearly a half-hour. I didn't know what to do. I wanted so badly to talk to someone, to find some help; but what would Gunther say? He'd warned me not to come back to work yet, and I hadn't listened.

I had to tell him. Gunther was the only person who could possibly make sense of what had just happened to me. I got a legal pad and a Papermate and wrote down as much as I could remember in note form, in case I lost my cool when I was talking to Gunther and left out something important. My penmanship looked childish and unfamiliar, probably because my hand was shaking. I was going to ask him about the cereal, too. I was going to ask him about that worksheet he'd made me do. We were going to set a few things straight, I decided.

Gloria wasn't at her desk. I looked at the candy dish out of habit: Tootsie Rolls. Gunther's door was ajar, and it sounded like he was on the phone. I raised my hand to knock before sticking my head in.

'—Really a think tank more than anything. We don't have a product to sell, but we provide an invaluable service to companies that do. What we do is analyze all the information relevant to your campaign and then synthesize a plan based on all known market factors . . .'

I put my hand to my temple. *What's he talking about?* An image of one of Serge's girls flashed across my mind. I felt a wave of dizziness and I reached out to lean on Gloria's fica, then realized it was only a plant and leaned on the wall instead. I felt cold.

'. . . Closely guarded secret. Our system analysis is not only unique, Marty, its success rate speaks for itself. We can tell you what ads will be successful across a broad demographic spectrum, independent of the Nielsens and *in advance*. Our predictive success is right here in these charts, and I think you'll have to agree that nobody else has come close.'

There was a silence. I hovered there, aware that I was eavesdropping and I'd look like a jackass if I got caught, yet unable to move away from the door.

Of course, Gunther wouldn't be talking openly about the war on the *phone*. We are a secret agency housed within a corporate structure. He has to keep up the fiction.

'Daytime TV, Marty, is our strongest area in these last six months. We've penetrated the cartoon market—'

But what about the memo?

What about the cereal? *The cartoon market?*

'—For the next offensive, where a full-frontal assault on prime-time will begin.'

What about Serge, drowning in the well; giving destruct orders? What about Arla Gonzalez shooting down my Gossamer, the traitor?

I put my notes on Gloria's desk and fled. I felt weak and ashamed. I slunk out of Dataplex without talking to anybody.

I didn't want to think about Gunther or his company politics. I'd been shot down. I'd lost the nex with Gossamer.

My self-pity was unsurpassed. Again I drove home baffled by the life I was living. I looked in other people's cars as they passed me on the Parkway. I looked in yards and at stores when I got to my neighborhood. I didn't know how to participate in any of this. I couldn't even see the point of it.

But at the same time, I was sad that I wasn't a part of this world with its cars and stores and jobs and TV. I was missing being someone who had a mother. I had never realized what an anchor she'd been for me, until she wasn't there anymore.

I had no niche in this world. I couldn't go to the movies on Friday night. I couldn't share the talk about the latest episode of *Remington Steele* with the other girls by the coffee machine. I had a whole chocolate cheesecake in the freezer and it was no use to me. I couldn't eat it. There was *no escape*.

Watching Serge get swallowed by the well had been horrible. I could still see her face disappearing in the honeycomb of well cells. I could still see her open mouth, her epiglottis moving. But the worst thing was losing Gossamer.

Don't get shot down, she'd warned me.

By the time I got home, I was bawling openly. I ran into my apartment with my head down, opened the freezer, ripped out the cheesecake, and threw it across the room. It landed in one of my mother's ferns.

I opened a tiny bottle of vodka that I'd saved from a plane flight. I sipped it and then spit it out. Vodka makes me sick even under the best of circumstances.

In the end the only thing I could think to do was take a bath. I sat on the bathroom floor where I'd spent so much time recently, vomiting. But I couldn't even enjoy the relief of being sick. Nebbie came in and jumped into the empty tub, flinching when the water splashed her face. She jumped out again. Rocky came in, tail making a question mark, and Nebbie jumped up on the side of the tub, spitting at him.

I clambered into the tub as it filled.

'I hate this,' I sobbed into Nebbie's fur. 'Why can't I channel Middle Earth or Narnia? Or Pern – I'd love to channel Pern,

I've always wondered what *klah* tasted like. Why do I have to have the Grid? The thing isn't nice. It's like a cancer. It's like when you see a melanoma on some white lady's back at the beach, it looks like she's got a well-done hamburger stuck to her shoulder, your skin crawls just looking at it. Why do I have to be in the middle of it? Why? Nebbie, I'm so miserable.'

Nebbie purred and pointed her pink butt at me. I was out of bubble bath, which brought on another flood of tears.

The water was too hot. I didn't get out, though. I made myself stay, hissing and puffing, until I got used to it. Slowly, the sobs began to subside and after a while I relaxed. I leaned back in the water and reached for a towel to dry my hands. I was just reaching for the copy of *Dragonsinger* that I kept on the toilet tank, to start rereading it for the umpteenth time. Then I saw my own legs.

Normally the bubbles would prevent this from happening.

I could see muscles. Those thigh muscles that are always aching from doing sumo stances. What do the weight-lifters call them? Quadriceps. *Quads*.

I was so surprised that I dropped the book in the water. I had to get out of the tub and fetch one of my spare copies from the bedroom.

I thought: I'm becoming *not fat*.

I thought: what next?

Never ask that question.

As soon as I got to work in the morning, Gunther called me into his office and wordlessly handed me my pink slip.

I stared at him.

'Is this permanent?' I said.

He didn't want to look at me. He was ripping the blue fuzzy hair out of a Troll doll.

'That depends.'

'Depends on what?'

'On whether they change their minds at Headquarters. I went to bat for you, Cookie. What can I say? If you can't see anything, you can't see.'

'I didn't say I *couldn't* see, I said I got shot down.'

Gunther shrugged. I could see my briefing lying in his in-box, still encased in its yellow-ochre interoffice-memo envelope. Had he even read it?

I added, by way of explanation, 'I'm not about to open the nex in case Goss has landed in the well. That would be dangerous, wouldn't it? It could cause feedback. Right?'

He didn't say anything. He was rubbing little balls of wadded-up Troll-doll hair between his fingertips.

'Plus, in light of everything that's happened with Dr. Gonzalez, isn't anybody at Machine Front interested in knowing *why* she shot us down? Look how she trapped Serge.'

Gunther gave the impression that he was thinking about this, but he didn't say anything.

'Gunther, can't we try to fix it? Maybe Goss can be recovered. Maybe we can re-establish the nex.'

He sighed, looked at the ceiling. He opened his mouth as if to say something, and then changed his mind. Scratched his head.

'Gunther?'

The phone rang. Gunther set the troll down, wiggled his eyebrows at me apologetically, and picked it up again. I could hear Gloria's angry voice on the other end. She made no effort to keep her voice down: not only did her words carry across the phone, I could actually hear her where she sat at her desk on the other side of Gunther's office wall.

'*You told me to give it two minutes and call you. So I'm calling you.*' Gunther hastily covered the receiver.

He gave me an embarrassed shrug.

'Gloria says I got to go,' he said, standing up. 'Big meeting with Bob Hagler. Take your time clearing out your cubby.'

'But . . .' I spluttered. 'What am I supposed to do?'

Gunther took his suit jacket off the back of his chair and tossed it over his shoulder like a part-time male model posing for the Stern's Supersale catalog.

'I'll give you a reference if you want to go over to Military Psychokinesis now.'

'And that's it?'

'Sorry. Sayonara, kimosabe.'

I went home, stunned, and took out a half-gallon of ice cream. I wanted so badly to binge, but it melted in my lap. I couldn't eat it. I couldn't get the spoon more than halfway to my mouth.

It's not as though I like the war. I hate it. But who am I going to be now?

While we were waiting for the guys to show up for pocketbook-and-broom practice, I told Miss Cooper that I got laid off and she said, 'Well, now you have no more excuses. You can get serious about your training.'

'I never thought about it that way.'

'Are they still paying you?'

'They're treating it as a disability.'

'So, you don't have to worry about money. This could turn out to be a good thing for you. I'll help you, if you want. Train.'

'Would you?'

'Yeah, of course. I think you could be really good, Cookie. You're strong and you're not afraid.'

'I'm strong?'

'Yeah! People don't think big people are strong, but they are. You're carrying around a lot of weight every day. You have good muscles. If you could lose the fat, you'd be really powerful.'

'I don't feel powerful,' I said. I hadn't eaten in weeks. I was amazed that I was still alive.

Mr. Vukovich and Mr. Adams came in to practice pocketbook-and-broom. The demonstration team has various set pieces that are performed to attract new students. Breaking bricks obviously is very popular; there's also the nail-bed demonstration that Miss Cooper does, where she lies on a bed of nails and Shihan breaks a cinder block on her stomach with a sledgehammer. There are weapons demonstrations, and self-defense for women – i.e. pocketbook-and-broom. We have several scenarios where we demonstrate a woman innocently going about her business: standing at a bus stop, sweeping her front porch, etc., and some guy comes up and grabs her or otherwise attacks her. Our job is to beat the guy up using our pocketbook and/or broom. It's all choreographed and nobody really gets hurt. The guys fly convincingly through the air when we throw them. We always know exactly what they are going to do and when.

It's supposed to be fun, and everyone laughs when they see our performance. But it kind of bugs me sometimes.

'Don't you think it's a little demeaning that we have brooms and purses?' I said. 'I mean, I carry a purse, OK, so maybe there's something in that. But what are the chances of me being attacked while I'm doing housework? Which I do with a vacuum cleaner anyway, by the way.'

'The point is that you can use everyday objects as weapons,' said Miss Cooper. She comes from Allendale, by the way. Her father is a dentist. I doubt she's ever had to worry about being mugged in reality. She'd probably be fine. But what could she know about using everyday objects as weapons, exactly?

I ought to have shut up. But I couldn't help it. I was feeling grumpy about everything.

'OK, but why do they have to be such sexist objects? Why not a hammer or a tennis racket?'

'Oh, come on, can't you see the funny side?' Cori said. I'd noticed that she took a sadistic pleasure in ramming the broom up into the attacker's crotch and watching him writhe on the floor. 'Don't be so touchy.'

If you hadn't had a good meal in a week, you'd be touchy too, I thought. But I shut up. I twirled my pocketbook. I couldn't fly. Miss Cooper was right: this was what I had now. I'd better make the most of it.

On Tuesday I did my first push-up. I mean a real push-up, not a girl push-up where you rest on your knees. Actually, I did three of them. My hips had shrunk and my upper body had grown stronger in the weight room.

I was so excited I saw stars.

I was seeing stars a lot lately. I had bought a book on fasting for health purposes, and I knew that I was getting near to the point where my body would start consuming its own vital organs. I didn't want to be sick again, but I knew I couldn't keep training without eating. So after my workout, I mixed orange juice with my water. I never tasted anything so sublime, and the sugar hit my veins like an electric shock. After that, I had so much energy that I decided to walk all the way to Miles's and surprise him.

Miles answered the door with half a pastrami sandwich in one hand. He waved me in. He was in the middle of debugging *Spazmonia!* He had his work up on the screen of one computer, and some text game on the other. He was in the habit of switching back and forth between work and play constantly. I always found it amazing that he could get any work done at all with all the distractions he needed to surround himself with.

As I moved a stack of computer paper off Miles's spare squeaky swivel chair and sat down, I had the feeling that I was just another convenient distraction. Miles looked glad to see me, almost gleeful. He said he wanted to show me some new miniatures he had bought at The Compleat Strategist so he could ask my opinion on the right colors to paint them. I went into his office and waited, glancing idly through the libretto for his newest comic rock opera, *The Marriage of Fig Newton*. The next-door neighbors had put the stereo speakers in their windows and Weird Al Yankovic blasted into the backyard while they splashed in the above-ground pool. I heard Miles go down to the basement to get the stuff. The phone rang, and then cut off. He must have picked up the extension.

As I sat there with the sultry breeze bringing summer in through the window, ruffling the pages of Miles's notebooks, an inexplicable sense of well-being crept over me. I could smell the warm, new plastic of the computer, and the static coming off the screen. Outside I swear I could smell warm maple leaves, too, and the inchworms on the leaves. I was in my own place and I was perfectly happy. Even the stink of Miles's half-eaten pastrami sandwich balanced on top of a Garfield coffee mug couldn't mar the perfection of this moment. I was in harmony with something cosmic.

I didn't know that was possible for me.

The cords of the venetian blinds flapped. It was going to rain later.

I don't know how long I sat there before I took a look at the text game that Miles had been playing. Pale green letters showed on the dark screen.

Light hitting the well is like a dog chasing a car. It
starts out frenzied. Where it meets the surface it

explodes against the fluid, producing a crystalline dazzle; but as it penetrates it starts getting tired and colors appear: amber turns green turns indigo as the dog's tail whirls in braking circles. Finally halts. The dog wanders off diffidently, as if giving up were always part of the plan. As for the light: it has been eaten, its energy dispersed, and all the while the well's honeycomb cells rock in a sourceless current.

Her experience didn't feel like drowning. It didn't even feel like being in water. She had the sense instead that she was floating high in the Grid, suspended by filaments fine as spidersilk, turning gently in the breeze. Motes of blown Grid-proteins came and some of them attached themselves to her as filings to a magnet. Others passed through her like subatomic particles tunneling through metal. She was being taken apart to be remade. She was having her clock cleaned.

There are no pronouns down here. The grammar is reflexive, the well's an inclusive set; all members commit feedback. There are no passengers. So that by the time *she* was herself, she was almost fully assembled, almost ready to leave and become something other than the well.

At first she didn't know where her own body left off and the well began. Strings of sensation passed from it to her and back again: a million tiny umbilical cords, tugged gently by the current, feeding her and feeding back to the well and feeding her again.

She felt the battle armor forming itself around her and realized she could move. She wasn't breathing. She felt the hair on her head sprouting.

The well spat her out, slowly, over the course of

a day. Shadows wheeled across her; smells passed,
some of them lingering a while. They must have
been pulling at deep memories, for they made her
mind swollen and uneasy with unconscious matter
that refused to name itself. She didn't know how to
distract herself from what was happening. She
could do nothing but stare at the lattice structure
of the Grid, above, until she lost herself in the
mosaic it made of the sky.

By night she had been cast up, full length, on the
ground or what passed for it here. She lay there,
not dreaming, until—

Miles came in whistling and the nex snapped like a
cobweb. He plopped a foam-lined box of unpainted miniatures down next to the pastrami and said, 'Check out the
manticore.' Then I could hear him rummaging through little
bottles of model paint.

I glanced back at the screen.

What do you want to do?
This probably isn't a good time to stop for a ham
sandwich.

I gathered that this was the text of the real game, which
was getting impatient with Miles for not entering a response.

The Earth cooled. Invertebrates appeared.

I gave a little shake and looked away. He closed the
window and switched on the air-conditioning. The sound of
the fans shuddering to life sent chills up the back of my neck.

'Cook? What's the matter?'

'Nothing.' I stood up, which was a mistake. Time seemed

to slow down and black patches formed on the periphery of my vision, moving like clouds across my eyes. My legs felt vague and the next thing I knew I was on all fours on the carpet, sliding in and out of consciousness like a little ocean licking the beach.

Miles brought me some water.

'It's this heat,' he said. 'And you're not eating.'

He took my pulse. 'You wanna lie down? You want me to take you to the doctor?'

I shook my head.

'Lifesavers,' I managed to say. I was still feeling strangely high and distant, and my heart swelled to include Miles, his computer, his air conditioner and his overgrown spider plant with an indiscriminate feeling of compassion.

'What? Cookie, you're being a little . . . huh-huh . . . Cookie?'

'Do you have any Lifesavers?'

'What? Yeah.' He rummaged in his desk. He had half a roll of wild cherry.

'Just one,' I said.

'Go ahead, knock yourself out.' He sat back on his heels and watched me take the candy. He meant to be ironic but the truth is, that Lifesaver earned its name. It hit my tongue and my brain like the first sunrise of spring must hit the Eskimos.

'You know who that was on the phone just now?'

Like I cared. 'George Lucas wanting to make the *Spazmonia!* movie?' I said dully.

'Gloria. She told me.'

'Oh.'

'Oh.'

'I guess you think I'm having a breakdown, too,' I said.

Miles said, 'Gloria said you left a bunch of stuff there. She's going to bring it to karate tomorrow night.'

I took another Lifesaver. I didn't suck it actively, in case it made me sick. I just let it lie on my tongue. Having any foreign body in my mouth, even a toothbrush, lately made me want to gag.

'Do you need any help with these people, Cookie?'

'What kind of help?'

Miles said, 'The other night at your mom's house I got a weird feeling off your boss . . . Wolfgang?'

'Gunther.'

'Him, yeah. I don't like the way he talks about you.'

Bizarrely, I heard myself defending Gunther. 'He's a really nice guy! You don't even know him.'

'OK. If you say so.' Miles didn't sound convinced.

'So, I was looking at your text game,' I said brightly, desperate to change the subject. 'Is that the one you were telling me about?'

'*Quark*? Yeah. I'm stuck right now. There's this underground chamber, see, and I can't find my way out of it. The game keeps describing something about ropes, but you can't climb them and you can't carry them and nothing happens when you pull them . . . it's some kind of trick and it's driving me nuts.'

I nodded slowly.

'Is there anything about . . . dogs . . . in that game? Or battle armor?'

'No – why? Do you think you figured something out?'

'Maybe. Can I take you up on that offer after all?'

'You mean you want the computer? Cool. Yeah, sure.' He grinned and picked up a little fanged horse. 'Do you think the inside of a Nightmare's mouth should be red or green?'

Late that afternoon a thunderstorm did roar down, and I had to go home and close windows and sing Nebbie out from under the bed with the theme from *Cats*. Miles set up the computer for me and showed me how to use it. After he left, I also dragged out Mom's color TV and set that up, too.

I had to take down a lot of books and rearranged my Dewar's crates until I had the TV and the screen of Miles's computer where I wanted them. Between this disruption to my paperback library and the intrusion of my mother's effects, the apartment was now more or less a maze of shoulder-high piles of heterogeneous *stuff*. Nebbie would have been in heaven, except for the fact that Rocky really liked her and she didn't feel the same.

I made lemonade.

Normally I'd eat cake with this (remember the Trixie Belden?) But I was beyond cake now. I was wearing size 14 jogging shorts. And a halter top. I felt like a kid again.

'OK, we'll warm up with something easy. It's only words on a screen. No pictures. It's just D&D,' I told myself and I squared off against the Apple IIe Miles had set up for me. 'It can't jump out and get you.'

See, I thought that *Quark* would be a good way to get myself used to the idea of doing it on my own. I hadn't watched real TV for years, not since the first hauntings began. I was too scared.

I thought that maybe I should try to pick up where I'd left off, so I had asked Miles to save the game at the point where he was stuck and let me try working on it. He had explained the basic commands. I didn't listen much. I was hoping that I'd find out everything I needed to know just by reading.

There were more thunderstorms. I remember hearing the first peals of thunder, because in her fright Nebbie knocked over a bust of Brahms that had belonged to my mother. It was hollowed out and Mom used to keep her stash in there ('in case of a raid,' she told us kids seriously). A plastic bag hit the carpet and a sprinkling of pot spilled out. Nebbie probably thought it was catnip because she licked it.

After that, I was lost to the world.

The Swatch had various dials and buttons, all very
tiny and difficult to manipulate. As light grew about
her she saw that incised on the edge were the
characters CAPT. B. SERGE N76. She studied the
wristband for a long time trying to remember how
to operate it. *Fabriqué au Suisse,* it said. She
flipped it open. *Dante,* she thought. How to call
Dante? She couldn't remember. When she tried to
operate the watch a visual floated out of it. It was
not Dante's face. It was a train. A girl and a guy,
kissing on the step, the girl's foot coming off the
ground like a dog pointing. A little song. *'Say
goodbye a little longer/Make it last a little
longer/Give your breath long-lasting freshness with
Big Red.'*

She snapped the holo down. She flashed a
memory of the way she had felt the first time she
had seen what intestines looked like. Her tongue
seemed to be clogging her throat. She had a sense
of betrayal, as if the world was declaring itself to
be something more obscene and ludicrous than
she'd heretofore been led to believe.

She didn't want to know those kinds of secrets.
She stood up.

Visually, the Grid was overwhelming from this
angle. She kept tilting her head back to try and
take it all in, which was impossible. She turned and
looked up and turned again, steadying herself
against a branch of the thing with one hand. From
the point where her hand touched she saw a faint
puff of dust, and an odor came slithering towards
her nose. She also felt something in her skin, a
kind of shiver that brought the hairs to attention
on the back of her neck.

Surface area, she found herself thinking. *It has a huge amount of exposure, very high surface-area-to-volume ratio.*

That idea sank through her mind like a stone in a muddy pond. She didn't have another thought as such for a while. She took her hand off the branch, and instantly there was a reaction in her head. The second thought took the form of a niggling irritation that she should have even bothered to think the first thing.

You know this already. You know all about the Grid, as much as any guy. Why don't you get with it already?

She could almost *hear* this one, in her mind. It had an accent, a stubborn twang that refused to change no matter how far its owner traveled from her place of origin.

Texas.

The word lodged in her memory like a burr in a horse's tail. She took a deep breath. Whatever she had been recalling, it was gone. *Texas?*

Then: *Horse?*

Burr?

She sat down with her back to the bole of the Grid. There was a faint thrum within the material, which was ever-so-slightly yielding – not like wood, more like some kind of plastic but with a current going through it, if that were possible.

A few things had come back different.

She heard a rhythmic clicking from inside her thorax at all times. It was not a heartbeat or a pacemaker or anything like that. It was more like a chorus of crickets sounding from beneath her skin, making wild rhythms. The chorus moved around

within her trunk randomly, or maybe according to
an algorithm too complex for her to figure out: the
angles of the branches? Orientation like a compass?
Temperature, or chemical composition of the air?
Who knew?

Plus, she could no longer remember what human
time felt like. The time she experienced was Grid
Time, and its pace was roughly equivalent to
attention. Sometimes it flowed thick and sweet like
Caro syrup. Sometimes it was staggered and
disconnected, crunchy, lively as Rice Krispies when
you first pour the milk in. Sometimes it seemed to
have colors, even, like Jell-O. Time was just a game
that played in her mind. Her Swatch was no help.
The digital display was now written in Roman
numerals, which she had only mastered well enough
to pass the quiz in fifth-grade math. And Time itself
seemed to have acquired an analogous character: it
altered its quality in a tangible way, like Ls
changing to Ms or whatever; V becoming less when
you put a I in front of it, and so on. It wasn't linear
anymore. It wasn't intuitive to her. Time seemed to
have the power to change itself retroactively.

I pulled back. This was hard going. My eyes were stinging
and aching. The room had gotten dark and the luminous
print on the screen seemed to attack my corneas. I felt
exhausted. I got up, stretched, rubbed my eyes, and looked
at the screen again.

I could see a flashing cursor and a question mark inviting
my response.

I tried to remember what Miles had said about how to play
these games. You entered simple phrases, like 'Take rock' or
'Jump chasm.' But all I could think of were questions.

One letter at a time, I typed:

What can she do?

I pressed 'enter.'

Her heart does not beat. She does not breathe.
She can go in the well and come out again at a
different point.

She can smell the Grid pollen just like Gossamer.

She can probe inside the golems but there is no
reality there.

Is she part of the Grid now?

She is in a room with a two-way mirror. The Grid
can see her, but she can't see it. Or so it seems.

Because she's filled with loneliness. Her physical
needs have been erased, but her sense of isolation
is so enormous that it bleeds over into the empty
spaces that once held hunger and thirst and
tiredness, until loneliness becomes something as
urgent as pain. She reaches inwardly, reaches,
reaches for contact with something like herself.

The Grid isn't it.

The Grid as a physical presence reminds her of
the insides of a TV, with plastic and wire physical
forms that have nothing to do with how the thing
hits you at the business end. She doesn't know what
the Grid is but she does know that the cables and
lightning rods and sculpted tree-faxes of its sensory
structure are illusory or at best, misleading.

What about the children?

She can't get inside them. From the outside, they
seem electrified, speeded-up, jerky. Their voices
seem to be able to imitate any sound at all,

however unlikely, and their music doesn't follow
the rules of music. They seldom speak words and
when they do she doesn't understand the language
and it sounds processed, like Herbie Hancock's
voice in that so-called song, 'Rockit'.

She feels disappointed by this because she thinks
it means they aren't real, either, and in her
loneliness she couldn't bear that.

I sat back. This was depressing. *I ought to go to bed*, I
thought. Still, there would be no job to go to the next day. I
could sleep late. I heard the disk drive whirring. I flipped up
the control panel to turn off the computer, and more text
scrolled down in a burst.

Then she touched one of them.

It happened while she was wandering from one
well pool to another, examining the radiance of the
Grid where it scored the surface of the well, and
the crosshatching of shadows that traced byzantine
shapes on the dull roof of sky.

She was engaged in a theoretical panic. She
wasn't breathing and her heart wasn't beating that
she was aware of, which robbed her of all ability to
experience her own emotions. The Grid had her. It
was inside her. It was free to operate, was affecting
her thoughts for whatever sinister purposes of its
own at this very moment, and just the idea of this
made her afraid to think. She felt like she had a
tapeworm in her brain.

Then the girl shot out of the well in front of her
like a macabre otter. In the Gridlight the girl's skin
was the dark green of an angry goddess's, and the
well fluid falling off her in sheets left her polished

to a high shine, like a dressage horse on show day.
She uttered an inarticulate noise, her tongue
thrashing in her mouth, and snapped her fingers in
Serge's face. Serge, or whatever Serge had become,
reached out reflexively and seized the girl's wrist.

It was warm. It was sinewy, and the veins pulsed
as they bridged the tendons. The Grid, too, pulsed
with Las Vegasian enthusiasm, slave to the light and
the random. And Serge's heart shuddered into action.
Blood drummed in her ears. Saliva moved at the tip
of her tongue. She took a startled, fiery breath.

The girl was deep in Serge's personal space,
which normally extended to a radius of several feet
beyond her physical body. She got all up in Serge's
face and cried, 'Ghaad-d-d-aaaag-huh-huh!' The
utterance went on for several seconds before Serge
shoved the girl away with a frightened violence.

'Get off me!' Serge croaked. 'Quit playing *Night of
the Living Dead*. I'm sorry, OK? Shit happens. I'm
sorry for what you are. I'm sorry I'm grossed-out
by you. I shouldn't be, right? Now I'm one of you,
we're all one big screwed-up family.'

She sat down and put her head in her hands.
That didn't help. Instead of not beating at all, now
her heart was beating too fast and her breathing
coming too quick and too toxic. With real physical
panic on the verge of claiming her, she pulled a
Bilbo Baggins and groped in her pockets. She was
hoping for a Snickers actually, but she had given
her last one to Gonzalez.

There was something else in her pocket.

It was a metal oblong, narrow and as long as her
hand. It had little rectangular holes all along its
length. It was heavy, but partially hollow. There

was a spiky thing with a knob coming out of one end. It had had a brand name, something beginning with a K, but she'd rubbed it out. She remembered doing that, when she first came here. She remembered playing it, to remind herself of the smell of sage.

She blew into it experimentally. A tune started up without her planning it; she felt she was listening more than she was playing, pouring the sound over herself. The sound was bringing back her world, pulling her memories up by their roots.

She slid it back and forth across her lips as she blew, using her free hand to warble in front of the exit point for the blown air. For their part, the girls listened and echoed and responded with their own bizarre assortment of soundmaking.

'It ain't what I'd call bluegrass,' Serge said eventually, breaking off. 'But it keeps me breathing, don't it?'

And she played some more. The dead and terrible feeling started to recede. Music always did that: made the world less a collection of passive objects being manipulated by people, and more a living vein of time packaged in many shapes and forms. She realized this now and, in the same moment, she understood something about the Grid. Its very refusal to be nailed down in object form made it musical. The Grid held the line, or curve, or membrane, or dodecahedron, between the possible and the actual. She rode inside this thought like it was a racecar changing direction at 180 m.p.h. until she lost control of it and it broke up.

The sound was all around her now. It issued not from mouths, but from air. Her little harmonica sounded plaintive and weird in the Grid's sonic clutch.

She didn't dare stop.

This playing was Serge swimming in the Grid's sound. It was the only way she had to hold herself together in the rapids of time and position. There were no words for what was happening through her soundmaking. It was not about food or sleep or sex or fighting or helping or communicating, even. It wasn't about exchanging information. It was about not flying apart into smithereens. Not giving in to the undifferentiated wasteland. Not being an unperson. Yet.

She thought: Yes. Music is the faultline. Music is the crack in the egg, the vibration of birth, the fulfillment of chickenhood, funky or otherwise.

Funky or otherwise? Dipshit.

She put the harmonica down. She felt exhausted. But she was remembering who she had been.

'I know what you're thinking,' she said. As one their faces swiveled to her, as flowers to a light source. 'You're thinking you can hog-tie me with a length of my own filtration tubing, then get hold of my Swatch and do your funky bring-out-your-dead thing with it in the well.'

Then she laughed.

'See, I know you're thinking that because that's what I would do, and y'all are just like me. Well, half me. If y'all had your daddy's impulsive streak y'all would've tried it by now already.'

She shook her head.

'Six would shit himself if he knew.

'Do you guys understand what I'm saying or what?

'It sure would be easier on me if there was just one of you. I feel real outnumbered especially the way y'all are just staring at me.'

One golem sat down. The others slipped away among the branches. She didn't know if they had dematerialized or were just hiding.

'We-hell,' she barked nervously. 'So you do understand. Wuh-ho.

'OK, well, I got some questions.

'Why don't I feel hungry? Why don't I have to pee?

'Am I dead? Am I one of you and if so, like, what am I supposed to do now?

'Is there, like, an orientation or something?'

She waited a while after each of these questions. The child was watching her closely, but Serge could not read her expression. The Grid kept humming and crackling restlessly.

'So you don't want to talk.' Serge's voice took on an authoritative tone. It was as if she resented having shown her vulnerability and now had to make up for it by coming over all General Patton-ish.

'You know,' Serge said, pausing for effect and to hawk and spit into the well. 'If this was a TV movie we'd all be coming to terms with our differences and getting our family values up to speed here. We'd be talking it over and I'd be uncovering some damn, like, gruff fondness for y'all. You'd come up to me with a bunch of Grid-flowers or some sh*t and I'd start crying and say I'm sorry I didn't have you even though I'm not and hell, who knows, we might even hug, and sh*t. I'd probably like that. No chestnuts, I really would. I want to solve this, you guys got to believe me. But the way this is going I

can't see that happening. I guess I'm just not
getting any cuddle factor off you guys whatsoever.
What I see is me, dead, and you guys going on
being . . . weird . . . forever. Just in and out of that
well, never growing up, never growing old, never
dying. I can't put my finger on exactly why that is
more of a dead-dog bummer than me being dead,
but somehow it is. Somehow just picturing that
picture makes me want to puke up a lung.'

The girl got up and started to move off through
the Grid. The others were visible in the shadows,
joining her, climbing away. They were leaving her
behind. She didn't want to be alone.

'It's just too ugly,' said Serge. 'And it's too weird,
and I'm *not doing it.'*

But they were disappearing, and soon she would
be alone. She sat there for a short while, listening
to her persistent heart and the fast ticking in her
chest that sounded suspiciously like a bomb, and
pretty soon she sprang up and followed them. She
could smell the Grid urging her on, dictating on a
cellular level. It was in her veins, in the tide of her
heart now. Her heart that these half-life children
had started again after what should have been a
final silence.

'It's obscene,' said Serge. 'I don't like it.'

They took her to the place where the missile had
fallen. It didn't look the same to her now. She was
still aware of all the misfit equipment arranged
above the dust bowl, but the importance of the
human artifacts seemed reduced in her new eyes.
She noticed now that the Grid was woven into a
spiderweb, a concentric series of irregular rings

crosshatched with pulsing beams of something forever caught in a state halfway between solid matter and sheer light. And she knew what had happened because the Grid's memory was a part of Serge: it lay in the bottom of her lungs, the coming of the MF missile with intent to destroy all life at the logic mines and being instead itself pulled down by the defensive system that these little girls had created.

Oh, they had built it, for sure. Six would have provided that aptitude in his ejaculate.

They had sacrificed miles of the Grid's sinew, wedded it to stolen stereo components and transistors, poached body parts thrown in for good measure; and now by the will of the Grid, whatever that was, the dead zone was coming alive in some sneaky and hard-to-fathom way.

The girls went down into the dust, proud of their creation.

She looked at them, jerky little Sergettes with music around them like a smell.

She was no longer wanting to have them exterminated.

She was well and truly screwed. What good was she, Captain Bonny Serge, with the Grid leading her around by the nose, literally? Information hung in the air. It thrummed in the branches. It simmered in the well. She was just another storehouse, a mobile one, but a member of the club now all the same.

'Holy Poobah,' said Serge. 'I'll never be just me again. I'll never be an individual. From here on out, I'm always a part of something else, something alive.'

She paused, chewing her lip.

'I don't like that.'

'You always were a part of something else. You were never you. That was an illusion.'

Serge jumped.

One of them was nearby, watching her.

Serge whispered, *'Did you say something?'*

'You ever see a stranded starfish?' The voice of her undead daughter was thin and clear. It carried Serge's accent like a strong odor. 'Just layin' there on the beach, out of his element? All flat and useless. It's sad.'

Serge stared. The kid had picked up the image out of Serge's childhood memories and played it back to her. The kid was inside her thoughts. Serge was laid right the way open, eviscerated like roadkill to a crow. Still she resisted.

She said: 'A starfish can't feel sad. He can't even think.'

'If a starfish was part of the Grid, then he could be sad. But he wouldn't have to be, because—'

'Because he'd never be stranded, he'd be part of the Grid, yeah I know. Sounds like a friggin' cult to me.'

'It ain't no cult. It's just a friggin' reality. Mom.'

'Since when you talk?'

The girl shrugged. 'Since you need us to. You didn't like the music. Even though it was like taking a bath inside and you needed it. You want to play human being. We can do that, until you see it's going nowhere and give up.'

'I never give up,' said Serge, but her words were hollow. 'What the hell *are* you guys, anyways?'

'There isn't a word. Union you express as marriage, two units producing a third but none of

them ever really touching or changing each other.
There is no behavior you've ever seen that
describes us. We are the weaving, the woven. We
are the river: that which divides and that which
collects and transforms itself on the axes of time
and distance. We move in and out of each other and
our home because there is no such separation for
us. We can make you. We can take you apart. And
you can do the same, now. If you allow it. But you
hold fast to your old patterns. You cannot forget.'

Serge considered this. Then she said:

'Does my ray gun still work?'

syntactical reversal

I woke up feeling depressed. I had crawled into bed, baffled by what I'd read on Miles's computer – and far too weirded out even to think about telling him. I wanted none of it to be happening. I wanted to be normal. Like other people. I wanted a huge stack of pancakes, with microwaved bacon on the side, nice and crispy. Real maple syrup. Fresh-squeezed orange juice.

But I knew that I might as well stick my finger down my throat because the result would be the same. I drank some water and wandered around my apartment, ignoring the invitations of the cats to play, and spent half an hour tearfully sorting through my mother's record collection. I played The Pointer Sisters in the hope of cheering myself up, and so I nearly didn't hear the phone.

'Hello?'

'I know you told me everything was copacetic, but I did some homework on your employer,' Miles said. He paused significantly. 'Do you think this is a secure line?'

I laughed. 'Do you want me to meet you under some bridge on the Seine at midnight?'

'I'm only saying. Remember, you aren't supposed to talk about your work. You signed a non-disclosure agreement.'

'How do you know that?'

'Aha.' I could hear him cracking his knuckles. 'Vee haff vays, jah?'

'I don't think Dataplex give a hoot what I do now. Just tell me what you found out, already.'

'OK, well, let's see. Where to start? They claim to have computer programs – highly secret, of course, aren't they always? – that purportedly take the transcripts of your debriefings and analyze the product influences. The subliminal content then becomes visible, and they know what's being transmitted to you successfully, and what isn't.'

'Subliminal content of what? What are you talking about? I'm looking at a blank screen.'

'Cookie, think a minute. They signed you up because you can see *other things* when you watch TV.'

'Oh, well, I can channel the Grid, yeah.'

'So it's not a blank screen. They're either showing you TV, or they're showing you some kind of video that they want to test, or both. Didn't you know that?'

'No, Miles, I think you're missing the point. My job is to gather intelligence. About what's happening. There. In the Grid. That no one but me can see. Well, the machines can see it, but they can't see everything.'

'Oh, dear,' Miles sighed. I pictured him rubbing the back of his neck. That's what he does when he's going to break it to you that a white dragon just Surprised you and you're about to get blasted with a Cone of Cold sixty feet in diameter and there ain't buzz-all you can do about it. 'See, I don't think you quite—'

'Nonono, *you* don't *quite*, Miles. Maybe they're *saying* that it's market testing,' I explained. 'But that's just what they use as a cover. Foreign Markets Research doesn't mean, like, Japan and Korea. It means *foreign* foreign. As foreign as you could get.'

Long silence. I wonder if I should tell him about the gravity-torsion generator in New Hampshire ... or was it Vermont?

'OK,' said Miles brightly after a while. 'Let's just explore a hypothetical situation. Say you were going to do some market testing. You wanted to find out how well your message was getting across. You found someone who was, say, a *sensitive*. Someone who could act like a barometer, a highly specific barometer, for subtle messages and influences. Subliminal content.'

'Subliminal content? I thought that was illegal.'

'Only the kind that's easy to detect. Flashing an image or embedding sound – that's illegal. But there are more subtle ways of delivering a message that can't be outlawed because they're part of the art of advertising. These are the ones Dataplex claim to be able to find, decode, and evaluate. They can do this better than the advertisers themselves, who are often using guesswork. And of course, the logical next step would be to use this same analytical ability to design ads and implant the ideas.'

'But I don't see TV, Miles. And I don't see things chopped up into segments. When I fly, I'm part of a continuous story that makes sense, at least to me. I don't see how I could be getting all that meaning out of being shown some TV shows that aren't even visible to me.'

'But you are. Your brain is organizing the mess they feed you into something you can recognize. Our brains make narrative out of whatever they're fed.'

I felt myself begin to pout.

'I thought it was my psychic talent.'

'You're special, Cookie, but you're not unique. This method could work on anyone. You're just more suggestible than most people, particularly when it comes to TV. That makes you an unusually effective subject. What you say about their advertising, their programs, whatever they throw at you, is more revealing than what the average person can glean. But you're really just picking up on signals that are there. You're not delusional, not in that sense, but you're not psychic, either.'

'I *am* psychic, Miles,' I said. 'You don't know what I've been through with the police and stuff.'

There was a silence. I could hear his fingers tapping the keys.

'And of course I'm not delusional,' I added.

Mile's computer chirped and beeped at him. He typed some more.

'Miles, I am definitely psychic. I don't read the tarot, I don't keep crystals, I don't want to be, but I am. I guess I inherited it.'

He was definitely ignoring me.

'Miles, I told the police where to find bodies. I told them the circumstances crimes had been committed under. I saw things I really didn't want to see. That was before I stopped watching TV.'

At last Miles said, 'Cookie, I'm sorry to be the one to tell you this, and you probably don't want to hear it, but I've talked to the Hasbrook Heights police about you.'

'Well, then, they told you.'

'They told me that you *thought* you saw crimes being committed. And then you *thought* you were being stalked by some guy who just got out of prison on bail pending his murder trial. They went to see the guy you identified to them and he turned out to be a UPS driver with a clean record. They asked you to stop calling them but you kept phoning in tips anyway. And then, mysteriously, you stopped. In the spring of 1982. Wasn't that when you started at Dataplex?'

I felt myself going hot. 'It wasn't like that,' I said. 'I don't know who you talked to, but it wasn't like that. That guy was a killer, he just hadn't committed the crime yet and I didn't realize that, I thought they caught him on my tip and he was out on parole but he hadn't even *done it* yet and he found out who I was and came after me. Check it out now, tell them to check it now – what kind of idiots are they in the police? I'M NOT CRAZY!'

There was a crackling noise. Miles was dipping into the Cheez Doodles.

'I don't think you're crazy, Cookie.' He didn't sound very convincing, though. His words came through muffled as he chewed. 'I think you have a problem dealing with some things, though. That's just an observation, not a judgment.'

'You sound like my father now,' I sniffed. 'He says I'm afraid of the world. I'm not! It's just that I don't want to live in it, as such. I know that deep down inside I'm somebody.'

'Well, of course you're *somebody*.'

'No, really, Miles. You don't get it – this isn't the world for me. How can I be the real me in a world of office buildings and highways and supermarkets and TV? It's all so fake. No, don't start with your back-to-the-wilderness stuff. I wish I really *could* be a warrior. I wish I could be a hero instead of stuck just watching wars on a screen. Unfortunately I've always been picked last for kickball teams and they don't teach sword-fighting in gym class.'

'There's always archery,' Miles offered.

'Besides, I figure my father's 'real world' isn't interested in me so why should I be interested in it? I'd rather play D&D and read Del Rey books – how is that any less legitimate than keeping track of what Meryl Streep wears to the Oscars or following the Yankees? At least my way has an element of imagination. And now I'm learning karate, so maybe I can become warrior material after all. And if I can't, at least I can enjoy pretending for a couple of hours every night in the presence of like-minded people. It's like a real-life RPG. And the black belts are *real warriors*, Miles. Maybe I have a chance after all. Maybe I could get there.'

'OK, OK. You wanna go to the arcade?' he said. Bravely. He's way out of his depth here.

'That's OK.' I made myself take deep breaths. Miles is my friend. I can't afford to alienate him. 'I have to go practice my pocketbook-and-broom for the demonstration. I want to look better than Cori, and she's already one up on me. She sleeps with her pocketbook and flies on her broom.'

The big tournament was fast approaching. Doing pocketbook-and-broom was now taking every molecule of my concentration, and afterwards I was reeling around like a drunken trout on a line while I tried to regain my equilibrium.

'Sorry, Miss Cooper,' I said weakly. 'It's my allergy medication. I'll be all right in a minute.'

For some reason I could endure the work in the weight room, and I could even jog a couple of miles at a time if it wasn't too hot, but the pocketbook-and-broom seemed to strain my body as much as it did my sense of credibility.

I passed out in the low horse stance a few times, too, and once I keeled over during a cat-stance drill and knocked into Cori, who banged her knee into a pillar and had to sit out (big surprise there). I used the excuse of helping her with an ice pack to sit out, too, until I could recover.

Miss Cooper cornered me afterwards and told me to eat something or she'd get me banned from the dojo for health reasons.

I checked my calendar. I hadn't had any real food for twenty-seven days.

Maybe she had a point.

I got a take-out slice from Tony's.

The fasting book said just to have dilute orange juice and

reintroduce food gradually, but I'm not patient enough for that kind of thing. I wanted to get this over with.

I brought a pillow and blanket into the bathroom, so I'd be right there on location when the time came to throw up.

Then I picked up an old, chocolate-stained copy of *Dune* and started nibbling. I only made it halfway through the slice. Then I sort of toppled over into the pillow and fell asleep.

I woke up reborn. My stomach was growling and my mouth tasted like an old soccer ball, but I bounced through the living room dodging piles of my mother's stuff like I was a puppy.

It was like, with Killashandra's Milekey transition, you know how her symbiont lets her see colors that she could never see before and heightens all her senses? It was sort of like that.

No wonder Gandhi always looked so cheerful, I thought. *All that fasting.*

I decided to play it safe and stick to orange juice, like the book said. I knew I'd have to start eating a more balanced diet soon. My body couldn't take much more deprivation. I just wanted to hang on to this clarity a little longer. I didn't want to go back to the way things were. I didn't want to be Algernon. And I was starting to see something now, like finding yourself in the crazed pattern of broken mirror, the fractured vision that was my talent or my curse. I was starting to think that I could make sense of this starfish thing after all, if only I'd try.

Or it could make sense of me.

Everything's in the grammar, isn't it?

It's like, the true diversity and strangeness of the world is something which continually escapes us. Or rather – case in point – we continually escape it. All the duplications and identifications we heap upon one another – golden arches

and red aluminum cans littering every last wilderness on
Earth – classification systems for every possible species of
creature, thing, illness, psychological state and philosophical
possibility – all are there to keep the Grid at bay.

Even the Grid's *name* is to keep the Grid at bay, for gosh
sakes.

We are so fragile. A bomb can blow you apart in gory and
horrifying ways. The Grid can do it cheaper and cleaner.
Like a clever sadist, it leaves no obvious marks. And the
worst part is, I can't be sure it's entirely a bad thing. I just
don't know.

It's like this:

They did trick me. They did use me.

Did they trick me. Did they use me.

If only by implication, such a simple syntactical reversal
changes everything.

Could reality also displace itself so easily.

Reality could . . . well, you fill in the blanks.

max fact unpacked

'What do you need a ray gun for? You already told Machine Front to wipe us out.'

'That's right, and it's only a matter of time before a big fireball comes down and ends this conversation. For the best. Really.'

'It won't destroy you. Only us. You are part of the Grid. You will be reabsorbed. But as long as our other body is somewhere else, we cannot return to the Grid.'

'What do you mean, you can't return to the Grid? I seen you. You go in the well all the time.'

'And come out again. We're the stranded starfish. Not you.'

But Serge was only interested in herself. 'What's that clicking noise in my chest, then? Don't you got me wired to blow up?'

'It's a monitor. The Grid can read your internal state through that sound.'

Serge's internal state, in point of fact, was jumpy and hostile – that was, more so than usual.

'The Grid this, the Grid that. What the peashooter is the Grid, anyways?'

Fear, because a headlong like water over pebbles overing undering throughing absolute impossible identityless the sigh of you never were will be again, the fear always tracks through us you them like blood bringing poison from the source to the extremities where it blooms forth. Heads rising from water or water-mockery, ersatz water wannabe neverwas can't you remember the difference between self and others YOU singing badly in the shower, Zestfully clean and splashing on the Jean Nate and THEY the originators of the collective golem-memories: men mostly, one walks his dog across the Delaware River, one remembers smashing gypsy moth caterpillars by the thousands in the summer of '81, riding over them with his Schwinn tenspeed in the year before he got his license, playing games to see how many he can squash as the sun sets Mt. St. Helens fluorescent puce and chartreuse thanks to all that ash in the 'sphere, and another breakdances even in his sleep, the muscles of his neck twitching in an effort of imaginary support but he is dead now, all are dead and golemed, we are of the dead and there is no room for life that preordained pinball game of habits and deeply grooved behaviors; no, here room only for the endless remix, sophisticated worm action in the poetry of the Grid's bronchial tracts, information routes and reroutes and routs again, algorithms run patterns are made and tweaked and unmade, the creativity is disgusting, obscene, yet you are it is you now, Captain Painter is home eating hay and you are forever here. So you have brought Captain Painter here, too, and the spirit of Bob's Chevy Lot on Route 8 and

*Palomino Corners Beauty Salon with the stylist
who always cut your bangs crooked because you
was a jap even though you wasn't no jap you was
part Eskimo what do they know about Eskimos in
Sagebrush County? And I can't find any
confederacy of humans here, I am just an old sieve
of electrical impulses and clotted beliefs, catching
what I catch, missing what I miss, if the Grid is
God it's a long time til next Sunday, maybe we
want to take a recount on that whole notion? Dead
dead dead just means out w/the old in w/the new,
get a new structure asap even a bacterial one is
OK—*

I'M DEAD

What?

'I'M DEAD,' said Serge.

'Then maybe you'd like to invent special godlike
powers for yourself,' said the girl.

'The Grid is in you,' another girl said. 'It is of
you, for you, with you, by you. Among other things.
The Grid can walk you through yourself and out the
other side. You're just a wind tunnel, Bonny Serge.'

'Yeah? It takes one to know one,' retorted Serge
glumly. And felt . . .

. . . *it begin again, like the raven tapping on
Poe's back door, a tipping and trapping of flown
essences, desires, possibilities, piling up and
swirling and exerting pressure like a dam about
to— no, not like that at all, more like a
laundromat's jumbo-sized washing machine full of
sloshing clothes and some f@*ker puts a bullet
through the glass during a holdup for the $23.75
in the self-service change-making machine and it
all comes spewing out, dirt, water, underwear,*

detergent, broken glass – all this STUFF is banging
on the periphery of her senses, saying I AM HERE
and YOU ARE NOT

Well f$%k it.

Maybe she should off herself, surrender her will
to IT and go for a ride but NO, IT had animated her
dead embryo, animated, grown, nurtured it on
human chemicals and human dreams and there
was no getting around that: do I dare peek inside
my own daughter(s), she thought.

And if they are human, then what?

What will happen to them?

When the MFeels come.

Serge looks at the thing the girls built.

'Why did you save the mines? Why did you pull
down the MaxFact and hide it in the well before it
could detonate? You killed parts of the planet to
build this contraption.'

'We had to save ourselves. No one else was going
to.'

'But you haven't saved yourselves. Listen, you
don't think you can fire that thing *back* at them, do
you? Because even if you could launch it, one
MaxFact can't blow away the entire colonization
effort.'

'We don't need to fire it. It's not a weapon
anymore.'

'Then what is it? *Where* is it? Nobody saw where
it went down.'

'You can go inside it and see for yourself,' said
her daughter. Her tone was that of an owner
offering a walk to her dog.

But Serge was afraid.

'It's not an invitation to a beheading,' said the child. Coming out of a six-year-old's mouth, the words are particularly ugly.

'How the *frig* did you get so smart?'

'We used what you gave us. Come see.'

Down at the bottom of the dust bowl that had once been the well, at the base of the scary tower made of stereo components and body parts, there was no more well anymore. No more missile lying quiescent in the pond-scum. Now there was a door lying in the ground. It wasn't a trapdoor, although it was lying flat instead of standing up. It was an ordinary door. Suspiciously ordinary. It looked like an illustration from a children's book. It was made of wood. It had brass hinges and a round knob and four rectangular wooden panels. It was the kind of archetypal door that Serge hadn't seen much of in reality.

Architecture is a projection of the body on the environment. Serge remembered this wisdom from watching Channel 13. It's an effort to extend the body, impose the space of the self on the space of the world.

Just like music.

Doors were significant in dreams and horror movies. Either way, she wasn't happy to see this one.

While she stood there thinking about it, the Grid crackled and popped and hummed. The Grid had an elephantine groove, a beat that didn't correspond to anything so mechanical as a heart, but was rather a mathematical statement whose meaning lurked almost below her awareness, never quite declared and never quite denied.

She walked across the pit, squatted down, and opened the door.

She received no memory of passing through. To gaze on this place seemed to be as real as to enter it. Already, without intending to, she was moving through the city of the Grid's children.

It extends in all directions without prejudice, turning corners and changing orientations as effortlessly as one of those optical-illusion Escher staircases. Every so often you glimpse something bright and blue, like sky, like water, but when you turn to look at it square on it yields to become nothing more than a mirror over a garbage dump, or the cat's cradle-work of a fancy, multidirectional bridge buried under an exuberance of bird shit. The falcons weave corkscrews through the alleyways, pausing sometimes to rend their prey on the stained lip of a concrete hole made to release effluvia into some bottomless gully, sometimes to preen themselves on the beautiful clock towers that stand on the green university hills, where libraries and music halls lie open to the rainless skies while the stars glimmer faultlessly in the bottoms of storm drains.

She was walking, though. Not climbing, not monkeying, not swimming: walking. One-two, one-two, like a gunslinger waiting for the ambush.

The girls were with her, eight of them like a posse she couldn't trust at her back.

'What does all this got to do with the missile?' she said, and her voice bounced off metal and stone, shocking her: she had gotten used to a constant background of Gridspeak, and now there was only silence torn by her echoes.

'The missile is the source of it,' the nearest girl stated proudly, capering a little. And she pointed to a building the size of a football stadium, looming ahead as though it had moved there of its own accord just by her mentioning it.

They approached the stadium through a cloud of paper fliers advertising something in Chinese that blew against their legs and stuck there momentarily before whipping away. After a few strides the stadium did not seem quite so big or far away. Details appeared: a buckled asphalt parking lot; loading bays; flagpoles with their cables flapping musically. The white façade of the structure was in fact grooved and the indentations furred with green and brown molds, dusted with diesel fumes. She didn't see an entrance as such, but a set of bright blue fire doors had been propped open with a surveyor's stick trailing an orange fluorescent ribbon. It seemed to take a long time to reach these doors across the parking lot, especially because she kept stopping to marvel at things she never would have found remarkable on Earth: tufts of grass coming up in the cracks. Red ants. The paper wrapper of a drinking straw plastered to the asphalt by rain.

At the doors she heard the humming, deep and resonant, coming from within. Cool, damp air flowed out through the crack between doors. Serge thought of generators and boiler rooms. It was dark in there, but when she stood on the surveyor's stick and pulled the flanged edge of the door to open it slightly, she saw the darkness wasn't total. There was an undersea glow coming from a warehouse-sized space within.

She slid her shoulder in and took a look.

This was a very large space. Her ears told her this, and the downdraft of cold air from far above. She couldn't actually see much.

It was like an aquarium, most of the space taken up by liquid trapped behind a transparent wall. The liquid was greenish and transected by numerous fibers, faintly luminous.

In the middle lay the MaxFact like a big penis or turd. The bright fibers were sucking on it.

She turned. The girls were giggling and standing on each other's feet and running around. She snarled:

'How did you do this? How did you do this?'

Shrugs; laughter. Infuriating.

'Six was a good mechanic, but this is crazy. What are those stringy things? Are they wires?'

The girls answer in that annoying way, bouncing the words back and forth between them. 'They're like veins. Implications made physical.'

'What?'

'See, the Grid has unraveled the machine. We didn't do anything, we just use what we find. And when we looked inside the rocket, we found a lotta stuff. This whole city, in fact.'

Serge made a face. They were taunting her.

'You could understand if you wanted to. You're part of it now. You could know.'

Serge propped the door open behind her and went in. The MaxFact looked small in this great space, and inconsequential. The girls followed her in, whispering.

'Bulls@*t,' she was muttering.

The missile was lying in a tank and around the

tank were platforms with stairs and ladders, workstations of some kind. She climbed up and the sound of her boots on the steel rang like gongs. There were clipboards with Japanese writing hanging from the metal frame.

'Too bad Klaski's boyfriend ain't here,' Serge snorted. She reached the top of the tank. It was open. The water lapped the thick glass just a couple of feet below the lip of the tank.

Only it wasn't water.

She put her hand in and touched it. It was well fluid.

The girl was right. She understood. From that tactile point of commonality, she could perceive the whole thing, like when a word breaks apart a dream you'd forgotten and offers it up all at once, glistening and strange.

'I heard of people taking their car apart and turning it inside out on the garage floor,' she said after a while. 'This is pretty extreme. You turned the missile inside out. You drew out everything that it implied.'

'Or that implied it,' sang the children.

The cart horses that pulled the wood that fuelled the fire that Copernicus wrote by are in that MaxFact. The battered wife who worked for rice for her children, fourteen hours a day making weapons in a tiny hut in Tokyo during a failed attempt to take over all the world that ended in mushroom clouds and the Marshall Plan and gave rise to the personal stereo. The dead insect species in South America that are ghosts to the rubber used in some of the synthetics. It goes on and on, an unspooling web of connections where everything leads to

everything else, into language and through math
and out again, behind the stars and under the sea.

With all of that information, building a city must
have been no sweat.

Yup, you had to give it credit. That MaxFact had
to be the ultimate in chic travel accessories: it
looked like a tube of mascara and unpacked like a
whole history of civilization.

My phone was ringing. The machine picked it up, but by
then it was too late – I'd lost the nex.

I rubbed my eyes and staggered into the kitchen, tripping
over Rocky.

'Cookie, it's me, are you there?' Miles.

I picked up the phone.

'Uh-huh,' I said.

'I'm going to Barnes and Noble. Wanna come?'

'OK.' Anything to get out of my own head for a while.

What I forgot was that Miles never goes to Barnes and
Noble for half an hour to pick up a few paperbacks. He
installs himself in the computer section and reads for hours.
I got a Roger Zelazny paperback and went outside, into the
heat, to wait for him.

I sat down on the concrete divider between the Barnes
and Noble parking lot and Einstein Moomjy. I watched
people going in and out of Einstein Moomjy, the heat shimmer,
the traffic. I tried to fathom it. How a piece of land that
was once a forest full of wildlife and Indians could become
so loaded with abstract thought. Road engineering. The
mechanics of cars. Architecture. Wiring schemae, sewage,
plumbing. The materials of the buildings and their petro-
chemical origins. Then there were the people, bred of every
possible ethnicity, tracing their past to innumerable cultures
and geographical locations, yet all of them brought here by

some circumstance to acquire a NJ twang and a MasterCard. What are these people capable of that they'll never even know? If they're anything like me, anything at all, then they aren't doing much with their lives.

But they're probably not like me or they'd be sitting here too, feeling baffled. And they're not.

They're shopping.

I saw a map of the human body in a book that Gunther used to keep on his desk. He has a lot of medical books. He says they're nice and heavy and make his office look more dignified, but I've caught him reading them from time to time. Anyway, the picture I saw was a cartoon scaled according to the density of sensory nerve endings. The eyes and lips were huge. So was the ding-dong (of course, it was a man). But the legs were puny and the feet were hardly there at all.

Miles finally came out carrying one big book in a plastic bag.

'What's up?' he said.

So I told him what I was thinking about. I asked him if a computer could remap the world according to invisible qualifiers. He sat down next to me and scratched his head.

'You mean like in geography, when they map the world according to economics or rainfall or something like that?'

'Yeah, I guess. But I was thinking about more than one factor on the map at once. I was thinking about mapping the connections.'

As usual, Miles instantly understood the idea and started vamping on it.

'OK, take shopping. What if we mapped Route 17 according to the content of its merchandise, and where everything came from, and what it's connected to and how? The complexity of Tower Records alone would require more bytes than I could even calculate. If you took into account the musical relationships instead of just reproducing tones like you do on a CD, you'd probably kill yourself trying to encapsulate it all. And the bookstores. It would be crazy. The world could disappear into its own navel. Then there's fashion, interior design, cooking – how does all of that manifest when you look beyond the physical? We never think about it because we hold it all in our heads. But try to write the code, Cookie. Then you'll see.'

I said, 'Like unpacking a very tightly stuffed suitcase.'

'What?'

'Never mind. I guess it all looks safe and predictable. Life in the suburbs. But it's wild, wild. It's all there, just waiting to be brought to the surface. And the smallest nudge, and the world could . . . well, I don't know now.'

I'm getting a little fanciful now.

I wish I could eat.

It's the antidote to thinking. The Club Med of the brain.

'Well, if you had brought this up a couple years ago, I'd have said it was impossible to map the world realistically with a computer. But now I'm not so sure. There's this guy, Benoit Mandelbrot, and he studies the mathematics of soap bubbles and stuff like that. He's very hot with the graphics people right now, but it goes a lot deeper than that. I read his book two years back and it set everybody on fire.'

In my mind's eye I saw giant bath bubbles drifting down Rt. 17.

'You can create mathematical representations of natural phenomena using his methods. Usually math and nature don't mix, but now you can get to what's underneath a physical representation.'

I said, 'So what would the underlying truth look like? If you could see its guts.'

"The underlying truth?" said Miles. 'Have you been listening to that Rush tape I loaned you?'

'Huh? No, I think that's 'the underlying fear'.'

Miles snorted. 'Same difference. OK, well, I mean, there are so many factors.'

'What about finance?' I prompted. 'The numbers behind the retail industry.'

'Good, Cookie!' praised Miles in his typical I-have-an-IQ-of-147 tone. 'Very true. And even more complex. I bet you'd need more than fractals. And then there's marketing. Advertising.'

I felt bile rise in my throat. I swallowed it and sat very still. Sweat was trickling down the back of my neck and into my tank top.

I said, 'I don't need a computer program. I don't need math. I know what it looks like. I know what the guts of marketing look like. They are luminescent and tangled and they swallow dead people and spit them out in quadruplicate or more.'

Miles didn't say anything. He seemed frightened. His knee started jiggling up and down like a kid who has to go to the bathroom. People act this way around me sometimes. It's annoying.

'Never mind,' I sighed.

Miles looked at me sidelong. 'You know, I have been thinking about what we were talking about before. With Dataplex and the way they were showing you stuff and then analyzing your . . . uh . . . visions.'

'Yeah?'

'It was working, wasn't it? I mean, they wouldn't pay you that much if you weren't getting something right.'

'No kidding. It was working. But I answered one of their surveys all wrong, and I guess they started to doubt me. And then I got shot down.'

'So what are they going to do now that they don't have you?'

I wasn't sure, and I said so. 'They do have other Fliers,' I added. 'But we're not allowed to talk to each other about the project. It's in the contract.'

Miles snorted. 'This whole thing is totally bizarre. You should do something about it, Cookie. Get to the bottom of it.'

Maybe I should. I didn't feel up to crusading, though. I said, 'My only problem is I'm crazy.'

There was a silence made conspicuous by the fact that this was Miles's big opportunity to contradict me. After a while I said,

'Could there be an ecology of the abstract? In other words, do abstract forms fight, and consume each other, and reproduce and stuff?'

'If they do, it all happens on an abstract level.'

'But is there evidence? Could you see it, like postulating dark matter? You know, could you find out about it indirectly, like when astronomers find out stuff by looking at other stuff.'

'That's a weird idea, Cook. But speaking of evidence, I think we need to take direct action with this Dataplex thing.'

'We?' I can raise one eyebrow. I learned how in grade school. It comes in handy at times like this.

'*We*. Listen carefully, Spock,' Miles said. And he told me his plan.

When I got home, I was all on edge. I didn't like the direction that things were taking, but I couldn't figure out how to get a rein on the situation without actually flying. And I was afraid to do that. Gossamer was down. I had never tried to fly outside of Dataplex. What if I turned on the TV and saw another violent incident, instead of the Grid?

Or what if Gossamer was . . . dead? What would happen to me then?

I could play more *Quark*; but what good could that do? It was only reading. It was just like the rest of my life: all observation, no participation. Serge was like a non-player character: I couldn't make her do anything.

And it's all very well, Miles and his direct action, but Miles doesn't have what I have. He doesn't have a direct line to the situation. He can't actually perceive what we're talking about. He can only imagine it. I can see it, feel it, smell it.

Taste it. I can still taste orchids.

Sooner or later, I'm going to have to find out what's happened to Gossamer.

So I fed Nebbie and Rocky a whole bowl of 9 Lives and a dish of Fancy Feast apiece, in case I was on the nex for a while. I cleaned their litter box, too. As a safety precaution, I set my alarm clock for 8:30 p.m. and put it on top of the TV.

Then I turned on the TV to Channel 1, which is always pure static. No chance of market influences there, right?

I sat down, and I waited for something to appear.

I didn't have to wait long.

too high-tech for *cosmo*

There's no time, like the present.

Nothing has changed.

You are no longer Flying. All sensation of the air, before so complex and subtle and thrilling, has been covered, dampened – crushed. You are in the snug grip of something which presses you like a flower inside a book. Gravity is beside the point. There's no depth in which gravity might pull. All the ants you ever stepped on return to mind, revenants splayed juicily across two dimensions, their final scent–parcels wafting towards you with the message: 'Now you know how it feels, sucka!'

But you don't really know how it feels. Gossamer's pain receptors have not been wired to you. And if you really were a squashed ant, you'd be dead now. You're still with Goss, so you figure Goss must be alive.

But she can't move. And something funny seems to be happening to her senses, or to the nex at any rate. Because you feel yourself dissolving. You travel down highways of luminous color; you see and feel globules that seem smooth from a distance and then leap at you and show themselves to be spiny, or pockmarked – or even geometrical like crystals – only to retreat, teasing, to join a larger liquid. At the same time you go juddering through a thicket of solid branches that grow in all directions. They cut right through you and yet don't destroy you. You break into fragments that still know each other, even as they drift apart to their separate destinies.

All of this seems to have been going on for an indeterminate time, an Alka-Seltzer effect persisting almost to the point of unintelligibility. *Plop-plop; fizz-fizz:* goodbye everything that used to compose you. You are now in so many places at a time that your awareness is a mist of non sequiturs. Your sense of identity hangs there like a kitten in transit, gripped by the scruff of the neck: no choice but to trust Mom.

Then, with a jerk, your senses return to Gossamer's body and you realize that she's been in the well all this time. Now someone's pulling her out like a wet kite.

Major Arla Gonzalez holds Gossamer at arm's length and squints at the wound made by the crossbow bolt.

'*Pobrecita,*' she croons. 'You'll be OK, Gossamer. But you're not going anywhere near that convoy.'

She shakes the well fluid off Goss and you feel like a mouse in a tumble dryer. Then the sky and the Grid and the ground reassemble themselves and you feel the cool hardness of battle armor against your dorsal side. You are hanging from something and looking at the Grid. Gossamer is limp, helpless. What is carrying you begins to move.

The four-point rhythm of a monkey climbing tells you what's going on. Arla has donned Gossamer like a cloak and she's making her way through the Grid.

Your first impulse is to scream for help from MF. But would they help you? *Could* they help you? *Reassignment and reprogramming* sounds suspiciously like *graft on a new brain and out you go with the leftovers.* And that was the offer on the table while Goss was still in one piece. She might not be worth repairing, according to the calculations of MF. Totaled. Written off.

On the other hand, you know where their MaxFact missile is.

You can verify the existence – and mortality – of the child-golems. Maybe you should call them . . . or maybe not.

Gonzalez has no trouble finding the rest of Serge's team. They have returned to their camp in the altered Grid; it's a logical place to wait for Serge, and also, from their point of view, a safe one. Its lines and forms remind them of home. The Grid seems tamer here. You are not at all sure if this is a good thing.

'I'm not a golem!' Gonzalez yells as soon as she can see them. 'Don't attack me!'

'Dr. Gonzalez!' Klaski cries. Her face is dirty and marred by burn scars, but she's still pretty.

'Sweet Jesus, it's her. Good to see you, dude!'

'Jenny Hendricks?' says Gonzalez. 'What are you doing out here?'

'I got bored doing paperwork at the clinic. Stupid, right?'

'Yeah,' laughs Gonzalez, a little hysterical. 'Give me four beige walls and a coffee machine any day.'

Nobody asks her why she fled. Everybody hugs.

The absence of Serge hangs in the air like an odor.

'I'm sure we'll be able to meet up with your captain soon,' says Gonzalez in that mellow, melting voice. 'She said she was turning her Swatch off temporarily for security reasons. Something to do with golems intercepting signals.'

'Can they do that?' asks Lewis, looking terrified.

'She said to keep you guys together and keep Klaski under control.'

Klaski bursts into tears.

'I let her down, I know I did—'

'Shut up, Klaski,' says Lewis impatiently, turning back to Gonzalez. 'Last we heard, she was under ambush. You saw her get out? How did you get separated?'

'She told me to take the Flier and get out of the area. She said she could take care of herself and I believed her.'

'S*$t,' says Hendricks. 'I hope she's OK.'

Lewis says, 'We'll get Goss airborne again and then we can

look for her. I'll see if we can get through to Major Galante. I wonder if she's been in contact with MF.'

Lewis flips open her Swatch and starts making calls.

'Have some water, Arla,' Hendricks says, offering a canteen.

'You better play careful with that,' Arla replies. 'We could be here a while.'

'What happened to Gossamer?' snuffles Klaski, reaching out as if to touch you.

'Golems,' answers Arla. 'I found her in the well. Got her out just in time.'

'Lewis can look at her. Maybe we can repair—'

'Not now,' says Arla crisply. 'That's a job best left to the experts.'

Not what you were hoping to hear. Now the guys are telling Gonzalez about the first ambush and how the golems mysteriously vanished when the girls came. The weird structures in the Grid. How they can't find Galante's convoy.

'Ttt, tttch!' Arla shakes her head. The fact that she is dissembling seems painfully transparent to you, but evidently not to the others.

Cup-a-Soup is broken out like champagne. Crackers are dunked. Everyone is excited.

'OK, guys,' said Arla eventually. 'As you know, I'm a medical officer, so I got nothing to prove when it comes to authority, OK? I'm not a soldier. You guys know that. On the other hand, I've survived out here on my own and I know my way back to N-Ridge, which is the closest outpost to us.'

'What about going back to X?' says Lewis.

'Without machines?'

'We could try and get ours back. Just one transport.'

'Yeah,' says Hendricks, 'we'll just take on about a hundred golems in full battle gear. That sounds like a good idea.'

'All I'm saying is what's the good of going on to N-Ridge? If the golems control the roadways, we might get stranded out there.'

Arla shrugs. 'Should we have a democracy? Is that what you

want? OK, let's vote. Who wants to go back through sixteen miles of Grid without machine support?'

Klaski sits on her hands. Hendricks looks at Lewis, who flips open her Swatch and says, 'Let's ask Dante.'

'It makes more sense to continue to N-Ridge,' Dante says. 'Major Galante has left a skeleton team there. You might even run into her convoy on the way.'

'Do you have aerials for us? Can you give us any extra information?'

'We lost our aerials when Gossamer took a dive. You're on your own, kids.'

Lewis chews her lip.

'I'd like a chance to repair Gossamer. At least we'd have a scout.'

Hendricks says, 'Yeah, let's see if we can get some pictures. We need something to go on. No radio contact with N-Ridge means we got no idea what state they're in up there.'

Lewis says, 'Maybe Major Gonzalez knows something about that.'

'I know a lot about that,' purrs Arla. 'It's a machine camp. It has a defended perimeter to protect the structured-materials mines. It's the most important region of the planet right now, and therefore I figure it's the safest place to be. More so than X, even. The profits we're looking for are going to be derived from what the machines find in the mines. Whatever Machine Front may do, they won't give up N-Ridge.'

'Why have us around at all, then?' says Klaski. 'If the machines are so great, why can't we just go home?'

'Stop whining,' Lewis said sharply. 'If you didn't want to be here, you never should have signed on.'

'I didn't think it would be like this,' Klaski retorts. 'I could swear I'm moving, like, two feet sideways every couple seconds, but I never go anywhere. The Grid feels weird under your feet. I didn't expect it to be so . . . physical.'

No one pays any attention to her.

'Major Galante has established control of N-Ridge.' Lewis's manner is slow and thoughtful. 'I think Dr. Gonzalez is right. We were supposed to rendezvous with Major Galante anyway. She's probably looking for us even as we're looking for her. She got sent on our tail because . . .'

Because she couldn't find the logic bullets at N-Ridge. Because Gonzalez is suspected of removing them somehow, at the time of the golem raid. Because only Gonzalez knows what really went down that day. The thoughts track across Lewis's face, all too obvious to you.

Then Dr. Gonzalez turns to face Lewis, and you can only see Klaski, picking her nose and tapping her foot like a rabbit's heartbeat.

'Then we're agreed. We make for N-Ridge.'

Lewis calls Major Galante and informs her, tersely, of their plans.

'Let me speak to Dr. Gonzalez,' says Galante.

Lewis's eyes flick towards Gonzalez, who is bent over Serge's abandoned kit, repacking it for the journey. You can hear the exchange perfectly well, but that doesn't mean Gonzalez can. Lewis is some way away across the floor of the Grid structure, and she's speaking softly.

'Ma'am, I'm sorry but that won't be possible,' said Lewis.

'What do you mean, that won't be—'

'Gotta go, Major Galante.' And Lewis snaps shut her Swatch. Gonzalez doesn't give the impression she's paying any attention. Every so often a ration pack or tampon will go flying through your field of view, tossed over Gonzalez's shoulder as she re-organizes Serge's kit. The air is thick with epinephrine and assorted other Grid-made uppers with unpronounceable names. You taste mint and cotton candy.

You watch Lewis. She rubs her hands on her thighs, smearing the battle armor with Grid pollen. Her close-cropped red hair is greasy and stands up in spikes, making her look like that singer with Eurhythmics, except older and more pinched. Lewis suspects that Gonzalez is up to no good. She knows that Galante, on the receiving end of such a clipped communiqué, will interpret the message either as an indication that Lewis has gone bonkers or as a distress call. Coupled with Galante's already-urgent need to find Gonzalez, either interpretation will get MF focused on finding them.

You can't understand why Gonzalez has allowed Lewis to call MF at all, though. Why has she bothered to hook up with Serge's guys, and why is she not more overt in her kidnap of them? Because this is effectively what she has done, and eventually they will realize it – or she will be caught by Galante.

You try to pick up a line to MF but there's too much interference. Your coms seem to be working, but your charges are low and you can neither give nor receive a strong signal. You put out an automated SOS anyway, hoping that it will break through if you reach a high point or a quiet patch in the Grid's electrical field.

This is very frustrating. You can't fly. You can only see what Gonzalez's position allows you to see. You've come back to the Grid so that you can finally *do* something. You've come here to act. And you can't.

You might as well be in New Jersey.

Gonzalez doesn't waste any time. They pack their camp, perform the requisite incinerations, and set off through the Grid. You find yourself looking back on the group. Lewis swings herself from limb to limb with smoke hissing from her gloves and boots where they make contact with the Grid. The faceplate of her helmet is smeared with some organic paste, probably a developing slime-mold or half-cooked flywing, but she doesn't wipe it away. Her eyes flick back and forth as she reads the chem-link's transmissions on the interior of her helmet, every so often shouting to Arla to change direction or to climb higher to avoid a dangerous region. Behind her, Hendricks follows doggedly, with less grace but an unflagging energy, bearing most of the equipment burden in a large backpack. Klaski brings up the rear, and sometimes she's so far back that the others have no choice but to stop and wait for her. She is perpetually red-faced and out of breath, and she has the shakes.

'It's my fault,' she keeps saying. 'It's my fault. What am I going to do?'

She shies away from the well whenever the group go near it.

'Her golems are going to come out of there. They'll come after me.'

Hendricks tries to encourage her but Lewis says, 'We don't know where Serge is, so stop talking about golems.'

'But what if she's—'

'Then it *is* your fault. Now shut up and stop whining. Life isn't all pop tarts.'

'You aren't *her*, so stop pretending!' Klaski flares.

Softly at first, as if she doesn't even notice the budding argument, Gonzalez starts singing 'You've Got a Friend' in quite a nice contralto.'

She sings with R&B flavor and plenty of vibrato, so that instead of sounding like Kermit the Frog – oops, that is, James Taylor – Carole King's song sounds like soul.

Pretty soon Hendricks and Klaski join in, too. Klaski mumbles the words and adds, '*Yeah, yeah yeah,*' but hopelessly out of tune.

Lewis doesn't sing. Possibly she is more sensitive to irony than the others. She keeps looking at her Swatch. You can't see Gonzalez's face, of course.

But you can see several sets of dark eyes appear and disappear in the Grid to either side and above. No one else notices; but your sensitive, Gossamer-enhanced ears can pick up the Grid humming along, a faint and eerie chromatic echo.

It's impossible to know which way Gonzalez is leading them, but she seems purposeful about it. She's holding something in her left hand – you glimpse it once, as she hastily hides it in her vest pocket when Hendricks unexpectedly appears to ask her a

question. It looks a little like a smooth grenade. You see her consult it surreptitiously and wonder if it's some sort of homing
device. None of your orientation points are available to you visually, and the Grid interferes with coms down here. You haven't got
a prayer of getting a clear signal until you can get aloft again.
And at the moment, that seems unlikely.

After five hours they break because Klaski is ready to drop.
Gossamer needs a recharge too or you'll lose hope of boosting a
signal to MF. But Lewis doesn't ask Gonzalez to hand over the flier
again. She knows Gonzalez isn't giving up the goods.

It looks bad for you.

Lewis says, 'Zero response from the Captain. I got a bad feeling
about it.'

They make food. Gonzalez tries to engage Hendricks in a
philosophical discussion on the meaning of golems.

'Don't you ever wonder about it, Jenny? If the well can make a
dead person's heart beat again, what could it do for a live person?
Could it make you immortal? Don't you wonder, just a little?'

'Don't want to be immortal, doc. I just want to get back to
Missouri.' She pronounces it 'Mizorah'.

Arla turns to Klaski. 'You're the quiet one,' she says.

Klaski manages a faint, obligatory smile.

'Serge was overdue for leave, guys.' Arla's tone is kindly, her
Latin tones purring as they stroke the air. 'She was incredibly
dedicated, but she should have taken a break. For her own sake,
for everybody's sake. Out here in the Grid, the emotions get to
you after a while. You have to get away. Especially if you're the
type to deny your emotions anyway.'

She watches Klaski, who is crying silently. Nothing new about
that. Arla goes over and puts her arm around Klaski's shoulder,
and Klaski collapses into her.

'I know,' Arla says. 'I know.'

Lewis keeps looking at *Redbook*, and there's a funny little dead
patch while Klaski sniffles and Arla stares into space. You are

acutely aware how artificial this comradeship is; how ill-at-ease and duplicitous. You are also aware of the Grid, humming and pulsing. Ever since reading about Serge's musical experiences, you notice its soundmaking more. You also keep thinking that you glimpse the girls, keeping pace alongside sometimes, or sometimes watching from above. It's hard to be sure. Gossamer's eyes aren't well-adapted to seeing into the Grid at such close range. You belong in the sky, not in this soup of uncertainty.

Then Hendricks barks, 'Hey! Beans are ready.'

Everybody jumps because she sounds just like Serge, who is gone.

The others watch Gonzalez eat. She makes faces and pleasure noises.

'It sure is nice to see somebody enjoying the cuisine out here in the field,' says Klaski. She looks at her own bowl. 'I wish this was pizza.'

'The interesting thing,' Lewis says, 'is how there are no carnivores in the Grid. The ecology is all based on the Grid itself.'

'I've noticed that,' Hendricks put in. 'Gossamer here feeds directly off the Grid, and it doesn't seem to mind. Nothing actually kills each other.'

'No, it only kills us.'

'Machine Front will finish that up,' Lewis says confidently. 'The Third Wave is already coming in, and once the new MFeels are here there won't be need for any personnel. So no killing. The effort can become purely scientific.'

Gonzalez breaks off eating, suppressing a belch.

'That depends what you mean by killing. The ecology of this planet extends to its electrical fields and its mineral substrate. Take the logic bullets. Structured metals.'

'But what *is* a structured metal?' Hendricks asks.

'Something you could make smartbombs from, apparently,' Lewis answers. 'Logic bullets. Fight the Grid with its own language. Something you could use in computers. Ask Klaski. She got into MIT.'

'Jo? What *are* logic bullets?'

'Something too high-tech for *Cosmo*,' says Klaski, looking annoyed. 'They're a way of encoding information. Kind of like a computer disk. But you can't stick it in your computer. Machine Front have been developing the interface and looking for ways to decode the information recorded in the planet's insides. The logic bullets are the result of a distillation of the Grid's whole way of processing information. Plug them into the right hardware and we should be able to predict certain things about the Grid.'

'I didn't know you knew all this,' says Hendricks. Klaski gives a wan smile. 'What things could you predict?'

Klaski shakes her head. 'Electrical behavior. Placement of branch arms. How the scent-language works. All the things that make it impossible for us to move effectively through the Grid, or over it, with machines.'

Gonzalez is chuckling. 'Is that what they teach you in school?' she murmurs, shaking her head.

'Do you know something I don't?'

'Logic bullets are going to be used back on Earth, to make our computers run faster and better, to solve problems we can't solve, to make the guys who get hold of them a whole lot of money.'

Lewis shrugs. 'Military technology always filters down for civilian use.'

'Maybe,' says Gonzalez. 'But I don't trust Machine Front anymore. I think they're in over their heads – actually, I think they're in over *our* heads.'

Lewis says, 'Maybe, but as long as my Swatch tells me the stuff I need to survive, I'm not trading it in, you know what I'm talking about?'

'That's OK,' says Hendricks airily. 'We don't got to talk politics. I'm thinking about doing my hair in cornrows. When I get back, I mean. This frizz is driving me nuts.'

'You should,' Lewis puts in with her mouth full. 'You'd look good with long hair.'

Klaski looks bothered.

'But, Doctor Gonzalez, everybody at N-Ridge—'

Lewis kicks her. 'Leave the doctor alone, Klaski.'

Klaski starts to pout, but Hendricks tries to smooth things over. 'We're eating. She doesn't want to talk about that stuff now.'

'It's OK,' purrs Gonzalez, and smiles at Klaski. 'What do you want to know?'

'I was just wondering how you survived all this time without Machine Front? How did you escape the golems?'

Gonzalez blows on her beans. 'They never seemed interested in me. Sheer luck, I guess. Maybe it was my perfume . . .'

Lewis casts you a lot of sidelong glances.

You are their best hope. Only you know where you really are – or would know, if you could just get into the open air. Only you have a silent link with MF – again, if you could get a signal. Lewis studies your torn wing whenever Gonzalez's turned back presents her with the opportunity. She's doing it now; but she must be aware that Klaski is taking the conversation too close to personal questions about Gonzalez and the Grid, and Serge.

Abruptly, Lewis says, 'Did you know that they do brain surgery without anesthesia?'

'No way. That's disgusting,' said Hendricks.

'They do. Your brain doesn't have any nerves. It can't feel pain.'

'I don't believe you.'

'It's true, scout's honor.'

'Yeah? Then that means a brain surgeon could operate on himself, right?' says Klaski. Her stomach is filling up and her confidence is coming back. Too soon, to your thinking. 'That's what I'd say before they could get me under the knife. "Hey, doc," I'd say. "Let's see you do it on yourself before you go doing it on me."'

General ha-has.

mr. potato head

I had to stop there, because at 9 p.m. sharp I was to meet
Miles in the parking lot of Dykes Lumber on Route 17.
Actually, I was a little early. The asphalt shone darkly under
a patina of oil, transmission fluid, and rain. Even at this hour,
the passing of truck traffic beat the air like huge wings, and
did some kind of synesthestic boogie in my head so that I
swore I could hear the susurrus of tires on wet pavement
even though I had my walkman playing Air Supply at
Volume 8. I was doing this to drown out my fear and it
wasn't working.

Miles loves to take charge of a situation: that's why he's a
Dungeonmaster and not a player. On his precise instructions, I had brought a small flashlight, some blank cassettes
and a steno notebook. Thank God I took shorthand in high
school. I knew that Gloria hid the keys to the filing cabinet
under the African violet on her desk, so I had no problem
there.

A shadow moved in the corner of my eye and I startled
like a cat. Miles was tapping on the window with one
knuckle. I turned off the Walkman and rolled down the
window, my ears ringing.

'Are we doing this or what?' he demanded, breathing minty toothpaste into the car.

I nodded.

'I'm driving,' he said. 'You sure you can handle this?'

'No,' I said. 'But I'll try.'

I locked the Rabbit and we got in Miles's car. An air of ordered serenity surrounded me; when it comes to his car, Miles is nothing if not tidy.

'Remember,' he said. 'If anyone catches you, refer them to me. Say, "You have to talk to Dr. Miles," and leave it at that.'

I looked out the window and rolled my eyes. Miles was going to pretend to be a Polish psychiatrist working with me on some new form of behavior-modification therapy, and I was supposed to just play potato and go along with him. I didn't trust this plan but I knew that Miles would only help me if he was allowed to do so on his own terms, and I didn't want to go it alone.

I fished for Tic Tacs and studied the highway. A grotesquerie of industrial buildings with their neon signs threw a stain of ambient light into the clouds. Red and white SALE banners flapped from gray concrete warehousely edifices. Blah blah blah. It's all the same, my world, and I can't see how any of it is justified.

Not far away from this place, immaculate Colonials with perfect gardens marched in decorous order down tree-lined streets, the smell of Rice-A-Roni and roast chicken drifting through doors and the muted studio-audience laughter of *Cheers* faintly penetrated the picture windows with the flicker of 21-inch TVs, and Golden Retrievers barked when you came within fifty yards of their five-hundred-dollar doghouses. Backyards with swingsets and jungle gyms, in-ground pools, two-car garages with the teenager's ageing Camero parked in the driveway. Everything so convenient. So easy. Who wouldn't want to be taken in by it?

But I just feel sure that it's all there to turn us into Pillsbury Dough Boys. I ought to know. I've eaten more than my fair share of cookies you bake from a tube.

We parked next to the nursery's fleet of white pickups with *Kroemer's* stenciled on the doors. So far it was all going to plan. The Supersweep Office Cleaner van was parked in the loading zone at the end of the building. Lights were on in the programming wing.

We waited. I wanted to put the music back on but Miles would object, so I sat staring at beads of rain on the windshield. Ever since I'd read Serge's account of being in the well, and then experiencing Gossamer's take on the same thing, I'd been noticing the elastic properties of time. Lately it was not unusual for me to fall into a reverie for several minutes without even realizing it.

'OK,' said Miles suddenly. 'This is it.'

The lights in the programming wing had gone down. I got out of the car and ran, bent over, across the parking lot and into the shadow of the building. I could hear the traffic on the Parkway nearly overhead. I could hear Def Leppard playing on a boom box in the lobby. I peeked through the plate-glass windows and saw that the lobby was clear. There was a floor-polishing machine parked near the reception desk. All the other activity had moved into the Marketing wing.

I dashed down the dark hall and into Gloria's work area. Got the keys out of her desk. Opened Gunther's door. Shut it quietly behind me. And opened the filing cabinet next to Gunther's desk.

There wasn't enough light filtering in from outside to read by, so I had to use my special flashlight. Under *Orbach, Karen*, there was a package full of cassettes from recent debriefings. I carefully copied out the notations on the labels onto my blank cassettes and substituted them for the sessions recorded immediately before Goss was shot down. I had to hope nobody would notice the difference between my handwriting and Gloria's and investigate further. It was a pretty safe gamble that nobody would actually listen to these in the next forty-eight hours, after which I could find some excuse to visit Gloria and replace them. I didn't dare take the paper files themselves, but I could make notes in shorthand, couldn't I?

I hadn't gotten past my initial medical reports and job application before I heard someone outside, near Gloria's desk.

There was nowhere to hide. I slid the packet of tapes into the back waistband of my sweatpants and closed the drawer. I clicked off the flashlight with my thumb and dropped it in the pocket of my sweatshirt just as the door swung open and a round industrial vaccuum cleaner came into Gunther's office, followed by a small blonde. She turned on the light, saw me, and gave a hoarse cry. My hand flew to my mouth. I was at least as surprised as she was, but not for the same reason.

I knew her.

It was Clarissa Delgado, one of several girls I'd known and hated in high school because her sole mission in life had been to insult and humiliate me at every opportunity. Clarissa was pretty but not too bright, and she wasn't above snickering at my tennis serve or making nasty remarks in the locker room during gym (the only class we shared because, like I said, she was not too bright).

What she was doing up here in Woodcliff Lake was any-body's guess. She looked six or seven months pregnant, and shoving the vacuum cleaner around probably wasn't a lot of fun. That ought to have given me some satisfaction, but I was freaked out to see her again. She sank against the wall, staring at me, and brushed her feathered hair away from her eyes, which were heavily lined in purple and shadowed with pale blue powder.

'Clarissa,' I said as neutrally as I could. I was conscious of the fact that my voice sounded like a bassoon. I can't see anything wrong with a woman having a deep voice, but people like Clarissa always make me feel like I have six legs.

Her eyes narrowed. 'I know you,' she said. 'You went to East Rutherford, didn't you?'

Experience had softened my accent and exaggerated hers. I snorted softly, then checked myself because I could tell that I remembered her a lot better than she remembered me.

'You work here or you breaking in?' she said sharply.

'I work here.'

'Working late, huh?' That sneering voice. Hadn't changed. She could read from a driver's ed manual and make it sound sarcastic.

'I fell asleep on the couch, waiting for Gunther,' I said. 'You just woke me up, now.'

She nodded. She tilted her head quizzically.

'So that's why the light was off.' She read the plate on the door. 'Gunther Stengel. He your boss?'

'Sort of. He's a colleague.' I wanted her to think I was on a par with Gunther, even though under the circumstances that would be pushing things in a stupid way.

'Where's your office?'

'I uh, don't have one.'

'You always come to work in a black jogging outfit? You *jog*, Cookie?'

She grinned. She had remembered my name.

'Fridays we dress down,' I said, clinging to the shreds of my sense of dignity.

'Uh-huh.' She tossed the handle of the vaccuum into the corner and let the door close behind her.

'I guess your job pays pretty good, then, right?'

I shrugged. I wasn't sure how to play this. Clarisssa must be hard up if she was working as a night cleaner. I probably shouldn't rub her nose in it. 'Can't complain.'

'Because this is the kind of thing I got to tell my supervisor about.'

'Oh,' I said, grokking. 'You don't have to bother him – or her – with *that*.'

'No?' She raised her eyebrows. I dug in my purse, thinking *Thank God I didn't listen to Miles and leave it behind.*

'Do you ever find spilled change when you're cleaning?' I said in a conversational tone.

'Yeah, but we got to report it.'

'Oh.' I held up a fifty.

'Two of those and I'll let you out the fire exit.'

We went down the dark corridor to the back of the building, she like a little pregnant elf and me like a big troll. My money had vanished into her bra. The envelope in my pants made me feel like I was wearing a diaper. It made shushing noises when I moved.

'See ya, walrus!' Claarissa called after me. 'Coo-coo kachoo!'

Her laughter followed me across the parking lot and into the rhododendrons, where I crouched for several minutes before I worked up the nerve to make my way back to Miles's car.

'Any problems?' he said, looking up from a Thomas Wolfe paperback.

I shook my head.

'Where's the evidence?'

'I'm sitting on it.'

I kept sitting on it, too, for several days, much to Miles's frustration. At the dojo, everybody was getting psyched up for the big tournament. It was scheduled for a Sunday, and on Saturday there was going to be a big test for new color belts and black belts. The Okinawan masters of the Budokokutai, our new organization, were arriving on Thursday and the exams would be conducted by Master Hideki and his younger brother, Masunobu, and the other senior members of their group who were flying over. Shihan Norman had been collecting money from us all year to pay for their trip, and everyone was excited because Okinawa is the island where karate originated and the masters from there are the best in the world. Shihan Norman's teacher, Shihan Ingenito, was coming in from California and Sensei Price was coming down from Buffalo, so our dojo was going to be hosting a lot of important masters and their students.

This meant extra cleaning, extra training, lessons on karate history and etiquette, Japanese vocabulary – you name it. Shihan Norman fluttered around like a big chubby chicken, his chinless mouth endlessly wagging and the light flashing off his thick glasses as he constantly scanned the dojo, seeking imperfections to point out.

Miss Cooper didn't have as much time for me, but I didn't mind. I was going full-throttle on straight exercise: weight lifting, jogging, stuff like that. I watched from the weight room as the black belts had special classes and lectures. Miss Cooper was being brought out to demonstrate all kinds of stuff. Evidently the Okinawans didn't allow their women to train at all, and Shihan wanted to make sure that he wouldn't be criticized over Miss Cooper. So she had to get even stronger, even more proficient, and she had to learn to keep her eyes down, apparently. She practically moved into the dojo, there was so much for her to do.

Miles called me several times a day and after a while I started letting the machine get it. Miles wasn't very happy with me. After my little adventure with Clarissa Delgado, I insisted on keeping the files to myself so that I could listen to them privately. He didn't like that. Miles liked to be in control. And he liked it even less when I didn't immediately tear into the information.

But I didn't like being pushed.

I just wanted a little time to not think about it. I was feeling uneasy and there was some kind of battle going on in my head. I didn't want to deal with things. I didn't want to do the things I knew I had to do. I was feeling sorry for myself, and when I wasn't at the dojo I spent a lot of time wandering around supermarkets with an empty shopping cart, looking for something I dared buy and eat without being sick. I hung out in the cereal aisle, hoping to catch a glimpse of somebody buying Cookie Starfishes, as if this would give me some self-insight, or some reification. I never saw it happen. People tended to buy a lot of Cheerios, though, which told me nothing.

No matter what I did, I felt like I couldn't get a break. *Quark* was the closest thing I had to recreation, and it wasn't even *Quark*. It was *Cookie's Hell Planet*.

'Nobody is going to tell me that what I'm seeing is just some stupid marketing shit,' I told Nebbie. 'Nobody. I don't know what's going on around here, but this is important and it's real and I'm going to find out more.'

Still, I felt queasy when I put the first tape in my stereo. This was a cross between reading someone's diary, and seeing dirty magazines for the first time, and the folded test paper that comes back to you and you have to open it and see the F written in huge red letters at the top. I was all nervous and miserable and eager and guilty and thrilled.

But the first half-hour was just me droning on about what I'd seen. It was old stuff from several months ago. Once the novelty of hearing my voice on tape had worn off, I got bored and skipped ahead.

A man I didn't know was talking.

Unknown Man:*'Dr. Stengel, what do you make of the references on Session C?'*

Gunther:*'Our lexical-analysis programs picked up* Apocalypse Now, Snoopy, *and* Blade Runner. *I have no idea what Cookie was looking at. You know this is a double-blind test.'*

Unknown Man: *'Those are all correct. There was something from Mr. Rogers's neighborhood, but it was fairly subtle. And The Jeffersons, of course.'*

Gunther:*'The Jeffersons we got weeks ago. It's been cropping up almost every time. I didn't bother to mention it, but you can check the records. What I want to know is, why was Serge wearing leg warmers?'*

Unknown Man: *'Flashdance, of course.'*

I stopped the tape. Since when was Gunther a doctor of anything? Nobody else called him doctor. And who was the other guy?

I kept listening, but the conversation turned into a technical discussion about the computer program that Gunther was using. Eventually Gunther said, *'Look at her history with music video. She nailed the theme song. Nailed it. Picked it off the tape with no hesitation, and* without the sound. Rocket Squad *were an unsigned band, we showed her a demo video, but 'Planetary Journey' charted for eighteen weeks. Everybody loves it. Kids love it. Adults love it. Black people, white people, everybody. I put a percentage of the success of that show down to Ms. Orbach's choice of music.'*

Unknown Man: *'Maybe. But without Orbach's input, our predictors picked* Faith Is Mine *and we'll never know how that would have done if we'd only pushed it.'*

Gunther: *'I know we're doing the right thing moving her out of video and on to TV. She's ready for the big markets.'*

Unknown Man: *'Are your analysis programs ready, though? I'm still not convinced we can accurately assess Ms. Orbach's results. I read through the transcripts myself and I picked up*

*things that I think your software missed. And let's face it, whatever
your enthusiasm over your patients—'*

Gunther: 'My staff, Bob.'

Bob: 'Your staff might be, it's the software that we ultimately
stand or fall by. Cookie as a raw talent is fine, as far as that goes.
But this is Dataplex, not the Woo-woo Institute. We need to turn
what she does into code, and we need to do it accurately. That's the
business we're in. Government grants might work fine for start-up
money, but we're in this for the long haul. We need to automate.
That was the whole point of the exercise. To troll the data and come
up with a formula, or formulae, that tell us what's successful.
Don't lose sight of that.'

Gunther: 'But they're my people. I'm proud of them.'

Bob: 'That's fine, for as far as it goes. Eventually we need to pull
your guys out. If word gets out that Dataplex are using nutcases
instead of science, we'll be ruined. You might as well advertise
crystal-ball readings.'

Gunther: 'Hey, I hear Ronald Reagan has an astrologer.'

Laughter. The tape cut off.

I sat there for a while, listening to the clock tick. No stopping
now. I put another tape in, skipping again to the analysis.
This one was recent. In fact, it was the session that Gunther
had reluctantly recorded after I'd spotted Gonzalez and got
driven away by the storm and ended up with the orchid
taste. My stomach clenched, remembering.

Bob: 'Did you get that part about Leroy Jones?'

Gunther: 'Yeah, I checked it out, there's no security leak.'

Bob: 'There has to be.'

Gunther: 'Not necessarily. Someone could have mentioned the
name, she could have heard it on the radio, on an interview or
something. Also, Jones worked as a minor illustrator on some net-
work specials. She might have seen it when she used to watch TV,
years ago.'

Bob: *'Or she could be watching TV now. Has anybody tried to check that?'*

Gunther: *'She's not. Believe me, she wouldn't. She's too scared.'*

'Hah!' I said. 'I'm not too scared now. This is really insulting. What games are you guys playing with my head?'

Bob: *'How did she get his social security number, then?'*

Gunther: (whistles *Twilight Zone* theme)

Laughter.

When I stomped off to the dojo that night, I was fired up to fight; but it wasn't going to be that kind of class. The Okinawans had arrived and this session was all about them inspecting the dojo, checking us out, and probably talking to us about their plans for the American branch of their organization. It seemed like every student who'd ever trained showed up, some of them coming out of the woodwork after absences of weeks and months. Everybody's gi was ironed. Troy's hair was slick with gel and he flashed me a smile over Cori's head.

The Okinawans entered en masse and we all bowed formally to them. Speeches were made. Miss Cooper usually led the class, but tonight Sensei Hideki, the younger brother of Shihan Hideki, the head of the Budokokutai, led the warm-up personally.

Sensei Hideki turned out to be a sixth-dan, one rank below our Shihan but a lot more physically capable. He gave all the instructions in thickly accented Japanese that nobody could understand. We all struggled to imitate him as he dropped into a full box split, did one-armed push-ups on his fingertips, and then jumped up and swung his leg rapidly up over his head like he was going to kick the wall over his own shoulder. After a long series of push-ups and sit-ups and various basic drills, he indicated that we should 'stretch out, own time' and then started hitting the makiwara like he was chopping down a tree. The whole dojo shook. He didn't break a sweat.

'Wow,' I muttered to Gloria. 'So this is the real thing.'

'He makes Shihan look like Mr. Potato Head,' replied Gloria out of the corner of her mouth.

The Okinawans were hard disciplinarians. They drove us like cattle in repetitive performance of basic moves, and then when we got to kata practice they made us sit in low sumo stances for minutes on end. Sensei Hideki went around shoving everybody down so low that our butts were practically on the floor.

They ignored the color belts, luckily. The black belts got picked on bigtime, but I guess we weren't worthy of their notice. It was oppressively hot but they refused to open the doors or turn on the fan. Cori fainted during Sei-enchin and had to go sit on the side.

What was funny about the Okinawans was how small and trucklike their bodies were. The tallest couldn't have been as tall as the average American woman, but they were all wide-bodied and they had huge, deformed knuckles from makiwara practice. They moved stiffly but with perfect geometrical form. They looked like little robotic bulls. I'd never been able to achieve this kind of hardness, no matter how much I practiced trying to make my gi snap when I punched. It's something I've noticed about Troy, too. I think it's a black thing. We can't move like little Nazis – why would you want to? We have a more flexible sense of time. We just don't fit in well with this perfect-form, perfect-time drilling and it feels unnatural to try. Look how Miss Cooper messed up my side kick when she tried to teach me to do it 'right'. Because I also notice that when it comes to sparring, me and Troy can get the job done.

Having said all that, I was totally impressed with the little Okinawans but it seemed they didn't feel the same about me. During practice of Saifa, Sensei Hideki walked right by me and then stopped to watch me perform my stomp-kick.

'Queen Kong!' he said. 'You break floor, you pay for it!'

Then he laughed uproariously at his own humor.

I felt myself go hot and I forgot the next move of the kata. I had to apologize and go kneel in zazen in the corner. They ignored me after that.

I glanced sideways at Cori. She was blushing and bowing to one of the masters, her braid swinging and slapping her butt as she nodded enthusiastic agreement with a little Okinawan no taller than five feet two, as if she was a Playboy Bunny and he was Hugh Hefner.

We all wanted to brown-nose. I'd probably have been doing it myself if Masunobu Hideki hadn't called me Queen Kong. We were so eager to have the Great Masters among us. We were so eager to be a part of the legends.

I wondered how long Masunobu Hideki would last in the Grid.

At the end of the training session, the masters gave a rousing speech in translation and everybody clapped and cheered. We all staggered up the stairs and went to Tony's for pizza and to compare notes. Everybody's quadriceps were killing them from all the sumo stances, which seemed like a sign that we were finally being initiated to the inner mysteries of the martial arts. Miss Cooper's eyes were alight with excitement. The Okinawans had paid a lot of attention to her. Evidently she hadn't disgraced the dojo after all, and she said that Shihan Norman had even said 'Nice going' after she'd finished her naginata practice in the private black-belt session upstairs.

'Pocketbook-and-broom is going to be great,' she said.

'Yeah, tell that to my nuts,' said Mr. Vukovich, to general laughter. 'Cori keeps getting past my cup with the straps of her pocketbook, dude. I hope I can still have kids.'

By the time I got home, I had decided that I was being grumpy about the Okinawans because of the Dataplex thing, and that wasn't right. I wasn't going to let one bad experience corrupt me for everything else. Karate had done a lot for me. Dataplex hadn't. It was Dataplex I should be going after – not the karate masters who held the key to my growth as a person, my physical freedom from food addiction.

I fed the cats and picked up the phone.

'Miles,' I said. 'Remember how you told me you could get into people's records and stuff using your computer? If I gave you a name and a social security number, could you find out whether that person exists?'

'Whether they exist? I can do better than that, I hope. What's it all about?'

I read the name and number off a piece of paper I'd copied from the tape.

'Who's Leroy Jones?'

'I was hoping you could tell me.'

holy toledo

Arla has long toes with red-painted nails. She is standing in a shallow well puddle, watching it change colors as it reads her.

She has taken you near to the dead zone. You don't know how far you are from the mines, but you know you are close to the dead Grid because of the reappearance of artifice in the Grid's structure. The foundation here is almost like solid ground.

'You'd like my golem, wouldn't you?' she taunts the Grid, throwing her head back and laughing into the whirl of web-arms, the moving tapestry that human assumption wants to call 'branches' or 'forest roof' even though nothing here is green. The colors of the gel around her feet, initially only pastel washes like bleeding aquarelles, begin to coagulate and form fine lines radiating from the edges of her skin. The lines creep outward and then, as if bent by an invisible current within the gel, they begin to curve around the edges of her foot so that they all point the same way. Many-stranded plaits of color flow along the sides of her feet and past her heels, arrowing towards the black of the well. When the strands reach the well they appear as luminous neon against the black backdrop; then, as if heavier than the surrounding substrate, they sink, wavering, until they are swallowed.

Deep in the well, near the limits of visibility, something small appears. At first its form is amoebic, but soon it begins to grow and resolve until you can see knobs of flesh over translucent bone, red and pulsing as if with blood from an unseen heart.

You hear a metallic click. There is a weapon pointed at the back of Arla's head.

'Step away from the well, please, Major.'

It's Klaski of all people. You recognize her voice and her Jean Naté after-bath splash.

'Don't be stupid,' Arla snaps. Her tone is completely different: no serenity, no I-could-be-a-better-mother-than-your-mother. No romance. You wonder what Klaski sees in her eyes. If they are still horror-movie yellow. 'It only has my feet. You can't make a whole golem from a pair of feet.'

'With all due respect, Major, you are placing yourself and this entire unit at risk. You don't know what the Grid can do with the information you're giving it. And what if you fall in?'

'F@*k off, Lieutenant,' says Arla. She names Klaski's rank sneeringly, like she's offended by Klaski's formality. But she steps out of the well fluid and shakes its residue off her feet. She pulls Gossamer tighter around her shoulders.

Klaski is shaking so hard that you doubt whether she could aim the weapon effectively.

'I'm going to have to ask you to hand over the Equipment as well, ma'am.'

Equipment: that must mean you. Arla is breathing hard. She's like a horse after an uphill gallop. She's blowing and shifting her weight from foot to foot.

'Don't make this personal, Lieutenant. You don't want to f*$k with me.'

'I don't know what the hell you're playing at, ma'am, but if you don't come out of the well I will shoot you.'

Arla comes out of the well.

'You must have misunderstood me,' she said softly. 'Give me the weapon.'

'No, ma'am, I can't do that.'

'I'm your commanding officer and you will follow orders.'

'I'm not a donkey, ma'am.'

'No? Maybe you *should* be a donkey, Lieutenant. You dis-obeyed your commander once and look what happened.'

'Ma'am, with all respect I don't believe you're one hundred percent in command of your full faculties, ma'am, and I cannot give you the weapon.'

Arla charges her. Klaski slips and falls to her knees on the edge of the well. Arla grabs the gun by the barrel.

'Now you don't want to drop that in the well,' she says. 'Gimme it.'

'Ma'am, don't make me shoot your hand off.'

Arla kicks her in the face and Klaski's head snaps back; then Arla jumps on top of her and wrenches the gun away. Klaski man-ages to squeeze off two shots: one shears Arla's hand neatly in half, leaving only her thumb and a bleeding stump. The other cuts a swathe through the nearby Grid, releasing a cloud of pollen and an enormous burst of rainbow light.

Arla roars. She sweeps up Klaski in both arms like a judo player, hoists her over one hip and dumps her headfirst on the ground. Klaski's forehead hit the Grid, her neck crumples and then, as Arla releases her, her body topples into the well.

Then Arla sticks her hand between her thighs and sways. You can't see her face but you can hear her gasping and grunting for control of the pain. Blood slides into the well and dissolves in pink puffs.

Lewis and Hendricks turn up within moments. Hendricks is pale.

'She . . . she was trying to kill herself. She jumped in the well. I couldn't stop her,' Arla gasps. 'I tried but she shot me.'

Hendricks runs to the edge of the well and looks down on Klaski's sinking body, horror-struck.

'We have to get her out! Is she dead? Arla, is she alive or dead?'

She leans in and starts dragging Klaski up by one arm. You can hear her grunting and cursing and making mewling noises of effort.

'Help me, Arla!'

Now Lewis is blocking your view. Lewis is bending over you, removing the dressing, checking the wound. 'Crossbow,' she mutters. 'I've never seen a golem with a crossbow before.'

You can hear Gonzalez consoling Hendricks, and Hendricks sobbing and raging. Lewis ignores them both. She whispers, 'Gossamer, you're going to have to get yourself up and out of here. This tissue isn't healed yet, Arla's not dressing it right at all, some friggin' doctor, she probably doesn't want you to fly. I'm putting some temporary mesh over it and spraying it, and I think you'll soon be able to unfold it without—'

'What are you doing, Lewis?'

'Just checking to be sure Gossamer didn't get damaged in the struggle. It's fine.' Lewis has quickly taken care of Gossamer's wound and now pats the dressing back in place, turns, and moves out of your line of vision. Arla is watching her suspiciously. She comes over to you and touches the edge of the dressing but doesn't remove it.

Hendricks has gotten Klaski out of the well, but Klaski is unconscious and has a lump on her head the size of an egg. Hendricks starts doing CPR.

'Pulse, pulse, where are you, pulse?' she chants. Arla ignores the two of them. She picks you up and dons you again.

'You won't last long out here if this is the quality of your unit,' she says harshly to Lewis. Lewis abandons Klaski and bull-charges Gonzalez. You feel the impact go through Gonzalez's body; she staggers back, bracing herself up against her straight-ened right leg as her left bends to absorb the shock.

You can't see Lewis, but after a few seconds you realize that Gonzalez must have her in a headlock. Lewis must have tucked her chin in or something, because she's still struggling and if

Gonzalez really had her around the neck she'd be unconscious by now.

'Hendricks,' croaks Lewis. 'Incinerate!'

You can hear her, but Hendricks is too far away. Lewis fumbles in her suit and drags out a star-shaped immolation charge. She chucks it at Hendricks, who catches it and looks at it with wide eyes. She is going to throw it at Lewis, and Arla – and you!

'Oh no, you don't!' cries Gonzalez, and throws Lewis on the ground, shoving her into the well just as she did with Klaski. But Lewis is still conscious, and she fights and scrabbles to get out. Gonzalez lunges at Hendricks and tries to get the charge off her. Hendricks drops the charge, but before Arla can get it Hendricks's ray gun goes off.

You hang there on Arla's back for several seconds before you are sure that Gossamer is still alive. Arla steps back a few paces, apparently unhurt. She's dragging Hendricks by the armpits.

'Don't die, bitch, or you'll blow everything.'

Hendricks slides into the well. Arla releases a stream of curses to the sky. She turns and stomps away from the well, giving you a full view of Hendricks's staring-eyed body sinking. Her chest is nothing but shards of battle armor, bone and blood where the ray gun got her. The well breaks up the blood like water breaks up oil.

The situation has taken on its own momentum now. You find yourself wishing Arla would get something right, gain some con-trol – anything would be better than this mayhem. Now she's trying to wrestle Lewis back into the well, but Lewis has got hold of the charge that Hendricks dropped and has coded it to fire.

'It's going off, doc,' she hisses at Gonzalez. 'We'll both be torches in a second, so do your worst.'

Gonzalez lets her go and dives for cover. She throws herself on her face and puts her hands – what's left of them – over the back of her head. You can see the whirl of the Grid overhead and the multiple flashes of the explosion. You are blinded for several seconds. Finally, when Gonzalez gets up, you see that a chunk of the Grid has been blasted to black. Small flames dance along its limbs and there's a smell, worse than burning hair. All you hear are jungle noises, deep inside your ears like a cloud of insects in your head. Gossamer's olfactories too ache from the overload.

You're still a passenger. Arla is running around hurling herself at random arms of the Grid, overcome by fury and frustration. Then she sort of collapses on her hands and knees and stays there for a while. She's losing a lot of blood from that wounded hand.

'This is no good,' you hear her mutter through the jungle noises in your head. 'Salvage something. You stupid f*%k!'

Arla bends over Klaski's body. She seems to have her head against Klaski's chest. You see her pick up Klaski's wrist and hold it, feeling for signs of life.

'Good CPR, Hendricks,' said Arla. 'I still have one subject. One last chance. Now for the fun part.'

And she rolls Klaski's inert body back into the well.

After a while Arla sits back and leans her head against a vertical slab of Grid. She dangles her feet over its bough, and her shadow falls not on the well below, but on the netting of fine fibers just above her and over her right shoulder. With one eye, you can see her shadow there. It's fractured and warped by the Grid. Below, the well glows and sparkles.

Your hearing is coming back, but one eye is completely obscured by being pressed against the Grid. Arla should be crushing you to a pulp, but it isn't possible for you to get any thinner than you already are. Gossamer's mouthparts emerge from their petal-like folds and attach to the Grid. If you could feel energy flowing as a sensation, then you would feel Gossamer's nerves blaze.

The batteries are charging.

'Oh, I can hear your footsteps, you thing, you Grid,' Arla whispers. 'I can hear you coming with that old-fashioned shoe sound, that grainy clicking walk, yeah like the cartoon Inspector at the beginning of the *Pink Panther* movies, and I can hear you striking the match. I wish I could disappear except for a couple of huge eyes.'

No, you don't, you think. *It's not all it's cracked.*

Arla's phrases come out one at a time. It's as if she's on the phone to someone else whose voice can't be heard.

'Oh my hand. Oh sh%*ohf?@k.' Deep inhale. 'Uhhhnnnn. I'm so loaded I'd probably jump in front of a freight train. You give me such good stuff to breathe. I feel better now. Thank you.'

A long pause. For a minute you wonder if she's gone to sleep.

'I can't save them. It wasn't my idea. Everything is your idea. No.'

You smell nitrous oxide. You wish she would be quiet. Gossamer's wound is starting to heal. Arla has botched it badly, probably on purpose, but simply by laying the tissue correctly across the butterfly gauze Lewis has gone a long way to solving that problem. The Grid feeds Gossamer enzymes and sugars.

Then Arla launches herself to her feet, staggering and almost falling because she can't use both hands to steady herself.

'You got what you wanted, you big bug!' she yells at the Grid in a rough, deep voice. 'Now where's my diamond ring? Where's my mockingbird?'

Gossamer has been ripped away from the Grid, only half-charged. But soon Arla sways, sits down again, puts her head between her knees. You hear her hissing and panting. Gossamer reattaches.

And Serge's daughters come creeping out of the Grid to watch Arla.

'I want to come into your world. Don't leave me out here.'

Hiss-pant.

Hiss-pant.

'Give me some sign. If Joanne Klaski steps out of that well, if you accept her, then you have to accept me. Right? Why else are you saving me?'

Hisssss . . .

'Jesus Christ, I just want some reassurance that it's the right thing, is that so much to ask?'

Arla gets up and looks in the well at Klaski. Again she turns, sticking her wrist under her opposite armpit and moaning. You see that Klaski, facedown, is sinking.

And Arla sees the girls.

'What do you want? Why don't you speak? Why are you doing this to me?'

Then the rhythm of her breathing breaks. Her voice is low and ragged.

'Not *you*.' This time you can't see who she's talking to. 'No, not you again.'

And you feel a thrum of hope run along the edges of Gossamer's wings, like an updraft.

When the newcomer speaks, her voice hasn't changed one bit.

'You said you wanted reassurance, Chicken Little. All that killing was a waste of time because I'm here to tell you that sure as marmots, the Grid is survivable. Now what are you gonna do?'

You can't actually see Serge because you're still facing the wrong way. You can still see the well-hole where Klaski got dumped, though. She's no longer floating on her face. She's vertical, and her arms are moving. It's like looking at a bug in a toilet bowl. At first you can't be sure if the motion of its limbs is down to the current, or if it's still alive.

But you think it's still alive.

Klaski. Of all people. Well, one thing is becoming clear.

Most things in life aren't real, they're in your head. When it comes to most things, you can give up and there won't be any big consequences. Like, personally, you always gave up diets. But for Klaski you can see that she can't think about giving up. She can't let it enter her mind. She's been close to dying all the time. You never knew what that meant, and you never thought about what that meant, and if you thought about it you probably thought it meant something profound. It doesn't. All it means is that the stuff inside you that has nothing to do with you, personally, takes over. Your ancestral stuff. Your biology. It's like a great invisible safety net holding you together. It's like a Grid in its own right.

And something lives in that net, something that you can't lay claim to with your ego, but something that also isn't just a relic from the past. There's a spark that gives you courage when you think there's nothing left.

Klaski has that.

It lets her fingers reach out and grasp the edge of the Grid. It recruits muscle fibers, takes their spindles past their default threshold of response, brings her whole body to breaking point, so that with an extreme effort she pulls her head out of the well fluid and takes a breath.

Once she's done that, there can be no possibility of giving up.

Arla sees nothing, hears nothing of Klaski's efforts because all her attention is focused on dealing with Serge.

'You did it,' Serge says. 'I know that now. I can remember it. You were there. You were in charge of the sexual-health clinic. You performed the abortion. You knew that ordinary mucus didn't affect the well, and you knew that blood cells and isolated tissues didn't catch, but you figured if a dead body makes a golem, then an embryo makes a golem. Am I right?'

'It was research. We thought we could save lives. Those embryos were going to be terminated anyway. They were already dead.'

'Only mine didn't die. It got adopted by a alien. And now you're still on the take. You're still looking for answers. What does it take to make you go home and turn on *Wide World of Sports* and open a beer?'

Arla's got her control back from somewhere. She's exited primitive mode and she's back to being the ship's doctor.

'I understand that you're angry. But I'm not your enemy. Whatever I did that you don't like, I did it for a good reason. I was working with an isolated patch of well fluid. In containment. The seals weren't supposed to be compromised. Nothing was supposed to get *out*, don't you see? But the system failed, and I think it failed for a reason. It's MF you should be worried about. It's them you should be angry at, not—'

'Angry? Why should I be angry? You gave me everlasting life. I can go on having a ant-free picnic here for theoretically ever. Why-hy, it's a bring-your-own-coleslaw extravaganza!'

'You were stupid,' Arla says. 'We could have pulled something out of the hat here. We could have brought evidence to Machine Front. We could have done a lot of things but you had to go playing pyro-bitch and ordering a wipeout on *your own offspring*. What is the matter with you?'

'You're insane.'

'You think I care about that? Do you have any idea what I've been breathing out here? I'm *allowed* to be insane, I'd be insane if I wasn't insane already after what I've been through. But *you* should know better.'

Serge is laughing. You can't see her so it's hard to be sure why, but considering what you do see – *who* you do see, dragging herself out of the well looking cute and blonde and pissed-off – you figure you can take a pretty good guess what's so funny.

'Serge!' screams Arla. 'Where are you going? Come back! Tell me what it's like!'

'Thought you got me, didn't you?' rasps Klaski, spitting well fluid. She's coming up behind Arla like an unkillable horror-movie villain. Her eyes look purple but she manages to get her helmet back on as she staggers forward. Her palms are ink-black, and the lines in her hands shine pale. You feel Arla stiffen as Klaski gets her breath back and speaks again. 'Did you kill Serge, too? And what did she mean about embryos? Is that what you did? You worked at the clinic with Hendricks, does that mean you put *babies* in the well?'

Arla turns and sees Klaski nearly on top of her. She begins to retreat. The Grid jigs and jogs in your frame of view as she tries to get her balance.

'Don't start with the babies crap. It was an extreme situation, and my intentions were good. So don't you try to lay that at my feet, you weak little . . . little . . .' Arla falters. Klaski has backed her nearly to the edge of the well, and she's scared. She is also losing a lot of blood, to judge by the crimson trail she's leaving. She angles her body so you can see Klaski in your peripheral vision.

'You can't do it, can you, Major?' Klaski says. 'You can stick your toe in and you can make other people go in, and you can flash your eyes at it and you can wear Gossamer on your back like a cloak, like a hunter wears a bearskin coat only you're no hunter, you're just some lady who bought a mink stole at the Fur Vault. If the Grid is so wonderful and if it's all so mind-blowing, why don't you just go in and join the party?'

'I was only trying to protect you,' Arla says, showing the palms of her gory hands to Klaski, to the sky, appealing. 'You were pointing a gun at me. You shot off my hand!'

'You said you were going in the Grid. I tried to stop you. That was my big mistake. If you really want to go in, then let's see it.'

'I don't!' blurts Arla. 'I was only fooling. And I was wrong what I said. I was naive. I made a mistake. Joanne, you got to forgive me – we're all alone out here, we got nobody else, nobody on our side. We got to make this right and be friends.'

Klaski looks up. The Grid hangs overhead, jewel-bright, like the web of a giant neon-spinning spider that wishes it lived in a cathedral and keeps trying in a low-budget way to make it so. It's horrible. She keeps shivering. Well fluid slides off her face and plops on her boots.

'I want to go home,' she says. 'Where are the others?'

And you can see it. She has capitulated. All Arla has to do is make reassurances, lie cozily, offer help in her beautiful, soft voice.

Arla makes a sinuous little movement with her head, almost imperceptibly.

'So . . . what was it like in there?' she asks. You recognize the tone. You know it well. It's the sound of an alcoholic asking the way to the bathroom so that he can check out the contents of the liquor cabinet en route, just to know what's in there. It's the sound of the junkie wondering if his grandmother has cashed her social security check yet, and of the compulsive eater sticking a couple of Hostess cupcakes in my – I mean, her – purse 'for emergencies.'

Klaski doesn't hesitate.

'What was it like? I'll show you,' she says, and launches herself at Arla.

Arla doesn't want to go in the Grid, after all. She doesn't want to die, either. Klaski has to beat her repeatedly about the head with Lewis's socket wrench, and then strangle her with a nylon packing cord, before Arla finally gives up and her heart stops.

Klaski has a big rage then. She storms up and down, kicking Arla's body for good measure every time she passes. You feel the blows shudder through Arla's flesh. Klaski is screaming at the dead Arla.

'What is happening to us? How could this get so out of hand? I never wanted this. I bet you never wanted it either. This has to stop. Now. I'm going to make it stop.'

She freezes.

Something has rolled out of Arla's dead hand. You can see it. It's the thing you thought was a grenade. While both of you watch, it rolls slowly, wobbling, until it drops into the well.

Klaski goes down on her hands and knees and peers into the depths of the well fluid. You can just about see what she sees. There is a cluster of black hand-sized oblongs in the well, all identical. You're pretty sure you know what they are.

They are logic bullets.

Klaski says: 'Holy Toledo.'

company picnic

It was painful to listen to the tapes that I'd liberated from Gunther's (or should I say Dr. Stengel's?) office, but after a while it became cathartic. One pattern became clear: Gunther was uncomfortable with what he was doing. That didn't excuse him, but it made me realize he too was vulnerable. I gathered that 'Bob' was our Vice President in charge of Development, Bob Hagler. I didn't really know him well enough to recognize his voice, but Gunther tended to spend a lot of time with him so the connection made sense.

On Friday Dataplex was having a half-day because the computers were all being serviced and were going to be down. Gunther had scheduled his annual summer office party for that afternoon; I knew because Gloria was going, and she had invited me. My initial instinct was to refuse totally, but after a few days of listening to the tapes and training with the Okinawans, my aching limbs and hungry stomach made me angry enough that I decided I would go. I called Miles and asked him to meet me there.

'When are you going to tell me what was on the tapes?'

'Tomorrow,' I said. 'It's all going to come out.'

'Cookie, don't be stupid. You don't know how to handle

this. You're going to mess it up. Talk to me, and we can plan a strategy together.'

There was no way I was telling Miles at this stage. He'd only try to take over. And anyway, it was time I started fighting my own battles, right?

Getting to talk to Gunther wasn't so easy, though. His backyard was mobbed with people and he'd acquired a couple more stray dogs, there were no less than three barbecues in operation, and then there was the above-ground pool which seemed to overflow frequently because people's kids were doing cannonballs into it. Gunther was busy grilling ribs and drinking Samuel Adams – no expense ever spared at Gunther's parties.

I went over to him and he looked genuinely glad to see me.

'How are you?' he said solicitously. 'Can I get you a beer? I'm so glad you came. The ribs are gonna be done in, like, two minutes. Gosh, you've lost a lot of weight.'

I didn't look him in the eye. All my wimp instincts would have kicked in. Instead, I read the notes I'd made from the tape. My voice cracked and broke. Gunther tried to stop me several times, and then he steered me away from the barbecue, looking around in a paranoid fashion – not that anyone could hear anything over the shrieking of Gloria's daughter and the barking of Gunther's various dogs.

'—'*Broken Wings*' by Mr. Mister?' I finished. 'Are you guys *kidding* me? I get shot down by a madwoman so I can't fly anymore, and I'm supposed to believe it's all about the fact that you were running a market test for some *video*? About martyrdom and angel wings? Oh, my *God*. I could puke. I *have* puked.'

'Well, actually, we had moved you out of video for the most part but this is going to be a special debut. I have a friend who does PR in the industry who asked me to do him a favor and find out if the hype was going to deliver.' Gunther drew his eyebrows together and gave me his sincere look. 'You were very good, you know, Cookie.'

'You don't deny it, then.' I was spitting mad. Gunther blinked and swallowed some beer. He was smaller than me; we both noticed it right about then.

'I've always said you were a terrific Flier. The best.'

'I don't mean that. Darn it, Gunther, you know what I mean.'

Gunther wrinkled his forehead and tried to take my arm. 'You want to go inside and talk privately?' he began, putting down his beef skewer. I shook him off.

'Cut it out.' My voice was getting higher and louder. I couldn't help it. 'Are you really admitting *all* of this?' I waved the notes. 'All of this is a fake? What the hell are you paying me for, then?'

People were looking at us. One of Gunther's stray dogs was stealing a chunk of raw meat from the plate by the barbecue.

'We pay you for your insights,' said Gunther in measured tones. 'You're our best source of information about what actually penetrates to a viewer's psyche. We're also paid a generous grant to study the UFO phenomenon, which provides you with a stipend.'

'My hazard pay?' I said. 'Is that what you're referring to?'

'Whatever terminology makes you most comfortable.'

'But . . . but . . . this makes me sound like a loony bird. I'm a *real psychic*. Don't you people understand that?'

'We know your history with the Hasbrook Heights Police Department. They didn't actually characterize you as a psychic, as you probably know.'

'I can't deal with this,' I said. 'I never volunteered to be a guinea pig in somebody's experiment.'

'Actually, you did. It's just the wording of the experiment that you don't like. The connotation, as opposed to the denotation.'

'Don't throw your intellect around with me, Gunther. I read books, you know. I'm not stupid.'

But of course I felt distinctly stupid, and he knew it. He was quiet for a moment and I had the impression that I was expected to gather up the shreds of my dignity.

'You know, Gunther, when you gave me that survey to fill out? For Bob Hagler? I blew it on purpose.'

Gunther looked at his shoes.

'I did. Did you think I just lost it? Because I'm telling you, I could fly just fine until I got shot down. But I won't fly for you. No way.'

I could see Gunther's brain smoking as he took this in.

'And I don't want your disability pay.'

'Look, Cookie . . .'

'That's Karen to you.'

He inclined his head regally in apology. His tone became formal. 'Karen. Ms. Orbach. I can appreciate that you're feeling unhappy with the current situation, but I would urge you not to burn your bridges with us. Your condition – being unable to get up there and see what you see – is probably temporary. We would be happy to review your status in, say, six months. You don't have to throw away your career.'

'My career? My career as a circus freak?'

'You're not a circus freak. You're a sensitive and valuable person in a predacious market culture.'

I threw up my hands. 'Oh, I give up. I'm going home. I wish there were dragons. I wish there were castles. I wish I could get on a spaceship. This world is just a big letdown.'

I didn't even care if I sounded childish. I stomped away, snorting to get the smell of charcoal smoke out of my nose. I wanted a bucket of Haagen-Dazs so bad – not that it would do any good. I went to my car and found I'd locked the keys inside.

Some guy in a white T-shirt and cutoffs came up to me. I tried to ignore him but he kept staring at me until I had to look at him.

'Hi,' said the guy. 'You must be Cookie. I'm Jake Davies, but everybody calls me Montana. You know, the sandworm archeo-biologist? I study extraplanetary artifacts and interpret the messages in the tracks of the Arrakis sandworm, but I also dabble in other areas. You may have read my monograph on replicating the tensile strength of sandworm skin in biodomes.'

I looked at him blankly for a minute. Then my mom-trained make-nice reflexes kicked in and I said, 'Oh, yeah. *Dune* was a great book, but I never could get into the sequels.'

He made a lemon face and added, 'I find there's a distinct lack of administrative support for my post. I keep asking for a language interpreter but I never get one. I put in a request for a planetary field expedition three years ago. I don't have to tell you that never happened.'

What a kook. I looked around for an escape.

'I'm gonna . . . get some water,' I said, edging towards the cooler where some guys from Accounting were standing. I was tempted to bolt, but thought I should at least try and brush him off onto somebody else.

His eyebrows came down like two caterpillars kissing. 'Are you mocking me?' he snarled. 'Water is the lifeblood. Water is the sacred text. Water—'

I ran for it. I dodged around Gloria's kids and almost collided with Gunther carrying a big platter of ribs smothered in Heinz 57 sauce.

'Cookie, there you are – no hard feelings, right? Can I tempt you with a—'

I swerved to avoid Gunther and instead crashed into

Miles. He had a beach towel draped around his neck and was still holding his car keys. *Thank heavens*.

'Can we leave?' I said.

'I just got here. Are those ribs?'

I grabbed his arm. 'Seriously. I need to go. *Now*.'

'Unhand me, wench. Into the chariot with you, then, and surcease your scowling.'

He opened the door and I sat down heavily in his front seat. He started the engine and pulled out.

'I was really looking forward to going swimming,' he said. Then he glanced across at me. 'What's going on with you? You look like you're going to cry.'

I *was* crying. I blotted my face on my forearm and took a couple of shuddery breaths to control myself.

'Never mind.'

'I found out about Leroy Jones,' he said. 'He does exist. The social security number matches his name. Now are you going to tell me why you wanted to know?'

I leaned my head against the window. The air-conditioning came up and ruffled the hairs on my forearms.

I said, 'Let me guess. He's a psycho killer. He tried to assassinate Walt Disney.'

'Walt Disney is already dead. No, Leroy Jones is a respected artist and illustrator. He's one of the creators of some new cartoon that has all the kids excited. I never heard of it – I'm a *Rocky & Bullwinkle* guy myself.'

He did a right onto Black Oak Ridge Road and took the opportunity to take a long look at me. I gave him my profile.

'What cartoon?' I said dully.

'Huh. Well, this is the funny part, but I'm not sure I should tell you because you're touchy about these things . . .'

'I already know. It's *Cookie Starfishes*, isn't it?'

Miles seemed disappointed. 'Then I guess you already have one,' he said.

'Have one what?'

'Look in the glove compartment.'

I opened the glove compartment and next to a map of Passaic County and a roll of Lifesavers was a stuffed purple starfish. When you squeezed it, it played the line *'I am the eye/In the sky/I can fly'* from that song 'Planetary Express' by Rocket Squad. The song I supposedly 'picked' somehow. So it was the theme song for *Cookie Starfishes*.

'Cute, huh? Come on, Cookie, cheer up. You've got a mascot.'

I leaned back in the seat and laid my forearm over my eyes.

'I'm losing all perspective,' I said. 'What's happening to me?'

'Did you know,' said Miles, 'that Genesis once wrote a song from the perspective of a lawnmower?'

the dead lamb's Mother

Klaski fishes the logic bullets out of the well, using the netting on Lewis's equipment pack. The task takes a while, but she goes at it with total focus. When they are out, she picks them up and lets them spill through her fingers. They look like jewels and smell like fertilizer. They seem to resonate slightly in her hands, like bells.

'This is what everyone wants so badly,' she says. Her voice is shaking. 'The mathematics of the Grid. The master key of creation. The code to an alien mind.'

Klaski sits back on her heels.

'So Arla had a secret. She took the logic bullets out of the mines and hid them in the well. I wonder if it's done anything to them . . .'

She smooths them in her hands, looking for signs of cracks or flaws. Not that she would know. She's never seen logic bullets before.

'I thought it was suicidal behavior but she was just checking on her treasure trove. What was she going to do with them? Keep them from MF?'

You can almost hear Arla now. *'The machines will use this. They'll build better weapons. They'll get control. They'll find the Grid's weaknesses, understand its thought.'*

Klaski laughs.

'Yes, it's true, folks – Joanne Klaski walks off with the door prize.'

She freezes. She has realized that someone is watching her. She focuses her eyes on the spaces within the Grid. There are several someones, actually, and they all look the same.

Klaski drops the logic bullets in a cascade of melodic tones and brandishes her ray gun.

'You keep away from me!' she yells.

Serge's little girls – they're like wrapping a live lamb in the skin of a dead one so the dead lamb's mother will accept it – is that what the Grid is doing? *Just getting under our skin, again and again.*

Because Klaski can't seem to bring herself to shoot them. Not unless they move first. They don't. They are scarcely more than eyes in a dark forest.

She flips open her Swatch.

'Major Galante? Machine Front? It's . . . it's Lieutenant Klaski, you don't know me, I'm under Captain Serge . . . you know, she had Dante but I don't know how . . . ? Hello? Machine Front? Mayday?'

She waits a while. Her Swatch plays Madonna's 'Borderline' and the cursor flashes. Then a mechanical voice says, 'Attempting connection to Major Galante. Please wait.'

'Galante.'

'Oh! Major Galante, this is Lieutenant Klaski – can you hear me?'

'Yeah, I got you, Klaski, where you guys been? I keep calling and getting no response.'

'Major, it's bad, I lost the others. I think they're all . . . they're not coming back. Uh, can you tell me how to get to your position?'

'My advice is to get your flier up again. We need Gossamer.'

'I can't. It's damaged. Shot down.'

'Gossamer's damaged? No wonder I can't get through. I've tried to call Sergeant Lewis about fifty times. What's going on over there? Let me speak to Dr. Gonzalez.'

'She's dead, ma'am. I'm the only one left and I—'

Her face is rubberizing and her voice bubbles with tears.

Galante is cursing freely.

'How close are you to the mines? You should be nearly at the perimeter. Get a grip, Lieutenant, and get yourself to safety. I can't come looking for you now, I got problems of my own.'

'I really need to talk to you in person, Major Galante. There's some things I just can't explain over a Swatch. Can't you send me your position and I can come to you instead?'

'Sure, if you think you can walk through about ten thousand golems and survive. We're under ambush. You don't want to be here. Get up to the mines. If you can make it that far, my guys will take care of you. Copy?'

'Yeah,' croaks Klaski tearfully. 'I copy.'

The link cuts. Klaski takes a shuddery breath. 'How am I going to get there from here?'

And you remember the dead Grid, cutting a road in the direction of the mines. Its edge is near here. You send files to her Swatch, hoping she'll take the hint.

The Swatch chirps a few bars of 'Red Skies at Night' and Klaski answers easily. She looks deflated when she realizes it's only a data transmission from Gossamer. Then she fishes around in the Swatch for a long time before she finds the visual of your flyover showing the dead Grid and how it leads to the mines.

'I hope this works,' she moans.

Klaski counts the logic bullets. There are forty-seven. She packs them in Hendricks's knapsack, dumping out various clothes, cassette tapes and toiletries in the process. After she's taken *Thriller* she incinerates these. She picks up Gossamer and drapes you across her own backpack much as Arla did. Then Klaski picks up Hendricks's pack with the logic bullets and hangs them around her front, like a kangaroo pouch, and sets off.

planetary journey

In the end I told Miles enough to get him excited about Dataplex. Culminating in the fact that I'd been watching *Cookie Starfishes* all this time when I was at work. But he didn't look especially shocked.

I prompted:

'Don't you *remember*?Don't you remember the night we got drunk and I told you I felt like a starfish? Remember? *Ringworld Engineers* in the bathtub, you said.'

It came out all jumbled, and Miles rubbed his eyebrows as he tried to follow my meaning. 'Oh . . . maybe . . . sort of . . . did you actually *say* 'Cookie Starfishes' at the time?'

'Yeah, I did. And then I saw the darn cereal in Shop Rite.'

He wagged his head from side to side, considering. I couldn't understand why he wasn't more shocked and horrified by the sinister implications of what Dataplex were doing. OK, maybe making these connections is the province of the paranoid schizophrenic – maybe I'm extra good at it. But to me there was a big unknown in terms of whether Dataplex was making me think and feel things, or whether my visions were truly there to be felt whether or not Dataplex existed. Whether the world on a TV screen was more real than me and Miles sitting in this car yakking about it.

But in that case, how could the Grid in some sense be inseparable from a cartoon about intelligent spacefaring snacks?

'Golems . . .' Miles murmured doubtfully.

I said: 'Come on. Do you really think I could make all this stuff up if I tried?'

'Well. Something's going on. Hard to say what it is.'

He didn't believe me. He didn't think I was lying; he just thought I was deluded.

But he hacked into Dataplex's personnel records and found that Leroy Jones had been paid as an outside contractor – just like I was – not long before I joined Dataplex. Miles also found his current address: a very swanky neighborhood in Alpine where people like Brooke Shields were rumored to live.

'Let's go out there tomorrow,' he said. 'What can it hurt?'

A confrontation? No, thanks.

'I don't know. I have to be at the dojo later, and . . . I don't know, Miles. What's the point?'

But here I was, Saturday morning after a weird bout of Friday-night TV with Klaski and the logic, sitting on Leroy Jones's couch in his Alpine mini-mansion, sipping iced tea and listening to Miles do a Barbara Walters on the great man.

'You know, I can't say where the ideas come from,' Leroy mused. 'Usually I'll be out running and an idea will just like *float* into my head. I'll get home, do a little sketch – like with the starfishes idea, the first thing I saw was Malkor, the wizard. At first he was a comical character. He had a magic cookie jar, and he used the cookies to cast spells.'

Miles glanced at me, but I didn't meet his eye.

'But then it kind of started to morph in my head, and the cookies became real characters, and they had their own stories.'

'Were you working for Dataplex then?' I said.

'If you could call it working! I went in and took a test. They play you some music and ask you to draw what you hear. At least, that's what I had to do, anyway – maybe the drawing part was because I'm an artist by profession. Then they gave me a whole stack of tapes, asked me to listen to them and bring in my sketches. So I did. I played them on my Walkman when I was out jogging. And then, one day, I got the starfishes idea. I worked on it for a while before I got up the nerve to show it to anybody. I took it to a friend of mine at Rodeo Comics, and he gave it to some TV chick he knew, and the next thing I know I get a TV contract. I quit the Dataplex project as soon as the real money started coming. I got too busy with the show.'

I wonder if that was when you died, I thought, looking for Grid parallels. *And became a golem.*

'What was on the tapes?' I tried to sound casually curious.

'Oh, music. Rock, pop, R&B, world music. A whole mix. Some stuff I've heard, but most of it was new to me. Some of it has come on the radio since then. One of the songs was actually 'Planetary Journey', believe it or not. You know, the *Cookie Starfishes* theme song. It hadn't even been released yet, but the producers picked it for the show and as soon as I heard it I recognized it from the Dataplex tapes. Neat coincidence. Good tune, too.'

'Did you know that Dataplex are still involved in the show?' Miles said.

Leroy waved his hand. 'Yeah, I hear they consult on the advertising or something. Everybody seems to think they know the secret of a show's success and they can tell advertisers which space to buy to get the best results. That's about the extent of it.'

'So you don't think your idea had anything to do with Dataplex?'

Leroy frowned. He was a light-skinned black man, with a sprinkling of freckles and a mustache, and until Miles said that his expression had been sunny and open.

'No. No, I don't. Not unless you want to give them credit for letting me take time off from my other jobs, giving me some headspace, which I badly needed at the time.'

'Of course, of course,' Miles said hastily. 'Well, thanks a lot for your time. Sorry to drop in like this. Come on, Karen.'

I didn't move.

'Mr. Jones. How did you hear about the Dataplex gig?' I asked.

Leroy chuckled. 'You're probably not going to believe this, but it was one of those ads – you know: Earn up to $500 a week in your spare time, no selling, type of thing. At the time I was pretty hard up. Keisha's mom left her with me, I had to put her in day care and work two jobs just to keep food on the table and pay the car loan. Actually, if I remember correctly, somebody put a flier on my windshield. I came out of my counselor's office and there it was. See, it was tough times. I was on antidepressants and all that crap, I had to see a shrink but I couldn't afford him. I saw the ad and I thought, 'What the hell?''

I looked around the villa. It had been tastefully decorated. Everything was in the kind of understatement that you can only buy in SoHo, except for a giant framed poster advertising *Cookie Starfishes*.

Leroy sure wasn't depressed now.

Then something flashed in my head.

'Do you remember your counselor's name?'

He cocked his head. 'Yeah. Dr. Stengel. Good guy. Very sympathetic.'

Keisha's Shetland pony could be seen grazing outside. How many Dr. Stengels could there be in northern New Jersey?

'*Gunther* Stengel?' I asked.

'I think so . . . yeah. Some kind of German name, or Swedish or something. You know him?'

Everything was clicking now. I could just see Gunther sending his secretary out to put fliers on people's cars while he had them on his couch talking about their childhoods. It was one way to recruit nutcases.

Leroy Jones was watching me curiously. Shaken, I babbled a breathless response. 'No . . . not exactly . . . well, it all turned out OK for you. That's quite a story.'

'Yeah.' Leroy Jones grinned and sat back, relaxing. 'It turned out great. We're going into syndication and I'm looking at cable deals, maybe a movie. Who says art doesn't pay?'

'Too bad they had to kill you first,' I murmured without thinking. When I saw his face, I leaped to my feet, horrified. 'I'm sorry. I didn't mean that.'

Miles grabbed my arm. 'Cookie doesn't know what she's saying sometimes,' he said. 'Please excuse us.'

Now Leroy was seriously annoyed. He followed us to the door.

'What's all this about?' he shouted after us as we ran down the front lawn. 'Do you guys really work for *Rolling Stone*? Hey! I thought you said your name was Karen!'

'It's a conspiracy!' cried Miles, hitting the steering wheel. 'An attempt to dominate the commercial market. Mind control. Shit.'

'Mind control?' I said. 'Where do you get that?'

'Dataplex planted the idea for *Cookie Starfishes* in Leroy Jones, using music. I wonder where those original tapes are now?'

'Don't be ridiculous, Miles.'

He took his gaze off the road and stared at me. Usually *he*'s the one saying that to *me*.

'Well, how do you explain the connection?'

'I don't know,' I said. 'But I refuse to believe that Gunther is capable of performing mind control. He can't even get his dogs to listen to him. He's a good salesman but he's no Franz Mesmer.'

'Who?'

'The first hypnotist. The word 'mesmerize' comes from his name, didn't you know that? My mother, she was into all that stuff.'

'I should have known.'

'See, why would Dataplex plant an idea for a hit TV show in the mind of an unknown cartoonist? If they knew they had a hit show, they would have run with it themselves. And besides, if they already had the idea, it had to come from somewhere. The original creator would be bound to object and probably try to sue them. It's not plausible. It's not even plausible to imagine that, with a plot like you've described to me, *Cookie Starfishes* could be a hit show. I mean, who would predict that? It sounds totally stupid in theory.'

'It's totally stupid in reality, too,' Miles said. 'I watched it the other day, just out of curiosity. But I could look into the lawsuit angle. You never know.'

'No, Miles, you were right the first time. Dataplex are looking to *predict* what will be successful. They're running experiments to try to find a method of knowing in advance what horse to bet on. That's what my debriefings have been about. That's what they're using me for.'

'And what about *Cookie Starfishes*?'

'I think Leroy's like me. He connected with the Grid, too. Maybe it was through that song that was on the tape that I saw and he heard. The song that also turned out to be a surprise hit. It was a hit because it connects to something bigger, and that's why it inspired Leroy. See, Dataplex are trying to tap something. They *are* tapping something. But they don't

know what it is. The connection between me and Leroy isn't
Dataplex. It's the Grid.'

'The who?'

I tried to explain. I told him about the Grid, which led me
into Machine Front and their Third Wave of MFeels. He
knew vaguely about the golems from things I'd let drop
before, but I told him about Serge's daughters and how they
were one person spread over several bodies. I told him about
the scent language of the Grid.

But it didn't go down very well. I had never acually con-
fided in anyone what went on when I flew. It was top-secret
information: I was only supposed to talk about it to Gunther
when he debriefed me. And I had always believed Gunther
understood and respected what I was saying. Telling Miles
about the Grid felt like taking my clothes off in public.

'A luminous web? You mean like in *Tron*?' Miles said, per-
plexed.

I sighed.

'I wish I had your brains, Miles. Or I wish you had my
imagination. Because the way things are, I don't know how
we're going to put this together.'

'I don't wish I had your imagination,' Miles said darkly.
'Cookie, this Grid, whatever it is, isn't real. You know that,
right?'

'Is the stock market real? Is Winnie the Pooh real?'

'Yes, and no, respectively. You shouldn't have to ask me
these kinds of questions, Cookie.'

Miles wanted to hang out and argue some more, but I had to
be at the dojo. Today was the last practice session before
tomorrow's tournament and my first demonstration, and it
was also going to be Miss Cooper's test for nidan. She wasn't
the only one taking a test; half the dojo was up for promotion, but most of us would be tested in a large group. Miss

Cooper would perform solo, and she would have to spar with all the other black belts in the dojo – including some of the Okinawans.

When I entered the dressing room she and Gloria were both there. Miss Cooper was tying her dishevelled blonde hair back into a fresh ponytail.

'God, it's hot,' she said. 'I could drink a lake.'

'How's it going?'

'Oh, man, it's awesome. I've never been so tired in my whole life, but also, like, so inspired? Sensei Masunobu is the best. Look at my arms.'

She showed me her forearms. They were covered with black and blue contusions.

'Knocking-hands drill,' she said. 'It's a Chinese practice. Cool, huh?'

'What happened to your knuckles?' I said. They were completely skinned, bloody – a wreck.

'Makiwara. They do a lot more makiwara than we do.'

Gloria tut-tutted. 'You better be careful, hon. You can get calcium deposits from that, it's not good for your joints. Plus you could get an infection in there.'

'Pfff!' said Miss Cooper. 'This is real training. I've learned more in the past week than I learned in the past two years.'

Gloria sniffed. 'Yeah, well, just look at the Okinawans and then look at our great master.' Her voice dripped with sarcasm. 'Did you see him doing Sanchin this morning? He was wilting. He kept sneaking off to drink Sprite in his office. Did you see his belly? That man looks like a giant adenoid.'

'Shh!' Miss Cooper started to reprimand us, but Gloria and I were giggling so much that she let up with her posing. 'Actually, you have a point. I wish I could go train in Okinawa. They really teach you. Masunobu showed me a whole bunch of applications for Sanseiru – we never learned those.'

'I saw,' said Gloria tartly. 'They mostly seemed to involve dumping you on your ass and laughing.'

'They do laugh a lot,' Miss Cooper said.

'Yeah, they laugh at us,' countered Gloria. 'See what you missed, Cookie? Where you been, anyway?'

'I . . . uh . . . I didn't know there was anything going on this morning. I thought it was afternoon and evening, today.'

'Shihan mentioned it last night. I thought you knew.'

'Am I in trouble?'

'I doubt he even noticed you weren't here. He's too busy worrying about being demoted. Apparently the Okinawans don't like it that he's a seventh dan. He might have to take a test, too. I hope he does. He probably couldn't pass a black-belt test. He's an embarrassment.'

I had never heard this kind of talk before, and I didn't know what to make of it. What about all the secret techniques? What about all Shihan Norman's experience and knowledge and wisdom? I found myself wanting to defend him.

'I'm not sure about these Okinawans,' I said. 'They keep talking about propagating the system and spreading the word – they make it sound like a religion.'

'Maybe to them it is,' said Miss Cooper. 'Karate is very big on Okinawa. Shihan Hideki is a highly respected community leader.'

'Yeah, but he can party,' Gloria snorted. 'Did you see him last night?'

Apparently, after I'd left some of the Okinawans had come to Tony's looking for entertainment and Gloria and Miss Cooper had taken them out to a club. Miss Cooper cracked up, telling me.

'Master Hideki was wearing this sharkskin suit, and he got out on the dance floor and started boogying like John Travolta.'

'I saw you and Masunobu slow-dancing,' teased Gloria, elbowing Miss Cooper. 'You know he has a wife, right?'

'Of course I do! He's, like, at least forty. He showed me pictures of his kids. He's really sweet.'

'When he's not dumping you on the floor and giggling at your bruises.'

'They open doors for you,' defended Miss Cooper. 'They don't let you sit down without pulling out your chair. And they're high-level masters. It's really strange.'

Gloria said, 'I wonder how high-level Masunobu was when he had his face in your tits last night on the dance floor!'

We all cracked up.

'Come on, he's not that short!' Miss Cooper protested.

One of the Okinawans barked something in Japanese from the training floor and we all dashed out, bowed, and scurried into position on the floor. We were about to be put through our paces again.

What stands out in my mind about that day was the way Miss Cooper performed her naginata kata during the test. In the sparring, she was more or less humiliated by the Okinawans. Whenever she tried to punch one of them, the guy would just ignore the punch, pick her up and toss her, then laugh. There wasn't much that she could do. She only weighs about 115 pounds, tops. She'd bow, stand up, be allowed to try again. I knew she could kick Masunobu in the head if she felt like it – she had a lightning-fast roundhouse – and at least score some kind of point, but she wasn't allowed to. The Okinawans frown on kicks higher than knee level as being too unrealistic and risky, and they don't allow them in sparring. She wasn't helped by the fact that the dojo floor was swimming in sweat and she kept slipping. Her opponents never seemed to slip because they never seemed to move. They just stood rooted to the spot and waited for her to try something. Every time she had to block one of their punches I could see the pain she was in from her ruined forearms. She had to fight one black belt after the other without a break, and by the end of it she could hardly get herself off the floor.

Still, after she was excused to change into her naginata costume, she returned looking really excellent with a white headband tied across her forehead and those wide-legged black pants on her legs, carrying the ancient weapon. Her kata was amazing, the best I'd ever seen her do, and Masunobu Hideki nodded his approval at the end. All of us broke out cheering, only to be shushed censoriously by Shihan Norman, who looked angry about something. Immediately after the session he disappeared into his office. The Okinawans ignored him. They seemed to think he was some kind of joke – which, frankly, he was.

Afterward a whole pile of us, Americans and Okinawans together, stormed Pizza Hut and pretty much destroyed every scrap of food they had. I use the term 'we' loosely. I ate some fruit I'd brought with me, and I nibbled some of Gloria's garlic bread. I couldn't face anything more substantial.

'I'm really proud of you,' said Gloria. 'You've stuck with the pact.'

'Yeah, too bad I can't afford a new car now,' I said glumly. I looked at the pizza, wishing I could remember how much I used to like it because now I'd just as soon have eaten a rat.

'Things will pick up,' Gloria said. 'Gunther's going to come to his senses any day now. He's not exactly batting a thousand without you.'

I didn't pursue it. I was afraid I'd start crying and tell Gloria everything. Maybe she even knew. She probably did. They all thought I was a cuckoo bird.

After Pizza Hut we went to the Hilton Hotel where the

Okinawans were staying and drank in the hotel bar. It was noisy and crowded, but the air-conditioning was powerful and it was nice to sit in the cool darkness and pretend I didn't have to go back to the Grid.

Troy and Gloria left together; Troy was tanked and Gloria was going to drive him home. 'You got to come in and tell Diane it was your fault,' he slurred at Gloria.

'Yeah, sure, I pried your mouth open and poured eight beers down it, tough guy.'

Miss Cooper waded across from the bar to me. She had a drink in her hand and a huge smile on her face. Just looking at her bloody, skinned knuckles made me wince.

'Are you coming up to Masunobu's room? It's getting too crowded here and the prices are ridiculous.'

I pretended to yawn.

'I'm really whacked. I want to be on form for tomorrow, so I'm gonna go. Don't drink too much, OK? We're going pocketbook-and-broom, not the Fifty-two Steps of the Drunken Monk.'

'I'm not drinking at all,' Miss Cooper said. 'This is tonic water. Don't you want to come up for a little while? It's only ten o'clock.'

I looked at the scene. Most of our group had left. Masunobu Hideki and about five or six black belts, most of them from other dojos around the country, were getting ready to repair to Masunobu's room with a boom box and a case of beer. Masunobu was snapping his fingers to Van Halen and the Americans were laughing and playing air guitar. I felt no urge to stay. How much time can you stand to spend with a bunch of drunk white guys who think Eddie Van Halen is a musical god but Prince is just some weirdo in eyeliner?

'I'll see you tomorrow,' I said.

'Are you sure? It'll be fun – come on, Cookie!'

Miss Cooper's eyes sparkled. She was excited, in her element. I hated to let her down.

'You did great today,' I said. 'Congratulations on your test.'

She laughed nervously. 'I don't know if I passed yet.'

'You deserve the promotion. Everybody's really proud of you. Now go have fun. I got to drag my big old butt home and get into a lukewarm bath.'

I went out into stifling heat, a barrage of cricket music and the smell of car exhaust off Route 23. Every muscle in my body was heavy and dragging, but my head was strangely alive.

I knew I wouldn't get into a lukewarm bath. I might not even sleep.

follow the yellow brick road

It takes Joanne Klaski three days to follow the yellow brick road of dead Grid to N-Ridge, and during that time she encounters not one single golem. That fact in itself is spooky. Klaski is an easy target. She does not move fast. Although she is using the structured area that borders the dead zone to guide her, she's climbing through an extremely high region in the Grid because she's desperate for radio contact with . . . well, with anybody. The upper Grid is a place of storms and visual incoherence, and she's not a swift mover even at the best of times. Still: there are no golems to be seen.

Presumably they have all gone to destroy Major Galante's party. Not a cheery thought.

The Swatch works some of the time, but Galante's receiver is set to messaging only and Machine Front merely confirm Major Galante's orders that Klaski is to go to N-Ridge. The Swatch responds to queries about war status and golem movements with channel-clogging quantities of statistics that Klaski doesn't know how to interpret. As a lowly lieutenant, she doesn't qualify to have a Dante-equivalent in her Swatch, and without Dante's personality and higher-reasoning components, Machine Front is about as interactive as a brick wall. So Klaski doctors Gossamer religiously, charges her in the Grid, and asks her to fly. Gossamer cannot travel more than a few yards before pancaking onto the canopy or spiraling out of control.

You are wanting to give up. Piggybacking a good-as-dead soldier on a futile mission is a form of torture. It's all you can do to stay on the nex, and you only do it out of hope that one day Gossamer will be able to fly for real, leave Klaski behind, and . . . well, you don't really know what you will do then. You just know that you are slipping into a depression because you can't do anything for yourself.

Then Klaski comes to the crest of the ridge, finds a high, strong branch that isn't dangerously charged, and takes a look around.

You can hear a little rattle in Klaski's chest when she flattens herself and lets her weight go into the Grid. She lowers her belly against the branch and dangles her arms and legs, a would-be puma in the jungle. She sets her cheek down. The Grid is vibrating like a bass amp. The sound fills the spaces where Klaski's lumbar spine articulates. It sets the jelly of her flesh trembling.

When her head goes down on the branch, you can see what's up ahead.

There is the dead zone of the Grid, scoring the luminescence of the Grid like a slash made with a graphite pencil. It can be seen stretching away into the distance.

And just ahead, instead of terminating in wild Grid, it ends in a man-made wall.

'Oh God,' Klaski breathes. 'I hope you're not jerking me around here.'

The logic mines lie there in front of you: no well, no electricity, no tangle of visual confusion. Just a rough gray pit, slaggy and wasted. There is a retaining wall, looks like a mixture of barbed wire and Play-Doh, with orange and blue wires protruding at intervals where they connect to rusty towers in the exact shape of giant D batteries. The nearest of these oozes something black from its positive terminal and gives off a zingy, ionic odor. The Grid doesn't cross this wall.

Judging by the gross creatures that tend to come up out of the well, not to mention its nasty organic smell, you would expect the well to be all sumpy and sludgy after it was drained. You'd expect to find bones and colorful, maggoty lumps of half-digested things down there. And the mine-pit is nothing more or less than what's left after the Grid has been shorn away and the well drained. But there is nothing lifelike about the pit. It's ashen-gray, a tumbled rubblescape of irregular crevices and mounds, bereft of geometry and aesthetic continuity. It's ugly in a point-less kind of way.

There is some kind of pumping station on the other side of the pit. It consists of pipes and walkways and smokestacks, all cobbled together out of flimsy aluminum and plastic. It looks like something out of that Pink Floyd movie, the one you walked out of leaving Jim Szabo alone with a bucket of popcorn and a hard-on, the one where people went into meat grinders.

Various other buildings huddle in a rough circle around the sealed pit. But there is no activity across the wall at all. No dust, no noise, no flashing lights. No voices. And, to judge by Klaski's fruitless efforts to communicate with N-Ridge via Swatch, no signal, either.

Strange. You know Major Galante well enough to expect that, in the absence of a stockpile of logic bullets, her first priority would be to get the mines operational again in case the missing logic was never found and the work had to start over. But noth-ing moves here.

Major Galante is still incommunicado. Klaski calls X and informs them that the mines are silent. Eventually, Machine Front routes her to an actual person in the control tower. There is no image – too much interference – but, judging from the voice, Klaski is talking to a male.

'We're having the same problem,' he says. 'We lost contact two days ago.'

'How do I get in, then?'

'Do you see any golems on the inside? We can't pick up anything, but naturally golems don't show up on satellite.'

'None that I can see,' answered Klaski.

'OK, well, can you point your flier at it and send us pictures?'

So you find yourself being used as a kind of Polaroid camera, and you don't like it. Klaski holds you up and asks you to send the images. The control officer starts yakking monotonously, something about processing and analyzing the footage. Klaski breaks in.

'Listen, I need *help*. When are you going to send help?'

'There is no more human help to be sent. I'm sitting up here on a stack of hardware waiting for Major Galante to get the logic bullets, and I can't send her to the mines because we already know the logic isn't there. She's going on a sweep south of you.'

'That's crazy! She should come get *me!* I'm the one she wants.'

'Calm down, Lieutenant. You might have to sit tight for a while. All the fliers have been recalled for reprocessing for the Third Wave. However, we have a large contingent of new weaponry waiting at X.'

'How's that going to help me?'

'As soon as Major Galante has completed her mission, we can use MaxFacts to detonate the N-valley area specified by Captain Serge in her final orders. Once that's cleared of Grid we—'

Klaski is starting to panic. 'No! That detonation zone is where *I* am, you idiots! You have to tell Major Galante to come and get me now. She wouldn't listen to me. She's got it all wrong!'

She's panting and shouting into the Swatch. It's obvious that she isn't making her point to the control-tower guy, but she's too upset to speak slowly and clearly and in words of one syllable, as Control Tower Guy seems to require.

'I know it's no fun for you, Klaski. It isn't fun here at X, either, but count yourself lucky to be alive. Hang tight. We have only a handful of logic bullets we can use to prime the MFeels. We can't do anything big until Major Galante recovers the main stash or the mines produce a new batch. When the MFeels get into action, we can get control of any golem hot spots and get the remaining humans, yourself included, out. We have to take care of the big picture first.'

'Then come get me!' cries Klaski. 'I've got the logic bullets. I've got them. Send a damn stretch limo up here and get me!'

'I don't copy.'

'Yes, you do – I said, I've got the logic bullets.'

She drags out a logic bullet and shows it to the Swatch.

'Hold the line,' says the man tersely. He comes back only moments later. 'Machine analysis indicates your chances are better inside the mines. Get yourself into the perimeter asap. If you can't get their attention any other way, then use one of the breaches in the wall or blow your way in if necessary. We will dispatch Third Wave aerial support to you immediately.'

'Oh, what a relief,' Klaski sighs, shutting the Swatch. 'I thought he was never going to get it.'

People always talk to themselves.

'OK, come on, pick yourself up and let's do it. Just one more thing to do and then you'll be safe. I bet they have food in there, too.'

Getting across the fence to the pit doesn't look like it's going to be a big deal. There is at least one breach-point where the cement has been inexpertly repaired – when you check your flight files from Galante's assault you are able to orient yourself based on your recordings of where the wall was breached during the last mission you flew over N-Ridge. Klaski has a good bootload of charges and Lewis programmed the timer back at X. Klaski monkeys her way to the nearest scrap of wall, plants four charges, hooks up the timer, and puts the second side of *Synchronicity* on her Walkman. She sets herself twenty minutes. Then she scoots. When she gets far enough away, she ties herself to a branch, just in case.

The explosion wipes out every sound except the slinking bass-line of 'Tea in the Sahara'. A jolt goes through the Grid and one of Klaski's bungee cords springs loose. It recoils and snaps her in the face, just missing her eye.

She doesn't cry. That's a big effort, and she wastes some more time there, pouting and hissing in self-pity. Crying would do her more good, but you figure that she's probably never been much good at crying without an audience.

She starts moving forward. The smoke has cleared and the heat from the blast has dissipated into the remains of the wall, the Grid, and the air itself.

Nothing stirs inside the perimeter.

Klaski climbs through the hole.

The place looks like a construction site on lunch break. There are diggers and cranes, dozers, backhoes, dumptrucks, you name it. They have been left at odd angles, some half-buried, others with doors open.

Every so often there's a burn scar. You remember these: they are the remnants of the personnel who served under Gonzalez. Klaski almost steps on one, then leaps back when she realizes what it is. She trips, falls backward, lands on her ass in the dust. There is something wrapped around her boots.

'What the—?'

She pulls off a strand of what looks like fishing line. 'What, is this place booby-trapped?'

She runs the Swatch and makes another futile attempt to reach the control-tower guy.

ALL LINES BUSY, says the Swatch. MAJOR MFEEL LANDING OPERATION IN PROGRESS. NO NON-ESSENTIAL COMMUNICATIONS PERMITTED.

'But this *is* essential!' Klaski rants, scrambling to her feet and untangling herself. She cups her hands around her mouth.

'Hello? Anybody home? Hello, HUMANS?'

Her voice echoes off the metal of the nearest building, a Quonset hut painted fluorescent orange and with cat's eyes embedded in the roof. Behind her, the Grid hums a warped echo.

She tugs the line, then starts to follow it. Soon it loops and crosses over another of the same, only to disappear under the dust and stones. Klaski moves with exaggerated care. She tiptoes towards the nearest piece of equipment, a crane. The access ladder has been melted into a lump, and she has to clamber up the crane's tread to reach the open door and then swing herself into the operator's seat. There is a set of noise-reducing headphones, a clipboard, and a computer printing outlet with a scroll of dusty paper spilling from it. The writing is faded but it looks like a blueprint. She punches up the MF com center.

'Hello?'

The lights are on.

'How do I reboot?' she mutters. You've heard Miles say the same thing, but you've never understood what it means. Klaski looks under the dash. That's when you see a fat bundle of the filaments, just like the one Klaski tripped over outside. It looks like a cross between the clear tubes they use in hospitals for Ivs and stuff, and fishing line. It's neatly bound together and coiled, and it seems to merge seamlessly with the structure of the crane.

When you look closely you can see pellets of something radiant shooting from the machines, through the tubes. Pulsing, but without a detectable pattern.

Klaski grunts and fiddles with things in the confined space. She bangs her head, curses, and starts to back out. Then she must see the filaments, too.

'That's weird,' she says, fingering them. 'When's that damned aerial getting here?'

She goes outside and squints into the sky. Nothing. Then she looks around at the nearby buildings. Besides the Quonset hut, there are a couple of sheds and some flattened tents that look as if they've been rolled over by Major Galante's convoy.

'Where's the actual mine?'

You know where it is. It's behind the Quonset hut, and there is a ramp going down into the earth. The doors were sealed last time you were up here.

The filaments are draped across the camp like spiderwebs, connecting pieces of machinery to each other and to the ground and buildings and perimeter walls. Some of the cables are so fine that they are only visible when the light shines behind them. Klaski picks her way across the open area of the compound and tiptoes into the Quonset hut. Her breathing is loud in the enclosed space, and her voice sounds sandy and loaded with treble.

'Hello? People? Yo!'

Stillness. There are offices in here, a lab at one end with its doors security-shielded, and a series of locked, environmentally controlled storage units. She goes to each unit and alters the pigmentation on the door until she can see through to the interior. Evidently there is nothing of interest until she reaches the fourth door.

Klaski recoils, backs up, then goes back for a longer look. Then she turns and walks away quickly. When she turns you see that the unit contains a steel table with a lumpy-looking body bag on it.

Klaski starts going through the offices, but she's nervous and random in her behavior. She rifles desks and spins computer monitors on their flexible necks, but she doesn't take the time to really find anything out. She has no method. Her breathing is accelerated; you can hear its hiss in the filters. She is panicking, as usual.

She finds some notes in Major Galante's handwriting scrawled with a red Bic pen. They're informal; almost personal. It looks like Galante was drafting a memo to whoever was taking over from her at the mines. There are orders about security and wall-repair, and suggestions for how to organize the team and which machines to deploy underground, in order to get more logic bullets. In the last paragraph, all pretext of officialspeak goes out the window.

The mines don't look right to me. I don't think any of this equipment has been used recently, and I'm not even 100% convinced there are *any logic bullets. There's no sign of metals extraction but there are indications of the Grid invading the camp. I'd like to seal this place down and get out. Watch yourselves, and keep an eye on coms equipment at all times. The Grid knows it can cripple us by sabotaging that.*

Klaski shudders and looks around, rubbing her arms like she's chilly.

All you can think is how the body bag doesn't make sense. This isn't a war that features people's bodies being returned to their relatives draped in flags. In the First Wave, after it was clear what the well did to dead bodies, soldiers were put in grave balloons for later pickup; but inevitably logistics failures meant that those pickups couldn't be made, and some of the grave balloons eventually got tangled in the Grid and ended up in the well. So the current policy is on-the-spot incineration to prevent golem reproduction.

Major Galante wouldn't have been careless enough to leave a corpse lying around.

Klaski goes into the coms room but nothing is coming up on any of the scopes but noise. There are piles of printouts lying around; some of them seem to detail the takeover by Major Galante, while others are copies of correspondence with MF and the analyses that MF has done to predict the outcomes of various strategies in recovering the missing logic bullets. The numbers recommend that Galante leave behind only a small crew to reopen the mines and start getting more logic, which is supposedly what she did. MF was going to take care of everything else remotely.

But the crew are nowhere to be seen and the coms aren't working, and Galante's warnings to her successor seem to have done no good. The place has a deserted air. Creepy. There is a small refrigerator and the milk in it is sour. Klaski finds a plastic-wrapped ham sandwich and eats it. You don't want to think what it tastes like.

Klaski starts fiddling with controls but gets nowhere. She shouts into her Swatch.

'What am I supposed to do, stand out on the tarmac and wave my arms at the sky? Do you guys know what's going on up here? Where are the crew?'

No answer.

'Typical Grid. Interference. I have to get out of here.'

There doesn't seem to be anything obviously wrong with the com system.

'I wonder if somebody retuned the satellite so it's pointing the wrong way.'

She starts looking at the direct radio links to see if she can pick up some signal there, but the power supply has failed. She drops to her knees and opens the console.

'Why can't I be like Lewis? I wish I could fix stuff.'

Filaments. Just like in the equipment outside. Transparent cabling lies in tangles and nested coils, invading the com system like a tumor in someone's guts.

Klaski leaps back, scrubbing her gloved hands on her battle-suited thighs.

'I need a com system. This is crazy. Where is everybody? What happened up here?'

Pause. Sound of Klaski breathing. You assume she is thinking.

'Come on, Goss, let's go. Let's go outside and see if we can fly you up like a flare.'

But she doesn't go straight out. She goes back to the refrigeration unit containing the body bag. She stands there. Checks the readouts.

The unit is still functioning. Klaski checks her suit filters anyway.

'It better not smell bad in there. Shouldn't have eaten that sandwich.'

She goes in.

On the steel table there is a green manila folder beside a bottle of spray disinfectant and a roll of breath mints with the brand name carefully blacked out. There is a post-it note on the folder.

Apparent indigene. When alive, specimen not picked up on photographic equipment. Photographs and autopsy notes by Dr. A. Gonzalez.

Paper-clipped to the rest of the notes are some Polaroids of a child's body. It looks flat and pathetic, and not immediately rec-ognizable as one of the feral children Klaski was so scared of, although it's hard to imagine what else it might be.

Klaski looks at the black bag in silence. The zipper is partly open. She pulls on latex gloves, then puts one of her gloved hands over her mouth as she slips the zipper down a little more.

And a little more.

You can hear the zipper going down, but you can't see what's inside. There's a puff of air scented with plastic, and Klaski jumps back, letting out a gasp. She turns her body slightly and you see that the bag is empty. There was nothing in it but air, and the pressure of Klaski's hand has forced this out.

'It isn't here. It's frozen. Major Gonzalez sent it back to X for study.'

The words are spoken by a single voice, iterated from several mouths, and they come from the main work area of the Quonset hut. Gossamer's eyes count eight girls standing just outside the lab doorway, replicas of the Polaroid – but very much alive. They are loosely grouped just inside the door of the Quonset hut. Silhouetted in the Gridlight of the door itself is the outline of a golem in battle armor. You recognize the figure.

Klaski stands motionless for a couple of beats, still looking down at the empty body bag.

She turns. Sees them. And looks around in a panic. No escape. She can only go towards them, and they are blocking the door.

'I wasn't . . . I didn't . . .'

'Arla Gonzalez killed me,' one of them says. 'She felt bad about it.'

The same sly smile spreads across all their faces. The words spread among them, passed like a hot potato.

'Not bad enough, though. Not bad enough to give me back to the well. Now I am broken. Forever. Machine Front has one of my bodies. Do you know what that means?'

'Um . . . not really.' Klaski smiles a nervous charm-school smile.

'Who wants to live with part of you missing? I have a hole in me now and it won't be healed until that body goes back into the Grid, or is destroyed. But Machine Front have taken it and will plunder its essence. And there's nothing I can do. I guess I got Arla into some trouble, after that. She wasn't strong, you know. Yes, you do know, don't you?'

Each sentence is spoken by a different girl; but they follow on seamlessly from one another, as if the speaker were a ventriloquist projecting her voice into different locations.

Klaski is shaking so hard that your vision jumps.

'We're trying to decide what to do with the place,' say the girls, gesturing around the interior of the abandoned hut as if they were talking about a house that needed renovation. Again, the commentary bounces from one body to the other. 'It has potential, don't you think? But what we could really use is another sample of Earth hardware. Something different from what we've already got. The cranes and backhoes were useful in helping decode the mechanical properties of the MaxFact, but if you've seen one of these machines, you've seen them all.'

They are eyeing Klaski acquisitively. Klaski proffers her Walkman.

'This is all I got. Seriously. Except breathing filters and you don't need those, right? And the Swatch is broken, trust me you don't want that.'

'Actually,' says a girl, 'I was looking at your cape.'

'My which? *Oh!*' Klaski's fingers grip Gossamer's edges and pull you closer around her shoulders. You've got one eye full on the girls now, and one looking out of Klaski's back. Confusing: like looking around a corner with a mirror.

'It's just a . . . it's damaged.' You can feel the tension in Klaski's body. You wonder if she's capable of fighting as ruthlessly on your behalf as she was when defending her own life. Probably not.

'Do you need help?' ask the girls.

'No, no, I'm fine. I'm just waiting . . . I'm OK, thanks.'

'Because we heard you talking to your people. They're sending some kind of transport for you.'

Klaski seems encouraged by this.

'Do you . . . do you know what happened to the other people who were up here? Did the . . . did the golems get them?'

'No, they went into the mine, looking for logic bullets.'

'Oh, uh . . . that's great. Well, I guess I'll go look for them, then. Do they, uh, do they know you're wandering around here?'

Klaski's shifting her weight from foot to foot, seeking escape. But it's no use. The battle-suited golem is still blocking the door.

'We waited until Major Galante left,' the girls tell Klaski, bouncing the words back and forth between them. 'Then we brought golems up through the mines and took control. We have linked the MaxFact to the logic mines, you see. It was a natural progression.'

You don't think Klaski is really taking this in. Why are the girls talking over her head? Are they talking to *you*?

'We started the golem attack in the hope that it would provoke the launch of a MaxFact, and it did. We had been preparing the capture of the missile for some time. But then Arla Gonzalez killed one of us and took the body, and she sent it to X for study. We think Machine Front have been trying to use our body to develop the logic drives in the Third Wave.'

'The logic that Gonzalez had,' Klaski said.

'Yes. She saved it so that she could negotiate with Machine Front. She knew they wanted her dead, because of her role in our death . . . and life.'

'But what happened to the people? Major Galante left staff behind. Where is everybody? And what are all those tubes out there?'

'We brought Major Galante's staff down into the mines, and from there to the underlying structure. They won't be coming out.'

'Oh. Um. You sealed off the mine? With people inside?'

'It's not a Virginia coal mine. It's not like that at all. They aren't suffocating in there.'

No, you think. It's probably worse, whatever's happening to them.

'I bet you're just saying that,' Klaski says. 'And what about those wire-thingies? The fishing line?'

'The fishing line isn't for catching fish. It's for interpreting information. Dragging all that heavy machinery into the well wouldn't be practical. You see, you mine for logic and the Grid mines you. It's a two-way street. That's the nature of the Grid. It operates according to an acausal connecting principle.'

'A *who*?'

'It connects things, but not according to the paradigms you would recognize. You can only relate to cause and effect. Subject and object. The Grid doesn't work like that.'

'Um,' says Klaski. 'Do you think we could have this conversation outside? See, I'm expecting a lift any minute.'

She makes a whirlybird motion with her forefinger.

'Oh. Serge will be disappointed. She wanted us to take you down to the city.'

The golem standing in the doorway now steps inside and folds its arms across its chest. Klaski still doesn't recognize Serge. Maybe she's distracted by the fact that a group of battle-suited male golems are now walking through the outer door of the Quonset hut. Klaski startles, inhaling so sharply that the air shrieks in her throat. The golems take up positions at the other exits, leaving the main doors open. Outside, many more golems are visible.

'What city?'

'The city we made from the MaxFact and the logic mines. The synchronicity.'

'Haha, very cute. Here, you want it?' And she pulls her Walkman off her belt and holds it out. The girls cock their heads in unison. You feel Klaski's pulse thunder in her neck.

'I'll self-immolate,' Klaski threatens. 'Just like the others. You'd better stand back if you don't want to get blown away.'

And she gropes in her pockets for charges.

The nearest girl glances over her shoulder.

'Serge has some questions.'

'Don't talk to me about Serge. I'm not going in the well, just you forget it.'

'Are you coming with me or do you want to stay here with the golems?'

And the children turn and walk out the main door.

Klaski waits a couple of beats and then bolts after them.

'I'm coming, see, so tell them to keep their distance.'

The girls don't say anything. They flash the same smile over their collective shoulders, though. Serge falls in behind Klaski. Outside are many more golems. They all start to walk across the compound, heading for the mine shaft. Klaski looks up. You can see the sky; there is no sign of an aerial carrier of any stripe.

Klaski stops suddenly and grabs you by the edges. She untangles you from her battle armor. Then you feel yourself thrown in the air like pizza dough, and Gossamer's skin feels all electric and alive for the first time since Arla's crossbow bolt brought you down.

'Fly, Gossamer, fly! Get help! Go to X and tell them! I've got the you-know-whats! Tell them to come get me!'

Serge leaps forward and tries to grab you, but Klaski is too quick. Other golems move in on Klaski, too. She shrinks below you, waving her arms wildly from beneath a football-scrimmage of golems.

The air flows over you, drags you upward, and you are free. You float into a feeling of perfection.

It's just like old times. On high, you have the glory. You own the sky. Gossamer aches with the effort; even that is a kind of pleasure.

But there's more than poetry up here. The transmissions of Machine Front come banging into your ears again, reporting the arrival of the Third Wave, calling you back to X with all urgency.

Below, Klaski is allowed to get to her feet; but now golems mass around her and the girls, pushing them towards the mine, until all you can see is the crowd of them, big and dead and numerous, carrying along the smaller figures like a tide. They go behind the Quonset hut and open the doors of the mine with a squealing sound. Then they disappear into a hole in the ground.

between a pathological phenomenon and a breakfast cereal

I found myself watching a 9 Lives cat-food commercial.

I straightened, rubbing my eyes. I was supposed to be looking at the static on Channel 1 . . . but instead I was watching the late-night movie on Channel 11. *The China Syndrome*. Hurriedly I switched back to static.

'Rocky,' I said. 'Have you been playing with the TV?'

He was lying on top of the warm console with one paw draped over the side. Rocky always liked watching baseball. My mom used to put the Yankees on Channel 11 for him and he'd bat the TV ball with his paw whenever he saw a pitch go in.

'Don't tell me you know how to turn on Channel 11,' I said. 'But the Yankee game is over. It's almost midnight.'

I got a little choked up there. Poor Rocky. Mom never told me he knew how to work the TV. He must be missing her.

Not that he showed it. He jumped into my lap and howled.

'Go away,' I said. 'You have plenty of food. And you don't even like 9 Lives.'

Nine lives, I thought, following Rocky into the kitchen. Serge's daughters had nine lives, and one of them was gone.

I opened some Fancy Feast for Rocky. Nebbie materialized from out of the chaos and spat at him. Absently, I broke up the ensuing scuffle with my foot. I had started wearing my mother's Snoopy slippers and Nebbie was afraid of them.

I thought:

You know what, those logic bullets don't look like bullets at all. They look like eggs.

Little metal eggs.

Eggs laid by a mechanical chicken.

Which came first, the chicken or the—

No, that was too simplistic. But . . .

Synchronicity. An acausal connecting principle.

I might not be able to watch TV, but you'd have to be blind, deaf and dumb not to know about that video with three bleach-blond guys in raggedy clothes on a junk heap.

I thought:

IS MY WHOLE LIFE GOING TO TURN OUT TO BE A BAD JOKE?

I dragged out a few of Mom's books and found some stuff on Carl Jung. What a weird guy. But reading psychological theories felt like a dead end. I was too afraid that I'd find out I *was* nuts, and then where would I be?

OK, I thought. *Let's see if we can put something together*.

The girls must represent some aspect of Grid intelligence, because they seemed able to control the golems. They staged the first golem raid on the logic mines. But in the process they lost one of their own number, and Dr. Gonzalez, recognizing the corpse as the product of one of her own *Island of Dr. Moreau* experiments and a potential biological bridge between the Grid and humanity, went straight to Machine

Front with the new information. She even sent them the corpse as proof that the Grid could make more than just zombie-like golems.

Machine Front made no effort to change its posture. It launched the MaxFact, but the missile didn't wipe out the mines because the girls had planned to capture it all along. This left the mines aswarm with golems and all the equipment and personnel at risk of assimilation into the well.

Gonzalez followed the necessary procedures and ordered a self-destruct for her team. But she didn't follow the order herself. She grabbed the logic bullets and took off into the Grid alone.

Meanwhile, the MaxFact went into the well, and the girls began to unpack it. They unpacked the obvious, causal associations first . . . and this process destroyed the Grid in a strip leading to the logic mines, while at the same time altering the Grid's structure in the areas adjacent to the dead zone. Making that structure more Earthlike.

At the same time, the golems (or was it the girls? Or the Grid? What was the difference, anymore?) took control of the mines and the humans couldn't get the logic bullets they so desperately needed for the Third Wave. It was a standoff.

Then Serge found Gonzalez still alive.

Gonzalez believed that MF were the source of all evil. She had no intention of giving them the logic bullets. For their part, the girls and the golems seemed to protect her. But for all her willingness to experiment with others, she was afraid to go into the well itself.

After the MaxFact had unraveled itself into a dream city, the girls began to link it to the logic mines. And – evidently – this was how it became the SynchroniCity, better known as a hit record. Because if we were talking about causality, this linkup between the MaxFact and the mines was the point where causality seemed to break down.

Because:

The logic bullets weren't bullets. The mines weren't a case of the colonists raping the planet. The Grid was eating the mining equipment even as it produced logic bullets. Which looked like eggs – to me, anyway. And which had been stored by Dr. Gonzalez in the well, floating like frog spawn, soaking up the Grid's essence.

So the raped planet produced seed. Rape. Seed. Rapeseed.

This word was vaguely familiar, so I looked it up and found out it was the old term for canola oil. Low in cholesterol.

I thought:

Should we check Gunther's ad base to see if canola oil is a product being pushed? I'M TOTALLY PARANOID NOW. I don't know what means which.

Besides, I hated myself for thinking this way or even using the rape analogy to think about the Grid. It was the old 'Did she ask for it?' excuse. Or – and speaking of Channel 11, Toyota *were* the official sponsors of the NY Yankees and the Toyota slogan was *You asked for it, you got it: Toyota.* So for all I knew, I'd picked up the whole idea during the commercial breaks for the Yankee game that had preceded *The China Syndrome.*

Which brought me right back to my problem of what to believe in – my own eyes, or not?

And anyway, leaving the Police out of it, there were other interpretations of the unpacked MaxFact meeting up with the logic mines. The term SynchroniCity could also be taken to mean an attempt to unify two kinds of thought: human thought, and Grid thought. To synchronize watches. And then to build this meeting-of-the-minds in physical form. So you could walk around inside the conceptual possibilities.

But thinking about this made me woozy, like quadratic equations in tenth grade. Too much like hard work.

OK: back to the facts.

At around the time Serge and Gonzalez encountered each other in the Grid, Galante recaptured the mines for MF. But the logic bullets were gone, and as soon as Galante went off to look for them, the personnel she left behind were trapped inside the mines – which were now a part of the SynchroniCity. Elsewhere, Serge was betrayed by Gonzalez, and went into the well alive.

Where she was now having a belated stab at motherhood, the only problem being that her offspring were not human.

Klaski of all people had gone in the well and come out again, apparently unchanged, and now intended to use the logic bullets to bargain for her own life. The Third Wave MFeels (possibly incorporating data mysteriously gained during examination of the dead girl's body? Was that even possible?) were waiting to launch against and destroy whole regions of the Grid, including the SynchroniCity, in response to Serge's own orders. Except Serge had captured Klaski and her intentions did not look good.

Whose side to be on?

It was all so ugly and unfathomable.

Lucky for me, I've never been one of those people who remember their dreams or I'd have been afraid to go to bed. By the time I turned off all the equipment and got into bed, it was only a few hours before dawn.

When my alarm went off, I felt like a rusty crane from N-Ridge. I padded barefoot down to the laundry room in my building's basement to drag my gi out of the washing machine, where I'd shoved it the night before. Someone had already started another load of clothes, and my gi was spread across the top of the dryer. It was nearly dry, but creased as hell. I took it upstairs and plugged in the iron. In the steam that rose off the ironing board I tried to send messages to my various body parts to get ready for the pocketbook-and-broom demonstration. I wasn't worried about my kata – I knew it wasn't very good, but I wouldn't forget the moves. I wasn't worried about sparring, either. We wear gloves and shin protectors and I'd promised myself I wouldn't sweep anybody and jump on them, no matter what names they called me. I'd be Bushido Girl. If I lost, I lost.

But I was deeply afraid I'd crack up laughing in the middle of pocketbook-and-broom and walk away from Mr. Evanovich even as he was hurling himself through the air to fake being thrown by me. Not that I couldn't throw him. He was only a small guy and I'm a big woman, which made the whole exercise even more absurd. As if some geeky little civil engineer like Mr.Evanovich – brown belt or not – was going to come up to a big sister like me at a bus stop and try to rob me! It was pure comedy.

'Just get through this, Cookie,' I told myself as I showed Rocky that he had the same cat food as Nebbie. 'You can quit the team after today.'

I was a little late arriving at Passaic High School and the tournament was already under way. There were hordes of people wearing all different gis and patches. Kids everywhere. In the gymnasium, different rings had been set up with corner chairs for the judges, and the stage had been laid out with all kinds of bricks and boards and other equipment for the demonstrations. The stands rang with the talk of the crowd.

I watched people warming up as I made my way through the throng and I couldn't help thinking they all looked like dufuses. How could anybody be so stupid as to practice a kata that looks like *that*? I found myself thinking, more than once. Or: why do they put their hands in front of their foreheads when they bow? *Duh, that's lame.*

Maybe they thought the same about us. But of course they would have been wrong. What we do is *real.*

Gloria hailed me. 'I'm so nervous about the sparring,' she said. 'I wish I could just enter kata. Did you see some of the girls in our division? They look like mooses.'

I craned my neck. 'There's no contact, is there?'

'No, only tagging each other. But still, they're scary.'

'You stand a really good chance in kata,' I said. 'Where's Miss Cooper?'

'That's what everybody wants to know.'

Then we spotted Shihan Norman.

'Excuse me, Shihan,' Gloria said, and we both bowed as he turned to us.

'Hello, ladies.'

'We were just looking for Miss Cooper – we wanted to say good luck on the demonstration.'

He frowned. 'She couldn't make it.'

'Couldn't make it? What happened? Is she sick?'

He looked uncomfortable. 'She's having some personal problems.'

Gloria and I exchanged shocked glances. Tanya, miss a demonstration? *This* demonstration, the day after her test? The day after the greatest day of her life?

'But who's doing pocketbook-and-broom?' I blurted.

'Mrs. Canalletto is going to fill in. She's been practicing the moves with Miss Knight. Now, I need you to go help Mr. Juarez organize the kids. Make sure they've tied their belts right and there are no runny noses, OK? Now if you girls will excuse me, I have to go talk to Master Hideki.'

We bowed to Shihan Norman again and he nodded back, then walked off.

'Do you ever get tired of brown-nosing this guy and calling him Shihan?' I said.

Gloria giggled. 'If he gets demoted we'll just call him

Sensei. So what's with Tanya? I wonder if she's just hung over from the party last night.'

'She wasn't drinking when I left. Maybe I should have stayed. It seemed like she wanted me to, somehow.'

Gloria frowned. 'I hope she's OK.'

'I'm sure she's fine.'

'I'm going to go over there and just check,' said Gloria. She made it all sound so sinister.

'We're supposed to be helping with the kids,' I said weakly.

Gloria made a face. 'Let Cori do that – look, she's flirting with Mr. Juarez again and he looks like he needs a break from her. We'll just slip off. Tanya only lives five minutes from here.'

I hesitated. 'Maybe we should call her first.'

'Let's just *go*,' Gloria persisted.

Miss Cooper lived in a one-bedroom above a pizza place in a Valley Road minimall. She answered the door barefoot, in jeans and a tank top. I had to admire her forearms. She actually had muscle where most people just have bone; where I still had sausages, even after weeks of weight lifting and barely eating. But her pale skin was almost as dark as mine now, except where some of the older bruises were turning yellow.

Her face was puffy and blotchy and her eyes were red.

Gloria and I burst out talking at once: 'Oh my God! Are you OK? What happened?'

'Oh, guys, hi,' she said stiffly. 'Yeah, I'm all right, listen, I'm sorry but I won't be able to be there today. I'll call you, OK?'

And she started to shut the door.

'Whoa, whoa,' said Gloria, putting out her hand and stopping the door. 'What happened? Is it your family? Can we help?'

'No, it's nothing like that, honestly. I just . . . I don't feel very well. I told Shihan. I'll call you later, OK?'

I would have left it there, but Gloria set her lips firmly.

'What is going on? Shihan had a really shifty look on his face when we asked about you. What *is* going on, Tanya? We're your friends. We can help you.'

Suddenly I had the feeling that Gloria knew more about this than I did.

'Let us in,' she commanded, and Miss Cooper took a step back.

'It's a mess,' she said. 'I'm a mess. You guys are going to miss the kata competition. Just go on. I'm all right, honestly. I'm being stupid.'

'Then come on, if you don't want to tell us, then wash your face and get your stuff and we'll all go over there together. OK?'

Miss Cooper shook her head so fast that her hair flew.

'No, no, I can't. You guys go, really . . .'

It went on like this for a couple of minutes and finally Miss Cooper said:

'It's Masunobu, all right? Something h-h-happened with Masunobu last night and I don't want to see him and I don't want to see anybody, I just want to be alone.'

'Something happened? What happened?' Gloria's eyebrows drew together in a fierce grimace. *'Was he fresh with you?'*

Miss Cooper started crying.

We all went into the living room and Gloria made everybody sit down. She seemed to know exactly what to do. She sat next to Miss Cooper and gave her a hug. Miss Cooper clung to her, sobbing.

'What exactly happened, sweetie?' Gloria said. 'I know you don't want to talk about it but you'll feel better if you get it out.'

'I don't even know how it started,' said Miss Cooper. 'We

were hanging out in his room and I was talking to Masunobu about the wars with the Japanese and how the Okinawans fought the samurai with wooden weapons. It was a whole bunch of us, playing music and stuff ... and then suddenly all the guys seemed to be leaving. You know Reggie, the guy from Sensei Price's dojo? When he was leaving he asked if I was OK and if I wanted to go with them. He was very protective. I didn't understand. I looked at Masunobu and Masunobu said, 'We talk goju history. We talk important stories,' and he pointed to me and himself. So I said it was cool and I'd see them tomorrow, and the guys all left. They didn't really want to talk karate anyway, they were going on about baseball the whole time and getting really, really drunk. They said they'd be in the bar if we needed them.'

Gloria let out a long breath. 'Oh, Tanya. Didn't you think?'

'I don't know, I don't know, it seemed harmless ... I guess Masunobu was pretty drunk but he's a master, what could I say? What could I do? He was telling me really interesting stories. I guess I was flattered. I never imagined ... I mean, he's married, and I never came on to him or anything. I'm taller than him!'

'Like that ever mattered a crock of beans,' Gloria observed. 'What do they teach you in college, anyway?'

'Not much,' I said. 'Go on, please, Miss Cooper.'

'At first I thought it was a joke. I thought he was just messing around. Then I started getting scared. He was on top of me and I couldn't get out from under him. He's so strong, Gloria, you'd never believe somebody so short could be so strong. He started taking my clothes off. He kept saying, 'This I like, this I like,' and 'You have face like doll.' I was like, 'No, no, please stop,' and I tried to get free but I couldn't. Then he stood up and took his pants down – no, Gloria, this is too embarrassing.'

'Honey, this is criminal stuff, I'm telling you.'

'It's cultural differences,' Miss Cooper said wildly, still crying. 'I'm sure it's not his fault.'

'Cultural differences my be-hind,' I snorted. 'Have you told Shihan?'

'I tried to. I kept crying when I was talking to him, though. He told me to stay home today and he'd look into it. But I don't think he understood.'

'What's to understand?' said Gloria. 'The guy's a menace. Tanya, did he actually force himself on you?'

Miss Cooper shook her head. 'I rolled off the bed and got to the door. He tried to come after me but he tripped over his pants. He was talking Japanese – I don't know what he was saying.'

'Well!' said Gloria, making a wry face. 'Is it true they have really small dicks?'

Miss Cooper started crying again. Gloria broke into a spate of apologies. I went over to Miss Cooper's speedball that she has mounted in her living room and started hitting it.

'I don't believe this,' I said. 'Everywhere you look, there's no integrity.'

'I agree,' Gloria said. 'If these are the people that Shihan is looking up to, then I think he ought to know what they're really like.'

'It's probably perfectly acceptable in their country,' said Miss Cooper, but even she sounded doubtful.

I said, 'I guess I'm just highly connable in all departments. I really believed that karate was about warriors.'

'But it *is*,' said Miss Cooper passionately. 'Maybe our Shihan isn't always the best example. Maybe Masunobu Hideki was out of line last night – and I'm not saying he was, I really can't be sure—'

'Ho!' cried Gloria. 'He was outta line already. I'm thinking about calling my cousin Paulie and asking him to go up to their hotel and have a *conversation*, you know what I mean?'

'Oh, I wouldn't do that! Your cousin could get hurt.'

'Pffff!' said Gloria. 'Gimme a break.'

Gloria's cousin vs. the Okinawan masters. I thought about what I'd seen in the pool hall. It hadn't looked much like a kung fu movie, had it?

Miss Cooper must have seen the thoughtful look on my face. 'Now, Cookie, you mustn't let this put you off. Karate is still pure. The spirit of Bushido is still pure.'

'So, what's the plan, then?' Gloria broke in. 'We're only purple belts. And fellow women. We came by to see if you were OK, and you're not. Are you going to the tournament? Or to the police? If I were you, I'd go to the police.'

'I can't do that! Shihan told me to stay here, and that's what I'm doing.'

So in the end, after a lot more talking, we left her there. What else could we do? I knew one thing. She needed to keep believing in karate. To do otherwise would shatter everything she'd worked for. I had too much empathy for how that feels to tell her that probably these masters would get mopped up if they had to fight for real, and anyway, I knew she wouldn't believe me if I did.

But I knew I was right. I just thought of Serge and I could see where all this karate stuff fit into the big picture. Yes, Miss Cooper could do fifty push-ups without putting her knees on the ground once. Then again, I could do five and so how hard could it be to get to fifty? Yes, Miss Cooper could do a kick to the height of somebody's face. So could the Rockettes. Yes, she knew all the moves to Seipai kata. But even Miles's dog had some choreography in his newspaper-catching routine – was Seipai *really that special*? Still, I knew that if you put everything together, Miss Cooper looked pretty good. Especially to me. I'd always been overweight and shy, I'd always believed in arcane knowledge and yearned to be part of an elite.

On the other hand, Serge moved like a rusty pipe. But I remember one time when Serge sat exposed on the perimeter of the N-Ridge mines with lightning hitting the Grid over her head and rain coursing down her back. Sat there for three days. For hours at a time she barely moved, watching the golems through her scope. She lived on rainwater, and I suspected her breathing filters were damaged because she kept taking them out and fiddling with them. She waited her quarry out, she used incendiaries, she completed her mission; and then she went back to X and got really drunk. And went out and did it all again.

Was that what made a warrior? Why had Serge done what she did in the end, right down to ordering her own destruction and letting herself be taken by the Grid? Her rhetoric declared that she was a patriot and a servant of the military. Yet nobody really believed that. Serge just couldn't back off – that was it. Didn't have the concept of it in her brain. Couldn't quit.

And Serge wouldn't have let some little toad grope her up just because he was a higher rank and she was in awe of that, whatever it meant.

Let's face it: Serge would have wiped the floor with Masunobu Hideki and then gone out to practice barrel-racing on her pony Captain Painter. But there I was, all these months and years, standing in line, practicing the moves, bowing religiously – thinking there was something these people could give me that was worth having. I broke the brick because Troy was baiting me and I was angry, not because I'd learned to move *ki* into my left toe.

Gloria was agitated.

'I just don't get it,' she finally said as we stopped at the lights on Alps Road. 'How could she be so stupid?'

'It shouldn't be about how smart she is,' I said. 'He should have left her alone.'

Gloria clicked her tongue. 'Hey, easy. It's not like I'm defending the little s%*t,' she said.

Just because something happens, does that mean it's destined? Is there a big picture, or is everything just a mess? Why would the Grid *really* offer up logic bullets that could be used to destroy it? Are the logic bullets really bait, like Serge thinks – will the Grid use them to turn Machine Front against itself?

Or will the Grid turn into Machine Front in the process of fighting it?

And just because something happened, does that mean the Universe wanted it to happen? Does the past justify itself, just by being the past?

Is Gloria right? Did Miss Cooper ask for it? Somehow? Toyota?

No. No, I can't put any of it together. I can't understand the Grid. I can't understand people. I don't understand myself.

Gloria parked her Lincoln Town Car on the far side of the Wayne Hills High School parking lot. The hot engine cracked and pinged as we got out. The cars all shimmered liquidly in the burgeoning heat. I was reminded of Gossamer's visuals during a pollen storm.

'I changed my mind about one thing,' Gloria said. 'I'm looking forward to the sparring now.'

We set off into the mirages. I was still thinking, hard. I said:

'I wonder when I'm going to learn. I can't seem to tell the difference between a psychopathological phenomenon and a breakfast cereal.'

'What?' Gloria said, turning her Ray Bans on me.

'I don't know the difference between reality and TV.'

'Oh,' she said. '*That*. Don't let them get to you, Cookie. You're OK.'

'I'm not OK. I can't tell the authentic from the BS. Why is this? Have I taken myself totally out of the equation? Am I always going to be behind the curve, out of fear, when I could be ahead of it, darn it? Am I going to let the fact that I'm a nutcase ruin my life?'

'I think we should just concentrate on what we have to do right now,' Gloria said. 'Let's get through today. I'm serious about calling Paulie. I just might do it.'

I wasn't really listening. I was still talking to myself. It wasn't that I expected Gloria to understand. I just needed to hear myself say it.

'No. No. Nonononononono. I'm going to be a nutcase and I'm going to be it to the best of my ability, starting now. I'm going to be an *authentic nutcase*. Thank you very much.'

I turned on my heel and marched away. Gloria called after me,

'Hey! Cookie! What about pocketbook-and-broom? What am I going to tell Mrs. Cannalletto?'

I waved my hands in the air to show I didn't care what she told Mrs. Cannalletto. I was going to try *Quark*/not-*Quark* again. Miles kept saying it was an interactive game. Well, maybe it was time for me to start interacting.

Time for me to get tough.

I reached my Rabbit and burned my hand on the chrome when I put the key in the lock.

'Shhhhhh— sugar!' I said.

That was very nearly a swear. It really was.

the american book of the dead

It's about time. Where have you been, deadbeat?

I typed: I don't want to play Quark. I want to
know about the mines.

Then you've come to the wrong place. Now,
where were we? You were trapped in a large
cavern, weren't you, and you still hadn't figured
out what those ropes were for. Shall we resume?

I put: No. We were in the Grid, with Serge. But I
need to see Klaski now. What have the golems done
to her?

I pressed 'return' and waited. Maybe it wasn't going to
work this time. Maybe I had taken it for granted. Maybe—

They took her down into the logic mine, but
nothing was like it was supposed to be.

It took Klaski a while to get this one. She
remembered the time her uncle Ed bought a
barbecue from Sears and inside the box was a lawn
mower. Ed kept looking at the picture of the Sun
Chef on the box, at the Sun Chef receipt, at the Sun

Chef instruction manual, and then back again at
the Lawn Ranger 909. He just couldn't come to
grips with the contradiction. The kids laughed, and
Aunt Bea went into a tirade against Sears, but
Uncle Ed had to go get a Michelob and stand there
drinking it and scratching his balls just to get over
the shock. Things like this weren't supposed to
happen and they could really mess up a guy's
head, not to mention what to do with the spare
ribs?

Klaski knew how Ed felt that day.

She had followed the golems down the shaft and
the doors boomed shut behind them; but they
weren't in a lit tunnel and they weren't in total
darkness, either. There was a feeling of open air:
damp, windy darkness like after a rainstorm at
dusk. The wind carried her sideways and she
stumbled, sprawling on her side with a curse. For
the first time since she had left X she had a truly
hard, unyielding surface beneath her.

Klaski rose to her knees, then stood. The
darkness around her was falling back to reveal
planes of concrete: floor, walls, but incomplete.
After the whorls and Grid vertigo, this smoothness
and predominance of right angles made her feel
rooted and secure, as if someone had nailed her
boots down. That was nice; but otherwise this
wasn't a nice place. It was a concrete wasteland:
the floor slabs were buckled and cracked, revealing
rusted iron reinforcements. Puddles lay in uneven
patches, and burn marks stained the walls.

Whatever it was, it wasn't a mine.

The girls seemed to have led her onto the top
floor of some partly bombed-out building, its jagged

edges hanging over a gulf. There was no more roof
and the walls were either destroyed or under
construction; it was hard to be sure which. Straight
ahead of her there was no wall at all: Klaski could
see a complex of other rectangles, an irregular city
skyline but without any of the light or noise. She
could see arching stairways that formed bridges
between high buildings. Figures moved across them.
Below, there must have been roads but there was
no sound of traffic. There was, instead, a humming
so faint as to be almost subliminal: an erratic
music.

'Where are we?'

'Do you like coffee?'

The girl walked closer to the edge of the
precipice. There seemed to be people here, but
something wasn't quite right about them. They
were out of focus. The girl walked among them and
Klaski realized that they must be golems. She
hesitated, looked over her shoulder. More golems.

Then she picked up the aroma and for a moment
she thought she was back home.

'Oh, I must be dead because that smell is
heaven.'

A strip of the enormous building had been
rendered into a coffee shop by the presence of a
green and white striped awning and a counter with
stools in front of it. Klaski could smell the brew.

Klaski sat down at a flimsy round table that
wobbled under the pressure of her palms. A
styrofoam cup was rolling slowly across the
puddled floor, describing a semaphore on the tile.
The jarring whir of the espresso machine shook her
dental work and made her tap her fingers on the

glass, which was gritty and wet. Golems were all around her, going about their business in a way that made sense evidently to them if not to her; but she couldn't get a bead on them, couldn't bring her attention to bear on anything but the inanimate, the fixed. The one exception to this rule was the sad release of smoke from a chimney stack on a tilted rooftop opposite, where a piece of guttering let loose a vapor of the softest, warmest pale gray. It sighed into the sky and quickly disappeared in random shapes and without violence. She watched it.

And realized that she was already missing the Grid's hellfire. The absence ached like phantom pain from a lost limb.

The girls sat down at a table. They look at Klaski as one. After a while she stood and went up to them aggressively, upset.

'I don't get this. Is it some kind of trick? We haven't taken a ship. This *isn't* home. This isn't my world.'

'It's under your world. This is your part of the the Grid.' The girls were taking turns playing with a crinkly brown-paper sack that used to hold, apparently, cement. They were making a paper airplane out of it. 'This is the Grid, having digested what you brought. All we did was join up the logic mines to the MaxFact that we pulled down. It's all the same thing. It's just a slice of paradigm.'

'The Grid, the Grid, the Grid. All I wanted was to get out of it. But this isn't right. It doesn't feel right.'

The other girls passed the words around.

'The Grid is yours. *The American Book of the*

Dead. It's the garbage dump and the graveyard, and
nirvana and Valhalla and hell and the sky. It's the
static between stations, the wood between the
worlds, it's twilight, the unconscious, the kitchen
sink. It's your mother and your undertaker.

'It's the only thing that will ever really know
you, and it doesn't give a fuck about you,' they
finished. The last girl to speak squinted at Klaski
across the partially formed wing of her airplane.
'To the Grid, you're just Play-Doh.'

Klaski's jaw went slack for a minute. The girl
licked her fingers and made another careful fold in
the paper. Klaski reached for a half-full mug of
black coffee.

'I wouldn't drink that if I were you,' said
another. And a third finished: 'It's full of unproven
theories.'

Klaski put the cup down, feeling foolish.

'So, what?' she snorted, trying to sound mocking.
'We're supposed to just give up and go home? Stop
the mining?'

A shadow fell over Klaski from behind. It was
bigger than a child's. She was afraid to turn
around.

'You people are mining your own birthright, and
you're doing it the wrong way.' The speaker
launched an airplane at Klaski, who ducked. It flew
over her head and she heard it hit something
behind her. The shadow moved to her right. She
hunched her shoulders in anticipation of a blow;
but she couldn't make herself turn. The girls said,
'By seeking to use a part or aspect of the logic of
the world without understanding all of it, you
create obscenity. The Grid is the infrastructure of

things. You try to use machines and mechanistic principles to understand it, the deepest reality of yourselves.'

And then a new voice spoke. A scratchy, phlegmy, ugly voice: one that used to figure in Klaski's nightmares. It said, 'But the machine truth ain't any more real than the Great Pumpkin. Every attack we made here was bogus, dude.'

Klaski turned around. And there was Serge, looking just the same. Just as ontologically pissed-off, too.

'So you survived. I should have known,' Klaski said. 'I guess you did what Arla wanted. You know it all now, right? You know what's on the Other Side.'

'I am what's on the other side.'

'And them?' Joanne pointed.

'The girls?' Serge's tone was amiable enough. This was unusual, and contributed to Klaski feeling herself losing what grip she'd ever had. 'Well, speaking of obscenity, I guess you could say they're obscenity run amok. They're the face of suffering, and of life, that rises out of the mess. They're the most terrible thing and the most wonderful thing. I never wanted them to be here, but now that they are, I got to save them.'

Save them? The notion was so romantic, so incongruous, that it made Klaski's stomach pitch.

Serge caught another airplane. The airplane's maker laughed, and the others echoed her. The genuine happiness in (t)he(i)r voice unsettled Klaski almost as much as Serge's declared intentions.

'And how are you going to do that?'

Serge said: 'Let me ask you one question. What do you think is going to happen to you now? I could kill you, or I could leave you to the Grid. Either way, it ain't no beauty pageant. I don't see no Fritos here. I don't see no working power supply and I sure don't see no batteries for your damn Walkman. Maybe you made it this far, but your clock's ticking.'

Klaski shrugged. 'I'm a one-trick pony in a one-horse town.'

'Is that supposed to be funny? You mocking the way I talk, *Joanne*?'

Without any warning, Serge picked Klaski up bodily and threw her a man's length. Klaski bounced off a solid wall and landed on a chunk of reinforced concrete with its rusted steel wire protruding from crumbled edges like broken fingers. This knocked the wind out of her. She lay there making a point of feeling pain for a while.

Then Klaski said: 'I take it you know that MF have put out your destruct order on the modified Grid structures? They have the coordinates you gave them, and they'll use Fliers to hunt down the individual members of the set. Ironic, isn't it? You caused your own doom, and your kids'. Oh, I know about your daughter, by the way. Or should I say that in the plural? Arla told me.'

'Arla – you guys are two of a kind. I wanna know how it is you could be so good at saving your own butt and roasting everyf%@ker else's.'

'So, what? Now everything's my fault? Excuse me for living.'

'Don't know if I can, Klaskoid. Let's try this out. Because of you, I got taken by the well. I couldn't capture Gonzalez, which I would have if I'd lived. That left her free to kill Hendricks and Lewis, and very nearly Gossamer, too. Because of you. Then you killed Gonzalez. And I'm supposed to believe you're some kind of helpless little victim? Gimme a break. I think someone in Personnel planted you on me. And I want to know why. What's it all about, Klaski?'

'N-n-n-no!' Klaski gasped, stunned by the whole idea. She started babbling, fast and defensive. 'It's not like that at all. It was all by mistake. There was no plot. I never wanted any part of this. I came out here to study the Grid, not to camp out in it and fight golems. I don't know why MF assigned me to your team. I never asked for it! I mean, your reputation . . . why would I . . . I just want to go home, that's the truth.'

'Yeah? And why should you get what you want when everybody else is f@&ked?'

Klaski didn't know what to say at first. She licked her lips.

'Well, maybe I can help you. You can use me to negotiate with MF. Or were you planning on walking back to X and doing that yourself? I bet they can't pick you up on a scope. You're a golem.'

'*I am not a golem.*'

'You're a golem now as far as MF are concerned. You sent those orders by robot and they can't be rescinded.'

Serge snorted. 'Let them come. The Grid eats MaxFacts – we've already seen that. The kids can unpack a MaxFact and recreate you-name-it from its guts. You'd be amazed if you saw what they're capable of.'

'Hmm,' Klaski said. 'MaxFacts are Second Wave,

though. Did you know the Third Wave Machine
Front Eels are here? What if they're able to use the
data they got from your daughter's dead body?
Machine Front are going to target your kids, Serge.
Major Galante said if you prime one of them with a
logic bullet, it can trace anything in the Grid.
Including golems. Once a Flier gets a lock on you,
the MF Eels can hunt you down. One by one.'

Serge dismissed this with a wave. 'We have the
SynchroniCity now. We can hide here if we have to.
And the logic bullets was destroyed in the N-Ridge
raid. MF haven't recovered them.'

Serge didn't know. She didn't know about the
logic bullets.

'Not yet,' Klaski said cautiously.

Serge didn't like the sound of that, did she?

'What's that supposed to mean?'

Klaski shrugged.

Serge looked and sounded like her jaw had been
wired shut as she said,

'Answer me, sh*$head.'

'Hey!' flared Klaski, climbing to her feet. 'Did I
hear a snapping sound a while back? I think it was
the chain of command. You need me more than I
need you, Bonny, so how about a little courtesy?'

Serge had herself on a punishingly tight rein. If
she relaxed her hold on herself one millimeter,
she'd probably *eat* Klaski. She took a long breath.

'Yeah? Since when are you so important?'

Klaski smiled. 'Since I found the logic bullets.'

And Serge's hands were on Klaski, tearing away
air hoses and filters, ripping protective clothing.
Serge's perfume – the Grid's perfume – came into
Klaski's limbic system and she went limp with

pleasant relaxation. Tendrils of Grid influence crept into the tears in her suit like fingers, like insects, like sand on a day at the beach. And Serge's voice was in Klaski's ear, panting, *come on, you piece of s@&t,* as Serge's hands gripped her sex and the back of her neck and began to drag her like a sack. Klaski felt the concrete floor yield beneath her like rubber and she heard herself laughing because the fear was gone: it could not remain in the presence of her limp and hollow body; it did not exist independent of the physical state that supported it and gave rise to it, so the fear went but the knowledge that this was bad remained, and she could do nothing.

Klaski's armor was coming off. Serge's golemized body slithered over her, its segmented armor parting and clenching on her exposed skin like lobster claws, gripping her flesh with weird little love bites.

Serge found the logic bullets and Klaski realized how stupid she had been to brag about them. Serge ripped the bag away and looked inside. She released Klaski and sat back on her heels.

She put her hands on the softly chiming logic bullets and seemed to commune with them for a long time. Klaski glanced surreptitiously around, wanting to make a break for it. The aerial would soon be here . . .

But there were too many golems, and she couldn't see the way back to the mines. If there had been a door or passage, it was no longer visible.

After a while Serge took a long breath and let it out, shaking her head like a disappointed schoolteacher.

'Listen to me, Klaski. Machine Front was built out of a long history of military one-upmanship. You get a strong weapon, the enemy builds a strong defense. You get a stronger weapon – or he does – and it keeps going up and up and up. But the Grid messes around with that equation. The harder you come in, the softer it seems. And the more dangerous it gets. That's why most of the boys got sent home and we're here instead of doing our hair. But that's not working, either, so now they got this idea they can mechanize the whole thing and that'll solve it. I don't think so.'

'So . . . if the logic bullets aren't going to destroy the Grid, you won't mind if I give them to MF so I can get out of here. Will you?' asked Klaski hopefully.

'My daughters are living creatures. They can die. They're part of the Grid. They're *fragile*. If MF do this thing, if they pull out the humans and send the MFeels, my girls are gonna be in the crossfire. I don't know what's gonna happen to the Grid or to the MFeels, but I know what will happen to us. We'll be changed. Probably destroyed.'

'OK, OK, I see your point. But, like, I still think the logic bullets could be really valuable. If we could understand how the Grid's intelligence works – isn't that why we're really here? The original purpose of the logic mines was to get a grip on what the Grid is. Bring something home that we could use. Everybody wants to learn from the Grid. That's how we'll move forward. That's really why we're here. The war is just something that happened because . . . well, probably because of a misunderstanding. So if we could understand *you*,

and the children . . . knowing how your mind
works . . .'

'Huh. And do you know how *your* mind works,
Klaskoid? Damn, the human mind doesn't really
work the way humans like to think. It's much more
crazed and folded. Backward, switchbacking,
switchbladed. Freaked. You humans can't handle
your own heads, and that's nothing personal,
Klaski, although I would have to add that you are a
good example.'

But Klaski wasn't discouraged at all.

'See, that's just what I mean. You have so much
to teach us. If we could just cooperate, I'm sure I
could convince Machine Front to step down the
hostilities. Won't you try? Help me explain. Help
me convince them to call off the attack. Machine
Front is a collective, so maybe they can appreciate
your being part of a Grid collective now.'

'Screw them,' Serge barked. 'Humans created
Machine Front to make them stronger and it has.
At the same time, it's made humans weaker. Take
yourself for example: you're lost in a world without
the free salad bar. What are you gonna do?'

'Why don't you lay off me, Captain Serge?'
Klaski flared. 'I'm alive. I must be doing something
right. And you can't just say, "Screw MF." That's not
the Serge I know. You were a true believer, Captain.
The well can't have erased that much of you.'

Something moved in Serge's face, and Klaski
pressed. 'Come on. Let's try it. Let's work together.
Let me take the logic bullets and talk to MF.'

Serge threw back her head and laughed.

'Save your breath, Private Benjamin. You can go
hang out with the rest of the mines personnel. I got

to figure out what to do with y'all, but for now you can roam the SynchroniCity. Who knows? You might learn something.'

And she whipped Klaski around and kicked her in the small of the back to send her away.

drano

It was the weekend after the big tournament. Troy had won first place in sparring. Cori Knight had gotten two opponents disqualified for excessive contact and so won a third place in her category without throwing a punch. Gloria had come fourth in kata and Mr. Juarez had broken five boards on stage. The Okinawans were going home the next day and today, Sunday, all the American masters were getting together for a tribunal to discuss what had happened between Miss Cooper and Sensei Hideki. At Gloria's behest, Miss Cooper had put in a formal complaint, although she had refused to involve the police.

I took her over to the dojo to sit on the tribunal. I had gone out to do my grocery shopping anyway; I was eating an almost-normal diet now in variety if not in quantity. I went downstairs with Miss Cooper and took what I meant to be a last look around the dojo. I knew that whatever happened here today, I wouldn't be coming back. I already had my Jack La Lane membership and I'd convinced Miles to join with me at half-price.

The dojo was draped in the old Okinawan flag. Shihan Norman had taken a door and turned it on its side on four cinder blocks to make a Japanese-style table. All the senseis and shihans sat there on the floor in their gis and black belts, and at one end sat Miss Cooper with adhesive tape on her knuckles, her eyes downcast. I didn't want to leave her there like that, but I had to. I bowed, backed out of the training floor and went upstairs, leaving my grocery bags outside Shihan's office. I walked out the door and closed it behind me.

Then I crept into the alley that led down to the riverbank and put my ear to the back door. The voices were muffled, but if I crouched down I could get my ear against a narrow crack between the double doors.

'I guess it could have been my fault,' Miss Cooper was saying. 'I thought he wanted to give me extra lessons. That's what he said. Or that's what I thought he said.'

'But you've already admitted you thought he was saying you had a face like a dog, and he was actually saying 'doll', right?' said Shihan Norman. 'So you could have misunderstood what he meant. Couldn't you?'

I felt the breeze blowing on my exposed eyeballs as my eyes widened. Shihan was taking up a position against his own student!

'Sensei Hideki gave me a lot of extra lessons, informally. He'd come up to me while he was drinking a cup of tea and start doing knocking hands. That's what I thought it was about.'

'How could anyone be that naive?' said Shihan Ingenito. 'You stayed alone at a man's hotel room after midnight. He'd been drinking. He'd already told you that you had a face like a doll. He'd already been friendly with you. Did you seriously think he was going to teach you secret bunkai?'

There was a silence. From the reaction of the men, I gathered that Miss Cooper had burst into tears.

'I'm sorry,' said Shihan Ingenito. 'See, this is the problem with female students. They can turn on the waterworks at any time.'

'It was all a misunderstanding, I'm sure,' said Shihan Norman.

'I don't know,' said Sensei Price. 'Doesn't sound like a misunderstanding to me. It sounds like sexual assault, and if Miss Cooper was my student, I would be challenging Masunobu Hideki to a fight.'

'Oh, please,' said Shihan Norman. 'This isn't *The Three Musketeers!*'

'No, but I already heard from two of my students that when they left Miss Cooper at the hotel they had reservations about what was going to happen, but they didn't dare intervene because of Masunobu Hideki's status. And the fact that they were afraid of what he'd do to them in a fight.'

'That's true,' Miss Cooper said. 'They kept asking me if I was sure I wanted to stay. I should have gone with them, but I just didn't think I was in any . . . danger. I mean, I still can't believe it . . .'

'Well, there you go,' Shihan Norman cut in. 'Miss Cooper admits she made a mistake in judgment.'

Price said, 'OK, John, so you're not going to call Masunobu out to fight and it's pretty obvious why.'

'Yeah, "why" is because I'm a grown-up.'

'I would fight him myself, but Miss Cooper isn't a member of my dojo and I'd be out of bounds.'

'Yeah, you would,' said Sensei Ingenito. Then: 'Do you think you could take him?'

'I really don't know.'

'Some of these guys can rip open your gut and tear your liver out with their bare hands.'

'I'll believe that when I see it,' said Sensei Price.

'Yeah, well, huh-ho, I hope it isn't your liver, man.'

Shihan Norman cleared his throat significantly.

'Whatever the case,' said Sensei Price. 'I think we should think twice before we commit further to the Budokokutai organization. I also think Miss Cooper deserves an apology at the very least. When I spoke to Shihan Hideki on the phone this morning, he didn't sound like he or his brother had anything to be sorry about. I don't think that's a good sign in terms of getting an official apology. Are you going to press charges, Tanya?'

Miss Cooper sniffed and gulped. 'I really don't know. I was hoping that everything could be cleared up today.'

Then the Okinawans came walking down the alley with their translator, talking in Japanese. I ducked behind some garbage cans before they could spot me. They entered the dojo, and a minute or so later I had my ear at the door again as they entered the meeting.

It didn't go on for very long. Through their translator the Okinawans announced that they would be handing out official grades and titles to all of the American teachers and their senior students, and that anybody who wanted to be on board would have to get with the program, by which I assumed they meant not only their way of training but their way of doing things. There was no question of a senior master's word being questioned by that of a young and impressionable female student. Miss Cooper showed promise, but she needed to know her place and keep her head down.

Sensei Price and Sensei Ingenito had things to say about Americans being different from Okinawans, and Shihan Hideki answered to the effect that karate was an Okinawan discipline and if they wanted to be in the organization they would have to toe the line.

Shihan Norman said, 'I want to take this opportunity to apologize for the uproar caused by one of my own students. Of course my dojo will implement all the changes. We'll expand our operations and we'll be sending a percentage of all our fees to the parent organization. We will also make sure that the masters have a sponsored trip to the US every year, and I was going to suggest that tonight I take you all out to Radio City Music Hall.'

'Ah! Rockettes!' said Shihan Hideki.

I leaned my cheek against the brickwork. It went on and on like that. After a while I couldn't listen anymore.

Miss Cooper was the first to leave. I wanted to follow her down the alley and talk to her, but I held back. Then the American senseis came out. They got to the end of the alley and started talking furiously among themselves.

The Okinawans were the last to go. Shihan Norman escorted them to the door.

Shihan Hideki said in English, 'Nothing personal in demotion, John. You do what we say, five years you in charge whole US operation. OK?'

'OK!' said Shihan Norman, beaming wetly and bowing a lot. 'Arigato gozaimus-ta!'

The Okinawans trundled away and he shut the door.

I waited a few minutes, then went in. I could hear John Norman downstairs, doing something in the sauna. My groceries were still sitting outside his office. I went down the stairs, whistling to announce myself.

I could see my grocery bags sitting there. My Weight Watchers ice cream would have melted by now. Shihan Norman was putting more coal on the sauna fire. He had spread out the bricks across the benches of the sauna.

'I guess that makes them harder, doesn't it?' I said.

He jumped and hit his head on the door frame.

'Miss Orbach. I didn't hear you come in.'

'I left some groceries here before.' I pointed to the bags, but didn't move to take them. 'So, baking the bricks makes them harder to break, right?'

'Yeah, something like that.' The light reflected off his big glasses.

'That's funny,' I said. 'I thought I read somewhere that heat makes brick more brittle. It takes out all the moisture that might have acted as a cushion. So the substance becomes more percussive. Yeah, I think I read that somewhere.'

'It depends on the kind of brick,' he said, curving his lips into a pained smile. 'But we aren't using these at the demonstration tomorrow, anyway. These are some ones I'm going to use at home, in my yard.'

'Ah,' I nodded exaggeratedly. 'I see.'

'So, it looks like your ice cream is melting there, Miss Orbach. Oh, Miss Cooper already left, by the way.'

I almost said, 'I know,' and then caught myself.

Instead, I said, 'I've been wanting to talk to you about something.'

'I've been wanting to talk to you, too, Miss Orbach. Come into my office.'

My palms were sweating as I sat down in the chair opposite his desk. He sat in his swivel chair, backed up by all his grades and titles in Japanese writing, and his photographs of himself shaking hands with Master Uechi and Master this and Master that and posing in front of the Shaolin Temple holding a pair of sai . . . and there he was doing Supairenpai kata in a lily pond with some other black belts. I mean, what on Earth was I going to say or do to this man in his own lair?

I was totally out of my depth.

'I've noticed you've been doing a lot of extra training lately. You're improving.'

'Thank you.'

'I'd like you to come in on Saturdays and help with the kids' classes. I'll give you some extra things to learn. It will be good for you.'

So Miss Cooper quit, I thought. *Or got kicked out.* I hadn't listened to the last part of the discussion. It was too upsetting.

'I was coming in to tell you that I'm quitting,' I said.

'Quitting?' His glasses flashed as his face registered surprise. 'May I ask why?'

'I don't think you have any business teaching people how to defend themselves when you can barely even do a push-up,' I said shakily. It had cost me everything I had to say it, and when the words were out of my mouth, they didn't sound nearly strong enough. They weren't.

'I'm not going to be insulted by that, Miss Orbach. Coming from you, well . . .' He laughed. 'Pardon the expression, but isn't that the pot calling the kettle black?'

'I'm not a seventh-degree black belt,' I said. 'Or, should I say, sixth?'

'You're way out of line, talking to me that way. Let me tell you something, Miss Orbach, if I was an Okinawan or Japanese master and a student said that to me, I'd throw you out immediately.'

'You can't throw me out, because I'm quitting.'

He shrugged. 'That's your choice.'

He wasn't even mad. He didn't even care.

'I think it's really horrible,' I said. 'People put their faith in you, and what do they get? A belt that doesn't mean anything. Troy won that competition the other day because he's a natural athlete, not because of anything he learned here. He beats up your black belts every time we have sparring in class. I've seen it.'

'Nobody beats anybody up in my dojo.'

'No, excuse me, I phrased that wrong. You're just supposed to touch the guy and that counts as hurting him.'

'Anything else would be barbaric. We're a brotherhood.'

This made me really mad but it's always the same with me. I just could not put my feelings into words. I couldn't get past that nice-behavior thing. *Brotherhood?* I wanted to say. *Is that what you call it when you gang up on a person who's been a victim and use her to advance your own career?* But I just couldn't say it. I tried.

'So, I just wanted you to know how I feel. I . . .' Again my voice was shaking. I gestured around the office, at the dojo trophies on the shelves and the assorted Japanese weapons, all of it. I wanted to say something really scathing but I just couldn't. 'I'm not too impressed with any of this.'

He just looked at me. No, he didn't care at all.

'I guess I better go,' I said, and got up. He pulled that smarmy smile again.

I threw myself over the desk at him.

I don't think he believed it was happening. He grabbed me by my arms but that didn't stop me head-butting him across his big flabby nose. He fell over backward in his chair and I was on top of him. He'd let go of my right hand and as I scrabbled around for balance in the crowded space between the desk and the wall, I grabbed the crystal paper-weight that held his state junior division bronze judo medal from 1963 – the highest honor he had ever personally won. I sat on his right arm and smashed it into his face again and again, feeling it grate and grind against his teeth.

Shihan shoved me back off him and my ears rang as the back of my head met with the edge of his desk. The phone fell down on the back of my neck and I shrugged it off. He was trying to kick his way out from under me but the desk trapped him in position and his eyes were full of blood.

The bag with my groceries in it had spilled on the floor. I saw an opportunity and, seizing hold of the bottle of liquid Drano, I ripped off the safety tab and squirted it at him. He screamed, choked, spat. I could see the incomprehension in his face even as he tried to get up. It was a beautiful thing. Very satisfying, that moment.

I crashed down on him with both my knees. I felt the wind go out of him and for good measure I ground the point of my elbow into his throat. He'd grabbed hold of my T-shirt and was trying to use it to tie me up, but I shrugged out of it and pulled away, leaving him scrabbling around on the floor like a fish on the deck of a rowboat. He couldn't get his breath. Drano dripped from his lips and nose, which was running with fresh blood. The last I saw of him he was groping blind, his hands patting and grasping his framed grades and titles in their Japanese writing.

I wanted to drag him into the sauna where he could bake to a state of brittleness together with his bricks, but a sudden, uncontrollable fear came over me and I ran out of the office, up the stairs, and out onto the street. It was a bright and sunny day in Minnehaha.

I was only wearing shorts and a 44DD Warners Cross My Heart support bra. Somebody in a pickup wolf-whistled me as I crossed the street. My left forearm was aching something awful. I reached down with my right hand, felt a bloody lump embedded in the muscle, and jerked loose one of John Norman's yellowed front teeth.

I went home and hugged the cats. I called Gloria and left a message on her machine saying I had to go away for a while and asking her to feed Nebbie and Rocky. I went out to Foodtown and stocked up on cat litter and food. I watered the plants. I took a shower and bandaged my arm and got changed into clean clothes with long sleeves to hide the bite mark. I picked out a few treasured books to bring along with me, in case things like that were allowed where I was going. I opened a can of chicken soup, heated it up and ate it with saltines. I unplugged the computer and hid the *Quark* save-game disk in an old photo album.

Then I sat and waited for the police to come.

It was Sunday afternoon. I waited until midnight, but nothing happened.

I couldn't sleep.

So I did what everybody else does when they run out of ideas. I turned on the TV.

You can fly again. It's the greatest.

The sky over X cracks and yawns open like a refrigerator door, light falling across the Grid in a chilly rhombus as the Third Wave ships sink through the atmosphere. It's obvious now why they're called MFeels: they look like eels in the sky, the articulations of their armor are so fine. The light shaft that carries them completely overpowers the luminosity of the Grid, so that it stands out in dark green and indigo against the new light, and for the first moments it looks like nothing so much as a tangled roll of barbed wire fence. The ships seem to swim down headfirst, eyeless but determined.

You have to dim the opacity of your visual inputs to handle the extra light.

As the ships get closer to X, the light fades and details appear on the arriving ships. Antennae are seen sprouting from the hulls, only to be retracted for entry into the docking bays that now iris open to receive the newcomers.

'Once they are primed with logic bullets, they'll be able to go through the Grid, swimming in the air. They can hunt golems with aerial backup from fliers like you and prevent them from damaging equipment,' Machine Front informs you. 'They won't be pervious to golem psychological warfare because the people will all be gone, and they can't fall into the well because they don't travel on the ground. They've been designed especially to cope with the anomalies of this planet. They represent the next stage of technological development: they don't need any human pilots at all. It's very exciting to see them finally arrive.'

There is little movement on the ground, though. Robot arms

are involved in preparing the MFeels, but most of these are housed under the roof of the compound. The tarmac is bare. Vehicles have been garaged or parked in neat lines and covered with tarps. There are some signs of a hasty exodus by humans, though: an occasional abandoned jeep or a radio kite blowing from a tower. Major Galante's convoy, blackened and torn from combat, is scattered across several fields of tarmac and some of the transport doors have been left wide open. There are some people standing at the foot of Tower Four: Galante's personnel, you assume, just in from the Grid.

Then you spot Galante herself, counting off her guys as they pass through the tower doors to safety.

She looks up and sees you. She smiles and waves, and you find yourself going down to her. Just like old times.

'I thought you were a goner, Goss. I'm so glad to see you. You're just in time. We have to execute Serge's final orders. I know if you're up there, this job will be done right.'

She pulls you out of the sky, Gossamer's skin draping her arms like silk. You thought this reunion would reassure you. You thought it would be like coming home, because Major Galante is nice and you always liked working with her. But it's not the same. You can't relax.

She doesn't notice, of course. No one notices how you feel, because they can't see you.

'I don't have time to do a full diagnostic and reprogram, Goss,' says Galante. 'You seem to be OK; that scar's not bothering you, is it? Let's see you fly.'

And you're up there again. The buildings fall away, the Grid falls away, everything that was wrong falls away and you're flying. That's perfection, and it always will be.

MF is in your headspace again.

PREPARE TO GUIDE THE TEST EELS, GOSSAMER.

Do you rebel? Do you refuse? Do you declare yourself an individual, with opinions, not just a passive conduit?

LET SOMEONE ELSE DO IT, you say, adding apologetically in a way that makes you hate yourself: I'M TOO SQUEAMISH.

That is the extent of your rebellion. Yeah, when it comes right down to it, you always capitulate.

GOLEMS HAVE SHOT DOWN MOST OF THE OTHER FLIERS. SYSTEMATICALLY. WE DON'T HAVE ENOUGH EYES UP THERE. SO GET OUT AND DO WHAT YOU WERE DESIGNED FOR.

You don't know what's going to happen but you can't get out of this one. Down in the seethe and rattle of the Grid you can feel the pull of the well. It's singing to Gossamer. Through the girls you know that it's building a city of the bones and breath of history, tracing the threads of possibility manifested in the MaxFact and every other object, word, concept brought here by humans. Tracing them back to their homes. It's calling up the ghosts that made the world of technology, revenants like golems but writ in the brick and human life that the MaxFact has eaten in order to bring itself into being.

The well would take Gossamer home any time, if you let it.

It would take her back to the beginning, and it would take her Earth-made eyes too, and unravel them and recodify or is it recognify their essence.

But what would that mean? For the Grid there is no separation between a concept and its execution.

You know that you'll never find out, because in the end you are obedient. You just don't have that kind of courage. Not you.

You start the flyover with a dead heart.

After so much time in the Grid, X looks like it has been scrubbed with disinfectant. Everything gleams. Everything is flat. Surfaces are level, still, lifeless. Machines are busy, gliding across the tarmac and manipulating the hardware that has settled in the landing bays. Everything functions according to machine rhythms that are alternately smooth and spastic, totally lacking in animal continuity. There are no signs of people, other than a couple of crookedly parked personnel carriers near the base of Tower Four.

You start to check the perimeter, and that's when you see your first people. There are two bipeds exiting a shed just outside the perimeter fence. As you watch, they approach the security net that borders the Grid. Even from here you can see they don't look right. Waxy lights scan them, and you tune in to the security readout.

The net has identified Joanne Klaski. It doesn't perceive her pint-sized companion at all. But you do. It's Serge's wayward daughter and she is going to enter X, carrying the logic bullets. Your head spins. What's going on? What did you miss?

You hesitate. If you let Gossamer watch them, you are at risk of MF demanding your images. But if you don't, you'll never know . . .

You decide to take your chances. You dive.

'I can't believe we're here already,' you hear Klaski saying. 'How did we get across the Grid so quickly?'

'That's an archetypal shed,' the girl replies, nodding at the structure they have just left. 'Everything in the SynchroniCity leads to everything else. But how are we going to get past this machine?'

'Don't worry about that. Just give me the logic bullets.'

The girl gives every appearance of being singular. Her voice sounds small and light and lonely, but determined. 'Not yet. Get me through anti-golem security. Get me to my body. Then you can have them.'

'I need them now,' Klaski insists, using a tone more like a nine-year-old's than the nine-year-old herself. 'Machine Front will think I lied if I don't prove I have them.'

'That's your problem. They have my body. I'm taking it back.'

Klaski pulls a gross-out face.

'It won't be very nice, you know. After all this time. Even if they've been careful . . .'

'I got you out of the SynchroniCity,' adds the girl. 'Now hold up your end of the bargain.'

'If a Flier or a person sees you, they'll kill you,' Klaski says.

'Not if I have the logic bullets.'

'But that's crazy!' Klaski whispers. You have to boost audio to pick her up. 'You can't stand up to them. They'll take the bullets and still use them against your . . . other bodies. Give them to me, and I can negotiate.'

'After I get my body. How many times do I have to say it?'

'It doesn't make sense,' Klaski grouses. 'Can you recover something from the body? Are you going to put it back in the Grid? I mean . . . when she died, you lost her knowledge, right?'

'No. All of the children of the well are supported by the Grid. You could say we're agents of it. When that part of me died, the rest of me had to take on more. So I remember her death. I experienced it. It was me.'

Klaski shudders. You hope that the girl doesn't intend to tell her what it was like.

The girl says: 'Can't you understand? I need that body. I'm going to take it back to the Grid – or see it destroyed. Anything else is just an open wound, and danger to me.'

'And what if something happens to you, here?'

'The others will absorb the shock.'

'So you have . . . huh-huh . . . you have nine lives? Why?'

'It's not really nine lives. It's just being in more than one place at once.'

'Fascinating. I could talk to Major Galante about you. Maybe you could come back to Earth.'

'There's nowhere to go back to.'

'That's just what you think. You have no idea what you're missing. Aren't you even curious?'

'You've already brought your world here. Your machines, your history. Arla Gonzalez, Jenny Hendricks . . . I have access to hundreds of dead. I know them all.'

'Oh.' Klaski watches the girl sidelong. She is lanky, long-legged, and outside of the Grid her movements have lost that spasmodic quality. Her six-fingered hands still look creepy – no way around that – and her black hair is matted and filthy. She's also missing some teeth, but not in a cute way. Klaski is developing the expression of a yuppy who has just inadvertently sat down on the A-train next to some run-down brother who sleeps on a subway grate and talks to God and has breath that smells like a dead horse.

The security lights flare and the girl throws her arms up over her eyes. A male voice belches out of the loudspeaker.

'Lieutenant Klaski? That really you?'

Klaski turns to the surveillance screen and waves at the camera eye nearby. There is a burst of interference and then a picture comes up on the screen. Chubby guy with glasses.

'It's me – Dave. You were talking to me up on N-Ridge.'

'You were supposed to send an aerial,' Klaski accuses.

'Christ, when we came to get you all we found was a whole lot of nothing. Where are the other personnel?'

'That will take some explaining,' Klaski says. 'The golems got into the compound through the mines somehow. Listen, leave that for now. I have the logic bullets, and I have a guest. We're harmless, OK, so no firing on me when you see me.'

'I have your position, Klaski. I don't see any guest, though. You want to explain what you mean?'

'Cameras can't tell you everything. Don't you have any binocs up there?'

'I'm in a radiation-shielded room. MFeels have been coming down hot and heavy from orbit. Last thing I need's binocs. Do you really have the logic? Our scanners aren't showing anything in your pack. Were you just s@$ting me to get a lift out, because—'

'I've got it, I've got it. Don't worry about it.'

'Come up to Tower Four. Major Galante's arrived and she's

boarding the last personnel. We're all leaving. It's a good thing you got here in time.'

The security net buzzes, then drops open and the two of them slip through, just like that, while you float nearby, disbelieving.

Klaski and the girl keep arguing. The girl seems more emotional without her seven other iterations. And more real.

'Serge will kick my butt if she gets hold of me,' Klaski is saying.

'She doesn't know everything.'

'She knows she's going to protect you.'

'She can't.'

'She's your mother!' Klaski fumes, flapping her arms in exasperation. You are careful to fly slightly behind her, so that she won't register your presence if she glances up momentarily in that God-help-me kind of way she has. 'Machine Front can see reason. I'm sure of that. Hell, they *are* reason. And nobody with any reason would choose war in place of mutual understanding. I'm sure of that. I'm really really sure. But forget this rescuing-your-own-body stuff. It will end in disaster, I'm telling you.'

'Come on,' says the girl. 'Just walk. The body for the logic bullets: that's the deal. Let's see you deliver.'

They start to walk. Everything is clean. No dirt at X; no garbage, either – too dangerous to allow, in case it should drift into the well. There are straight lines again, well-behaved surfaces, continuity. Klaski has been in the Grid a long time, and she doesn't have her land legs yet. She stumbles like a drunk.

X is bleak and deserted. It's like the set of the ghost town from the Grand Canyon episode of *The Brady Bunch*. All it needs are some fake tumbleweeds. Klaski is jumpy as hell, and the girl keeps stopping and balking.

'I don't like this.' Her teeth chatter, presumably with fear because it's warm enough. 'It's too open. It's horribly simple. Everything's exposed.'

Klaski tries to act sympathetic but is all on edge herself. The girl is as spooked and irrational as a wild animal.

'Come on,' Klaski urges. 'You'll get used to it. It's not far.'

'Where is my body? I don't want to go to this Tower Four.'

Exasperated, Klaski says, 'It's probably in Tower Four. They're probably going to take it back with them. We'll find out, but first things first. Come on . . . uh – hey, do you have a name? Did Serge give you one?'

The girl shakes her head.

'Come on, then . . . what should we call you? I know. I'll be Butch Cassidy, and you can be the Sundance Kid, OK? We'll pretend we're going to Bolivia.'

'On that basis, I should be Cassidy,' says the girl, poker-faced. 'I have more brains than you.'

'Whatever.' Klaski rolls her eyes. 'Come on, Cassidy! Move your little butt.'

My front door was opening. I heard the rustle of paper bags and the miniature thunder of cat feet as Nebbie and Rocky raced to greet Gloria.

'Hi, guys! Are you hungry?'

Quickly I switched off the TV. It was evening; I'd been on the nex a whole day, just flying.

'Oh, Cookie,' she gasped, patting her heart to show that I'd startled her. 'I didn't think you'd be here. Are you all right?'

I nodded. 'It's kind of hard to explain,' I said. 'I'm OK, but would you mind if I didn't say anything for now?'

Gloria looked at me in that slow way she has. 'OK,' she said after a while. 'You, uh, don't still want me to come by every day like you asked?'

'Please. If you don't mind. The situation . . . might change.'

'OK,' she said again. She took a deep breath and let it out. Then she sat with one hip on the back of my love seat and Nebbie jumped up beside her, purring. 'I guess you're not interested in stupid gossip. I just thought you'd find it interesting.'

'What?' I said, more out of guilty obligation to hold up my end than real curiosity.

'Oh, Sensei got whacked yesterday. Beat up real bad.'

The room vanished from around me and I was floating in an empty space. Everyone could see me. Everyone knew.

'He's in Holy Name hospital recovering from surgery. His wife told Mr. Ryan it was a break-in. Six guys. They had clubs and knives. He's lucky to be alive. They figure it was his karate that saved him.'

I could feel the hum of my own blood. It sounded like a vacuum cleaner in the next room.

'They get much?' I whispered. I heard Gloria going into the bathroom and running the water in the tub for Nebbie.

'Yeah, I guess he had a couple grand in cash from the monthly dues on the kids' classes. He was counting it to put it in the bank today. Hey, your sink's clogged.'

'I know,' I said. 'I ran out of Drano.'

seven pairs of kenneth cole

Absolutely nothing happened to me. I couldn't understand it.

I told Gloria that I wasn't impressed with Sensei Norman and I thought the whole karate thing was probably a load of boloney.

'I think it's all playing dress-up,' I said.

'It's weird,' Gloria said. 'Everybody's leaving. Sensei – did you know he got demoted to fifth dan? We can't call him Shihan anymore. Troy's going to do kickboxing in Paramus. He got that ribbon in the tournament, he figures he could be a good fighter.'

'What about you?' I said.

'Sensei asked me to teach the kids' class. Tanya quit.'

'Are you going to?'

'I guess. I want to get my black belt, Cookie.'

Soon after that, Miss Cooper called me.

'I'm leaving the organization,' she said. 'Sensei Price said I could drive up to his place and train, but Sensei Norman vetoed it. He said either I'm his student or nobody's student. So I left. Watch him scramble to find somebody to teach all the classes for him.'

'What will you do now?' I said. I didn't mention that Gloria of all people was replacing her.

'I don't know. Maybe something totally different. I still think the Okinawans are really cool, even after everything that happened. I'd like to go there. But I'm under a cloud right now. I might go to the city and study kenpo.'

And that was that.

Gunther called me, too. He asked me to come in. I still hadn't gotten around to replacing the tapes I'd stolen, and I figured he wanted them back. After all, I had more or less admitted to stealing them when I'd quoted parts of them to him at the barbecue.

I chucked them in a Shop Rite bag and went in. All the doors of the assignment room were shut. Some had green lights; some had red lights. The red lights meant some sucker was in there having their innermost thoughts plundered for money. I wanted to throw open all the doors and rip off the headphones, kick in the TV screens.

But there I'd be again, Cookie the maniac, Cookie the crazy.

I stalked into Gunther's office and chucked the bag on his desk.

'This what you want?' I said. 'I found it in the garbage. Cleaners must have thrown it out.'

He didn't even look in the bag.

'Cookie, I've been talking to Bob and we've come up with a salary package we think will be really appealing to you. I'm really delighted with this, and I think you will be, too. Sit down, please.'

I stared at him. He wasn't kidding.

'I can't come back to work, Gunther. Not after everything that's happened.'

'Don't worry. We can take care of things. John Norman's not a problem; he's too embarrassed to press charges. He told everyone he got attacked by a gang. Do you think he's going to want to admit one of his own students beat him up?'

I thought my heart would stop.

'How did you know about that?'

'Well, uh . . . he called us up and told us. He wanted us to know that we had a crazy person working for us. He wanted us to fire you.'

'And you told him you already did that.'

'We told him we stand behind our employees and he'd better get a lawyer if he had anything else to say to us.' Gunther looked really proud of himself.

'And? Have you heard from the police?'

Gunther shrugged. 'They might figure it out eventually. But I doubt it. Norman himself wants to keep it quiet. And if that changes, there are steps we can take. We have lawyers. You're a valued employee. There are ways around this stuff. There's your . . . condition.'

I did my best to give him the dead eye.

'Cookie, I know you're mad right now—'

'Yeah, mad as a hatter.'

'Sorry, poor choice of words. I know you're *angry*, but the truth is that you have a gift. And with that gift comes the obligation to use it.'

'For the betterment of humanity?'

'Well, yeah, maybe.'

'To make people buy more *Cookie Starfishes* merchandise? Or is it really the next Cyndi Lauper you're looking for now? What does that guy at the barbecue do – the one who thinks he's a sandworm expert? What are you using him for? Stock-market prediction?'

'That's confidential. He shouldn't have introduced himself that way. I've had a talk with him.'

'Oh, that's good, Gunther. That's real good.'

'Cookie, what can I say? We all gotta live. You walk out of here, what do you think happens? You're going to get a job where? At the Grand Union? At Macy's, like your mom?'

'There's no dishonor in that.'

'There's no future in it, either. It's up to you, Cookie. I'm not the bad guy. Neither is John Norman, you know. We're not evil villains. We don't own our own islands and laser people down with death rays. We're just regular guys trying to get by, make a living, go to the movies on a Friday night. So do me a favor and stop looking at me like you want to put a brick between my teeth too, all right?'

'Fine.'

'Fine. So what do you say? Don't you want to see the package we've put together?'

He proferred a sheet of letterhead.

'Stick it where the sun don't shine,' I said. I wished I could be ruder than that, but it just won't come for me.

'Come on. Don't make me beg. You're the *best*, Cookie.'

'Read my lips, Gunther.' And I mouthed F-U to him.

'OK, OK, well, go away and think about it. When you change your mind, my door is still open.'

I laughed. 'You don't know how open your door is, Gunther. You really don't know what you're playing with.'

I turned to go. I opened the door and looked at him. I was hoping he would ask me to elaborate. Maybe there could have been a chance for us then. Maybe we could have worked together, if only he'd entertained the possibility that I knew something real.

But he had a sneering expression on his face that said he thought what I'd said was pretty weak.

'Cookie, if you're afraid to fly, if there's a problem, we have people you could talk to.'

'I know,' I said. 'And pills I could take.'

'I'm only trying to help.'

I rattled the door handle.

'See ya, doc. By the way, when you call the police to give them a tip about me, make sure you tell them I'm only a green belt and I was unarmed. Maybe people will think twice about signing up for lessons with a guy who got wasted by a fat chick with a bag of groceries.'

I stalked out of the office and past Gloria, who was pretending to be on the phone. Gunther followed me, tie flapping.

'I never said I was going to make such a phone call,' he shouted after me. 'I can't understand this paranoia. You should see someone about that. It's a new symptom.'

'It's not paranoia, it's premonition. Check your Amex statements while you're at it. Your ex-girlfriend has bought herself seven pairs of Kenneth Cole shoes in the last month. I'd change my card number if I were you.'

And I left. I was all scared and shaky and expecting the wrath of God at any moment. I got to my car and thought about going back to apologize. But I didn't.

I sat in the Rabbit and measured the space between my stomach and the steering wheel. There was plenty.

Which gave my belly plenty of room to bounce around as what I had said to Gunther finally sank into me. I laughed and laughed.

'Seven pairs,' I gasped, wiping away the tears. 'Good for her.'

Then I went home, called the police and told them I could tell them all about the attack on John Norman if they wanted to come over and take my statement.

'I am *not* afraid to fly,' I told Nebbie. 'Unfortunately, there isn't time now. The squad car will be here soon.'

Nebbie was sitting on the windowsill, washing one of her hind legs. Rocky was watching her, tail twitching, thinking about pouncing.

'But just to prove I'm not afraid, I'll play a little *Quark*, OK?'

I looked at the dark TV.

Quark made more sense. I'd never be able to get into Tower Four as Gossamer. And what if MF saw me following Klaski and demanded to see my images? What if they saw the kid? What if I tried to hold the images of Cassidy back, but couldn't?

I was not afraid to fly. I was being circumspect. That was all.

thank you, ma'am

Once Cassidy had been persuaded to climb Tower Four, Klaski finally began to hear evidence of human activity. Voices and the sounds of boots on metal rang down the steel staircase. Cassidy seemed less frightened when she was climbing, and ascended nimbly. They came to a hatch in the ceiling.

'They must be loading the ship,' Klaski said. 'Stay here until I've explained the situation. I'll just get Major Galante to come and talk to us about the logic. She'll be very interested in you, Cassidy, I'm sure of that.'

She pushed the hatch open. There were guys hurrying around carrying crates and bags. They looked like they had just come in from the Grid: there was still a lot in the way of battle armor and weapons, and in the close space things didn't smell too hygenic, either.

Major Galante's voice rang out from somewhere above. 'OK, people. Let's ditch the battle armor, grab rations and get on board. We don't want to be here any longer than we have to.'

'You stay here,' Klaski repeated. 'Give me the logic.'

Cassidy didn't dignify that demand with a response. Her eyes flashed a warning.

Klaski blew out her breath like a horse snorting and climbed through the hatch. The first thing she saw was the barrel of Galante's ray gun.

'Where the *hell* did you come from?' Major Galante cried, and Klaski could see almost nothing of her irises. Her nostrils were flaring wide.

'Easy, ma'am,' croaked Klaski, showing her empty palms. She tried to grin. 'A guy called Dave sent me.'

Galante motioned Klaski away from the hatch with the gun. She pointed to the floor. Klaski sat.

The major flipped the privacy switch on her Swatch, so that Klaski couldn't see who was on the other end.

'This is Tower Four,' she snapped. 'Ah, Dave. I have somebody here identifies herself as Lieutenant Klaski, of Serge's unit. She says you know about it. *What?* Well, now. That's interesting. Send her up.'

She ended the call and addressed Klaski.

'We thought you guys were dead.'

Klaski smiled weakly. 'Not only am I not dead, ma'am, but I have something that I think you'll be very glad to see.'

She glanced at the hatch cover. She was trying to think how to phrase this. She'd had her speech all worked out in her head while Cassidy was leading her through the SynchroniCity to X, but the look on Galante's face was throwing her.

'See, you were right about the logic bullets,' she began. 'They weren't in the mine when you surrounded it. Dr. Gonzalez took them. She went a little crazy. That's why I—'

Through the open hatch, she could hear boots ringing on the metal ladder. She spun on her butt and half-crawled toward the hatch, yelling, 'Cassidy, no, not yet!'

Then she remembered that Cassidy wasn't wearing boots.

But Serge was.

She came up through the hole in one fluid movement, towering over Klaski and pushing Galante backward toward the milling activity of the crew with their crates and cables.

Galante and Serge nodded at one another. Klaski had never seen Serge fail to salute before. Serge glanced at Klaski, and Klaski gulped.

'But you can't be here. You're a golem.'

'Count me,' said Serge. 'How many of me you see?'

'One.'

'So I ain't no golem. Right?'

'I . . . I . . . I just assumed.' Klaski was only really flummoxed for a second, though. Then she rallied. 'Why didn't you come before? Why did you stay in the Grid?'

'You know the answer to that. Stupid.'

Major Galante spoke in a flat, calculated tone. 'I'm amazed to see you again, Captain Serge. The last we heard, you were issuing automated destruct orders to apply to yourself and a whole swathe of the Grid. Of all the officers in the Second wave, you're considered the most . . .'

'. . . Idiotically loyal?' offered Serge.

'I was going to say devoted to the Effort,' Galante

continued. 'But yes. This is quite a shift in
thinking.'

Galante looked small, and Klaski knew she was
afraid. Dangerously so. She said:

'Well, get on board then, Captain. We're almost
ready to launch.'

Serge snorted. 'One thing at a time. I need to
rescind those orders I gave. There's about a
discount-outlet warehouse full of stuff you don't
understand.'

Galante shifted her weight to one hip and folded
her arms across her chest.

'Really? Enlighten me. I'll give you five minutes.'

Serge relaxed infinitesimally. Klaski could detect
a faint collegial atmosphere between the two
commanders, a mutual respect.

'First off, I been in the well. That's why Klaski
here thought I was a golem. But I'm not. I been
translated into the Grid and back, and I can't say
as I like it much. Don't feel like telling you about
my personal problems, either. But I got
responsibilities.'

Klaski's glance went to the open hatch. She
couldn't help it.

'See,' Serge said, 'this is people and the Grid. It's
like when a mama bear tries to teach a baby bear to
go fishing. The baby bear sees the mama bear take
her great big paw and slap the water and come up
with a nice juicy fish, and so the baby bear thinks if
he splashes the water, he'll get a fish, too. So he's
splashing away, imitating her, and catching nothing
but water. And that's what's happening to y'all with
the Grid. You people just don't know where the fish
really is, so you're slapping.'

She paused significantly. Galante was interested. Who wouldn't be? Serge had crossed over to the Other Side and returned to tell. Galante wanted to hear Serge's revelations.

'Only you're not the mama bear, Serge,' said Cassidy's voice as she drew herself up through the hatch. 'You're just a baby bear, too.'

'Cassidy, you *nerd!*' yelled Serge. 'Get your butt back to the SynchroniCity before—'

'Don't shoot!' screamed Klaski at the same time, diving forward in a futile effort to grab the barrel of Galante's ray gun and turn it aside.

But Galante glanced at the security monitor and saw that it did not register Cassidy. She stepped neatly around Klaski. The ray hit Cassidy and she fell, just a simple collapse of limbs, an act of gravity. Like getting knocked down in the playground. But she didn't get up.

It happened so fast. Klaski found herself on the floor, kicked effortlessly to one side by Galante, who now fired on Serge. Serge jumped down the hatch and could be heard crashing around below. Galante's guys went after her.

'You stupid shit!' Klaski screamed, disbelieving. 'Don't you think before you shoot that thing?'

Major Galante turned and regarded Klaski stonily.

'You know the policy for dealing with golems.'

'THERE'S A HUMAN BODY ON THE SCOPE, COMMANDER,' said Galante's Swatch. Galante checked the visual, looked at Cassidy's body, then turned aside and bent over, hands on her knees, shaking. For a minute Klaski thought she was going to vomit. There was a shuffling sound as the

remaining crew members behind her moved and
murmured in reaction. Below, boots echoed on
metal as Serge fled her pursuers.

'It was a golem. It was a golem. It wasn't on the
scope.' Galante straightened, turned to look at her
subordinates.

'It's on the scope now,' somebody said.

'These girls are not golems. When they die, they
die,' cried Klaski. 'You knew about the body Arla
sent back. You saw the girls in the Grid. Didn't you
understand any of it?'

Galante's Swatch said,

'THESE GOLEMS REPRESENT A PERNICIOUS
THREAT. THEY HAVE TAKEN OVER THE MINES
TWICE AND HAVE STOLEN A MAXFACT FOR SOME
UNKNOWN PURPOSE. CAPTAIN SERGE HERSELF
ORDERED THEIR DESTRUCTION, BEFORE BEING
CORRUPTED BY THE WELL. THEY WILL BE THE
FIRST TARGET OF THE THIRD WAVE.'

'What? That's the stupidest thing I've ever
heard. Get Serge back and listen to her. You've got
an opportunity here to understand the whole—'

Klaski's prepared speech was cut short. Major
Galante dragged her by the arm and threw her into
an office to one side of the loading bay. She pointed
her finger at Klaski's face. 'Shut up. Stay there,'
she said. She closed the door and locked it.

'Mohammed! Stand guard. Debbie, pick up that
body and bag it. We'll put it in the hold with the
other one. The rest of you, get on with the takeoff
preps.'

Klaski found a chair and sat down in it. Her ears
rang and the room seemed to pitch and flash, as if
the Grid still had a hold of her sensory perception.

She couldn't believe what she had just seen. But what was she supposed to do about it?

Her mind felt like a wilted lettuce. The futility of it all.

Oh, well.

After a while, not very long, the emotional color began to fade.

It was nice to be back indoors. Maybe there would be a shower in her near future. And a bed . . .

Eventually she noticed that there was a Tupperware box of cold rice pilaf mixed with chicken and vegetables on the table: someone's interrupted lunch. It didn't smell bad. While she was eating, Klaski looked at the computer screen and saw supply lists and orbital timing schedules.

Major Galante came back in. Klaski licked rice off her dirty fingers and swallowed.

'Joanne Klaski, I could kiss you,' said Major Galante. 'Forty-seven logic bullets, all of them functional, recovered from the alien body outside. And you brought them in. You're a hero.'

Klaski glowed. This was more like it. Finally her contribution was being recognized.

'Ma'am, the scopes can't find Captain Serge. Do you want me to go out and look for her personally?'

'Don't be crazy,' barked Galante. 'Leave her to MF. They'll find her. What do you think Fliers are for?'

Then she came around behind Klaski and slapped on the restraints.

'Don't get me wrong, Klaski. You saved my ass. However, officially speaking, our records show you

responsible for the loss of your commanding officer
in one incident of recklessness, and for the wilful
murder of Arla Gonzalez in another. I'm sorry
about this, but you're under arrest.'

Klaski felt waves of indignation and
disappointment surging up her throat. Then Galante
said,

'Now get into the ship and consider yourself
lucky. You can forget about the Grid. You're going
home.'

And she pushed Klaski ahead of her into the last
transport vessel.

'Thank you, ma'am,' sobbed Klaski as the airlock
thudded shut.

Half an hour later, Klaski was listening to Major
Galante's Walkman and singing along to Men at
Work.

A hand tugged the headphones off her ears from
behind. Klaski whipped her head around and saw
the barrel of a ray gun about an inch from her
mouth.

She actually let out a feeble squeak and took a
couple of fish-gulps of air before she recognized it.
The Grid had altered it. The gun's shape was the
same, but instead of lead-gray metal and plastic
casing, it had an iridescent snakeskin look, and the
barrel itself was a lurid chemical orange. From
within the barrel came a faint neon gleam.

The crew were strapped in their seats with their
backs to Klaski, facing the viewscreen, preoccupied
with coms and last-minute checks. It was noisy.
Major Galante was arguing with her personal zebra
about flight trajectories.

'I failed,' Serge said in a low voice. 'I failed to hidewhip the Grid and then I failed to save it. Why did my girl bring them the logic bullets? Do you know why, Klaski?'

'Please,' Klaski whispered into the barrel. 'I just want to go home, ma'am.'

'Home? Where's that?'

Klaski was already crying, because it came easiest. Serge was always so sarcastic.

'Back to Earth, ma'am.'

She heard Serge sigh; but the barrel didn't waver.

'I hate to burst your Hubba Bubba, but there ain't no such rutabaga, Klaski. Or if there is, you're already there.'

Klaski could hear a little flute solo coming through the displaced headphones. It sounded remote and insignificant.

As usual, she couldn't really follow Serge's meaning. Wasn't a rutabaga some kind of vegetable?

'You know why she did it, don't you, Klaski? I ask her and I ask her and she just says it's to do with being a starfish above the tide. What the hell is that, Klaski?'

Klaski licked her lips.

'She wanted her body back. She said she couldn't be whole as long as the body was somewhere else.'

Serge didn't move. Klaski didn't think she was breathing. After a while she said, 'Thanks for that. Kid.'

The barrel moved away from Klaski's face and pointed towards the viewscreen, where the attention of Galante and her crew was focused.

'Ever since I got gobbled by the well, I been wondering,' Serge said, 'whether this here equipment still works, after all it's been through.'

And Klaski lifted her gaze, over the Grid-stained battle armor that covered Serge's chest, past her chapped lips to her flared nostrils, and finally to a pair of black eyes, where the reflection of the gun's flash shone pure white before Serge's pupils had time to contract.

easter

DATAPLEX EXPLOITED MENTALLY ILL EMPLOYEE
By Susan Briggs, staff writer

The Mahwah woman recently convicted of aggravated battery against her karate teacher may have suffered from mistreatment in the workplace at Dataplex Corporation, it emerged today.

Karen Orbach was routinely expected to work up to 90 hours a week in Dataplex's Woodcliff Lake R&D department, according to her lawyer, Rita Schickworth.

'Our information indicates that Dataplex executives were aware that Ms. Orbach suffers from a mild form of delusional schizophrenia which is aggravated by stress, yet they took no action.'

Schickworth added that Dataplex 'will be investigated by the appropriate state and federal agencies in connection with my client's complaints.'

At her trial last week, Ms Orbach declined her option to plead guilty by reason of insanity and received an 18-month prison sentence.

A Dataplex spokesman said that the gruelling R&D project in question has been 'indefinitely suspended.'

The victim, John Norman, returned to his Wanaque home Tuesday after a five-week hospital stay involving reconstructive facial surgery and treatment for a ruptured spleen. Norman is a fifth-degree black belt and the founder of Minnehaha Karate Academy.

'Violence never solves anything,' said Ellen Payne, MSW. Her name tag glinted on her cheap polyester blouse, one of those with a ribbon-tie neckline that was supposed to disguise its wearers' flat-chestedness but never did.

'Karen, were you ever abused as a child?'

'Um, no,' I assured her, shaking my head. I could feel myself pulling the old politeness around me like a fur coat. The deference. It was safer.

'OK,' she said, sounding doubtful. 'Because if you had been, I think it would be really beneficial for you if we could talk about it. Abuse isn't always physical. Did your parents take drugs?'

I could almost see the mental checklist she was running down, ticking off the boxes, categorizing me. Questions about whether Uncle Marty had ever asked me to sit on his lap were bound to follow.

If there's one thing that really annoys me, it's people insulting my intelligence. What would Gloria do now?

'You know,' I said softly. 'I'm really offended by this line of questioning.'

'Do you want to hit me?' said Ellen Payne, MSW.

'Not yet,' I said. 'Violence never solves anything.'

'You're being sarcastic.'

'Well!' I laughed.

'What do you mean by 'Well'?'

'*Well*, is that really what you think? Have you ever seen a movie where violence isn't the solution? Have you read the paper lately? Violence seems to be the preferred solution all over the planet, and if it's officially sanctioned it's wonderful heroism and if it isn't it's a crime. I lost my temper with that . . . that . . . *A-hole*.' I couldn't quite bring myself to say the full curse word but I think, for me, 'A-hole' was big progress. 'And I'm glad I did it because he deserved it and nobody else was going to step up to the plate. If I could do it all over again, I'd do exactly the same. Did he threaten me? No. Did I hear voices? No. Am I a mental case? Maybe. So what? I have every right to be here, Ellen Payne, MSW. So stop trying to make me feel like I'm broken and I need fixing. I don't want any counseling. I don't want to be rehabilitated.'

She listened to my outburst dispassionately, then cocked her head a little and pursed her lips.

'You know, Karen, most of the inmates here have below-average intelligence. Many of them come from deprived backgrounds or an abusive home life. Some of them have emotional problems. You're going to have to live among them for the duration of your sentence. You could have gotten an insanity plea, but you wouldn't even consider it. You ought to have been on medication in the first place. You are on tranquilizers now, I see from your file. Is that right?'

'I don't need them,' I said. I rolled my tongue around in my mouth. I had a celery string stuck between two molars.

'Does that mean you're not taking them? Come on, I know there are tricks. Are you not taking your medication?'

'Of course I'm taking it,' I lied.

'Well, it might be very satisfying to you to sit there and tell me that you don't want to be rehabilitated, but when reality sets in I think you're going to change your mind. You don't belong here, Karen. Wait until you make a wrong move. Wait and see who's the aggressor and who's the victim when you're up against some of these women, and then you can tell me that violence is a good solution. It wasn't a good solution for you, and if you can't see that now, you're going to.'

I sighed. Nothing like a good lecture on top of a bad night's sleep and an inedible breakfast. 'Now,' Ellen Payne, MSW continued. 'Something went wrong in your life to make you do this thing, and I'm here to help you work out what that was and how you can make sure nothing like this ever happens again. If you cooperate with this process, you could get out sooner.'

'Maybe I'm not interested in that.'

'Well, frankly, I'm having a lot of trouble understanding why.' She stood up and gathered her stuff. 'I'll check back with you in a few weeks, in case anything changes. I hope you'll reconsider.'

'I hope you reconsider your Aunt Pat's nursing home,' I heard myself say. 'She gets bedsores and the nurses steal her romance novels. When was the last time you went to see her?'

Ellen Payne, MSW slammed the door. I heard her heels go tripping down the corridor. She sounded like the seventh race at Belmont.

That night, I went to the TV room for the first time. The cigarette smoke made my eyes water. I wasn't the fattest person there. I wasn't the blackest, either. A sister the size of Rochelle Park took up most of the sofa. She was talking back to the TV.

'Aw, come on, can't you see that little weaselly guy done it? How stupid you want to get?'

'It can't be the little guy, it's always the guy with the English accent.'

I folded my arms across my chest and looked sideways across the TV. Playing safe.

The big woman glanced at me, said, 'Got a cigarette?'

I shook my head. I was petrified. Four skinny girls were crammed into a loveseat, whispering to each other and giggling. I could tell they were talking about me but I didn't dare look at anyone directly.

'Check it out,' a middle-aged redhead said, 'She's like a friggin' statue. You see that show the other night about them stone idols, she looks like one of them. What was that place called?'

'Easter Island,' answered one of the skinnies, couldn't

have been more than nineteen. 'Hey, Easter! Newgirl, I'm talking to you.'

I looked at her.

'My name is Karen,' I said.

'You do voo-doo, Easter?'

I snorted. 'Do you?'

She licked her lips, wiggled her fingers in front of her face. 'Cuz I heard you spooked out Microtits this morning. Told her a message from her dead auntie or something.'

'I didn't mean to spook her out,' I said seriously. 'I just accidentally said something I shouldn't.'

'Don'tyousmokethen?' It all came out as one angry word, from Rochelle Park.

'No.'

'You know who did it, Easter? Who killed the heiress?'

At first I didn't know what she meant. Then:

'I don't like to watch TV,' I said, still deliberately avoiding looking at the screen, although I could hear the sound.

'Everybody likes to watch Tom Selleck,' said the redhead in her flat voice. 'Unless you're a dyke.'

I didn't want to be marked as a dyke in a women's prison, did I? Reluctantly, I turned to the screen.

It wasn't the Grid. It was Hawaii. Even I knew who Magnum was, because I often read *TV Guide* so as not to appear totally clueless when chatting with colleagues at the watercooler. But it was hard to follow the story. The women were making a racket, talking back to the TV, occasionally throwing wadded-up gum at it, making fun of people's clothes and imitating their voices. '*Oooh*,' they'd say frequently to Magnum. 'You gonna take that from him?' Or: 'Psych! Lookit her face, any more mascara and she's gonna need a forklift just to get her eyes open.'

I'd never seen anything like it. In my houses, and my friends' houses, we always watched TV quietly. It was rude to do otherwise. These girls kicked their legs in the air and threw stuff at the screen.

Where were you guys when I was letting the Grid freak me out? I thought.

Then I started to join in. Nothing big, but I couldn't help laughing sometimes, or pointing, or muttering remarks of my own. And the TV stayed TV. No other planets.

It was pure magic.

'Get a nose job,' I heard myself say to one of the cops. The redhead heard me.

'Hah! You hear that? "Get a nose job," Easter says.'

'Don't mind Shannon,' said Rochelle Park to me. 'She don't know you beat up a karate master. Otherwise she wouldn't call you Easter, she'd call you Kung Fu.'

'What are you in here for, Shannon?' I managed. I wanted to smile but I couldn't make my face do it.

'Armed robbery. Oi, look out he's gonna—'

'—Left-hook you,' I finished, wincing empathetically as Magnum went flying over a table.

Maybe that's the key. Don't just watch. *Don't just let them use you.*

Maybe it's time for a little audience participation.

Back in my cell, I spent my nights working on a game plan.

It was no good being able to watch TV and interact with it and not see the Grid, if what I wanted was to see the Grid and act *on* it. What good is watching *Magnum, P.I.* in that situation?

It was true that at home I'd used a TV tuned to the static between channels, but I couldn't do that here because any private use of the TV had to be sanctioned through Ellen Payne, MSW, and I wasn't about to confide in her. All she knew was that I had delusional problems when watching TV. I could ask for therapeutic TV time, but if I then tuned in to dead air the guard would tell that to S.P., MSW, who would think I was yanking her chain.

Then again, there had been that time when Rocky had tuned in to Channel 11 in his attempt to watch Yankee baseball. I had flown through the Friday-night movie. I could do it.

But I had to do it right this time. I had to try to duplicate the conditions that had been used at Dataplex, but take control of them on my own terms. I was pretty sure that Miles had been right about what I had been shown at Dataplex: videotapes, not a blue screen at all. The blue screen probably came up when the nex snapped – when the video ended, in other words, or someone turned it off.

And the video I had been shown, complete with proposed commercial advertising, could only have been one thing.

Cookie Starfishes came on at 5:30 a.m. and again at 1:30 p.m. There was no way I could get to watch it in the afternoon during *All My Children* because, as I'd learned in the past few days, beautiful young Jenny had recently gone to New York to become a model and had no idea that the virginity she'd kept from and for her beloved Greg was about to be stolen and her good name besmirched by unscrupulous underwear-catalog photographers. Not to mention the fact that she was being stalked by a psycho.

So 5:30 a.m. it would have to be.

Ellen Payne, MSW did not come to see me again. I guess the Aunt Pat thing had upset her. Instead, she informed me by memo that a viewing could be arranged for my benefit on Thursday. Wednesday night, I didn't sleep. At the appointed hour, one of the guards let me into the TV room with a muttered, 'There ya go, Easter.' I was hungry, shivering, sweat-palmed as the guard went into the observation area and picked up the remote contol. The TV came on in a blast of happy music.

I sank into a chair and licked my lips.

'Right,' I heard myself mutter self-consciously. 'Interact. Talk back. Give 'em hell.'

The guard had her head down. She was doing paperwork.

'I'm not doing it, Dante,' I said, louder. The guard didn't even twitch. Who would, after the antics of Shannon and Rochelle Park – whose name turned out to be Malinda (car thief), by the way – and their cohorts?

'Go ahead and try me and let's see what happens,' I added. I leaned forward in my chair. I gesticulated. 'I'm gonna fly now and I hope you recognize that I don't belong to you anymore. You can't make me do anything. You can't make me do anything.'

I kept repeating it, but pretty soon I couldn't even hear my own voice, because I was *there*. The sky was loud with eventuality, with the sound of things being finished once and for all. I kept opening my mouth and forcing air past my vocal cords anyway, talking myself into existence just like the girls had sung up their city within the Grid.

I won't stay quiet anymore.

into the wishing well

When the MFeels first came down they looked like Thread. And maybe, in that they were mindless and blind, they *were* like Thread.

Now they're loaded up on logic bullets and, like Miles on Cheez Doodles, they're coming after whatever they consider to be a problem. The problem of the day is the girls of the Grid. You lie on the air and watch the MFeels' metallic, muscular bodies undulate and dive among the branches of the Grid. You watch them shrug off pollen and dodge lightning flashes. You watch them skim the well and then, bouncing invisible questions off Gossamer's eyes, they home in on each child.

At first it's like watching a polar bear try to catch a seal. The children simply scatter, slip into the well, and disappear, only to pop up again elsewhere as if diving through holes in the ice. But, like polar bears, the MFeels hunt in packs. And they have the predators' persistence, too. Their strategy begins to unfold. They are driving the girls together, sheepdogging them, wearing them down and cutting off their options. They are backed up by the full force of MF – no longer concerned about the consequences for life on the surface, MF are letting loose all their favorite toys. Explosions roil the surfaces of the well – first one, then two, then ten at once as MaxFacts are dropped all around. Soon there are no nearby pools for the children to dive into. They are driven into the higher branches. Clouds of indigenes rise, making it hard to see – a temporary reprieve.

You can hear the Grid, even from on high. It howls and chimes, but its music is not mysterious to the MFeels: they pulse in resonance; they have internalized its rhythms.

'There are some things you shouldn't see, Cookie,' Mom used to say. 'They get in your head and you can't ever get them out. There are some things you don't want to look at.'

Case in point. What she didn't tell you was that, by seeing some things, you could make them happen.

You watch the first MFeel catch up with its prey. The child, so frightening and atavistic to Klaski and the others, so dangerously unreal with that faster-than-fast movement and unpredictable mosquito-like direction-switching behavior, now appears desperately ordinary. In the context of the sinuous MFeels she looks particularly human. She scrambles clumsy and panicked like a wounded animal in the branches of the Grid. She's trying to get to the blasted region that the girls make their home. It looks like she's trying to get to the door in the bottom of the pit, X-marked, visible from the air like a helicopter pad. The door to the MaxFact city. But the door is closed.

The child takes a wild, swinging leap, arms and legs flying in reflexive abandonment. She sprawls on the closed surface of the red door. She has something in her hand: a Grid-modified whip-cutter. She begins to hack at the door with it. The door splinters, breaks at the edges; she claws, starts to open it, can't lift it at first.

And the MFeel comes at her from behind. She never sees it. It gores her with its sharp head and begins to burrow into her small body. You see her ribs part as it buries its voracious head in her thorax. Her black-haired head slumps. The logic bullet within the MFeel's translucent body glows like a live coal. It jerks, shakes itself with a wave motion undulating all down its length, and for a moment you are reminded of a cat killing a snake by smashing it against the rocks: only it is the child who is being killed and the snake that is thrashing with obscene animation. It is changing. Its skin breaks open and wings sprout. It lifts its head and shifts its mechanical snout from side to side, eyeless but no longer mind-less in the way it moves. Lights flash across its belly like Smaug's jewels or the instrument panels on *Star Trek*: jelly-bean lights, here splashed with blood.

That's enough. That's really a hundred percent enough. The inner voice has taken on a warning tone like a playground monitor about to blow into the whistle around her neck. Mom doesn't like this. You don't like it either.

No, I won't do it, I won't see it, I won't do it.

But it goes on and on, and you can't close your eyes. The metal dragon-thing raises itself into the air, flapping awkwardly, twist-ing its body from side to side and thrashing until limbs spring out from where they must have been straitjacketed within what was its casing and is now its flesh.

Still blind, it comes into the air, flits across the roof of the Grid, picking up colored pollen as it goes. Its wings seem to be grow-ing as it flies.

Below, the corpse of the child, a husk, left behind by her sisters or other selves. She never stood a chance.

Her sisters have followed her. They reach the door, scrabble at it, force it open. MFeels scream after them. The girls drop through the trapdoor in fast motion and the MFeels follow in a crowd, jostling one another like salmon on the spawn in their efforts to get inside.

You experience a moment of pure relief as you realize that, once inside, the MFeels will not be able to see their quarry, because you are their eyes and you are out here.

They will escape.

You urge Gossamer higher; but she doesn't listen. Just like before, the Grid is sending her a different message. The Grid is calling her to the door.

NO NO NO.

You try to pull Gossamer back from the door. You use all your will. It doesn't have any effect at all.

They are using you, using you, using you – don't you care? STOP, drat it!

It's all about willpower – you've got to resist.

But what kind of willpower could we be talking about, when you've never even been able to resist a Twinkie?

Gossamer whips through the aperture and you are flying through the MaxFact city. You seem to have entered via its underside. The MFeels have scattered, confused by their lack of vision, and the girls have a momentary advantage while MF regroups, using your eyes.

Close your eyes, close your eyes, don't look.

You can't stop.

See the wild children: they are running now, pell-mell like frantic, anonymous civilians in a Japanese monster movie. They run through the streets and down the steps and up the walls of their impossible concept-labyrinth, panicking because they can be killed.

They aren't the only ones. Golems appear like zombies from doorways and up from sewers, and are cut down without ever being seen because the only humans here are the ones running for their lives. Machines see only lightning and storm; you see a mother defending her young as the city itself seems to open up in front of the children and close down on their enemies. You see the Grid bare its teeth in anger and pain.

The children scatter, making multiple targets of themselves. It is not enough. They are being speared.

Again and again, you watch it happen. The helpless child killed; the precision machine brought to life. Dragonish weapons abandon their murdered prey and fly to roost in crooked towers and on radio antennae. Their logic bullets beat like hearts.

*

It seems like destiny. Are you supposed to support it because it looks like destiny? Is this one of those things you just have to accept and try and look on the bright side, feed the cat, go on with your life?

Nothing can change how you feel. No matter what you tell yourself or what Machine Front orders, you still see small children being pursued by monsters.

Serge's Gridborn girls are not just information-states. They are not just placeholders in some bigger schema. To *me* they live, and the knowledge that they will die, out here without help, neither human nor Grid, abandoned to the neverbefore/neveragain, written-off – to me this knowledge comes like a terrible ache in the gut, the one we all dread asking a doctor about because we know it must be the end of us, sooner or later. To me these children are not just some trick. Even if they are, to *me* they are *not*.

Yes, to *me. Me me me. I am here*, so shoot me. I admit it; I exist.

The MFeels must see the children to hunt them.

They can only see the children because of *my* eyes.

My eyes see this dream city. They see floodwaters pouring out of pipes in the walls, gushing brownly into a canal below. Behind gaps in the brickwork shines a red machine light. There is a smell of rust. All this dead structure has reassembled itself in living pieces. It has a logic, this arrangement, but the logic is extrinsic to the form of its parts. Rules change according to scale. Like Miles and his irritating new physics.

And I am part of the mind that does this reordering. We, Cookie/Gossamer, are already fused. We already live in more than one place. We already are/I already am more than one thing.

I could think my way into action.

I could stretch across the concept barrier, starfish beyond the known dimensions.

I will take my eyes away. I will not give my eyes over.

And damn you all. Including you and your company picnics, Gunther. By the way.

I can still fly, which is more than most can say. I take Gossamer away from the fray. I refuse to look. I study the architecture; I gaze *into* the architecture, seeking its antecedents, its associations, its paths of truth backbackback deep in the suitcase of the MaxFact, disarraying the carefully folded costumes of organized human time. I don't look for targets; I look inside them. This confuses the MFeels.

Machine Front are not having this. They try to make me help with the hunt. Gossamer jerks and writhes in my grip. They are overriding me. They are calling her with cheap electrodine cattle-prod tactics.

GOSSAMER TO TRACKING. REPORT NOW OR BE TAKEN OFFLINE.

Other fliers come swarming from the fake sky, ready to replace me.

Oh, no, you don't. Not this time.

In the middle of the city there was a green place. It was shaped like an eye and it consisted of cypress trees buried up to their knees in brackish fluid. It consisted of circuits and battery acid. It consisted of ink and barbed wire. It was a dream.

It could have been a park or a graveyard. All I knew was that the well steeped the roots of electric trees like neon everglades. And in the depths of the well lay golem bodies, blurred by decay or growth; hard to tell the difference, here. Their memories fed the collective. They no longer scared me.

Up in the high air the music of the Grid could be felt where my teeth should have been if only Gossamer had had teeth. The Grid had a pulse of sorts, a numerical array expressed as sound of the variety that stuns bats and annoys people. I nestled, listening, into a space between axonic impulses and their silence, and far away in my own body I drew a deep breath because boy did I need it. I heard my heart beat five times. Then I brought Goss down like a kamikaze kite, burying me and her and our eyes in the deepdeep fluid substrate of everything that was the well.

My two eyes converge to become one Grid-swallowed Earthmade Gossamer eye. It pulses in a static field, rises into being from the depths of the city where cabling and pipes snake-dance around each other and plunge in and out of a thousand staircases. The eye emerges from the well in greengrass: a scrap of abandoned baseball diamond long since built over with more useful structures. Buildings shadow it. Warped and twisted aluminum bleachers writhe in a semi-helix, bent over like an osteoporotic spine, and on the places where people are expected to put their butts I can see the inky scrawl of somebody's handwriting plus a scrap of that famous sketch of a male body within a circle – Michelangelo's graffiti. Standing guard in a watchful semicircle, old billboards flap burned paper like dead skin. Ads.

Their words have long since been rendered in bone.

This is Gossamer's eye. The well is doing what the well does. The well is changing it, making its mechanical properties into something alive. I am within the membrane, looking both ways, two-dimensional, like a Janus-faced playing card.

Gossamer's eye is large. The iris opens tall and narrow, like a cat's.

The pupil pulls like a vortex.

The nerves of this hybrid eye are like roads between worlds. I can see both worlds. I can see the prison TV room where the guard is blowing the steam from her Folger's. I can see the devastation of the ruinous city. I can see the last of the girls running towards me, pursued by the last of the MFeels.

The last one.

The last Cassidy runs up to my eye. She looks into me. I have been seen. For the first time, I have looked and have been seen in turn.

'Take me back,' she begs. I see her lips move. 'I don't want to become one of them. Take me to where you are. Please.'

I am in the place where seeing is acting.

The nex is still open.

I have no thickness at all; I am infinitely thin and permeable, and I am pulling the world through my self like a drain sucking water.

I take her. Starting with the MaxFact suitcase unpacking and peaking with the girl, I take it all. And I am Serge and her undead offspring. I am the bodies of the soldiers, plundered for their logic. I am the machine guts and nerves, stratae of meaning lying on one another like colors in a sand painting. In this moment, I am the Grid.

I can make a parting, or a curtain, or a door.

Gossamer's eyes will feed back, like a guitar amp.

The world will look on itself.

So this child can escape her fate. I will do this.

I won't leave her there, alone. I won't see her turned into some rending, killing *thing*.

I want to save someone. I want to make something come right.

I pull the girl through unharmed. I smell her green-stained body and feel her oily fingerprints. I hear her essence like a voice. She slips through me and out the other side, losing all substance, vaporized or transformed into thought; I don't know.

Then comes her pursuer.

I try to close the eye, stop the action here, but the well is stripping Gossamer away from me, casting me out as it remakes her machine parts into something alive. I'm losing the nex.

I see the blind snout arrowing towards me. As if it has already tasted of its next meal, the MFeel breaks all the rules and begins to change as it enters me. I see metal nostrils, green flame, cabled wings and articulated vertebrae. I see corrugated skin like the side of a metal garbage can. I see flashes of circuit board and intestine, white bones like an X ray. It's a visual tornado and it fills me entirely in a flash.

Then I flinch, and, like a spirit leaving its body, perforce I flee.

But I am still here. I was always here.

I'm sitting in a vinyl-covered orange chair looking up at a 19" color TV that's bolted to the wall. Tinny synthesizer music is playing. Credits are rolling, partially obscuring the puffy little purple and yellow starfish that cavort across the galaxy, studded with chocolate chips and grinning.

my coffee with reality-substitute

Miles came to see me.

'Well, at least they put you here. Rita says it's a nice jail.' He glanced around doubtfully. 'She says places here are few and far between. Especially for violent offenders.'

'You're still mad at me,' I said, because it was obvious.

'I just wish you would have *told* me. There are untraceable, really nasty things we could have done to the bastard by computer. Why'd you have to go all berserker? This *isn't* D&D, Cookie.'

'I know.'

'Rita could have gotten you out of it, you know. I wish you could have just pleaded.'

I shrugged. 'Maybe I'm better off staying in here. Did that ever occur to you?'

Miles gave me a dark look. 'Why do you say that? You don't think Dataplex would come after you?' I could almost see the thought-bubble form outside his head: *Industrial conspiracy? Or paranoid schizophrenia?*

'No, not Dataplex. Never mind. Look, this lawsuit is silly. You're wasting your money. Gunther kept telling me to take time off. You haven't got a case.'

Miles said, 'I want to shake the tree and see if any monkeys fall out. Don't worry about money. I've just started a contract with IBM for big bucks.'

I beamed. 'That's great! Congratulations. Do you have to wear a tie?'

Miles actually banged his fist on the table.

'Can you be serious for one minute! Are you truly aware of what you've done?'

'Quit talking to me like one of those darn psychologists, Miles. I poured Drano on the guy's face. I know what I did. I'd do it again, too.'

Miles sighed.

'Thanks for your staunch support, Pimpernel,' I added.

'Sorry. It's just that, I thought we had a shot at getting somewhere with . . . you know . . .' He gave a conspiratorial shifty look at the room around us '. . . Our *project*.'

I avoided his gaze.

'I, uh . . . think I've taken that as far as it can go,' I said.

'Meaning what?'

'Meaning . . . well, I guess I'm cured now. I watched *Hill Street Blues* last night.'

Miles stared at me. Embarassment clouded his face. He was thinking that I was just a fruitcake and everything we'd talked about was all part of it. He wasn't sure, though. He was looking at me like he'd find some sign in my eyes that he hadn't just been wasting his time all along.

'So,' I said, and my voice was shaky. 'How's the opera going? Speaking of *The Marriage of Fig Newton*, did you know that your eyes are the same color as Fig Newton filling?'

He gave his head a rapid shake like a wet dog would. He kept looking at me, and twisting his visitor's pass in his hands. It was starting to look sweaty and fuzzy. This was all too much of a stretch for him. Couldn't he see how risky it was for me to talk to him? He hadn't believed me when I'd told him about the Grid. What if I told him about Cassidy and the dragon, and he laughed?

I took a breath. Wished I had a candy bar. Took another breath.

'Miles, what if TV became real?'

He cocked his head. 'You mean, like when Daffy Duck starts talking back to the illustrator and this giant pencil comes into the frame and erases parts of him?'

I rolled my eyes. I should have expected this.

'Not exactly.'

'Or cartoons and people in the same reality? I think Gene Kelly did it in like the 1940s. What if dreams became real?'

'I don't remember my dreams.' I tried to explain it better. 'What if you could manifest your thoughts? You have a vision of a monster, say, and it becomes real.'

'Ah! *Ghostbusters*. The Marshmallow Puff man. And I bet Stephen King's done it. Or like how about that TV movie where they go back in time and meet Sherlock Holmes. I mean – hello? Sherlock Holmes is, like, a *fictional* character?'

'So everything's been done. It's all movies.' I couldn't keep the disappointment out of my voice.

'Like I always say, Cookie, better movies than reality. I'd rather eat my popcorn and go home.'

'Say you see something on TV and then it happens.'

'You're talking about the Grid again, aren't you? Golems. Mechanical flying . . . eels, was it?'

Miles's tone wasn't particularly sarcastic, but it was hard not to be defensive all the same. I tried to stick to the facts.

'They were called eels, and I guess they looked like eels at first. But they ended up more like dragons.'

'Didn't we establish that this was all marketing stuff?'

'Yes. No. Maybe. Look – what if the thing could *cross over*? Using you. I mean, me. What if it became actually, really real?'

'Mm-hmm.'

'And nobody believes you. No – I take it back, the only people who believe you are kooks.'

He shifted in his seat. 'Ah, now I'm with you. Well, if you're really serious about this, you should get tested. There are scientists studying precognition and stuff. Then you'd know, objectively. There would be proof. Right?'

I shivered. 'I don't know anymore. I thought that was what Dataplex was all about. I thought they knew what they were doing. I thought I wouldn't be alone. But it's been all about using me.'

Miles said, 'I wish you would let me pursue this. I'm sure I could nail Dataplex for *something*.'

I shook my head. 'What's the point? It's too late. I've let the thing happen. There's no going back now. I think I've . . . brought something over. From the Grid.'

My voice trailed off. I couldn't say it. I sounded too stupid. Besides, Miles was getting sick of me. I could tell. I couldn't blame him. Everything he said, I shot down. Then again, everything I said, he came up with a movie he'd seen it in.

But I wasn't really prepared for what came next. He leaned forward and put his elbows on the table.

'Cookie. I'm your friend. I have to say this to you, and if you get mad, there's nothing I can do, but I'll still be your friend if you let me.'

'Yeah? What?'

He wrinkled his brow. He looked very sincere.

'You have a . . . problem. With reality.'

I laughed. 'You think I'm a shithead.'

There! I said it! I actually said 'shit.' Incredible.

'I *don't* think you're a shithead. I'm just saying—'

'No, no, no, don't back off it, Miles.'

'I'm not backing off it, Cookie. On the contrary. I've seen

what's in your medicine cabinet. I know the stuff they've prescribed for you. Doctors don't just hand out Thorazine for fun.'

'And I don't just *take* it for fun – in fact, I don't take it at all.'

'Maybe you should.'

'Maybe the doctors are wrong. Maybe the doctors are stupid. Maybe— You know what? Hey, I do have a problem with reality. How can you *not*? Take Clarissa Delgado. What is she doing every day? What is the meaning of her life? She eats, sleeps, watches TV and goes shopping. And cleans offices. For what? That's reality? Being Clarissa Delgado for what purpose?'

'Who knows? It's not for us to say. Maybe she'll give birth to the next Edison. Or maybe she'll save somebody's life by giving blood, or smelling smoke and pulling a fire alarm. Or maybe she won't. But you can't judge people. You're not God.'

'I'm not judging her – I'm asking why she gets out of bed in the morning.'

'Habit, probably. Why do any of us?'

'Aha. Exactly. Well, I'll tell you. Food was why I got up in the morning. It was the meaning of my life. It was my reason for doing things, my reward, my stopgap to fill up dead time. It was my cushion, my defense, my weapon. It was the thing that anchored me to reality, if we're talking about reality. You got sugar-substitutes, right? Sweet 'n' Low? Well, I took my coffee with reality-substitute. Now I can't take it anymore. I can't use food. I don't have my security blanket and everything is naked and ugly. People are going on with their pointless routines and I'm one of them. There is nothing else.'

'There's being dead,' Miles replied amicably. 'Besides, not everybody's a drone. People do amazing things. They skydive. They invent things. They act in plays and climb mountains and play the stock market and save the whales. It's called free will. You should check it out.'

'I did check it out. I took up karate, and that turned out to be bogus, too.'

'You can't give up that easily.'

'Yes, I can. Look, those people you're talking about, the skydivers? They have their act together. And you know what? People like that never seem to have much imagination when it comes to the bad things. They never seem to think very deeply. Or if they did, they'd be too depressed.'

'Like you.'

'I'm not depressed. I'm confused. I want to know what the rest of us are supposed to do in this so-called real world of yours. I'm not a mountain climber or an ice diver. I'm twenty-five years old and I see things on TV that I'm not supposed to see. I thought it was the future, or something very far away. Now I'm not so sure. And the people I thought I could go to for help are only interested in predicting the next Cyndi Lauper or the next *MASH* or the next . . . Orville Reddenbacher microwave popcorn, I guess.'

Miles sighed. 'I don't know what to tell you, Cookie. All I can say is, we have one world. D&D is great, but it's a game, *Blade Runner* is a movie, *The Hobbit* is a book. We have one world, and this is it, and you've got to find a way to live in it.'

'Thanks for the Tough Love, Miles,' I sneered.

'Come on, come on, don't be like that. I'll tell you what. The whole point of escapism is to escape. So we'll keep playing by letter. Or over the phone. I'll go down to the Compleat Strategist and get you a new miniature. Unless you're really giving up Monty.'

'Yeah, I'm really giving up Monty. Being a paladin sucks.'

Miles looked sad. 'I thought you were a good paladin,' he murmured, turning away.

And that was pretty much the end of me and Miles. We said some other stuff; I can't remember what. He said he'd write me but I knew he wouldn't. Then he left.

But I'm OK. You know what, bottom line? I really am OK. I miss Gossamer, but I don't miss the rest of it. No more Machine Front, no more gore, no more orchid-taste in my mouth. I work out a lot. They have a gym here and hardly anybody ever uses it. The only thing the inmates want to do is Jane Fonda or Richard Simmons.

I pump iron.

I eat, too. But not too much. The food is awful. If you want to lose weight, commit a crime and go to prison.

I guess it's a reprieve. As long as I'm here, I don't have to think about the other stuff.

Maybe it can't last.

OK, definitely, it can't last. Sooner or later I'll have to go back out there and deal with what happened when I let the Grid feed back through me.

I'll have to find out where *she* is. The one who came through my eye.

What she is.

I mean, talk about damaged.

Oh, what a can of worms I got myself there.

Yeah, so for now I'm happy to lie low, bide my time.

And I've got a lot of *Love Boat* reruns to get through.

objectivity

Over the Hackensack skyline, the silhouette of City Hall a regal puce rectangle sunk in a bed of orange-stained cloud, Miles saw and felt the wings. He was looking idly through the plate-glass floor-to-ceiling window of Garden State Checks while a raven-haired woman with a teenaged daughter went to the window and fished a driver's license out of her gigantic pocketbook, and a tiny Latina who must have been standing on a box behind the bulletproof glass slipped a form across the counter.

In that moment, Miles glanced up. The downdraft had hit the back of his neck like the rush of a passing tractor-trailer, only there was no sound. The wings cast a shadow over Main Street. In the illumination of the sign CHECKS CASHED 24 HRS he could see the dark green veins in the webbing, and the tiny hairs – or were they pin feathers? He could see the shadows of circuits in the translucent body, too. Just for a moment.

Saliva caught in his throat and instinctively he threw himself flat on the sidewalk. He looked up just in time to see the trident of the monster's tail vanishing over the courthouse.

The thing broke up into sound. Not thunder; not words;

but snatches of what might once have been music, some-where, in some other air – like a record played backwards, upside-down, inside-out – reflecting an unknown-to-him intelligence. It petered off, leaving a sonic jet-trail in its wake that faded until Miles couldn't distinguish the strange sound from the ordinary traffic noise.

Trembling, Miles stood up, expletives dying on his lips as his mind worked feverishly to tell him a plausible story about what had just happened. He stood there like an aban-doned marionette for what must have been several minutes, because now the woman came out of Garden State Checks stuffing her wallet into her purse, which she clutched pro-tectively. The teenager trailed behind, scuffing the toes of her unlaced basketball sneakers against the sidewalk. She had Joan Jett spiky black hair and colored lengths of chain wrapped around her forearms, and a Deep Purple concert shirt. She saw Miles in his immaculate Dock Siders and Rush jeans jacket, motionless for no reason on the sidewalk. Miles gawked and the girl gawked back, almost challengingly. Then the girl tossed her head and turned away, running to catch up with her mother. The two started walking north.

Miles closed his mouth and looked around. Everyone else was going about their business. He wanted to stop someone, say, *'Did you hear? Did you see?'*

But he knew better than to set himself up for that one.

Maybe it was a hallucination. Maybe he had a brain tumor. Maybe someone had doctored his hot dog at lunch.

Miles shivered and stuffed his hands in his pockets. Out of the pillow of air between his jeans jacket and body he got a nasty whiff, some residual odor . . . sulfur?

He looked at the sky again. With a last burst of twinkly high notes, the dragonsong blended into the noise of rush hour.

'Well,' Miles whispered. 'Sink me.'